A MORNING AFFAIR

A MORNING AFFAIR

JANICE KAPLAN

NAL BOOKS

NEW AMERICAN LIBRARY

A DIVISION OF PENGUIN BOOKS USA INC., NEW YORK

PUBLISHED IN CANADA BY
PENGUIN BOOKS CANADA LIMITED, MARKHAM, ONTARIO

PUBLISHER'S NOTE

This book is a work of fiction. Names, characters, places, and incidents either are the product of the author's imagination or are used fictitiously, and any resemblance to actual persons, living or dead, events, or locales is entirely coincidental.

 NAL TRADEMARK REG. U.S. PAT. OFF. AND FOREIGN COUNTRIES
REGISTERED TRADEMARK—MARCA REGISTRADA
HECHO EN DRESDEN, TN

SIGNET, SIGNET CLASSIC, MENTOR, ONYX, PLUME, MERIDIAN and
NAL BOOKS are published *in the United States* by
New American Library, a division of Penguin Books USA Inc.,
1633 Broadway, New York, New York 10019,
in Canada by Penguin Books Canada Limited,
2801 John Street, Markham, Ontario L3R 1B4

Library of Congress Cataloging-in-Publication Data

Kaplan, Janice.
    A morning affair / by Janice Kaplan.
      p.   cm.
    ISBN 0-453-00653-1
    I. Title.
    PS3561.A5593M6   1989
    813'.54—dc19   88-30113
                                         CIP

Designed by Joe Zepé Ola

First Printing, May, 1989

  2   3   4   5   6   7   8   9

PRINTED IN THE UNITED STATES OF AMERICA

This book is for the boys: Ron, Zachary, and Matthew.
And, of course, for Mom and Dad.

ACKNOWLEDGMENTS

The characters in this book are fictional and not based on any producers, directors, or on-air personalities I know. But I am grateful to the smart and talented people at *Good Morning America* who showed me the good side of life in television. Among the stars I came to admire on both sides of the camera are Pat George, Phyllis McGrady, and Joan Lunden. My thanks also to Dorothy Schefer at *Vogue* for her constant support, and to Maureen Baron for her terrific editing and enthusiasm. Also thanks to Esther Newberg—there's nobody in publishing I admire more.

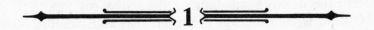

1

Jackie Rogers became an instant celebrity in Boston the day the senator from Massachusetts, Harrison Tark, smiled at her from the podium during a press conference and said it was a pleasure to answer the questions of someone so well-informed. Older political reporters, mostly male, twisted around in their seats to see the look on Jackie's face. As always, it was pleasant and controlled; there was no way Jackie Rogers was going to blush when the television lights were on.

"Thank you, Senator. It's been interesting to study your enlightened plan," said Jackie. At twenty-seven, she was the youngest person in the room, but she had already been a television reporter for five years, and she was a solid professional.

The senator's comment could have been the start of juicy headlines for the tabloids: *Brilliant bachelor senator and gorgeous gal reporter fall in love at press conference!* But such rumors wouldn't go far because everyone had to admit Tark's observation was true. Jackie was informed. For the previous twenty minutes, the senator had been briefing the press on the intricacies of budgetary reform, and when the reporters started asking questions, he was clearly frustrated. Apparently, nobody had been following him, or understood the subtleties of his plan. Then Jackie stood up, asked a sharp question and two quick follow-ups that not only got right to the point but showed she had been studying the budgetary programs in Washington. That was when the grateful senator made his comment.

Though the press conference on budget matters was boring, the senator—barely forty, liberal, handsome, and unmarried—was always news, so his compliment to Jackie appeared in both Boston newspapers, and on Channel Five's six- and eleven-o'clock news.

Jackie knew that none of the attention was going to hurt her career. In fact, everything had been going so well lately, she was only mildly surprised when her agent called a few days later to say that the network was looking for a new correspondent for *A.M. Reports*, and she was being seriously considered.

"Terrific," said Jackie. "Tell me what I should do."

"Nothing special, I just need an audition tape. Do you have a reel of your best spots?"

"I do, but it's not updated. I'll see if I can get a tape editor to help me with it tomorrow. Do I get to include the senator's testimonial?"

The agent laughed. "No, but don't worry. I'm making sure that everyone in New York hears about it."

"I'm sure you are."

Jackie got to work early enough the next morning to watch *A.M. Reports* from her desk in the WCVB-TV newsroom. The network show was hosted by Bradley James and Darlie Hayes, though as far as Jackie could tell, it was the Bradley James Show, with Darlie appearing often enough to satisfy anyone who wanted something nice to look at in the morning. Like the morning shows on all three networks, this one was a mix of news, entertainment, weather and interviews. It was fast-moving, with a maximum of five minutes allotted to each of the day's newsmakers and celebrities. Competition among the network morning shows was fierce, and Jackie had heard that *A.M. Reports* was trying to distinguish itself by putting a greater emphasis on news stories, many done outside the studio. If so, it wasn't obvious as she watched.

Her own newsroom was relatively quiet at that hour, except for the jangling of the wire-service machines. The station news director, Ernest Flanagan, got up from his desk behind a glass partition and came over to Jackie while she was watching the show.

"You need a tape editor this morning?" he asked.

She looked up at him sharply. "How did you know that?"

He shrugged. "Why else would you be in so early?"

"Maybe I have work to do, or maybe I just couldn't sleep."

He loosened his tie, which was already loose. "Don't be coy. This is the news business, remember? I heard yesterday that you were up for the job at *A.M. Reports*. You manage to keep a good secret. If you need to make a reel, Judd is in edit room one this morning. Tell him I told you it was okay."

"Thanks." She smiled, and didn't bother telling him that she too had heard about the job possibility only yesterday. "Let's say it's a long shot. The job hasn't exactly been offered to me yet."

"It will be. And you'll grab it."

She glanced at the television screen. "I don't know. It doesn't look like my credentials as an investigative reporter are going to mean much there. The show seems to be ninety percent fluff."

"What do you want, blood and guts at seven A.M.? It's the number-one show in the morning, and the executive producer is one of the smartest guys in the business. Steve Cawley. Old chum of mine, actually."

Jackie grinned. "Okay, I'll beg. Can you call him for me?"

Ernie shrugged, made a face. "What do you want me to tell him, that senators flirt with you at press conferences and you know how to investigate the waterfront? Come on, Jackie, you know the business. If the demographics say they need a blond from California or an Oriental girl from Texas, they're not going to hire you. If they can stand having someone smart and eastern, and a Radcliffe girl no less, it's yours."

"So you won't call him?"

He patted her hand. "I already did."

Jackie gave him a quick hug and went to find Judd. She had spent most of the evening before in the tape office of the station, watching news cassettes and trying to decide which of her stories were good enough to send to the network. It was hard to be objective. She'd lead the reel, of course, with the stories that had won her the National Reporter's Award a month ago—a series of investigative pieces, culminating in two live spots on the evening news, which revealed a multimillion-dollar kickback scam at the loading docks on Boston's waterfront. It had taken endless work and received plenty of publicity. Jackie always had the feeling that most people didn't have any idea what the story was really about, but they knew it was big, and it was definitely good television.

In edit room one, Judd played the tape of the live spots again, and Jackie decided they were as good as anything she had seen on network television. But as she watched Judd transfer the tapes to an audition reel, her attention drifted to thoughts of how Alden Taft, her lover of the moment, had responded to her work. The thought of leaving Alden to move to New York and work in network television, gave her only the slightest pang. Alden wasn't exactly disdainful of her career—he was too smart for that—but he found it enormously inconvenient. He wasn't sure why she was so devoted to her work when she could transfer that loyalty to him.

"Why in the world would you want to go to New York?" he had asked on the phone last night, when she told him about the job possibility.

"Because it's one of the most prestigious jobs in television," she said. "Network morning shows and network evening news are as good as it gets in this business."

"But you're doing fine in Boston. You're happy. We're happy. Why push your luck?"

"Figure it out, Alden. If your company asks you to become CEO, are you going to say, 'No, thanks, I'm happy as a vice-president?' "

"Of course not, but that's different."

"Ah, yes, male breadwinner must rise to the top, sweet female should be happy where she is."

Alden paused, took a different tack. "Jackie, the truth is that I'm worried you'll be disappointed. In Boston you're a big fish, but New York is an awfully big pond. It's going to be harder to succeed than you realize."

"If I get the job, I'll take the risk," she said, feeling a cold fury rising.

"For your own sake, I hope you don't get it."

She got the job. Two interviews with Steve Cawley, a meeting with a network vice-president, and she was able to trade in her credentials as a local news reporter for the cachet of being a network correspondent. Exactly six weeks later, Jackie moved from her cozy brownstone on Beacon Hill to a modern, one-bedroom apartment on East Fifty-third Street in Manhattan. The woman in the network business office who had helped her find the apartment assured her that it was in a luxury building, and it was: the doormen wore uniforms and white gloves and swung the revolving door with vigor each time someone walked in. The lobby decor was almost excessive with its huge crystal chandeliers and spurting fountain. Jackie was convinced that New Yorkers must spend more time in lobbies than at their homes, since the actual apartment was spare—white walls, hardwood floors, and white formica cabinets and countertops in the kitchen. But the apartment was on the seventeenth floor, and Jackie felt a definite thrill when she looked out her windows. The views were south and east, and she could glimpse the distinctive art-deco spire of the Chrysler Building from one window, bridges arching over the East River from another.

For some reason, the movers arrived from Boston before she did. When she got to the apartment, they had already disappeared, having chosen to put all her furniture in the living room and all her boxes in the bedroom. She needed someone to help her put everything where it belonged. She sighed. So there was going to be a reason to miss Alden, after all.

Alden Taft had been the love of her life since college. They had met her first day at Radcliffe when Jackie spotted him in the dining hall, a handsome, broad-shouldered blond who looked as if he had just stepped out of a Ralph Lauren ad. Dressed as she was in a pink polo shirt, with a yellow cotton sweater tied at her waist, Jackie might well have been photographed next to him. Alden took one glance at her lithe body with its gentle curves, her long slender legs, her easy, inviting smile, and gestured for her to sit down with him. Their first date was that night. Soon they were going to hockey games and football games, spending late nights studying together at the library, and holding hands in Harvard Square. Alden even became close friends with Dana Hall, Jackie's best friend, roommate, and confidante.

Alden waited until Jackie was a senior at Radcliffe and he was at Harvard Business School to cure her of her virginity. It was a successful cure, more successful, in fact, than he had wanted. For Jackie, it was like the first time she tasted caviar: she didn't understand why she had waited so long, and she couldn't wait to try all the varieties. Alden proposed marriage at the end of the year, but she declined, on the grounds that she wasn't ready to settle down. At twenty-one, she wanted fame, sex, and adventure —not a husband.

"Besides, it wouldn't be fair to you," she told him. "You're the first man I ever slept with. If I don't have more experiences now, in twenty years, I'll start wondering what I missed."

"I'm willing to risk that," said Alden.

"I'm not."

"Then tell me what experiences you need," Alden said in a cold tone that was the closest he ever came to getting angry. "Would you like me to wait while you screw around with three more men? Half a dozen? Or are we talking the entire Green Bay Packers football team?"

"You know I don't like the Packers," Jackie said. "I was thinking more along the lines of the Miami Dolphins."

"Very amusing." Alden was exasperated, and she was careful not to look at him, afraid that if she spent too much time contemplating his WASP perfection, she'd give in and decide to push prams around the playground for the rest of her life.

After that, they stopped seeing each other, turned their attention to careers and money. They both stayed in Boston and heard about each other through Dana: Jackie knew Alden had joined an investment bank and was getting rich; he knew that she was making a name for herself as a reporter on the local evening news. Jackie often thought that they would be the perfect couple—if only they could bear to talk to each other. They ran into each other occasionally—at a party, the Harvard-Yale game, a restaurant in town—but each time, one or the other of them was with someone else, and was too proud to admit that it just wasn't the same.

After all the time gone by, it was Dana who finally got them back together, or at least back into bed. She had invited them both to a New Year's Eve party at her apartment in New York, plied them with champagne, and offered them the extra bedroom.

"I can't believe how long it's been," said Alden when they woke up the next morning. "Four years, or is it five? God, I've missed you."

From what Jackie had heard, he had dated two airline stewardesses, a *Vogue* model, and a Chinese architect since they had last seen each other.

"This *was* nice," she said, "but it was one night and we were both drunk. Let's see what happens."

Alden pursed his lips but didn't say anything. They flew back to Boston together later in the day, and Jackie was surprised at how easy it was to resume old habits. She felt herself falling back in love, couldn't remember what it was that had driven them apart except some vague feeling that Alden was uncommunicative. They began dating again that winter, a cautious dance of passion and hurt, love and anger. They talked about marriage, but more often, they talked about careers. It seemed safer.

"I'm not sure you trust me," Jackie told Alden one night, over a dinner of take-out Chinese food.

"Let's say you don't have a fabulous history of loyalty," he said.

"Do you want to talk about it?"

"I'm not sure there's a lot to say."

"Should we try?"

"I'd rather eat."

So they ate, and Jackie silently vowed to try being loving and faithful, let time do its trick of healing.

Despite her plans for extensive sampling, Jackie had dated cautiously in the years apart from Alden. Her television work demanded time and attention, and she wasn't going to allow her career to be threatened by any misalliance. Boston, for all its sophistication, was a small town where people's attention was piqued by the local television faces. Heads turned now when she walked into Boston's Café Budapest for dinner with Alden. The maître d' knew her face if not her name, and gave them a prominent table. She didn't mind the attention, and neither did Alden. She was glad to have kept her reputation clean.

One night, several months after they had started dating again, Alden was supposed to go to an important black-tie dinner in honor of one of his clients. Jackie bought a white ruffled dress, short and sleek, which she showed off to him that morning while he drank a cup of coffee in her sunny breakfast nook.

"It's perfect," he said. "You could pass for a businessman's wife any day."

She dropped the dress on a kitchen stool, kissed him on the top of the head. "If that's a compliment, it stinks."

But they both laughed, and she handed him a small velvet box.

"For you," she said.

He looked surprised, opened it carefully.

"They're antique cufflinks and studs," she explained. "I happened to see them at an antique show I covered last week, and they reminded me of you."

He smiled. "Because they're old?"

"No, because I thought they were dignified. Classic. And solid gold—just like you."

He kissed her. "They're beautiful. Thank you."

She left for work then, promising she'd be finished early and ready to meet him at seven o'clock.

That was the day that the scandal on the loading docks, the story she'd been covering for weeks, broke wide open. A dockworker was shot. A union official was taken into custody and questioned by the police. There were rumors that a deputy mayor had been involved in the kickback scam and was going to be charged with corruption.

Jackie's story was the lead item on the six-o'clock news on Channel Five. Ernest called her at noon, asked her how much time she needed, and when she said six minutes—most stories ran three—he agreed, without any questions.

"I want to go live," he told her over the remote phone. "It'll have more impact."

She stayed on the docks all day with a director and a crew, and by five o'clock, she knew they were going to scoop all the other local stations. The story was going to be incredible. Nobody had as much information as she did—all the tough, grimy details of the scandal. It was a hot day, and she was wearing a billowing pink skirt with a pink-and-white polka-dot blouse. The director positioned her on the edge of one of the docks, with three muscular dockworkers looming in the background, well within camera range. The contrast worked. Live remotes always made her a little nervous: there was no room for error, no chance to go to the edit room and correct a bad shot or a slip of the tongue. When the director pointed his finger at her at 6:02, she felt a surge of adrenalin, knew she was going to be all right. This was *her* story. She had uncovered it, and today's events were proving her right.

The live report went without a hitch. As previously planned, she finished with a toss back to Harvey Nicholas, the anchorman in the studio. He thanked her, then asked the two questions she had given him. It was a technique Ernest liked—let the anchor-man get involved, look like more than the news reader he was.

Jackie had asked for return video, and because the story was big, she had it—a small monitor at her feet, so she could not only hear what was on the air, but see it as well. The studio director cut from a final long shot of her at the waterfront to a close-up of Harvey, peering intently into the camera. *"Fascinating story, Jackie, thank you again,"* he said. *"As most of you know, Jackie has been investigating this story for five weeks now, and her efforts have helped uncover the scandal. She'll have another live report from the waterfront at eleven. Now, in other news . . ."*

The field director gave her a thumbs-up sign, and Jackie pulled out her earpiece.

"Was it okay?"

The director grinned. "It was brilliant. I don't know how we're going to top it at eleven, but we'll try."

"Maybe we can get some fresh interviews to cut in. Another union leader, or someone else we haven't spoken to."

"Good idea. Want to get to work?"

"Let me take a short break."

Exhilarated, Jackie ran to a pay phone to call Alden. The first two tries she got busy signals, but the third time, irritated, she got through, and rapidly told Alden about the day.

"Did you see the six-o'clock news?" she asked him.

"I'm afraid I missed it," he said. "But I heard what happened at the docks."

"Well, watch at eleven if you can. I'm going to be on live again. God, what an unbelievable day this has been. Honey, I'm sorry about missing the dinner. Maybe I'll come over later—after all this is through."

There was silence on the phone.

"Is everything okay?" she asked.

"Not exactly," he said. "I was counting on having you with me tonight. No way you can break away for a couple of hours?"

It was noisy at the docks, and Jackie figured she probably hadn't heard right. "Alden, this is a big story. It's the kind of thing that can make a career."

"Going alone to an important dinner is the kind of thing that can ruin one."

"You must be joking." She looked up from the phone booth, saw the director motioning to her. Dick O'Connor, the union vice-president, had just appeared at the dock, and if Jackie wanted to interview him, she was going to have to grab him quickly.

"Listen, I've got to go. If anyone wants to know where I am, tell them to turn on the eleven-o'clock news."

More silence.

"Alden, I've got to go, all right?"

"Of course," said Alden. "But I'm not sure why you had to wait until six-twenty to call."

"Are you kidding? I haven't been able to breathe all day. This is the first time I've stopped in hours. I'm sorry. But what difference does it make?"

"If you'd called earlier, I could have made arrangements to take someone else."

She opened her mouth, then shut it again. The director was talking to O'Connor, and the cameraman was sending panicked looks in her direction.

"That's totally obnoxious of you, but we'll talk about it another time, okay?"

"Sure."

He hung up.

Jackie tried to talk about it the next day, but Alden's contribution was to say merely that she was right—everyone at the dinner knew about the story going on at the waterfront, so it wasn't embarrassing for him at all.

"In fact, I was very proud of you," he said. "One of my partners said I was going out with the Carl Bernstein of the Boston docks. I was pleased." He sat down and gave her a look that indicated the discussion was over.

"I'm glad everything worked out," she said, "but I was really hurt yesterday. It was probably the biggest day of my professional life, and all you could do was worry about going to dinner alone. You took all the joy out of it."

"Okay, let's forget about it," he said. "It's not going to happen again."

She glared at him. "Of course it's going to happen again. And again. This is what my job is all about."

"I understand," he said. "It will be fine." He picked up a *Wall Street Journal* and began flipping through it.

She wanted to throw something at him.

"Is this what Harvard Business School does to a person?" she asked.

"What?"

"Or maybe it's all these years as an investment banker. Something has turned you into an emotional cripple."

"That's charming, Jackie. Thank you." Alden shook his head. "I don't understand the problem. I said I was proud of you. Could you please tell me what's wrong now?"

"Don't you get it, Alden? I don't want you to be proud of me because one of your goddamn partners says to be. This is a modern relationship, remember? We're supposed to be equals."

He sighed. "Of course we're equals. But this is the real world. All the things that sounded so nice in your women's group at college don't mean much anymore."

"They mean something to me."

Alden shrugged. "Fine. I just want to make sure I mean something, too. I'm never quite sure where I am on your list of priorities."

"Where would you like to be?"

"If we get married, I think I deserve to be number one."

"And will I be number one for you?"

Alden closed the newspaper and sighed. "Jackie, this is getting ridiculous. I hate these conversations. Could we just skip it?"

"Of course we can skip it. We can skip everything, as far as I'm concerned." She was furious at Alden for being chauvinistic and arrogant, and making it impossible for her to marry him.

She might have reconsidered if the incident at Senator Tark's press conference hadn't occurred a few weeks later, making Alden difficult once again.

"Maybe Ernie Flanagan should issue a statement saying you and the senator have a purely business relationship," said Alden.

"That's ridiculous. There haven't been any rumors, just some good-natured joking."

"Maybe you think it's good-natured. I don't like it."

"Come on, Alden, it should make you feel good to know that Senator Tark was impressed with me and let everyone know it.

And if you could manage to think of something other than your own business concerns, you might see it that way."

It struck Jackie as ironic that the waterfront story and the Senator Tark comment, the two events that seemed to be precipitating her into a network job, had also given her a new view of Alden. The job possibility itself was dividing them—she was thrilled, but he was edgy.

"What will happen to me?" he asked.

"God, you're selfish."

"Because I don't want my girlfriend to be two hundred miles away?"

"I hate being called your girlfriend. It's demeaning. But we can commute, you know."

"That doesn't work."

"Nothing in this relationship works anymore," she said.

A few days later, when she got the job, Alden didn't bother sending flowers to congratulate her. She celebrated by drinking a Diet Coke alone in her apartment and having a long conversation with her mother. The day she left for New York, Alden was tied up in a meeting, and she never got to say good-bye, which was fine with her, because their good-byes had already been said.

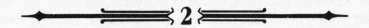

2

Jackie met Julian Beardsley after she had been in New York for exactly three days. She met him at a party at his penthouse to which he hadn't invited her. He hadn't invited any of the guests. The guest list had been provided by his friend Feodor Zerkov, a Russian Don Juan. Julian assumed that Feodor's acquaintances would include a variety of pretty women, and he was hoping that one of them would be sufficiently interesting to get him over the heartbreak of a long love affair that had ended that week.

So the first thing Jackie learned about Julian was his taste. His apartment didn't make a bad first impression. Floor-to-ceiling windows looked out over most of New York—uptown, downtown, and Central Park. The furniture had been designed not to compete with the view. There were a lot of white sofas and chrome tables that some interior decorator had probably decided were safe. A large Matisse canvas hung in the foyer, and the hallway leading to the living room looked like an extension of the Museum of Modern Art: paintings by Jasper Johns, Larry Rivers, Frank Stella, and Jackson Pollock lined the walls. In the living room, the track lighting was dim, and a wall of mirrors faced the windows. In the daytime, the mirrors probably reflected the incredible view, but tonight they just seemed to double the number of blondes and redheads circulating around the room. Jackie felt as if she were in a sorority house at UCLA. It was the first time in her life that her brown hair stuck out as unusual.

She looked around for someone to talk to, but there didn't seem to be any likely prospects. The woman standing next to her was wearing a green mini-dress, and seemed drunk; she was talking to another woman who had on tight, low-cut red party pajamas that Jackie would have considered too daring to wear to bed. Jackie got a glass of wine, and was saved by Feodor.

"Come meet Julian, darling," he said in his deep, Slavic tones. Feodor had been in the country for ten years, but he'd never gotten rid of his Russian accent, and Jackie was convinced that he never would. She had met him in Boston, while she was researching a story on immigrants who had made it in America. Feodor had obviously made it, but ultimately she decided not to include him in the story since his only obvious means of support was his rich friends. Feodor was proof that style could triumph over substance.

As he took her hand to lead her across the room, he said, "I've missed you, darling. Thank goodness you have come to New York. My bed has been lonely without you."

Jackie had never been in his bed—but Feodor was seductive on general principles.

She laughed, tossed her head. It was impossible not to flirt and be coquettish around Feodor, even if both of them knew it would lead nowhere. "You're never lonely," she said. "But I must know. How many of the women in this room have you already slept with?"

"What you think of me, darling." Feodor shook his head. "None of them mean anything. It's you I want."

"Uh-huh."

A tall man wearing tortoise-shell glasses and a kind of eccentric-genius grin turned out to be Julian Beardsley. He was in his mid-forties and looked like a college professor—though college professors don't usually have four beautiful women standing in a tight little circle around them.

Feodor introduced Jackie to her host, and Julian tried to introduce his entourage.

"This is Vania and Tess and Ingrid and . . ." He hesitated when he got to a slim blonde in a magenta dress who was quite literally hanging on his arm.

"Merry," she said, lifting her glass. "I'm Merry. Very."

Very Merry tightened her grip on Julian's arm.

"I seem to be surrounded by actresses and models tonight," Julian said, turning to look at Jackie. "What do you do?"

"I don't fit in, I'm afraid," she said. "I'm a journalist."

"Ah, our darling little Jackie is too modest," said Feodor, interrupting. "She's a television star."

"Hardly. I'm a reporter."

"The newest and best in New York," said Feodor. He put his arm around her, acting as if he were her lover or her agent, or both. Julian looked at her curiously, adjusted his glasses.

"Your art is incredible," said Jackie pleasantly, looking around. "I've seen prints of the Jasper Johns you have in the hall, but it certainly looks different in real life. I never realized it was so large and vivid."

Julian looked pleased. "It's one of my favorites. Where have you seen prints?"

"I'm embarrassed to admit it, but it was probably in a course in modern art I took in college. Radcliffe."

"No wonder you have such good taste," said Julian, a grin spreading across his face. "I went to Harvard. But it was a lot of years before you."

They discussed Cambridge and a few professors each had known, discovered that an old classmate of Julian's had been Jackie's instructor in a political science course. "He taught a class in libertarian history and comparative political culture that was brilliant," said Jackie. "But I'm sure he wouldn't remember me. I was always too intimidated to talk to him."

"I doubt that," said Julian.

"I hate to interrupt," said Merry, who had been clutching Julian and tapping her foot through most of the conversation, "but I need another drink. Could you get me one, Julian dear?"

He signaled to one of the waiters to bring another glass of champagne.

"Thank you, darling," said Merry. She put her very red lips close to Julian's ear and whispered something, and when Julian laughed, she glanced triumphantly at Jackie.

Jackie suddenly found herself thinking of all the boxes she had in her new apartment, still unpacked after just a few days in the city. Julian was interesting, but she hadn't come to New York to compete with the likes of Very Merry. It was time to leave—and she did.

The next morning, as Jackie was sorting through a box of scripts she had brought with her from Boston, Feodor called.

"Darling, I have surprising news," he said when she picked up the phone. "Julian called me just now. He wants to know if he can ask you for a date."

"I don't understand."

"I know, darling, I don't understand either. All the beautiful girls at the party, and he chose you. I thought it would be Merry—but I was wrong. He wants to go out with you."

"I didn't realize the party was Julian's personal hunting ground," Jackie said, trying not to sound annoyed. "But what I actually meant is why did he call you instead of me?"

"Julian doesn't like to waste time, darling. Millionaires are like that. He will not call if a girl isn't interested. Are you?"

"I'm interested in a date, if that's what you mean."

"You have to be interested in more than that, or I'll tell him not to call."

Julian called later that afternoon and asked if Jackie would be free that evening. She was. After a shower, she stood staring into her closet for several minutes before settling on a slim gray silk skirt with a herringbone pattern, a gray-and-white silk blouse, and a single strand of pearls. Not exactly New York chic, perhaps, but her style. If Julian wanted a red mini-dress, he would have asked one out.

Jackie took a cab to the address Julian had given her in the Village, and arrived at a dark, smoky café where a lot of people seemed to be talking German. Looking around, she spied Julian sitting at a small table with a bald, older man. As she made her way toward Julian, her heart started pounding. She had to tell herself firmly that she was not sixteen, and this was not her first date.

Julian stood up when she got to the table and pecked her cheek. "Good to see you. This is Heinrich Braun, the filmmaker." He looked at her intently while she shook hands with the bald man.

"Nice to meet you," she said. "Are you the same Heinrich Braun who directed the German expressionist films in the 1950's? Let's see, one was *The Three Miseries*?"

"Indeed." He turned to Julian. "So you have already briefed the young lady on me?"

"Not at all," said Julian. He looked at Jackie, a big grin on his face. "I'm impressed. Not that Heinrich isn't famous in some circles, but how do you happen to know of him?"

"Just one of those things you know," she said. It was always satisfying when her Radcliffe education actually came in handy.

They chatted amiably for a few minutes until someone near the front of the café announced that a movie was about to begin. The lights dimmed, and Jackie swung her chair around to look as a scratchy, black-and-white picture appeared on a tiny screen. She tried to concentrate, but the movie was in German, and if there were subtitles, she couldn't make them out. It occurred to her that this was a strange place for a millionaire to take someone for a first date. Clearly there was more to Julian than his money.

When the lights finally went on again, Julian reached over and grabbed Heinrich's hand. "Brilliant," he said. "Absolutely brilliant. Why have I never seen this one before?"

"It was one of my earliest," said Heinrich modestly. "There aren't many copies. I'm grateful that you both came tonight."

"Let's go celebrate," said Julian. "Come to dinner with us? We're heading to my favorite steak place in midtown."

"My pleasure," the director replied.

They waited for a few minutes while a number of people came by to congratulate Heinrich and make flattering comments about the film. Finally, they all climbed into Julian's limousine, which had been waiting outside, and drove to the Palm.

The restaurant was noisy, crowded, and expensive. Julian ordered steak and onion rings for everyone. Jackie hadn't eaten red meat since college, and she had to be thin enough to start her job in two weeks, so she ordered a green salad and a glass of white wine.

After dinner, they dropped off Heinrich at his apartment and continued on to Julian's penthouse. Julian led Jackie into the study on the first floor and poured two glasses of cognac. She thought the study was the best room in the house—all wood and leather and lined with bookshelves. No chrome, no mirrors, and no white sofas. She wondered if it was where Julian felt most comfortable—or if he had already figured out that it was the only place she would be comfortable.

Julian settled into a deep leather chair, and without too many preliminaries began discussing capitalist morality. He insisted that Heinrich's film was an allegory about life and death in a free society. Since Jackie didn't speak German and hadn't understood a word of the film, she didn't argue. He quoted Immanuel Kant on moral evil and vice, and she tried to remember enough from Philosophy 101 to keep up her end of the conversation. She didn't do badly—another advantage of a Radcliffe education was learning how to talk without saying anything.

Finally Julian yawned and announced that he was going to bed, and would she follow him? She said it was probably time to go home, so they launched into another intellectual conversation—this time about why anybody would have theoretical objections to sex.

"I hardly know you yet," she said. "I don't feel anything."

"I don't feel anything either," said Julian. "You feel things when you get into bed. You don't feel them sitting in the study drinking cognac."

Jackie shrugged. "It's silly to argue. If you were looking for someone for bed, you should have picked out someone else at the party. Very Merry, perhaps."

Julian laughed. "You're right. She was definitely available for the night. But that part always happens eventually, and I wanted something more. I made the right choice." He leaned over and kissed her good night, then left the room and walked upstairs. Jackie got up, walked to the foyer, and stared at the Matisse. The obvious choice was to let herself out of the apartment and take a cab home, but for some reason, she didn't want to. So she went up the stairs, peeked in a few rooms, and finally found Julian's bedroom. He was sitting on the bed reading a book, and looked up, his genius grin in place, when she walked in. "I'm really glad you're here," he said.

The view from the bedroom window matched the one downstairs, and Jackie stood staring out while Julian got into bed. She noticed that he put on a clean, white T-shirt and nothing else. She went into the bathroom which had two sinks, a sunken tub, a free-standing shower, a sauna, and a Jacuzzi. She washed quickly, ignoring all that equipment, put her blue underpants back on, and walked into the bedroom.

"Why are you still wearing your panties?" he asked.

"Why did you put on a T-shirt?"

"I always put on a T-shirt to sleep. It keeps me warm."

"I get cold on the bottom."

"There are better ways to stay warm there."

She crawled under the covers, feeling tense. Julian rubbed her back very gently, then kissed her sweetly on the neck, the cheeks, the lips. They talked some more, and pretty soon she discovered that Julian was right—there were better ways than blue panties to stay warm.

Julian woke up at six o'clock the next morning and whispered that he had to get to work, but she should stay in bed as long as she wanted. Instead she jumped up, got dressed, and kissed him good-bye before he had finished shaving.

When she stepped outside, the city seemed quiet—at least quiet for New York. The doorman asked if she wanted a cab, but she said no, she was going to walk. She strolled along Fifth Avenue for a while, trying to decide if she felt very good or very guilty. Still musing, she crossed the street and went into Central Park. The park was filled with joggers, exercising before they went off to work. They all looked firm and lean. Jackie decided that sex always made her feel fat, so she hailed a cab after all, and went to the exercise club she had joined the day before. She changed into the gray sweatsuit she'd left there, noticing as she did that she was the only one in the locker room not putting on designer exercise clothes. The hot style seemed to be a brightly colored unitard worn with leggings and a loose T-shirt. She was planning to work out on the Nautilus equipment, but an aerobics class was just beginning, and she joined it. Following five other women who were traipsing into the gym, she lined up with them behind an instructor named Chris—notable for her short blonde hair, demonic smile, and tight butt. Jackie stared at that butt for a full hour while Chris exhorted the group to kick higher! work harder! get those heart rates up! By the end of the class, Jackie couldn't breathe, and every muscle in her body hurt, so she assumed it had been a good workout.

When she got back to her apartment, she devoured two muffins, a bowl of cereal, and a big glass of orange juice, thinking all the while that it wasn't true what the women's magazines wrote about exercise dulling your appetite. There were two messages on her answering machine from the night before: one from her mother, telling her to call back "whenever you get in," and the other from Alden Taft. She called her mother first, explaining that she'd gotten in too late the night before to call. Her mother didn't ask any questions, so they chatted for a few minutes and hung up.

Jackie went back to the answering machine and listened to Alden's message again. "Just calling to say hello. Hope all is going well with you. We'll talk."

Jackie picked up the phone to call him, and then put it down again. She didn't have anything to say to Alden right now. She was happy where she was—in New York, leaving someone else's penthouse at dawn.

Jackie didn't hear from Julian all that day, or the next day. To prove she didn't care, she went to Saks Fifth Avenue and amused herself buying two alligator belts, three pairs of shoes, a snakeskin evening bag, and a silk scarf. Not essentials for a career woman, but nice to have—just like Julian. Still, she told herself that if that one date turned out to be the end of their adventure together, she wasn't going to be crushed. It was, as her mother would say in a different context, a good experience. But she felt a surge of pleasure when her doorman buzzed two nights later to ask if a Mr. Beardsley could come up.

"Certainly," she said, and a few minutes later opened her door to Julian.

"I just wanted to say hello," he said, giving her a kiss on the cheek and loping into the apartment. "I was driving by—actually driving myself for a change—and there was a perfect parking spot right outside your apartment building. How could I resist?"

"I'm glad you didn't." He was strolling around her apartment, peering briefly through her venetian blinds, as if to check the view, and staring at her shelves of books.

"I gave the bag lady who was sitting on the corner ten dollars and asked her to watch out for my Mercedes."

"You're joking."

"Not at all." He grinned, pulled down a leather-bound edition of Kierkegaard's *Either/or* and flipped through it. "Nice collection. Do you read these things?"

"At some time or other. What do you read?"

"Obscure economics manuals that will give me an edge in business because nobody else can make their way through them."

"Have you always been the Beardsley of Beardsley Enterprises?"

"It's not a family business, if that's what you mean. I started it right after I got my second Ph.D. at Harvard. I'd always planned to do theoretical math and physics."

"What made you change your mind?"

"Pure greed. I had a brilliant idea—excuse the immodesty—on how to use mathematical theory in the commodities market. I tried doing it on the side, but for one thing, it started taking too much time, and for another, I made more money in a week than I could make as an academic in a year. Maybe a lifetime." He put the book back. "That's the kind of screwed-up values our society has. I'd probably be doing a lot more good as a theorist, but nobody pays you much for doing good."

"I don't know much about the commodities market. Are we talking wheat, corn, and pork bellies?"

"We're talking commodities as in silver, gold, and platinum." He grinned. "By the way, I see why the network hired you. You're a good interviewer."

"Thanks." She riffled through a stack of transcripts on her desk.

There was an awkward silence. It was late, and Jackie was wearing what she pretty much always wore at home—faded dungarees and a polo shirt, hair pulled back, no makeup. Damn him, why hadn't he called before he just appeared?

He was still looking around the apartment.

"Would you like a drink?" she asked.

"No, I don't think so." He stopped and turned around, looking a bit abashed. "I didn't really come for anything. I just thought of seeing you when I drove by. I've got to be getting home."

"Want me to come with you?"

He looked surprised.

Maybe a woman who intellectualized sex the first night wasn't expected to proposition for it the second—but she wanted to be with Julian tonight, didn't want to close the door behind him now and be alone.

He turned around and began pacing—one length of the room, which, despite the fact that this was a New York apartment, was fairly long. He glanced out the window again, then came back—eyes sparkling, genius grin back in place.

"I'd love to have you come."

"Good," she said, a little surprised at his hesitation.

He kissed her lightly. "Do you want to know what made me decide?"

"No."

"I'll tell you anyway," he said. "Your breasts. I have to go to Chicago tomorrow morning on a seven-o'clock plane, and I have about a dozen things that I should do at home tonight. But when I walked around the room and closed my eyes, I kept seeing how your breasts looked the other night. That did it."

Jackie had always rather liked her breasts, which weren't particularly large, but were nicely firm and rounded. Alden had never mentioned them, probably because no true-blooded WASP knew what to call body parts when he was in bed with a woman. It was silly, but hearing the compliment from Julian—when she was tired of being the career woman and the intellectual, and feeling like any other insecure girl—was enough to make those breasts perk up proudly against her shirt and to make the rather solid heart that beat under them melt just the slightest degree.

On Friday, Jackie met Dana Hall, her best friend from college, for lunch. They met at the Harvard Club of New York, a place not noticeably different from the Harvard Club of Boston, which was not notably different from Harvard, period. Thick leather chairs, deep red carpet, a lot of men. In case there weren't enough real men around, there were always pictures on the walls of Harvard men who had become famous, or who had at least made enough money to have their portraits painted.

Once, while Jackie and Dana were still in Cambridge, a much-honored retiring professor had arranged to have his own picture and his wife's painted. He commissioned one of the most respected portrait painters in the country to do the pieces, and they were exquisite. When he died a few years later, he bequeathed both portraits to Harvard, with the stipulation that they be hung together. It was the delicious revenge of a Marxist history professor on his beloved but elitist Harvard. At last a woman's face would grace the walls! The portraits hung in a main hall for a few months after the professor died, and then they disappeared. Official word was that they were out being cleaned, though why three-year-old paintings would have to be cleaned was never explained. They stayed down while the administration apparently tried to decide what to do, and then came the brilliant stroke. The pictures were such classic examples of their type—modern American portraiture—that they would not be hung in the college, but would be on permanent loan to the Fogg Museum. None of the Marxist's protégés could complain, and the walls of Harvard College would be kept blessedly clear of women.

Dana and Jackie had been roommates all four years, put together originally as freshmen by some computer, which had apparently found it amusing that Jackie had gone to Dana Hall—and now would room with one. It took the real Dana Hall, who came from Owl Creek, Minnesota, a little while to understand that a classy girls' school in Boston also carried her name. It took Jackie a little while to understand that anyone could come from Owl Creek, Minnesota. But she rapidly forgave Dana her name and realized that she was lucky to be sleeping on top of her—more or less literally. They had bunk beds that first year and various other tight accommodations after that. Sophomore year, Dana convinced Jackie that she should go out with someone besides Alden. A handsome medical student named Hal Marsh tried dating both of them. They didn't realize it until he came to pick Jackie up for a date one night and cheerfully announced that he'd recently slept in her room. They both dumped him, on the grounds that their friendship was a lot more important than a date.

"He was great in bed," Dana told Jackie, after they'd made their pact. "Best oral sex at Harvard."

"Sorry I missed it."

"Don't worry about it. I can always show you what it was like."

Dana considered herself a sexual sophisticate, far more experienced than Jackie with men. She thought Jackie's involvement with Alden was sweet, and giggled when Jackie told her about her chaste prep-school dating habits—usually limited to concerts at the Boston Pops, ice-cream sodas afterward, and some groping in the back seat of the car. "We didn't bother going to plays and concerts where I grew up," said Dana. "We went to Owl Creek Hollow to fuck."

They joined Radcliffe Radical Feminists, and Dana once gave up men for an entire semester. "I'm not sure if it's a political statement or I'm just sick of them," she said. She tried to convince Jackie to sleep with her, on strictly feminist grounds, but abandoned the idea when Jackie convinced her that it might ruin their friendship.

Jackie was ten minutes early getting to the Harvard Club, and sat down on a comfortable chair in the lobby with a copy of *The New Yorker*. A few minutes later, she heard a familiar voice behind her.

"What kind of reading is that for a prize reporter from Boston?"

She glanced up quickly, then smiled. "Senator Tark!" She stood up to shake hands. "How nice to see you. What are you doing here?"

"Meetings, conferences, the usual rounds in a senator's life. The crisis of the moment is trying to decide if I should throw my support behind the Family Support bill that a women's group wants sponsored. But that's off the record. Right now, I'm lunching with an old classmate. What about you?"

"Same—lunch plans."

"I missed you at my last press conference."

She smiled. "Actually, I'm not in Boston anymore, Senator. I'm about to join *A.M. Reports*."

He raised his eyebrows. "Good for you. If I can ever help you out, let me know."

"Thanks. Same from my end."

They shook hands again, and he headed toward the elevator. As Jackie sat down, she wondered why Dana hadn't arrived yet. It was always exciting to meet Dana after some time apart, because Dana was the one person Jackie knew who was constantly recreating herself. Dana's opinions were strong and immutable—for as long as she chose to hold them. Then they would change, and her new position would become equally entrenched. Trying to point out these swings to Dana was useless—she was unyielding in her current sentiments. Given Dana's capriciousness, Jackie was often surprised at how firm their friendship had been over the years. Once, half-joking, she had asked when she was likely to fall out of favor, and Dana had responded with bafflement and hurt.

Dana walked in to meet Jackie at the stroke of one, wearing a navy cashmere dress that clung impressively to her tall, firm body. She was carrying a large Mark Cross briefcase, and her jet-black hair was newly short and stylishly slick. Several men in the lobby stopped to stare at her. Dana was striking, if not beautiful, and she carried herself with an air of confidence—something she had acquired during the years Jackie had known her.

"I always wanted to look like you when I was a kid," Dana had once told Jackie, enviously. "I was tall and gawky, and I desperately wanted to be one of the pretty little girls who got voted onto the cheerleading squad."

"But my looks are boring," Jackie complained.

"Perfect isn't boring."

Jackie had always been average height and slim, with a classically pretty face—big green eyes, peaches-and-cream skin, a perfect heart-shaped mouth. Her thick brown hair framed her face like a halo. People had been telling her she was pretty since she was five years old, so during college, Jackie tried to spice up her style—red highlights in her hair, a chic cut, extra bright makeup. But it was all wrong—"like painting stripes on an apple you'd just picked from the tree," Dana had said. Jackie was meant to look fresh and natural.

"You'd look more at home in Minnesota than I do," Dana had said.

"Funny, people used to tell me I looked as if I came over on the *Mayflower*."

"That too. Face it, you're just the all-American girl."

Jackie had stopped fighting it, knowing that simple good looks didn't hurt in network television.

Now Jackie caught Dana's eye across the lobby, and she hurried over. "You look fabulous," Jackie said, giving Dana a hug. "But you don't look like a lawyer anymore. What happened to the blue pinstripe suits you used to wear?"

"Gone," said Dana. "Meet the new Wall Street woman. Elegant. Sophisticated. Sexy. Dressed in Donna Karan from head to toe."

Jackie shook her head. "I can't keep up with you. I'm just a kid from Boston, still wearing her Calvin Kleins. Is it bad for your image to have lunch with me?"

"Probably. But at least we're not on Wall Street," she teased, and hugged her again. "Welcome to New York. Anyway, look at you. You look marvelous. What did you do to your hair?"

"I went to a shop on Fifty-seventh Street this morning for a trim. It cost seventy-five dollars, which is enough to make me think that I must look all right."

"It's very New York," said Dana. "And I mean that as a compliment."

They laughed and began chatting eagerly, not pausing until they were sitting down in the dining room next to two men who were smoking cigars.

"Do you want to change seats?" Jackie asked.

"Forget it," said Dana. "I've given up my campaign against smokers and may even come to love the smell of a cigar. I firmly believe that the requirements for making partner at my firm include smoking cigars—preferably illegal ones from Havana—and drinking double Scotches."

"I thought the proper drink now was white wine. Or maybe Evian water with lime."

"Not anymore, and definitely not at a Wall Street law firm." Dana smiled. "You won't believe all the things I've learned since one of the senior partners happened to mention that he considered me, quote, partnership material, end quote."

"I thought you were planning to get a few years' experience at the firm and then move on."

"To something more meaningful, right? Isn't that what I used to say? Listen, I've been busting my ass at this firm, and it's finally occurred to me that if I keep it up for a few more years and get voted into the partners' club, I can spend the rest of my life being counsel to corporate America, at a salary guaranteed not to go below one hundred thou. It's not a bad deal."

"Is this the same woman who was director of the Legal Aid office in Harlem while working her way through Columbia Law School?" asked Jackie.

"It is. We all change, alas."

The waiter came by to take their orders—white wine for Jackie, Scotch for Dana, spinach salads for both.

"At least you still eat spinach salads," said Jackie as the

waiter walked away. "It's nice to know that something about you hasn't changed."

"I get bored, Jackie—you know that."

"It hasn't been that long since we've seen each other."

"So I get bored fast. But speaking of the last time we saw each other—what's happened with Alden?"

"Gone."

"For good?"

"Who knows? But I think it's going to take more than your champagne and bedroom to get us back together this time."

"Do you care?"

"I don't know. At the moment, I'd rather worry about my job."

"I know what you mean," said Dana. "Whoever started the myth that you can have everything is full of shit."

"You always have a delicate way of putting things."

"Sorry. But I've learned to take my career seriously and take my men to bed."

"Clever." Jackie laughed. "But I have one question. If you're taking this Wall Street business so seriously, why are you wearing mauve eye shadow?"

"Don't you think it's subtle?"

"Subtle until someone stares into your eyes. Which I suspect partners do quite often."

Dana rolled her eyes. "We roomed together for too long. You know my secrets."

"I won't even ask how many partners you're sleeping with."

"None, though we'll get to the details of that soon." She sighed. "You have no idea how fucked-up the politics are in my office. We have forty-three partners, and if I had to guess, I'd say forty-two of them have wives who stay home and work for the Junior League. Or maybe the Garden Club. They haven't figured out what to do with a woman in the office. They know I'm smart, so they like working with me—but I always get the feeling that one wrong word, and I'll be forever labeled a castrating bitch."

"Wall Street sounds terrific."

"Is television any different?"

"A little. The men aren't as old and the women aren't as smart."

Dana picked up the Scotch, which had finally been put in front of her. "Here's to young men and beautiful women. Or old men and smart women. Whichever combination happens to work."

They drank. "Tell me what fabulous cases you're working on," said Jackie.

"It's too tedious. The only excitement is that I'm going on a business trip next week with Herman Osterfeld."

Jackie knew Osterfeld's name well. He was often quoted in the *Times* about some pressing point of law, generally offering an erudite statement about the true meaning of the Constitution.

"Are you working with him now? That's terrific."

Dana made a nasty face and tasted her salad. "I wouldn't quite put it at terrific," she said. "Prestigious, maybe. Interesting, definitely. Lucrative, possibly—since Osterfeld's word on who gets to be a partner is almost final. But terrific? No, I wouldn't say terrific."

"What's wrong?"

"Osterfeld uses people up like tissue paper. Toilet tissue, I suppose, would be a more graphic simile." She bit furiously into a breadstick. "I am the associate of the moment, which means I'm the only one he trusts with his big cases and Supreme Court briefs. Of course, I'm so honored that I work twenty-four hours a day for him, taking time only for the occasional nap in which I dream about how I can do an even better job."

"So what's wrong? It's not like you to mind working hard."

"I don't mind. But I know he's had favorites before. And if the past predicts the future, he will, at an appropriate time and for reasons which still aren't clear to me, kick me out of his office and turn his attention to the next associate."

"You're being paranoid."

"I'm not."

"Is there a sexual dimension to all this that I'm missing?"

"I never thought so, but this business trip makes me nervous. I think the Great God of Law is putting me to the test."

"Forgive me for being naive, but I haven't figured it out. Do you fall out of God's graces if you do sleep with him or if you don't?"

Dana tossed back her head and laughed. "That's what I was hoping you'd tell me. I suspect that he considers the Constitution far more important than sex, and wants to make sure that I do, too. On the other hand, I could be misreading it, in which case, I lose the chance at fulfilling one of my favorite fantasies."

"Isn't he a little old?"

"That's part of the fantasy. Osterfeld is a walking symbol of power. He isn't part of the inner circle, he *is* the inner circle. You don't get that power at our age, darling."

They talked about other men—including a lawyer named Mark whom Dana was dating. He was an associate at another law firm on Wall Street, and both of them were working such long hours that going out together required something just short of a state occasion. According to Dana, he was agreeable, smart, and very boring.

"He sounds like someone you should marry," Jackie said.

"My mother would love it. I bring him to all family occasions and firm functions. He is a fine escort and will make a fine husband."

"So?"

"So, you idiot, I'd rather spend my time dreaming about Herman Osterfeld, God of Law."

They both laughed, and Dana asked about Jackie's current loves. Jackie claimed that she hadn't been in New York long enough to have any.

"You're lying," said Dana, picking up her briefcase from under the chair. "I can always tell. But I have to get back to work, anyway. Just remember, next lunch I want to hear everything."

They hugged again at the door, and as Dana headed back to Wall Street, Jackie wondered why she had been so intent on keeping the name of Julian Beardsley from her very best friend.

Her job at *A.M. Reports* didn't officially start for another two weeks, but Jackie decided it was time to stop by and look around, let Steve Cawley know she was in town. Cawley, the executive producer of the show, was short, heavy, and balding, with a pencil perpetually stuck behind his ear, as if he were on the news desk of a local newspaper.

Ernest had filled Jackie in on Cawley before their first meeting, telling her that Cawley had been in his job for five years, which was considered an eternity in television, and *A.M. Re-*

ports had been on top of the ratings for most of that time. His reputation was unequaled; everyone said he had a magic touch. He had admitted to Ernest that he sometimes panicked when he heard people say that, afraid that the magic would disappear as quickly as it had come. Meanwhile, his bosses, terrified that he might leave, sweetened his contract at each yearly renewal. The money meant that alimony payments to his wife were easier to meet.

Cawley's instincts were the best, and the network executives had come to rely on them. It had been their idea to bring in another reporter on the show, but Cawley's idea to make it someone like Jackie—a good, solid reporter rather than a sexy star. At the first interview, they had liked each other immediately. Cawley had told her bluntly that it wasn't going to be easy to convince the powers-that-be to hire someone with brains, but if he could do it, the job was hers.

The receptionist at the front desk was yawning noisily when Jackie got out of the elevator, but perked up when Jackie told her who she was.

"We just got a memo about you," she said. "Aren't you the new field reporter?"

"I am. I'm just coming by to say hi to Steve Cawley. Is he around?"

"Sure."

Jackie found his office and knocked on the door.

"Who the hell is it?" The voice inside was gruff, sleepy.

"It's Jackie Rogers. Hope I'm not disturbing you."

"Jackie?" There was some shuffling inside, and a moment later, the door was flung open.

"Good to see you. Come in."

"I have a feeling it's a bad time."

"Never a bad time to see you." He slouched into the big chair behind his desk and motioned for her to sit on the sofa. "Actually, I was taking a nap, but it was time for me to get up, anyway."

"I'm sorry."

"No way for you to know." He smiled wearily. "One of those days. I was in at four this morning. Did you see the show? We had an exclusive interview with a survivor of that train crash. Good stuff." He glanced at his watch. "Meanwhile, tomorrow's show is still totally unbooked. Nobody'll be out of here before ten tonight."

"Long day."

"I shouldn't be telling you this. You'll be having them, too."

"I'm ready."

"Did you see the ratings this week?"

"I didn't." She was momentarily embarrassed, hoping it wouldn't be obvious that she hadn't been watching the show lately.

"We were number one by far. Killed the *Today* show. Had our highest rating in a year."

"I'm not surprised."

"I'm surprised every week that we win." He slouched deeper into his chair. "But if I get home in time tonight, I plan to celebrate the ratings with two slices of pizza and a very cold beer."

"You make it sound so glamorous to be at the network."

"Of course it's glamorous. I just happen to like working sixteen-hour days." He ran his hand ruefully over his shirt, and Jackie noticed that the buttons pulled tight at his waist. "Do you have a few minutes? I'll introduce you around."

"I'd love it."

He made a couple of phone calls, and then reported that the co-hosts of the show, Bradley James and Darlie Hayes, had already left for the day.

"They were in early," he explained apologetically.

"So were you."

"Right, but nobody cares if I have dark circles under my eyes," said Cawley, getting up from behind his desk. "Let's see if any of my staff considered it worthwhile to stay around this afternoon."

In the hall, he knocked lightly at a door across from his own, then walked in before anyone answered. The office was half the size of Cawley's, but crowded with tapes, awards, and TV memorabilia. A television was on, tuned to an all-news station, and it took Jackie a moment to realize that the strikingly handsome man lying on a couch by the television was fast asleep.

"Apparently, we all nap at the same time on these long days," whispered Cawley. "But that's Jeff Garth, one of our top producers."

Jeff's eyes opened and he stared right at Jackie. "Why is there a gorgeous woman in my office?" he asked.

Jackie laughed. "Sorry we woke you."

Jeff looked at her disarmingly. "A pleasant vision for a man coming out of a sound sleep. A beautiful woman is standing in front of me, and I had a dream that my boss referred to me as one of his top producers."

"That's what I heard," said Jackie, smiling.

Jeff stood up and stretched. He was six feet tall, his arms and chest nicely muscled. "Ah yes, top producer today because I got him the train-crash victim this morning. But I'm sure the compliment runs out at midnight. Tomorrow morning he'll want to know what I've done for him lately."

Cawley, ignoring the banter, introduced Jackie. "Jeff does much of our producing on the road, so you two will be spending a lot of days together."

"And a lot of nights together," said Jeff.

Looking at his tall, firm body and curly brown hair, Jackie thought of saying that she wouldn't mind that at all, but she resisted.

Jeff seemed to be studying her intently as well, and when she returned his gaze, he said, "You have gorgeous green eyes."

"Thank you," said Jackie. "You have terrific brown eyes."

They shared a smile, and Jackie sensed a spark between them. But Jeff changed the mood quickly, turning to Cawley. "I can't remember—Jackie just arrived from the boonies, right?"

Jackie raised an eyebrow, then interrupted. "Not exactly. I was at the network affiliate in Boston."

"All the same," said Jeff with a shrug. "Boston, Boise, whatever. Ain't New York."

"It's New York now," said Cawley as they walked out.

Jackie felt slightly shaken, unsure if it was Jeff's come-hitherness or his final put-down that had gotten to her.

Cawley closed Jeff's door. Not helping matters, he said, "Women around here are all nuts about Jeff. God knows why."

Jackie hoped that she'd find out.

"You haven't met Dominique, have you?" Cawley asked, continuing down the hall. "I think she's in editing. Let's stop there."

Dominique LaFarge was the other field reporter at *A.M.*

Reports—said to be beautiful, dumb, and friendly in bed. She had been discovered four years earlier by a network vice-president who had seen her singing in Las Vegas and found his heart beating fast. He brought her back to New York and put her on the air. What else he did with her was a matter of speculation.

In the edit room now, a tape editor told them Dominique had stepped out for a moment. Cawley and Jackie sat down, and two minutes later, Dominique returned. A waft of Obsession perfume preceded her into the room. She was dressed casually in tight black stirrup pants and a fluffy white sweater. But she was wearing a gold-and-diamond bracelet and matching earrings, and her thick red hair was pulled back, held in place by a black velvet bow. "It's a pleasure to meet you," she said, when Cawley introduced Jackie. Her smile was white enough for a toothpaste commercial, but her voice was a surprise—deep and throaty, a husky singer's voice. "I've been wondering what the new kid on the block would be like."

"A little nervous," said Jackie, "but pleased to be here."

"Aren't we all. I read the press release about you. Is it all true? Radcliffe? Award-winning investigative reporter?"

Jackie laughed. "Guilty as charged."

"Good. We need you here." She said it simply, honestly, but Cawley looked at her anxiously.

"I think Jackie will be able to add a new perspective to some of the stories we do," he said carefully.

"Don't worry, darling, I'm not insulted," said Dominique. "The most investigative reporting I've ever done was that five-part series on Linda Evans' wardrobe."

Cawley shrugged. "It was a good series. By the way, I've been meaning to ask if you want to follow up with an investigation of Victoria Principal's beauty secrets?"

"Sure, but isn't that the kind of heavy intellectual stuff you should give to Jackie?" She winked at him, her pouty mouth curved into a half-smile, and Jackie saw why the network exec had fallen in love. She was sweaty-palms material, all right.

"I think you can do it," said Cawley. "Anyway, Jackie isn't with us for another couple of weeks—and we can get Victoria for an interview next week in Malibu."

"I thought you were joking. You mean this is a real assignment?"

"You got it."

"Okay." She sighed. "Do I get to say that Victoria's beauty secret is that she's married to a plastic surgeon?"

"No."

"Just a thought."

"We didn't hire you to think," said Cawley affectionately. "Anyway, you better get back to editing. We need those voice-overs done this afternoon."

Dominique turned to Jackie. "Be prepared. It's a dog's life here. But let me know if there's anything I can help you with."

She sounded as if she meant it, so Jackie thanked her warmly and watched her saunter over to the soundproof booth where she was recording.

"She's gorgeous," Jackie said, as they headed back to the lobby. "Even better-looking than on the air."

"You noticed," said Cawley.

"She was also nicer than I expected."

"Everyone likes Dominique. She's terminally perky." He rubbed his eyes. "I happen to know that she's not as dumb as she pretends, but there are still some stories I wouldn't let her do, and she knows it. Even if she could handle them, she's got the wrong image. When people see Dominique on the air, they want to smile. They don't want to hear about foreign policy."

"So I get the stories that don't make anybody want to smile?"

"I wouldn't put it that way. You've just got a different style. You're serious and believable on the air. Sort of like Dan Rather."

"As long as you don't expect me to be like Dominique. It didn't strike me that we're two peas in a pod."

"No, you're not," he said seriously. "And I have to tell you that Dominique gets more fan mail than anyone else on the show. But she's right—you're going to be good for us."

"Thanks." Jackie pushed the button for the elevator. "Think I should borrow some of Dan's sweaters?"

"Can't hurt." He held the elevator door as she stepped in. "Just make sure they're low-cut."

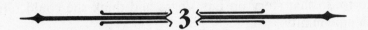

3

Dominique LaFarge woke up on Sunday morning feeling as if she were going to cry. A wonderful way to greet the day, she thought, glancing at the Sunday newspaper on her night table. She used to consider it one of the charms of living in Manhattan, that you could get the Sunday paper on your way home on Saturday night, as if the city were so far ahead of the rest of the world that even the next day arrived sooner than elsewhere. But this particular Sunday, getting the paper twelve hours early just meant that she had an additional twelve hours to be miserable.

Dominique was afraid that no matter how long she stayed in the business, she'd never stop being affected by the nasty rumors in the press. Today's gossip hurt particularly because it was so gratuitous. First there was the blurb about Jackie Rogers coming to *A.M. Reports*, which was fine, even though the thrust of it was that she was a genius coming to bimbo-land. All right, let her have an easy start, she seemed nice enough. But was the rest of it necessary? *"Jackie joins Dominique LaFarge, the show's other correspondent,"* wrote the columnist. *"Jackie seems to have been selected for her fine reporting. Dominique, as you'll remember, was hired for her fine body. And speaking about that lovely body, what are the rumors we hear about Dominique and the vice-president of a* different *network? Dominique and the gentleman were seen leaving the Plaza Hotel early the other morning. Maybe a breakfast meeting, maybe something else? Could it be that Dominique is looking to switch networks? Come on, Dominique. Negotiating is supposed to take place in the* boardroom.*"*

When she saw it, she wanted to throw up. She thought she'd moved beyond that, been accepted in New York. She'd certainly been accepted in the rest of the country. Cawley told her that her personal ratings kept getting higher, and her stories were getting better and better. So, she had been naive enough to think that the rumor-mongering was all over. But it had been a mistake to do that story on Las Vegas and think she could return with equanimity.

She'd had several singing engagements lately in Atlantic City and some in Vegas, and Dominique had to admit that she still loved getting on stage, wooing an audience. But it was different to try to return to Vegas on television; her critics clearly thought she was mocking them. And the spot really had been too suggestive, reminiscent of what she had left.

She couldn't blame Cawley, because the idea made sense. In fact, it had been hers. Bradley was doing a story in the studio on compulsive gambling, talking to two men and a woman whose lives had been ruined by gambling.

"It's so grim that it knocks you over," said Cawley, during one of the more or less regular meetings he held with talent and producers.

"Then you're not being fair to the gamblers," Dominique said, "because gambling isn't all gloom and doom. It starts out being very seductive and glitzy. Frankly, I think that's what addicts people. Gamble enough in Vegas, anyway, and you're treated like a king, with palatial suites, your own harem—ask for it and you get it."

"Good," said Cawley, "let's show it. We'll lead into Bradley's live spot with a tape piece you do on Vegas glitz and glamour. Maybe open with a round-up of the gorgeous rooms the high rollers get to stay in for free."

"Provided they gamble away a million bucks a night," said Bradley.

"I don't know," Dominique said slowly. "Isn't there a problem with my talking about Vegas on the air?"

"None," Cawley said. "You're an insider, which is good."

"Do we have to advertise it?"

Cawley smiled. "Don't worry about it, you're one of us now. The past is forgotten."

Dominique did the spot, despite her misgivings. She allowed the producer, Raleigh Anderson, to open with a shot of Dominique reclining in the marble-platformed whirlpool in a gambler's suite at the Sands Hotel. Then she interviewed an executive of the Las Vegas Hilton, sitting with him at the Egyptian-style bar. The end of the spot showed her lying on a huge round bed in Caesar's Palace, explaining how difficult it was to resist all the lures and enticements. Then she pushed a button, and gauze curtains descended around the bed as she lay back.

The funny thing about doing a spot like that was that she never really thought about other people seeing it. She and Raleigh—who had become a good friend—would dream up the terrific shots, and then just do them, as if they were alone, two girls showing off for each other, the outside world almost forgotten.

Dominique got out of bed now, threw the Sunday newspaper in the basket, opened her closet and stood very straight in front of the full-length mirror. Her bureau was the height of a ballet barre, and she reached for it now to begin the series of leg kicks and stretches she did every morning. She had done the same exercises virtually every day for the seventeen years she had been on stage and on television. No—eighteen years. Damn, she had been lying about her age for so long, she couldn't even remember what it really was.

Putting her leg on the would-be exercise barre, she brought her chest to her knee and bounced gently. It didn't really matter how old she was, she was as lithe and limber as ever. Of course, she had to work at it a little harder now than she used to, but she was determined to resist aging, just as she had resisted so many of the other problems that beset women like her who had to make their own success. For however many years she'd been in the business, she had nothing to hide. How many of the women who started out with her could say that? She knew any number of actresses and models who made a name for themselves, then waited in a constant state of anxiety for past indiscretions to surface in *Penthouse*. Well, it wouldn't happen to her. Like the other girls in Vegas, she'd had offers to pose for nude pictures when she was younger—big money, not much work. Most of the girls figured that there was no downside. If you didn't want to screw with the photographer, you didn't even have to, since most of them were—like the girls—interested in the money, not the sex. Better to get a great body in a picture than an average body in bed. The photographers who got too pushy also got a reputation, and the best girls stayed away.

But Dominique wasn't willing to sell her body for the pictures, even when the thousand or two thousand dollars she was regularly being offered really meant something. She always had a vision of the future, knew there was going to be a break that would depend on her talent, even her integrity, and not her looks. Despite what the gossip columns wanted people to believe, you couldn't make it to the top on your back. Maybe you could get up a rung or two, but after that, you had to get off the couch and prove yourself.

Dominique had gotten her break a few years ago, and now she loved being on *A.M. Reports*, in part because it was the only way that her mother, who lived in a town of sixty-two hundred people in rural Nebraska, ever got to see her. Dominique LaFarge, born Debbie Lane, admired her mother who had raised seven children all alone, after her husband died in a tractor accident. Dominique was the youngest, so she didn't remember much about the years that the family lived on a farm in Iowa. She did have a vivid image of her mother working constantly, never raising her voice, keeping seven children well-dressed, fed, and happy. When the children got older, her mother sold the farm—by sheer luck she got a good price, selling before the farm depressions. The family moved several times, in search of better jobs and schooling.

Dominique often wondered how her mother managed to accept her children with such equanimity—understanding and encouraging their diversity. Her oldest brother was a priest, others were teachers and accountants, one sister was a nurse. It was always clear that Dominique's talents lay in a different direction: she danced and sang her way through elementary school, watched old movies at the local theatre and dreamed of being a star.

Mrs. Lane suspected that her daughter would never be happy in a small town. So when at eighteen Debbie told her mother she wanted to change her name to Dominique LaFarge and try her luck in Hollywood or Las Vegas, Mrs. Lane gave her blessings. Maybe she was sending her daughter into an amoral world, but she trusted that Dominique was strong enough not to be corrupted.

Dominique held a variety of jobs, struggled first to make a living and then to make a name for herself. She had been around a lot before she got to *A.M. Reports*, and she was sometimes surprised at the naiveté of many of the people who worked there. It wasn't that they were young—though many were—so much as that they were sheltered. The two young women who booked most of Dominique's stories for her were typical. Both had grown up in New York and majored in journalism in college. Their clothes and manners were sophisticated, but their worlds, Dominique thought, were very limited. Once, when she first got to the show, Dominique suggested to one of the bookers, named Laurie Spinner, that they do a story on life behind the scenes at a Broadway musical.

"It's too New York," Laurie said, rejecting the idea. "Not the kind of thing anyone cares about in Iowa."

"What do you mean?" Dominique asked.

"This is a network show," Laurie explained airily. "We can't just do what we're interested in, we have to appeal to the whole country."

"You don't think people outside New York are interested in theater?"

"I know you can't imagine this," Laurie said, "but people outside New York don't know what theater *is*."

Dominique decided not to correct her, and she gradually learned that television people in New York said "Iowa" whenever they wanted to talk about people "not like us"—mysterious midwesterners with unfathomable taste. If a story flopped or a show got low ratings, it wasn't because anyone at the network had made a mistake, it was because they didn't understand it in Iowa. It gradually occurred to Dominique that nobody at the network had ever met anyone from Iowa, and it was extremely unlikely that Laurie Spinner could even find the state on a map. Dominique decided that disclosing her own background would serve no purpose.

Dominique finished her stretches, pulled off her T-shirt, and went to take a shower. Don't let the bastards get you down, she told herself, waiting for the water to get hot. She was glad that she had arranged to have brunch with Peter today—it would keep her from brooding all day. As she was about to step into the shower, she heard the phone ring. Grabbing a towel, she wrapped herself in it and went to answer.

"Dominique? It's Cawley. I'm going to kill you if you're upset."

She laughed. "Hi, Steve. I'm okay. You read the lovely things about me in the paper today, I take it?"

"Lies, jealousy, and envy. Not to mention slander and pure bullshit. Whoever writes that trash should be shot."

"Thanks for the support."

"It's not just me. Bradley thinks you're terrific and getting better every day. Between you, me, and the lamppost, he's starting to put on some pressure to get rid of Darlie. I can tell you who he'd like instead."

"I'm flattered."

"Happens to be true." He paused briefly. "One quick question?"

"Shoot."

"Nah, forget it. I don't believe anything I read. I can just tell the brass here that I'm personally confident that you're not negotiating with another network, can't I?"

So that's what the call and the extra charm were about. If she didn't like Cawley so much, she'd be annoyed. "The truth is that I did have an early breakfast meeting with a certain vice-president from NBC. Notice how they never mention the *guy's* name, Steve? I guess you can malign women, but not men. He's on the board for muscular dystrophy and asked me to sing at the New York benefit, which I said I'd do."

"Good for you. Tell him we'll buy a table to come see you."

Dominique hung up, took a quick shower, and got dressed for Peter. Having Peter Tully in her life made her feel so normal. They had first met when she did a cereal commercial that his advertising agency had created. She was used to men falling all over her, but for some reason, Peter didn't. She made a play for him which he ignored. When he finally took her out on a date, he didn't even kiss her good night. It was six weeks before they slept together. After that, he couldn't seem to get enough of her. She knew that he liked being seen with her, and that was okay. In an ungenerous moment she had told him that she thought his favorite possessions were his Porsche, his tape deck, and her—in that order. He had looked hurt, and she immediately apologized, even though it was true.

Dominique thought that Peter was simply insecure, eager to prove he had made it in the world by living in the right apartment, eating at the right restaurants and driving the right car.

Since Dominique wasn't excited by any of that, Peter tried to impress her with his career success, using his influence in the advertising world to get her several commercials. She didn't want to do most of them but was afraid he'd be hurt if she said no. Peter wasn't very good at distinguishing his job from his soul.

At thirty-nine, Peter had never been married, and Dominique sometimes suspected that he was the classic commitment-phobe, the kind women's magazines always wrote about. But she didn't think the fear would last forever. Sometimes she caught him gazing at her with a slight look of amazement, as if he found it hard to believe that someone as beautiful as Dominique would actually like him, would want to be with him whenever she could. Actually, she wanted even more than that. She wanted to marry him. It was time. She had done everything else.

Peter was ambitious for her in a way that she wasn't for herself anymore, and she often wondered if he even liked the person underneath the image. But it didn't matter, because he was kind and attentive. When he had called her the night before from Los Angeles, where he had been for the week, she told him she was lonely, and he offered to take the red-eye flight to New York, go home for a quick shower, and take her out for brunch.

"You don't have to do that," she said.

"Actually, it makes more sense. That way I don't have to waste the whole day Sunday traveling."

She dressed carefully for Peter, aware that he noticed. Funny, they'd been together close to a year, and she didn't think she'd ever worn blue jeans or a sweatshirt when he was around. He liked her being stylish enough to make people look twice when they walked down the street.

Peter arrived looking slightly tired, but as well turned-out as ever in cotton chino pants, an impeccable striped shirt, and an expensive oversize leather jacket. It was the style he sported for work and weekends. He had given up wearing a suit and tie long ago, having decided that this more personal look immediately showed clients that he was creative and original, full of one-of-a-kind ideas. The only problem, as far as Dominique could tell, was that every creative director in New York had done exactly the same thing. Chino pants and leather jackets were as much a standard on lower Madison Avenue as the three-piece suit was on Wall Street.

He kissed her briefly, looked approvingly at her very short suede skirt and loosely draped silk shirt, accented with the Hermès scarf he had once given her. Peter knew labels.

"I've made a reservation for brunch at Mortimer's," he said. "You all set?"

"Sure," she said. She was a little tired of Peter's brand-name restaurants; he went wherever his clients were likely to be. She thought of suggesting a little neighborhood place that had just opened around the corner, but she knew Peter wouldn't approve.

They took a cab to the restaurant, even though it was a beautiful day, and not many blocks away. Mortimer's was crowded, and as they waited at the bar for their table, Peter said hello to enough people to make the visit and the mediocre brunch worthwhile.

"How about a walk in Central Park?" Dominique asked when they were finally outside again. "It's so lovely out. There aren't many days like this in New York."

Peter looked dubious. "As long as I'm back in town early, I should really get a little work done this afternoon. Feel like coming down to my office?"

"Oh, come on," said Dominique. She slipped her arm through his, snuggled against the leather jacket. It was a delightful September day, warm with a gentle breeze and perfectly blue sky. "How about renting a boat and rowing on the lake in the park? It looks so romantic."

"It doesn't look that way close up," said Peter. "The lake is dirty and the people are scuzzy."

"There must be something I can convince you to do just for fun. A museum? Window-shopping on Fifth? The Frick?"

They settled on a drive in his Porsche, and took another cab to the garage where the car was parked. The attendant brought it up quickly, and Peter looked it over for scratches or dents, then removed the canvas hood protector slung over the front of the car.

"You're the only person I know who keeps a diaper on his car," said Dominique, sliding into the passenger seat and slamming the door.

"Just an extra precaution," he said.

They pulled out of the garage, moved through the city streets which, even on a Sunday, were crowded with cars. Dominique wondered why it was necessary to have a car that went one hundred sixty miles an hour when it was rarely possible to travel faster than a crawl.

Peter drove to the Henry Hudson Parkway where traffic was finally light and headed north. He turned on a classical music station and opened the sunroof. Slipping on a pair of sunglasses, Dominique tilted her head upward and sighed with satisfaction. She loved the feel of the wind in her hair, the sun beating down.

"Where are we going?" she asked as Peter paid the toll that officially took them out of Manhattan.

Peter shrugged. "I seem to remember an estate nearby, right on the river. Might be a pretty place to stop."

Dominique nodded, glad that he had gotten into the mood, after all.

The estate was mostly empty, but a sign promised that it was a public park, so they wandered in, through carefully constructed English gardens and overarching chestnut trees.

"Doesn't anybody else in Manhattan know about this spot?" Dominique asked, reaching for Peter's hand.

"There's not much to do here," he said. "I know about it because we had a company picnic here once."

Dominique thought that looking around and breathing the air gave them plenty to do, but she didn't say so. They wandered over to a steep grassy hill overlooking the Hudson River and sat down. The distant water was glimmering, a freighter moved slowly along, pushed by a tugboat that seemed far too small to maneuver the larger weight. Dominique put her arm around Peter and leaned her head on his shoulder.

"Sometimes I think I miss all this," she said. "I know I've been in New York for too long when peace and quiet seem such special treasures."

"You're never in New York for too long," said Peter. "You're always traveling."

"I bring New York with me. Doing a story out of town for twenty-four hours doesn't exactly bring a sense of calm." She stroked his neck lightly. "Don't you ever need an escape? A place in the country where we could go together?"

Peter swallowed visibly. "I like the city. I'd get bored elsewhere."

"Could you imagine raising kids in the city?"

"Why not?"

"I never even asked, honey—do you want kids?"

"Of course I do."

She kissed him softly. "I do too. And I love you, Peter. I want to have kids with you." She let her knee caress his thigh and kissed him deeply. Peter put his arms around her waist and pulled her closer as he lay back. Glancing around, she saw that there was no one in sight, and moved on top of him. Despite the burden of clothes, she could feel his desire rising. She stroked his cheek with her long nails and moved her hips gently as they kissed, pleased that Peter wanted her. She had dared to bring up her secret desire, the true underpinnings, for her, of their relationship, and he hadn't run away. As they kissed on the grass, she had the feeling that maybe, just maybe, he was thinking of her, and not the Porsche.

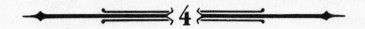

Jackie spent Monday being introduced to the network brass she hadn't yet met. She quickly realized that it was the merest formality—each of the executives wanted to believe he was so important that no new talent could appear on the air without his prior approval. No executive wanted to be asked about the "new girl" at a cocktail party and have to admit he hadn't even met her.

Walking with Cawley from office to office, Jackie wondered why a network would possibly need so many vice-presidents. Most of them blurred together, a group of fiftyish men with large offices, numerous phone lines, and pretty secretaries. The only standouts in the group were the one woman she met, who was the vice-president for personnel and seemed pleasant and efficient, and the vice-president for daytime programming named Winston Axminster, who seemed insufferably arrogant. He spent their brief meeting chomping on a cigar and leering openly. Jackie wondered if he could have been Dominique's benefactor.

Jackie got back to her apartment at dinnertime, and hoping for another surprise visit from Julian, kept on makeup, jewelry and silk suit. By eight o'clock, she realized that she was acting silly, and at nine she got sufficiently angry at herself to put on jeans and begin scrubbing the kitchen floor—something she hadn't done since she moved in. She was halfway across the floor when the phone rang, and it was Julian—wanting to know if she'd had dinner yet.

"Of course I've had dinner," Jackie said. "It's late."

"Oh. Well, how about having dinner again?"

"I can probably manage it."

"Good. I'm calling from the car. I'll be there in about twenty minutes."

She tried to decide if twenty minutes gave her enough time to shower and wash her hair. Since she smelled of ammonia, she decided she had better.

Forty-five minutes later, the doorman called to say that Mr. Beardsley was waiting. Jackie went downstairs to find Julian sitting in the back seat of his limousine talking on the telephone. She sidled in next to him. He blew her a kiss and returned to his conversation, which seemed to be about some wild speculations in the Hong Kong gold market.

"Sewall, you don't have any guts," he said at one point. "Do you want me to come there next week and work it out with you?"

Jackie couldn't hear what Sewall said, but Julian laughed and glanced at her. "No, I don't have any ulterior motives," he said into the phone. "I just want to see what the hell you're up to. I'll be there in a few days."

Julian hung up and grinned at her. "It's good to see you. You look beautiful." He ran his fingers through her hair, which was still a little damp.

"Hard day?" Jackie asked.

"More or less as usual. I spent half the day on the phone with Washington. Damn government regulators are trying to take all the fun out of this business. How about you?"

"My business is still fun," she said. She described her visit a few days earlier to Steve Cawley and the meeting with Dominique. "Cawley already warned me that Dominique is the hot property on the show. It makes me nervous, because I can't figure out exactly why they hired me. Maybe they think that between Dominique's sex appeal and my brains they have one good field reporter."

"There's nothing wrong with your sex appeal."

"You're partial, but thank you. Now tell me what's happening in the commodities markets. Should I buy or sell?"

"You should stay out. I don't think you'd have the stomach for it. Which reminds me—that was the head of our London office on the phone. He's been screwing up royally, and I'm going over to check up on him. Want to come?"

"Thanks, but I don't think so."

"Why not?"

She looked at him closely, surprised to see that he was serious. "I've got a lot to do before I start my new job," she said.

"Fine, you'll do it in London. I'll make sure there's a desk in
the room. I always have a suite."

Jackie laughed. "I wasn't worried about the accommodations."

"Good. Then it's settled."

"We've been out on two dates, Julian. You might decide
you're sick of me before we even get there."

"It's three dates if you count tonight. I'm willing to take my
chances."

"It all sounds vaguely improper."

"It seems to me we discussed sexual proprieties the first night.
Giving in hasn't turned out to be that bad, has it?"

"Not bad at all, so stop looking for compliments."

He grinned. "You'll come?"

"Of course."

They managed to squeeze in a few more nights together before
Julian left, and Jackie was pleased to discover that they weren't
getting tired of each other, after all. Julian had expanded his trip
to include business stops in Germany and Paris, and since Jackie
wasn't eager to chase him all over the continent, they agreed to
meet in London.

The flight was long, and Jackie didn't sleep. She flipped
through a novel by Balzac that Julian had given her before he
left—along with a first-class plane ticket. But she couldn't concentrate. She watched the sky turn from black to a brilliant,
red-streaked dawn, high above the clouds. It seemed such an
auspicious start to the trip that she didn't even mind when the
plane, plunging through the heavy clouds over London, landed
in the gray chill of Heathrow Airport.

She grabbed her carry-on bag, passed quickly through customs, and ran into a uniformed chauffeur holding a sign that
said BEARDSLEY GUEST.

"I guess you're looking for me," she told him.

"You're Mr. Beardsley's young friend?"

"That's right. Jackie Rogers."

"Welcome." He took her bag and led her toward a waiting
car. "Mr. Beardsley called with the message that he won't be in

from Paris until early this afternoon. I'm at your disposal until it's time for me to meet his flight."

"How nice." She settled into the car, trying to decide what you did when you had a chauffeur at your disposal.

"Are you familiar with London?" he asked.

"More or less," she said. "It's always been my favorite city."

"Care for a quick tour?" She agreed, so he took a circuitous route, driving past Buckingham Palace and Westminster Abbey and around Piccadilly Circus.

"Perhaps you'd like to stop in Harrods before you go to your hotel?"

"Definitely not," she said. Her last trip to London had been to cover Prince Andrew's wedding. Since the royal family wasn't about to grant interviews to a reporter from a local television station in Boston, she'd had to improvise—and had spent two days in Harrods, doing spots on all the gifts that Sarah Ferguson was likely to get. Her favorite was a china beer mug in the shape of an English sheepdog. She'd hoped that Fergie got lots of them.

They drove past Hyde Park, and pulled up at a plush-looking hotel across the street. In the lobby, an elegantly dressed woman greeted Jackie and explained that Mr. Beardsley always stayed in the Imperial Suite. "I'll accompany you to make sure that everything is in order," she said. They rode up in a gilt-edged elevator, went into a suite that was considerably larger than Jackie's apartment in New York and much better furnished. In one corner was a desk with a typewriter.

"Anything we can do for you?" the manager asked.

"Just tell the driver that I'm going to take a quick nap, and then maybe he can drop me off at the British Museum."

"Shall I have the maid come turn down the bed?"

"That's all right. I can handle it." Jackie shut the door behind her and wandered around the suite, wondering when Julian would arrive. She pulled down a corner of the heavy chintz bedspread and crawled under. Maybe a very quick nap.

The next thing she heard was Julian's voice whispering sweetly in her ear, "Welcome to London, Sleeping Beauty." Then a soft kiss on her cheek.

Jackie struggled to wake up. She hardly remembered falling

asleep, but according to the digital clock on the night table, it was 2:15 P.M.

"I didn't mean to be asleep," she said, feeling slightly disoriented.

Julian laughed. "Why not? It's the only reasonable thing to do after a long flight."

She yawned and pushed back the covers as Julian leaned over to kiss her again.

"I missed you," he said.

"Good."

"I have the entire afternoon free and I'm with a beautiful woman in my favorite city. What should we do?"

"I'll leave it up to you."

"I have one very good idea," he said, stroking her hair.

She smiled. "Shouldn't we go exploring London?"

"Other things to explore first. Like you." He went over to his small suitcase—Jackie marveled at how little luggage he had brought on the trip—and took out a pale blue bottle. "I brought you a glimpse of heaven from Paris."

He handed her the bottle, and she noticed a handwritten label: *"L'Huile des Dieux. Pharmacie de M. Herbert, 14 Rue des Jardins."* "Oil of the Gods?" asked Jackie, translating.

"A special formula," said Julian. He splashed a little on his palm, rubbed it gently on her neck. It was a light body oil, with a delicate scent of almonds and roses intermingling. "Monsieur Herbert is an old friend. When I told him about you, he offered this as his special *potion d'amour*." Julian reached to her blouse, began unbuttoning it. "Can I offer a body rub?"

"I don't think I could resist."

Julian slipped off her blouse, smiled when he saw the creamy white, silk camisole underneath. "God, you're sexy," he said. He brought his hands under the camisole, pulled it off over her head, then looked appreciatively at her body, bare to the waist, her nipples rising at his gaze. Jackie tried to decide what it was about Julian that made her feel sexy and free, less proper than her normal style.

"We'll start this as a back rub," Julian said. "A little relaxation after your flight." Jackie lay down on her stomach, felt Julian's strong hands, slippery with his Parisian oil, begin to caress her back and shoulders. He stroked firmly at her upper

back, releasing the tension, grazed down slowly to her waist.
Almost without pause he removed the rest of her clothes, continued to massage her buttocks and thighs, moved down to her
feet and sensuously anointed them with the oil.

Jackie turned over, reached for his hands. "Come here. I
want you." She heard her own voice, thick with desire. In
response, Julian kissed her languorously, then continued the
massage by sprinkling the oil on her breasts, slowly rubbing in
each droplet, doing the same on her stomach, her inner thighs.
She reached for him, and once more he resisted, intent on
continuing her pleasure. She sighed deeply, glorying in the
massage, her flesh responding to Julian's hands. "I want you,"
she whispered again, and finally he moved on top of her. She
sighed as he filled her, massaging deeply the place his hands had
missed. She groaned and moved forcefully under him, her flesh
finding its point of desire as she clung to Julian, arching against
him, calling his name. The fragrance of the oil joined with the
scent of their togetherness and Jackie, her body finally calm, felt
overcome with contentment.

The London fog had lifted, and the air was clear and sparkling
when they finally stepped outside.

"How about a walk through Hyde Park?" Julian suggested.
They crossed the street and strolled into the park, holding hands
like teenagers. Julian stopped to throw some pennies into a
small fountain.

"What an amazing park," he said. "It's been around since the
sixteenth century, and every generation finds something new to
do with it. For awhile it was used for military maneuvers. Then
Henry VIII stocked it with deer and kept it as a royal hunting
ground. It wasn't until the Restoration that it was reclaimed for
the public. Now . . ." he shrugged as they walked by a bench
where an old woman sat, surrounded by a half-dozen shopping
bags, feeding the birds.

"How do you know all that?" asked Jackie.

"I used to spend a lot of time in London."

"That doesn't explain it. I grew up with the Boston Public
Gardens virtually in my backyard, but if I had to give you a
tour, all I'd be able to say is that it's green and has a lot of
flowers."

"Should I stop lecturing?"

"No. I love learning from you."

He ushered her out of the park and into the limousine waiting by the gate for them. She wasn't sure how it—or they—had arrived there.

"How about a look at the National Gallery?" Julian asked.

Her look of surprise made him laugh. "I have good sources of information. I always know what you want."

They got into the car, and the driver pulled easily into the traffic. Jackie decided that it wouldn't take much to get used to having a chauffeur.

"Would you mind a brief detour to the Tate?" asked Julian.

"Where all the Turners and Constables are?"

"Right. My son is a big fan of Turner. He doesn't have bad taste. I guess it's something about the fire, ships and water— it's the same feeling as the war pictures that kids have always liked, but these have a little more dignity. Makes them acceptable for a card-carrying member of Students for Nuclear Disarmament. Anyway, I promised him I'd pick up some posters for his room."

"How old is your son?"

"Fourteen."

"I thought fourteen-year-olds put up pictures of punk rock stars and *Playboy* centerfolds."

"The sixteen-year-old does that. The fourteen-year-old is the sensitive one in the family."

"Ah, two boys." Jackie sat back in her seat, wondering why she felt like a giant balloon had just popped.

"The boys live with their mother?" she ventured.

Julian nodded.

"Break it to me right now," she said. "Are you divorced, or am I having an affair with a married man?"

"Divorced," Julian said. "Aren't all men my age divorced?"

"I never really thought about it."

It had occurred to her, of course, that her current lover must have had a previous life. Before she left to join Julian, she had taken Feodor out to an expensive restaurant for lunch, primed him with two vodka-tonics and one fairly hefty steak, and pumped him for information. He told her that Julian was reasonably faithful and very generous. He had recently broken off a long-term relationship with one Alexis Wilson—the parting was amicable and by mutual consent—and had set her up at a financial firm in midtown where she was now drawing a phenomenal salary. After two more vodkas, Feodor told her everything he knew about Beardsley Enterprises, including the fact that it had just come out clean from an investigation by the Commodities Futures Trading Commission—the CFTC—which was the government agency charged with overseeing commodities trading.

All that, and she had never thought to ask about an ex-wife, or two sons who liked to decorate their rooms with posters. So much for my credentials as an investigative reporter, she thought.

They stopped at the Tate, bought four prints for Julian's son, and went on to the National Gallery, where Jackie happily lost herself in the art. She knew some of the paintings well, and seeing them again was like meeting old friends. But then she remembered the information she'd learned in the car, and she couldn't concentrate on the pictures anymore.

"How does your son feel about Rembrandt?" she asked as they stopped in front of his self-portrait.

"I don't know," said Julian. "Was he your teenage hero?"

"God, no. I used to think he was dark, boring, and not worthy of his reputation. I was convinced that if the cards in the museum said 'Joe Smith' instead of 'Rembrandt,' nobody would even take a second look."

Julian chuckled. "And now?"

"It took years of art history classes to make me see the light. Or the dark, I should say. Though, by the way, have you ever noticed the difference in color between the Rembrandts here and the ones at the Metropolitan Museum in New York?"

"Frankly no," said Julian.

"The Met has a huge department of art restoration—though I had a professor at Radcliffe who used to call it art destruction. They've scrubbed all the Rembrandts as if they were dirty shirts. They're a lot brighter now, but they weren't *supposed* to be bright. Someone said they've turned *Night Watch* into *Day Watch*."

"Now you're the good guide," said Julian. "Tell me more."

Jackie sighed. "How did we get onto this? I didn't really want to talk about Rembrandt—I wanted to talk about your son. Your sons. And your ex-wife."

"Nothing much to talk about," said Julian. "You'll meet them when we get back to New York. Marianne still lives in our house in New Jersey with the kids, and I go there on weekends whenever I can."

"How cozy. You might as well still be married."

"Not exactly. Marianne leaves when I'm there, and we don't spend a lot of time dealing with each other. She's got a great life now. She takes my money, but she doesn't have to bother talking to me."

"I think talking to you is a lot more interesting than taking your money."

"Ah, that's what girlfriends always think. It's not what wives think."

"Do I detect a trace of bitterness?"

Julian made a face. "Mild. Marianne left me five years ago because she said I was swallowing her up and she needed her own identity. I understood that—I even respected her for it. But when it came right down to it, she wanted to be on her own as long as I was still supporting her."

"And you are?"

"Of course I am. Marianne now owns and runs a little art gallery in SoHo. Guess who bought it for her."

Jackie shrugged, not sure that she was ready to take sides, her loyalty to Julian skewed by her general belief that it was women who got hurt by divorce. "Were you blameless in all this?"

"Of course I was." He laughed. "I never screwed around—so what more can you want out of a husband? Marianne would say I was too busy sleeping with my business to notice her or anyone else."

"Should I call her and tell her she was wrong?"

"She'd never believe it. Actually, I don't think she meant to divorce me, either. She thought her leaving would make me realize how much I missed her and start paying more attention."

"But you started paying more attention elsewhere, instead?"

"Right." Julian looked reflective for a moment. "Marianne was rich and bored and thought a little *sturm und drang* would add some excitement to her life. I didn't. I'm too busy to waste a lot of time being brokenhearted."

Though it sounded callous, Jackie was sure he didn't mean it that way. He was simply too rich and practical to enjoy the fine art of agonizing about love.

Julian put his arm around her, and they walked on through the museum, stopping at a special exhibit of photographs of Windsor Castle.

"It would be nice to be royalty," said Jackie after they had examined the pictures from every angle, "but I think I've seen enough of the queen's bedroom."

"What would you like to see now?"

"My own."

Dressing for dinner, Jackie put on the one slinky black dress she had brought along, and a necklace of coral and pearls. She swept her hair into a knot on top of her head and noticed that some of the curls slipped out. She didn't try recapturing them. She could never think of herself as sexy—but she had to admit that tonight she at least looked fetching.

As she stepped into the living room, Julian was opening the door to their dinner companions. Erwin Sewall, who ran Julian's London office, was the consummate Englishman in three-piece blue suit, highly polished shoes, and a blue-and-red club tie. Jackie thought he looked a little like Alden. His wife, whose name was Samantha, reminded her of one of the Garden Club ladies Dana had described. They shook hands and looked each other over carefully.

Julian started to ask what everyone wanted to drink, but Erwin interrupted him.

"Too late, dear fellow. I've taken the liberty of ordering up two bottles of Dom Perignon and just a touch of caviar. It should be here momentarily."

A small smile danced on Julian's lips. "Just what are we celebrating?"

Erwin, seated, made a half-bow toward Jackie. "It's in honor of the lovely lady you brought to London. To your good taste."

"I'm glad to drink to both my good taste and to this very lovely lady," said Julian amiably. "But I've never known you to spend money on champagne when you could put it into something more substantial."

"Like a gold deal?"

Julian raised his eyebrows. "That's right. The one you didn't have the guts to try."

There was another knock on the door, and a tuxedo-clad

waiter came in, begged their pardon for interrupting, then pulled in a table with roses, champagne, and caviar. As soon as he left, Erwin picked up one of the bottles and fingered its label.

"Julian, you know I'm opposed to some of the speculations you've been suggesting, but this is still your company. I decided to go along with your decision." He popped the cork on the bottle. "To you, dear fellow. Your phone call last week paid off royally."

Julian grinned and reached for a glass. "How much?" he asked.

"Numbers?"

Julian nodded.

"It's not over yet, but I guess we'll make two million pounds on this one. Maybe three million." Erwin filled Julian's glass, then poured glasses for Jackie and Samantha.

"And to you," he said.

"I'm afraid I haven't made a dime this week," Jackie said. "Or a shilling, for that matter."

"Then stay close to Julian," said Erwin.

They drank the champagne, and before her second glass was empty, Jackie heard another cork pop and saw Erwin reaching to refill her glass. She continued sipping, and let the conversation swirl around her head. The fatigue from the flight, the long day, and the champagne were combining nicely to dull her senses. Julian and Erwin were talking about silver and gold, futures and options, markets and arbitrage, but she couldn't concentrate, and the conversation drifted by. She would learn about Julian's business another time.

The champagne gone, Julian asked if they were ready for dinner. Jackie pulled herself back to the moment and stood up. "Give me a few minutes," she said. She slipped into the bedroom and closed the door behind her. She caught a glimpse of herself in the mirror, noticed her eyes were bright, her face flushed.

She heard the bedroom door open and close softly again. She watched Julian in the mirror as he came up behind her and put his hands on the V of her dress. His fingers slid down, and he cupped her breasts, pulling them from the dress. They rose in his hands, above the black silk material. Julian swayed gently, rubbing against her. She could feel his body tensing; in the mirror she watched his head move to her shoulder, and then she abandoned the vision to turn slowly and meet his lips, his tongue. He kept stroking her breasts, and she reached with one hand to hold his buttocks.

"It's good," he whispered. Still holding tightly, she could feel his erection, firm against her hips. He took a few steps backward, sat on the edge of the bed, and pulled her toward him, his mouth eager on her nipples. But now she wanted him. She tugged at the buttons of his English-made pants, and Julian groaned slightly as her tongue danced over his groin. He lay back and she found his rhythm: quickening, powerful; they moved together until she tasted the acrid, sour gush of his satisfaction.

They lay still for just a few moments, and Jackie rested her head on Julian's stomach, caught between the damp mystery of his expended penis and the crisp starchiness of his shirt.

"You're good to me," he said softly, running a finger down her cheek. "Come here so I can return the favor."

"Later," she said. "Erwin will wonder where we are."

"Erwin can order more champagne and charge it to me," said Julian. He began teasing her with his fingers, then slid down closer to her, his tongue darting and gliding. She closed her eyes, swaying, pleasure rippling through her.

"I could stay here forever," Julian said between breaths. She moved with him then, not wanting to stop, until her release was complete. Then she held on to him, breathless, waiting for the world to resume its normal pace.

When Julian got up, Jackie disappeared into the bathroom, splashed water on her face and repaired her makeup. Everyone was standing up when she returned to the living room, and Erwin announced that he had reservations for them at his favorite restaurant. Jackie allowed herself to be ushered into the limousine once again, and they sped through London. Dinner was gay and giddy—more champagne, a meal that arrived without menus, courtesy of Erwin's nod to the maître d' and a suggestion to bring the usual, but make it a bit more special. Jackie wasn't sure what she was eating, but tasting truffles and lobster, she wondered why the English had a reputation for dull food.

As they were finishing pastries and coffee, Erwin suggested they stop by his club for an after-dinner drink.

Back in the limousine, they returned to the Hyde Park area and pulled up in front of a dark, foreboding building. Erwin knocked at the door, flashed a card at the peephole, and the door opened.

"Mr. Sewall, welcome. It's a quiet night here. We're glad to have you."

Erwin nodded to him and exchanged a brief pleasantry. There was a long stairway immediately inside the door, and they climbed it in the dim light, Julian offering Jackie a steadying hand. At the top, they went through another set of double doors into a room that at first glance looked like any other expensive London bar—lots of shiny brass, hanging glasses, and a long marble bar-counter. A few well-dressed men and women lounged at the bar. But the focus of attention seemed to be in the corners of the room where there were crap tables and backgammon boards. Off to one side, Jackie noticed a group of people playing blackjack. It was a very small and elite gathering.

"Welcome to the bankers' club," Erwin said.

"Club or casino?" asked Jackie.

"Both. Betting is legal in London in private clubs. So all the bankers who get rich during the day by being conservative come here at night to get richer by gambling."

Julian said hello to several people, and Samantha went off to join a group of women who were lifting their glasses at the bar.

"Do you play craps?" asked Erwin.

"Never have," said Jackie, "but I'll watch. Maybe I can learn."

She followed him to the craps table, and caught herself wondering if *A.M. Reports* had ever done a spot on London's clubs. She'd have to suggest it when she got there—even though it was probably the kind of story Dominique would be assigned.

Jackie couldn't follow the craps game at all, but she noticed that Julian and Erwin were soon out of chips. Julian purchased more from a man sitting at a Victorian desk and handed them to her.

"Your turn," Julian said. "The rule is: whatever you win, you keep. What you lose, you don't owe me."

"That's not one of your better investments," she said.

"Oh yes it is."

She sat down at a blackjack table and quickly won four straight hands while Julian watched.

"Incredible," he said. "What's your system?"

"Pure ignorance. I've only played once before in my life."

"You should come work for me," said Julian. "I like people with an instinct for making money."

She picked up the chips she'd won and held them out to him. "Here you go. This is all the work you're likely to get out of me."

"Does that mean we can call it a night?"

"No way. I'm just getting hot," said Jackie.

"You can always take your hot streak to bed."

"Now there's something I hadn't thought of."

Julian went off to work early the next morning, and Jackie spent the day wandering through the city, visiting antique stores and second-hand book shops. She found a very old copy of Stendhal's *The Red and the Black* and bought it—not sure whether she'd give it to Julian or keep it. Then she went back to look through a dusty pile of old books and picked up a slim volume of poems by Elizabeth Barrett Browning. It seemed very old and fragile, and when she flipped to the front, she realized it was a first edition. The price scrawled on the inside cover was one pound. She went back to the clerk and, heart pounding, handed him the book and the money. He didn't pay much attention—he just put the book into a bag and gave it back to her. While he was brushing the dust off his fingers, she slipped out of the store, feeling as if she had just stolen the Hope Diamond.

When she got back to the hotel, there was a message from Julian. He had called at three o'clock to say he would be late—but that she should go ahead and call room service for dinner. She crumpled the note and tried to control her annoyance until she got to the suite. Did he really expect her to sit alone in the hotel all night, waiting for him to return? She picked up the phone and had the operator get her the number for the NBC News Bureau in London. She got through to Lance McDonald, the director of the bureau, whom she had met covering Prince Andrew's wedding.

"What are you doing here?" Lance asked on the phone. "Don't tell me there's another wedding I don't know about."

"No way," she laughed. "I'm just here for a couple of days, and wondered if you were free for dinner."

"You're on," he said.

They met at a cozy bar near Fleet Street that had antiques on the walls and candles burning in Chianti bottles on the tables. She listened avidly as Lance told her all the network gossip. He was impressed that she had moved to *A.M. Reports*, and told her that Prince Charles had once given a terrific interview to Darlie Hayes.

"She didn't ask any intelligent questions, but she looks a lot like Princess Di. I think Charles sympathized with her," said Lance.

They drank dark beer and ate mutton pie. "This makes me feel like I'm truly in London," said Jackie.

"You are." Lance glanced at his watch. "I know I'm in London because I never sleep at a reasonable time. I have to get back to the bureau."

"Now?"

"That's right. The evening news runs at seven P.M., New York time, and it's taped at six-thirty. That's half-past eleven here."

"And you have to be there?"

"Not always. But tonight there's a story from our bureau, and I should be around to make sure that everything is all right."

"What's the story?"

Lance grinned. "Can't divulge. You're with the competition now."

In the cab going back to the hotel, she felt a pang of guilt, wondering if Julian had already returned. But the room was empty when she walked in, and relief slowly turned to annoyance. Why had Julian asked her to come with him to London if he couldn't be around?

He came in well after midnight, apologized, and began telling her excitedly about the deals he had been setting up. She listened carefully, aware of how little she actually knew about Julian's business. Though it was late, and she wanted Julian in bed, her journalist's instincts got the better of her, and she prodded Julian with questions, tried to follow the trail of the gold and silver transactions he was describing.

"Are the laws that govern the markets very different in London and New York?" she asked at one point, as he was relating an intricate ploy.

Julian stopped suddenly, touched a finger to her lips. "I told you once what a good interviewer you are. You make me talk too much."

"Not too much—just enough. I want to know everything about you."

"Let's save a few things for another time."

They snuggled into bed, and for a moment she wondered why her question had brought Julian up short. She felt briefly unsettled. Something in his account tonight suggested that he was dancing on the edge of the law. But that was foolish—Julian was rich, but he wasn't corrupt. Anyway, he had his arms around her now, and as she nestled against his chest, she decided to think about it another time.

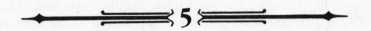

The day her job was to start at *A.M. Reports*, Jackie woke up in Julian's New York apartment in time to flip on the television set from the remote control by the bed, and watch Bradley James interview a rock star who seemed stoned. It was a few minutes before eight o'clock in the morning, and the singer was on live from Las Vegas, where it wasn't quite five. It was a good bet that he hadn't bothered to go to sleep the night before. The interview was embarrassing, and Jackie wondered why Bradley James didn't just end it, but he struggled through his list of questions. Jackie threw back the down coverlet and looked around for her nightgown. Next to her, Julian was still sleeping soundly. She didn't know what time he had finally fallen asleep. She had drifted off sometime after two, while Julian, sitting naked and excited on the edge of the bed, stayed on the phone with his traders in Hong Kong.

"The silver market is going wild," he had whispered. But she had fallen asleep anyway, having finally learned that a market swing that caused Julian to win or lose a million dollars didn't necessarily affect many other people. When you were playing with fortunes, the drop of a point or two was an apocalypse. But it wasn't anything to report on the morning news.

The television obviously wasn't bothering Julian, so Jackie left it on. She found her nightgown and ambled into the bathroom. Even now, half-awake, she marveled at the room, and the perspective it gave on life and the city. The skylight windows opened up to the blue heavens over Manhattan rather than the gray sidewalk below. Julian had admitted that the fixtures were all inlaid with fourteen-carat gold, and the intricate Italian tiles that covered the walls had been hand-painted.

When she got out of the shower, she glanced at the television set. The interview with the stoned singer was finally over, and Darlie Hayes was now chatting with a dog trainer who was trying to be amusing with stories about his experiences on the set of a big hit movie. She went back into the bathroom. *This is what your new job is all about,* she murmured to the reflection in the mirror. *Entertaining America during its morning pee and shower.*

She dressed carefully, combed her hair, and wondered what to do about the first-day jitters. When she came out of the bathroom, Julian was sitting up in bed staring intently at the television.

"You told me about the redhead," he said. "What's her name again?"

"Dominique."

"She just did a commercial for dog food."

Jackie nodded. "I'm not surprised. It's probably easier to make money hawking dog food than maintaining your integrity as a reporter."

"Which will you do?"

She smiled. "It's easy to maintain one's standards when nobody has offered to corrupt them. At the moment my integrity is safe."

"Good to hear." Julian stretched. "I'm running late this morning. Why don't you have Derek drive you to work—then he can come back and pick me up."

"Sweet of you, but I'll take a cab. I won't win a lot of hearts pulling up to my office the first day in a limousine."

Julian shrugged. "Whatever you think."

The same receptionist was sitting at the front desk when Jackie came in. She waved and motioned her in. Jackie hesitated, unsure where to go. She thought of ducking into the ladies' room to compose herself.

But before she had the chance, the elevator opened again, and Steve Cawley came rushing off. Seeing Jackie, he grabbed her arm.

"Thank God you're here," he said.

She laughed. "That's a nice welcome."

"It's serious. Come on." He began racing down the halls—the offices of *A.M. Reports* bore a striking resemblance to a rabbit warren—and Jackie followed, thinking that she would never find her way out again. They got to her office which was small but pleasant, filled this morning with sunshine and a small vase of daffodils.

"For you," he said. "The producers' welcome." He sat down, pulled the pencil from behind his ear, and began fiddling with it. "I'm in a bind. I've got a big hole in the show tomorrow, and a big story I want to fill it with. There's no time to break you in slowly. Think you can handle it?"

"Tomorrow?"

"Yup."

"What's the story?"

"Even hear of Dantil?"

She wrinkled her brow, trying to place it. "Oh, of course. It's that drug that some women were claiming caused birth defects. It got a lot of publicity a few months ago."

"The company took it off the market," said Cawley.

"Only because of the publicity, as far as anyone can tell."

"Whatever. A judge just ruled on the case six women brought against the manufacturer. Didn't give them a dime. Said there was no proof that the drug did anything to their babies."

"Sounds right," said Jackie.

Cawley looked surprised. "Well, we want a piece on it. The booking department's just arranged an interview with one of the mothers in Ohio who originated the suit."

"What's the angle?"

"Sob story. We'll show the baby, get Mom to cry, shoot the empty bottle of Dantil that she took while she was pregnant. Then you'll go to the courthouse and report on what the judge said. He's refused to be interviewed—said his decision explained everything he could."

Jackie couldn't sort it out yet—she needed some facts, research. "I'm sure I can handle it," she said. "But I don't know about getting it on for tomorrow."

"No choice," said Cawley. "All of the shows are going to do something on the decision. If we don't grab this woman in Ohio for an exclusive, someone else will." He pushed the pencil back behind his ear. "Sorry for the initiation by fire. But as I said, thank God you're here."

He walked out, and Jackie sat down behind her desk and looked around. *Well, you wanted to be at the network. Here you are.*

The telephone rang, and she jumped.

"Hello?"

"Is it really you?" She recognized the voice of Julian's secretary. "I've been transferred about a dozen times. Nobody seemed to know who you are or where you were."

"I just got here."

"Apparently. Hold on for Julian."

She waited and heard Julian click on the speaker phone.

"How's my celebrity?"

"I've been here under five minutes and received my first assignment."

"Good. I won't keep you," Julian said. "But I forgot to tell you that Erwin's coming into town tonight. What time can I make a dinner reservation?"

"I don't know. I have a story for tomorrow."

Over the speaker phone, she heard other people come into Julian's office, realized that he was distracted. "Nine o'clock at Le Cirque?"

"I might not be able to make it at all."

"You're working all night?"

"Who knows? But it's not a day to make any plans."

"Ah, the price we pay for fame and glamour," he said, and laughed.

Half an hour later, Jackie was in a company car, heading to the airport. A young woman who identified herself as "Sarah from Transportation" had handed her tickets and directions, and "Arthur from Research" had given her a huge folder of papers. Raleigh Anderson, her producer for the day, was sitting next to her, talking loudly on the car telephone. Jackie assumed that she was setting up last-minute details for the shoot, but she hadn't said anything except, "Excuse me, I've some calls to make" since they got in the car. Raleigh was a tall, horsey-looking blonde of indeterminate age; perfect clothes, makeup she had thought about, bleached hair. Either a well-preserved fifty or an old-looking forty, Jackie decided. Raleigh's usual beat was wherever Dominique went, and she wasn't thrilled about taking a new reporter on a tough story.

Jackie pulled out the packet of research and tried to read it. She turned pages quickly, realizing that she didn't have much time to make sense of all of it—balance the facts, decide what mattered.

Raleigh hung up and half-turned to her. "You all set?"

"I don't know. Have you read through this? It's complicated."

Raleigh looked out the window, looked back at Jackie, face set. "Let's make sure we have the same point of view on this. We're doing human interest. A woman with a sick child. Her anguish. And then we ask: could it have been prevented?"

"I don't think we know," said Jackie softly.

Raleigh shrugged. "We're not trying to prove anything. This is a people story, as we say."

They got to the airport, stood in line to get seat assignments.

"Do you smoke?" asked Raleigh.

"No."

"I do," she said abruptly. "Guess we won't sit together."

Once on the plane, Jackie tried to read the research again, but she couldn't concentrate. She stared out the window, watching the patterns in the clouds. In the row behind her, Raleigh was smoking a cigarette and reading the newspaper. The rest of the first-class section was empty except for two Japanese men in the front row, huddled together over a calculator and a long balance sheet. This is ridiculous, Jackie thought. She got up from her seat and sat down next to Raleigh.

"Sorry to bother you. But do you mind talking about the story for a minute?"

Raleigh looked at her over the top of her newspaper. "What's the problem?"

"I'm worried about the focus—the kinds of questions I should ask."

"I'll tell you what to ask when we get there," Raleigh said. "The crew's meeting us at the house. We're shooting there first, then going to the courthouse." She picked up her paper again, and Jackie felt herself getting angry, tried to fight it back.

"Actually, I'm used to thinking things through and asking my own questions," Jackie said. "I'm a journalist, not a pretty face. Please don't treat me like Dominique."

Raleigh put down the newspaper and glared at her, fire in her eyes. "I won't treat you like Dominique because you're not in her league," she said. "Dominique is a seasoned correspondent here, which you're not. She also knows how to work with producers. I don't know what you learned at the local station"— she spit it out like an epithet—"but you're at the network now, and you're green." She sat back again, haughtily, her face hard and unpleasant. "Now if you'll excuse me, I have some other things to prepare."

Jackie crept back to her own seat, waves of anger mixing with embarrassment. If Raleigh was trying to put her in her place, she had done a pretty good job.

At the airport, they rented a car, drove in silence. Raleigh made some quick turns through a neighborhood of shabby houses, pulled up in front of one that needed a new coat of paint.

"This is it," Raleigh said. She got out of the car, took long, easy strides up the front walk, a picture of studied casualness. Cold bitch, Jackie thought. She pulled together her papers, slammed the car door, and hurried to join Raleigh.

A plain-looking woman with a drawn face and anxious eyes came to the door immediately, as if she'd been waiting for them. She was holding a child of about three in her arms; his face was dirty and his shirt was stained with grape juice, but he was long-legged and cute.

"I'm so sorry about your misfortune," Raleigh was saying as Jackie approached. Raleigh turned to her with more warmth than she had shown all day. "Jackie, this is Mabel Greeves. She's being kind enough to let us into her house and tell us her story." Jackie looked up sharply, startled by the false sweetness in Raleigh's voice—but Mabel Greeves, obviously charmed, relaxed noticeably.

"It's my pleasure," she said.

Raleigh led the way into the house, looked around briefly at the bland furniture, worn carpeting, and dusty drapes. "We shouldn't have any trouble shooting in here," she said, smiling warmly at Mrs. Greeves. "It's perfect. Lovely."

"It's really not much," said Mrs. Greeves. Her voice was shaky, but she looked pleased.

Raleigh turned to the child. "Now this must be . . ." She paused, trying to remember the name from the research she had barely skimmed.

"This is Michael."

"Hi, Michael." Raleigh smiled at him, and he smiled briefly, then buried his head in his mother's shoulder. "I didn't expect him to be so big," Raleigh said.

"Oh. This isn't . . . I mean, this is Michael. My other son is the one with the . . ."

Raleigh nodded sympathetically. "With the problems. I'm sorry to be confused. I don't know much about children." She said it proudly, the successful career woman too busy to know much about children.

Mrs. Greeves shifted Michael to her other arm, seemed suddenly on her guard. "Jonathan is only eight months old," she said. "He's sleeping. Should I get him up?"

Just then there was a cry from the back room. Mrs. Greeves muttered a comment about perfect timing and hurried away.

A moment later she was back, holding the screaming baby. Jackie braced herself to look at the child, and was surprised to see that there was nothing very remarkable about him. His head seemed slightly smaller than normal for a baby, and his skin had a bluish cast. She reached out to touch his small hand.

"He's very cute," she said.

"He has a deformed heart," Mrs. Greeves said. Her hands were trembling, and the baby began to scream louder. "He's a difficult baby."

"Can I hold him?" Jackie asked. Mrs. Greeves handed her the baby. Jackie rocked back and forth on her heels, and the child began to calm down.

A few minutes later, the crew arrived—a cameraman who happened to be a woman, a sound engineer, and a lighting man. While they set up to shoot, Raleigh and Jackie took a brief walk outside the house, discussing the questions Jackie would ask.

"It's a piece of cake." Raleigh tossed down the cigarette she was smoking and ground it out with her toe. Jackie listened as Raleigh outlined the basic questions—How much Dantil did you take? How did you make the connection between the birth defects and the drug?—and since they were obvious, she just nodded. "After that, get her onto the court decision," Raleigh said. "She's got two kids, no husband, and no money. Ask her how she's going to survive now that she won't be getting any money in damages."

It occurred to Jackie that plenty of single women raised children without getting money from legal suits, but she decided not to say so.

"It's a cute baby," Jackie said instead. "I expected some more obvious deformity."

"I know," said Raleigh. "One of the other kids from the suit was born without a hand. That might have been a better story. But this is fine. You can't lose with cute-baby shots."

Jackie shrugged. "I get the feeling that Mrs. Greeves doesn't want to hear anything nice about that baby. She looks at him and sees trouble. I wonder if there's a way to ask her about that."

Raleigh lit another cigarette and inhaled deeply. "I know you think you can do this interview, but I'm going to give you some advice. You get a lot of points with our audience being sympathetic, and you don't get anywhere being nasty. We're not that kind of show."

They went back inside, and Raleigh headed into the living room to talk to the crew, while Jackie wandered into the kitchen. Mrs. Greeves stood at the counter, pouring something into a glass. She turned, startled, when Jackie walked in.

"Almost ready for our interview?" Jackie asked pleasantly.

"Sure." As she put down the bottle, Jackie saw it was an inexpensive brand of Scotch, and the bottle was almost empty. Mrs. Greeves gave a little laugh. "I'm pretty nervous about being interviewed, I guess."

"You shouldn't be."

Mrs. Greeves drank the Scotch quickly, poured another glass, and gulped that, too. "Want some?" she asked.

"No, I'm fine, thank you. But we should probably get started."

Mrs. Greeves began the interview by explaining that she started taking Dantil for her nerves when she was two months pregnant and her husband had left her. The drug was supposed to be safe. After Jonathan was born with all his problems, she heard of another woman who had taken Dantil and was bringing a lawsuit. She decided to join her since she thought justice could be done.

There were tears in her eyes, and Jackie noticed Raleigh motioning the camera to come in for a close-up.

Poor little Jonathan had so many special needs. And Judge Baker—how could he say there wasn't enough proof? Wasn't poor little Jonathan all the proof anyone needed? Maybe the judge just didn't understand about a mother's love. Mrs. Greeves sniffled, pulled out a crumpled handkerchief and dabbed at her eyes.

Jackie mentally applauded the terrific performance.

She asked a few more questions, as full of false sympathy as Raleigh had been, elicited some more tears, and got a sign from Raleigh to wrap it up.

They finished shooting in the house and headed over to the courthouse.

"That was great stuff," Raleigh said in the car.

"It was all bullshit."

Raleigh set her mouth in a hard line. "Sorry you won't be winning the Pulitzer Prize your first time out." She tossed her a piece of paper. "I wrote your stand-up. We'll shoot it on the courthouse steps."

Jackie looked at the two paragraphs she had scrawled: "Right here, in this courthouse, the fate of a young mother and her badly deformed child were sealed yesterday. The damage was done by this man—Judge Walter Roy Baker . . ."

Jackie held the paper tightly, felt her palms getting damp.

"Are you convinced the judge was wrong?" she asked.

Raleigh shrugged. "I told you before—it doesn't really matter. We're talking about one woman's struggle." She glanced at Jackie out of the corner of her eye. "Why, do you disagree?"

"Well, one thing struck me in the judge's opinion. He said . . . Let me find the quote." She flipped through some papers, found what she wanted. "Here it is. He said, quote: These symptoms are too reminiscent of more common problems to believe they were caused by the drug—end quote. I wonder if Mrs. Greeves is an alcoholic."

"What?"

"Fetal Alcohol Syndrome. Babies born to alcoholic mothers can have heart problems and look a lot like this kid did."

"That's out of left field, isn't it?"

"I saw Mrs. Greeves belt down two drinks in the kitchen right before the interview. And did you notice that her hands were shaking?"

Raleigh stopped in front of the courthouse and turned to look at her. "No, I didn't notice, and it's a little hard shooting a story when my correspondent wants to play Nancy Drew. Now, if you've memorized that stand-up, we can get going."

Jackie took a deep breath. "I'm not going to say anything on the air that I don't believe."

Raleigh looked at her angrily. "I'm not asking you to. I'm

asking you to talk about this woman's problems. How many times do I have to say that?"

"I think we should bring up the possibility that her problems are caused by alcohol."

"Based on one drink before an interview?"

"Two drinks."

"Ever hear of libel? You're going to make an accusation like that on national television with nothing to back it up?"

"What about the accusations you want me to make?"

"I don't want you to make any. I just want you to get off your high horse and do a good story. For a smart girl, you're acting incredibly stupid."

Raleigh stormed away, and Jackie, feeling a huge lump gathering in her throat, wondered if she was going to cry. Christ, that would be terrific.

The camerawoman, Annette Glass, was already lining up the courthouse shot. She called to Jackie, asking if she'd stand on the steps for a minute so she could focus. Jackie wiped her eyes and nodded.

"You okay?" Annette asked as Jackie came over.

Jackie shrugged, suddenly needing someone to talk to. "I guess so. It's just I've never worked with Raleigh before, and we're having a little trouble."

"Yeah, not a surprise. She's tough. But if it's any consolation, she puts together a great story. I've seen pieces look like shit in the field, and when she gets done in the editing room, you wonder if you've even been on the same shoot."

"Good to hear," Jackie said, though it occurred to her that the story Raleigh would put together might not be the same one she herself had in mind.

"Don't worry," Annette said. She patted Jackie on the shoulder. "You're doing fine. I'll do some background shots right now. You better go fix your makeup."

As Jackie went off to find a bathroom, she walked behind Raleigh and heard her barking at the lighting man about shadows. "Give the new kid a break! She's got enough to worry about without your putting black streaks across her face."

Raleigh turned to walk away, and Jackie stood there, stunned. After all their fighting, why was Raleigh so worried about getting the most flattering lighting for Jackie's face?

She fixed her makeup, went back to Annette.

"Is Raleigh rude to everyone?" Jackie asked.

Annette laughed. "You stop noticing after awhile. She wants everything to be right, and she doesn't trust anyone. If she could run the cameras and do the stand-ups herself, she would." Annette played with the focus on her camera. "You've got to understand it, though. It is her story."

"Funny," said Jackie. "I always think of these as *my* stories—not the producers'."

"Good way to get a reputation as an uppity bitch," said Annette, not unkindly. "Remember, it's your face on the air, but it's her ass on the line."

Jackie laughed, went to stand on the courthouse steps while the camera and lights were adjusted. She turned over the paper Raleigh had given her, jotted down a new stand-up. When Raleigh came over, she handed it to her, asked her to look at it.

"I think the idea is the same as what you wrote," Jackie explained. "This will just sound more natural coming out of my mouth."

Raleigh nodded. "Fine."

Jackie looked at her, bit her lip. Fighting with the producer was not the way to get a good story—or a good reputation. And when it came right down to it, who cared what they said on the air about Mrs. Greeves? Drugs or alcohol, her fault or someone else's . . . I'm here to do a good television show, Jackie told herself, not to save the world.

"Hey," she said to Raleigh. "I've got a great idea on how to end this piece."

Raleigh looked at her, trying to decide what was coming.

"If you want to get some sympathy points with the audience, maybe we should set up a fund to help Mrs. Greeves pay for poor little Jonathan's surgery. Then we're not saying who's right or wrong, we're just getting involved."

"What gave you this brilliant thought?" Raleigh asked.

Jackie grinned. "I decided to get off my high horse and play the game."

Raleigh finally smiled. "I hate to admit it, but it's a damn good idea."

At six o'clock the following morning, Jackie walked, exhausted, into the makeup room in the studio and plopped down into one of the two empty chairs. A tall, slim man wearing blue jeans and a violet sweater came up behind her. He had thick blond hair, slicked back in a mock-fifties look.

"Can I help you, darling? I'm Barry, and I do gorgeous faces."

"I'm Jackie Rogers, the new correspondent."

"I know *that*. This is gossip central, right here in the makeup room."

Jackie sighed. "Then do you also know that I don't usually have dark bags under my eyes? And that I'm making my debut on this show after pulling my first all-nighter since college?"

"Of course I know that." He played with her hair a bit, studied her face in the mirror. "Poor darling. It's awful how they treat people around here. But don't worry. I'll get Reuven to start on your hair, and then I'll do your makeup. We'll make you look gorgeous for the air."

Jackie relaxed and decided that everyone needed a gay makeup man after a night without sleep.

They had arrived back in New York about ten o'clock and started editing. At midnight, Raleigh asked Jackie if she wanted to go home, but she decided to stay, saying she'd sleep in the morning. When Steve Cawley came in at five o'clock, they were just finishing. Cawley watched the piece, announced that it was terrific, and suggested that Jackie do fifty seconds of live follow-up on the air with Darlie.

"This morning?"

"Right. Good way to introduce you as one of our regulars."

Jackie wished desperately that she hadn't stayed to edit, but there was nothing to do about it. At five-thirty she went home, had the cab wait while she showered and pulled on her favorite red-and-white-striped Anne Klein dress.

Now she heard Barry's voice telling her to open her eyes so he could put on some mascara. "Then you'll be done, darling."

She opened them, looked in the mirror. "You're a genius. How did you get rid of the dark circles?"

"I'll never tell."

"Okay, tell me where Darlie's dressing room is, then."

"The lion's den, you mean?"

"Right. I have to brief her on a story."

"Bring your whip, darling. It's the only way to talk to Darlie."
He gave her directions, and she left the comfort of the makeup
room, walked down a short, dimly lit hallway, and knocked on
Darlie's dressing-room door. A mellifluous voice called, "Come
in!" Jackie opened the door to find Darlie sitting by her dressing
table, pulling on a pair of pearl-gray panty hose. She frowned at
them as Jackie introduced herself.

"Hi," Darlie said. "What do you think of this color? Will it
read too light on the air?"

A strange greeting, Jackie thought, but decided to plunge
right in.

"What are you trying to match it to?"

"Let me find it." Darlie looked around. The small room was
totally packed with clothes. Floor-to-ceiling clothes racks lined
three walls of the room; the fourth wall had shelves stuffed with
sweaters and blouses. About three dozen pairs of shoes were
lined up on the floor, and two full-length mirrors peeked out
from around the clothes. The only clue that this wasn't a designer's showroom was a tiny table crammed into one corner. A
very neat script was on top of it, apparently unopened.

"According to the schedule, I wear the gray-and-yellow St.
John's knit today," Darlie said, pulling it off a rack. "But
sometimes I wear what I want."

"Who makes the schedule?" Jackie asked curiously.

"My loyal assistant Joanna. No, Diana. I've had three loyal
assistants in the last four months, for some reason. Then Steve
Cawley approves the list. But what does he know about clothes?"

"Very little, I assume," said Jackie. "But he seems to be
pretty good at everything else."

Darlie shrugged, and Jackie looked at her closely, surprised to
realize that in person, Darlie wasn't as striking as she was on the
air. She had a face made for television—sharp angles and high
cheekbones that the cameras softened into classic beauty. The
almost-black hair that seemed to glow on camera was mottled
with gray. Her narrow shoulders and small breasts made her
look slight on the air, and since she was always sitting down,
nobody was aware of the chunky thighs and somewhat heavy
hips that were now modeling pearl-gray panty hose.

"I'm sorry to bother you while you're getting dressed,"
Jackie said, "but Cawley wanted me to brief you on the Dantil

case so you could ask me a question after the tape piece. We have about fifty seconds for live follow-up."

"What am I supposed to ask you?"

"Whatever you want, I guess."

"Nonsense," said Darlie, immediately exasperated. "We have a staff of five writers who get paid to write questions. I get paid to ask them."

"Are any of the writers around now?"

"No, everything is written the day before." Darlie sighed. "Cawley is going to hear about this. Okay, go ahead. Tell me about it. You don't mind if I fix a nail while you talk, do you?"

Jackie decided to skip the details of the case, explaining instead that the only question left at the end of the spot was whether other women who had taken Dantil should be concerned.

"Should they?"

"Probably not. The company pulled it off the market here, but there hasn't been any real scientific evidence linking it to birth defects. And it's still used in forty-five countries."

Darlie, bent over the chipped nail, looked up in surprise. "Forty-five countries?"

"I think that's the figure."

"That's incredible. I didn't know there *were* forty-five countries." She studied the nail. "How many countries do you think there are altogether?"

"I never really counted them. Maybe three hundred?"

"Amazing. I couldn't name a dozen." Darlie got up, gave a final glance of approval at the nail, and pulled down a new package of panty hose from a shelf. "I don't like this color after all. But thanks for the briefing. If you'll excuse me now, I should finish getting dressed."

Jackie walked out of the dressing room, pulled the door closed, and quite literally bumped into Jeff Garth standing in the hall. They both laughed, and as Jeff reached over a hand to steady her, he said, "I don't usually loiter outside Darlie's dressing room, but Cawley asked me to check that you hadn't been eaten."

"Noble of him. And you, too. But I appear to still be in one piece."

"I'm glad. Someone should have warned you about Darlie. She can be difficult. She considers every pretty woman in the world a personal threat to her job."

"I guess I'm not pretty enough to be threatening," Jackie said. "She was very civil. A little strange, but civil."

"That's a surprise. I would have assumed that one look at you would have been enough to throw her into a state of uncontrollable rage."

"I'm flattered," Jackie said, smiling. "But we got along fine."

As Jeff glanced at the clipboard he was holding, Jackie appraised his strong features and handsome profile. God, he's sexy, she thought. Why wasn't *he* my producer today?

Jeff looked up again, caught Jackie's gaze, and smiled. "Anything I can do for you?" he asked. "Or are you all set with the live follow-up?"

"I think we're set."

Jeff flipped the page on his clipboard, started to walk away, then turned back to her. "Maybe Darlie didn't have her contact lenses in yet this morning. That would explain her civility. I, however, have perfect vision—and if I were Darlie, I *would* be uncontrollable seeing you."

He ambled down the corridor, and had turned a corner, out of sight, before Jackie fully understood what he meant.

Jackie's fifty seconds live on the air, cut down to thirty-six seconds due to time constraints, passed uneventfully. Afterward she slipped out of the studio, thought of stopping off to see Julian so he could admire Barry's makeup job, but decided she was too tired. She went home, washed her face, and crawled into bed. But she couldn't fall asleep right away. She kept replaying the story in her mind, trying to decide if they had been fair. The Jonathan Greeves Heart Fund was sure to raise some money—and attention—but everyone who contributed would assume that Dantil and the judge were in the wrong. The positive side of it was that Raleigh didn't hate her as much as she had at the start of the day. And that, Jackie figured, was worth something.

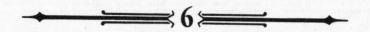

Dominique LaFarge was determined to be friends with Jackie Rogers, in part because everyone assumed that they would detest each other. The friendship had gotten off to something of a shaky start when Dominique called to congratulate Jackie on her first spot. After telling her how good she was, Dominique mentioned in passing that Jackie should be more careful what she wore on the air. That red-and-white dress made her look like an American flag. And besides, it was *last year's* Anne Klein—which was unacceptable in the up-to-the-minute world of television. Dominique thought Jackie had reacted badly by saying it was the story, not the look, that really mattered. Dominique said she was just trying to help. And to be perfectly honest, that's all she was trying to do.

To be friendly, she stopped by Jackie's office the next morning and found her staring with a baffled look at a huge basket on her desk. It was wrapped in clear crinkly plastic and tied up with black and gold ribbons. Dominique glanced at it and smiled. "Let me guess. A welcome-to-the-show package from Henry Gray Public Relations?"

Jackie looked at the card she was holding and nodded. "How did you know?"

"I got one a lot like it last Christmas. Henry represents a number of cosmetic companies and tends to send out packages filled with samples whenever he has a good excuse. The lipsticks are wonderful, by the way. Best I've ever used." She peeked through the plastic. "At least he had the good taste not to send you the face elixir-lift serum."

"What's that?"

"Wrinkle cream, darling, but you're too young to know about it. The rest of us kill for it."

Jackie looked at her intently. "You must be joking. You have gorgeous skin."

"Maybe because I'm a regular user of the magic serum."

Jackie smiled. "I doubt it."

"Anyway, you'll get to recognize Henry's packages, because he also represents a lot of food companies. Darlie had a four-foot-high chocolate Easter bunny in her office last spring. I'm waiting for Henry to make the connection between his various accounts and send a basket with Perugina chocolate and Clearasil."

Jackie laughed, but didn't make a move to untie the ribbons. "I shouldn't keep it, should I?"

Dominique shrugged. "You doing a story that conflicts?"

"Not that I know of."

"Then it's really just goodwill, not payola. He's hoping you'll think of the products if there's ever an appropriate time. Anyway, network rules say you can accept gifts worth up to seventy-five dollars, as I remember. Henry's pretty good about respecting the rules." She perused the package again. "Well, maybe he figures seventy-five dollars wholesale."

Jackie played with the ribbons for a moment, finally pulled off the plastic and looked at the elegant boxes inside. "Why don't you take a lipstick," she said, handing Dominique one of the small packages. "That way I'm sure I don't go over the limit."

Dominique took it, slipped it into the sleek pocketbook she had slung over her shoulder. "Listen, if anyone ever sends you one of those gorgeous Chanel pocketbooks, you should give it to me. It's way over the limit. I'll make sure it's sent back, of course." She grinned, and Jackie laughed.

Somehow, the exchange seemed to put them in the same camp, make it clear that they had more reason to be friends than enemies. After that, Dominique began stopping by Jackie's office every morning to say hello and chat briefly about the stories they were doing. What started as a formality quickly turned into an expected part of each of their days.

Dominique actually liked having Jackie around, because it meant that Jackie could handle stories like Dantil and leave Dominique more time for the glitzy, celebrity pieces she thrived on. Cawley had just suggested a week-long series on Hollywood's Sexiest Men, and Dominique couldn't have been happier.

She had spent two days in Sun Valley interviewing Robert Redford, and was about to fly to Los Angeles for Dustin Hoffman and Jack Nicholson. An A-list week if there ever was one. If Cawley promoted it enough, it should send their ratings through the sky. But she couldn't do everything, and when there was a scheduling conflict, she had suggested that the final interview with Paul Newman go to Jackie.

The morning of the interview, Dominique stopped by Jackie's office with a mug of coffee and a bagel to see how she was doing.

"Badly," said Jackie. She seemed frazzled and her desk was covered with crumpled paper. "I'm due in Paul Newman's hotel room in two hours, and I've managed to write exactly one question. It was a nice thought to give me this interview, Dominique, but why don't you take it back?"

"I can't. I'm on a flight for Los Angeles in two hours."

"Well, you've got to help me at least."

"What's the problem?"

"The problem is that I don't do celebrities. I've been staring at the research and a blank piece of paper all morning, and I can't think of anything earth-shattering to talk to him about. He's not a politician, there's nothing to investigate—what the hell can I ask him?"

Dominique sat down on Jackie's small couch, blew on her coffee. "It doesn't have to be earth-shattering, just interesting. Don't you have any curiosity about the guy?"

"Of course I do, but as I said, celebrities aren't my specialty. And in case I forgot about that, I have Arlette coming by every ten minutes in a total tizzy, telling me what I should and shouldn't say. She's furious that you gave him to me. Newman apparently gives very few interviews, and she's been working on getting him for months. Now she's acting like she's just gotten an interview with the burning bush, and I'm definitely not Moses."

Dominique laughed. The fact that Arlette, the show's head celebrity booker, was having fits wasn't surprising. The woman had the thickest Rolodex in the business, but very little common sense. She liked to think that celebrities came on the show as a personal favor to her, and nobody bothered to disabuse her of the notion or point out that celebrities and talk shows lived off each other. Arlette thought of every star she spoke to as a buddy, and didn't seem to realize that if she ever lost her title at *A.M. Reports*, she wouldn't have a friend left in Hollywood.

Dominique sipped her coffee. "Do me a favor, and forget about Arlette, and also forget that you don't do celebrities. If Paul Newman came sauntering down the hall right this minute, what would you ask him?"

"Since I and everyone else in the office would be on the floor in a dead faint, I'd probably ask him what it's like to know that every time he walks into a room, half the women are going to drop dead."

Dominique grinned. "Terrific. Write it down. It's question one. Now, assume that you pull yourself off the floor and make it back to your seat. What else would you like to know about him?"

"Whether he thinks he would have been such a big star if he had brown eyes."

"Fine. Question two."

"You must be joking. I can't ask that."

"Why not?"

"He'll laugh at me. I'll sound like a jerk."

"No you won't, you'll sound human. And he'll either give you a straight answer, which will be interesting, or he'll do something like blink his eyes and smile, which will be a nice moment. People eat up that stuff."

Jackie looked dubious, but scribbled some notes on the yellow pad on her desk. "Will you listen to my next question? I was going to ask him if he considers his race-car driving to be a metaphor for the high-risk clashes in the movie business."

"You can ask that," said Dominique, wrinkling her nose slightly.

"You think it's a rotten question?"

"It's not a rotten question, but it's not something you'd ask naturally—at a cocktail party, for example. It's the kind of question you have to write down first, if you know what I mean. That probably works for news interviews, but it sounds fake when you're doing celebrity chat."

Jackie pulled another sheet of yellow paper off her legal pad, crumpled it and threw it in the wastebasket. She looked disgusted. "Maybe I'll just bring a jar of his spaghetti sauce and one of Aunt Millie's and see if he can tell them apart in a blind taste test."

"Actually, it's not a bad idea," Dominique said. "The point is to get something human out of these guys. The sex-symbol stuff you were just talking about is good. If you want to ask him about race-car driving, ask him the things you really want to know. What does it feel like to go so fast? Would he rather die in a race car than die of old age? As for the spaghetti sauce, it's almost a joke, isn't it? Could Paul Newman put his face on anything and have it be successful?"

Jackie scribbled furiously, then looked up at Dominique in amazement. "You're good at this."

Dominique laughed. "I'm good at cocktail parties, too."

"No, I really mean it. These are terrific questions. They're not boring, and they're not overdone, either."

"I like celebrities. Unfortunately, if there's any meat to a story, I usually miss it."

"I'm not so sure. Anyway, I don't know how to thank you. Ten minutes ago I was getting as hysterical as Arlette, and now I think the interview's going to be great."

"Never get as hysterical as Arlette," said Dominique as she left. "It's not worth it."

Dominique stayed only one night in Los Angeles—just long enough to interview Jack Nicholson, who was unbearably sexy, and Dustin Hoffman, who thought he was. Actually, Dustin was a good interview, even though he seemed terribly self-absorbed. He didn't seem to mind when she asked him the question that was really on her mind; how could a short man with a big nose become an international sex symbol? At least he'd laughed.

Dominique hurried back to New York to get ready for a weekend stint at Trump Casino in Atlantic City. She hadn't told many people at the show about her singing appearance—even now she liked to keep that part of her life somewhat under wraps—but when she called Jackie the next day to make sure that everything had gone all right with Paul Newman, she invited her to come to the nightclub. Dominique was somewhat surprised that Jackie actually appeared early on Saturday night with a rich friend whom she introduced as Julian Beardsley. Dominique liked him at once. At her instruction, they were seated at a table near the front with Peter, and despite the lights, the music, and the pandemonium, Dominique could hear them applauding wildly every time she appeared on stage in one of her sexy gowns and belted out another song.

That night, Dominique managed to turn a near-tragedy into a smashing success. In the middle of one of her numbers, a spotlight came crashing down on stage, splintering into a million pieces and sending a gasp through the audience. Dominique barely missed a beat before she called, "Come on, boys, let's clean it up." She kept singing, and when two men with brooms tried to sweep up unobtrusively, she pulled them center stage and started singing and dancing with them, twirling their brooms like batons. The audience roared its approval.

"You have incredible stage presence," Jackie told her after the performance, when Dominique sat down with them for a drink.

"I've just learned not to worry," said Dominique. "I figure if I'm having fun, everyone else will, too."

"I wish I could do that." Jackie glanced at Julian. "I manage to worry everything to death."

"I worry about only one thing," said Dominique, throwing her arm around Peter. "When this guy will marry me."

Peter looked embarrassed, and Dominique cuddled up to him, stroking his cheek with her well-manicured fingers. There was a moment of silence at the table.

"Wait until I tell you about my next assignment," Jackie said to break the awkwardness. "From the charms of Paul Newman, I go to covering the Little Miss World pageant in Hollywood. I just read the press kit. Apparently, there'll be a bunch of six-to-eight-year-old girls dressed up like Lolita, doing all the embarrassing things they do on the Miss America pageant, and proving that poor taste has no age limit. My favorite moment so far is seeing a picture of Little Miss Texas, age seven, dressed in a string bikini."

Dominique shuddered, disentangled herself from Peter. "I don't know whether that's sexism or child abuse. Maybe you should call Gloria Steinem and suggest a protest, à la Miss

America 1972. In this case, I guess it would have to be an undershirt burning instead of bras."

Jackie laughed. "Hey, you know your feminist history."

"I'm not as dumb as I look," said Dominique flippantly. "I always figure that if everyone is going to call you a bimbo, it's nice to know in your heart of hearts that you're not."

Jackie and Julian laughed, but Peter looked uncomfortable.

"Don't put yourself down," Julian said, warmly. "Nobody can sing the way you do and have your composure and be called anything but a star."

"I'll second that," Jackie said.

Dominique smiled. "Well, thank you, fans. You can't imagine how nice it is to have friends in the audience."

"We're glad to be your audience anytime," Julian said.

"I don't know where you found this man," Dominique told Jackie, "but hang on to him. He's got the right line for every occasion."

When Dominique finally got home at two A.M., she was feeling wonderful. Julian had been charming, Jackie was sweet, and dozens of people had stopped by their table to congratulate her on her terrific performance. The adrenalin rush she always got on stage lasted most of the evening—in fact, the only disappointment had been Peter, who seemed sullen.

Dominique wasn't sure what was wrong with Peter the last few days. She was in love with the man, that much she knew. Much as she loved hoofing and singing in Atlantic City, and running around for the network, she might be willing to trade it all for Peter, a house, and a white picket fence. In a funny way, Jackie, who had ambition written all over her face, had made her realize that. A few years ago, Dominique would have felt threatened by Jackie, but now she felt: Good luck, kid, it's your turn.

Dominique liked to do things for Peter—slip into his apartment when he wasn't there and leave dinner in the oven or a dozen roses on the table. She knit him a bulky fisherman's sweater for his birthday, which he loved and put on immediately. When she told him she had made it, he thought she was joking.

She shared everything with Peter—he had met her family, and

even knew she was from Iowa. But she hadn't yet gotten the courage to tell him that if they married, it wouldn't be her first wedding ceremony. That event had occurred when she was twenty-one and unbearably naive. She had gotten a job as a showgirl in a small nightclub in downtown Los Angeles where the owner, Bert Poole, lavished endless attention on her. He was exactly twice her age and twice divorced. Generally crude and loud, he tried to be more gentlemanly around Dominique, recognizing that she was sweeter and more vulnerable than most of the women he knew. She didn't like to drink, so he bought her a Coke—or sometimes a rum-and-Coke—after every show. He doted on her, promised to make her a star, told her she was too young and pretty to be in this business without someone to protect her. She was entranced by his affection. It was hard to say how they ended up married. A psychiatrist would probably explain that she was looking for the father she never had, but she had never gone to a psychiatrist because she knew it was simpler than that. Bert surprised her one night with a fur coat, and she determined that the only way to express her gratitude was finally to submit to his advances. When she awoke the next morning, no longer a virgin but still a Catholic, she decided to marry him. He later told some friends that he was marrying the only virgin in America who was over the age of consent.

They married almost immediately—in a church, at her request—and she wasn't unhappy with him. She continued working in the club, and got to do a solo number. He remained mostly kind and protective, though less attentive, until one night, six months after they were married, when he came home drunk and stoned.

"Let's screw," he said, pulling at his pants as he staggered in the door.

"You're incredibly drunk," she said. "Should I get you some coffee?"

"I don't need coffee. I need your ass." He grabbed her arm and she shook it free.

"Come on, you're going to feel rotten in the morning. How about a big glass of tomato juice? I read somewhere that prevents hangovers."

"Bullshit. Take off your clothes. I've already fucked two of the whores in the chorus, and now I want to fuck my wife."

She took a step back, appalled, not sure that he wasn't joking. "Maybe you should just go to sleep," she said. She turned to walk away, but he leapt for her, spun her around, and slapped her across the face.

"I said I want to fuck my wife."

She screamed, and he hit her again. She tried to push him away from her, and as he stumbled—more from the alcohol than her assault—she ran into the bathroom and locked the door. He started to holler and bang on the other side. Trembling, she flung open the window and clambered out to the street. She spent the night at a neighbor's house. Early the next morning, she let herself quietly into the house, found Bert asleep on the living-room floor. The door to the bathroom had been smashed in, and the room was in shambles. Not finding her there, Bert had vented his fury on the medicine chest. Her makeup was flung around the room, and he had shattered the mirror. One of the towels was smeared with blood, and she guessed that he had cut his hand on the broken glass. She shuddered and said a prayer, wondering how much more blood there might have been if she hadn't escaped. She left with nothing but her pocketbook and some money she had saved, and got on a plane that morning to go to her mother's. Within a year, the marriage was annulled.

She didn't know if she would ever be able to tell that story to Peter. When she thought about it now, it seemed as if it had happened to someone else a long time ago. It certainly wasn't the kind of story Peter would immediately understand.

The week after Dominique's performance in Atlantic City, Peter broke two dates, including one for Saturday night, explaining that he had to work on the presentation for a new account. Dominique was cheerful and understanding on the phone, but had a gnawing sense that something wasn't right. She thought of calling his office on Saturday night, just to see if he was really there, but couldn't think of a good excuse. She didn't have the nerve to call on his private line and hang up if he answered. It would be too obvious. She'd just have to wait and wonder.

He finally stopped by her apartment late Sunday evening, looking distraught. Dominique gave him a gentle kiss and a glass of wine, which he sipped nervously. He put it down on her lacquer coffee table, spilling a little, as he did, on her Chinese rug.

"Dominique, I have to talk to you," he said.

"Is something wrong?"

He nodded. "I feel rotten about this, and it's not going to be easy for me to say. But it's time."

She swallowed hard. This is it, she thought. He's tired of our relationship. Forget the babies and the white picket fence.

Peter looked at Dominique, who was struggling to maintain her composure.

"I guess you know what it is." He sighed. "You didn't get the job. The orange-juice council picked someone else to represent them and do their commercials from now on."

"What?"

"I'm sorry. I fought for you, but as their advertising agency, we can only advise. They make the final decision."

Dominique tried not to laugh. She had all but forgotten that she was up for the job. Was this why he had been so morose lately?

"How long have you known this?"

"Over a week, but I didn't tell you because I didn't want to spoil your night in Atlantic City. Please don't cry."

Her lips were quivering, and she was trying to control them, but it was amusement, not tears, that she was holding back. Peter looked thoroughly miserable.

Finally, she went over and put her arms around him. "It's okay, sweetie. I'm not upset. I'm glad you tried."

"You're being very brave," he said, giving her a hug.

This time she did laugh. "Come on, Peter, it's not the worst disaster of my life."

"What are you going to do?"

"Do? What can I do? Maybe I'll represent the pear council. Or the apple board. Heck, there are a lot of fruits—not to mention vegetables. Could you see me as Miss Zucchini?"

He shook his head. "I'm glad you're taking this so well. I wasn't sure you would."

Dominique wished he knew her better than that. "Why would I get upset about losing a commercial? I still have you. That's all that really matters."

"You mean that?"

"Of course I do." As he sat down, looking puzzled, she realized that he didn't totally believe her. She stroked his cheek, which was smoothly shaven and smelled of lemony after-shave. "Want to hear a story?"

He nodded.

"When I was a little girl—I think I was about ten—my mother gave me a pearl ring for my birthday. I thought it was the most beautiful thing in the world. Then I went swimming one day in a murky pond, and it fell off. There was no way I could find it, and I cried and cried. I was so afraid to tell my mother. Finally, my big brother ratted on me, and my mother came outside and found me behind a tree, where I was still crying. She put her arm around me and said, 'Stop it. You never cry about losing things. Things don't matter, people do.' "

Peter looked at her blankly. "That's it?"

"Yup. I never forgot it."

He smiled. "It's a nice story." He glanced at his watch. "I guess I should be going. Don't you have an early flight tomorrow?"

"Seven A.M. to Detroit. Something about robots in the G.M. plant. Not exactly my kind of story, but I'm just a working girl. Do what I'm told."

He laughed. "You're a doll, is what you are."

She gave him a quick, tight hug. "So are you. Thank you for worrying so much about me. I love you."

"Mmm. I love you."

They said good night.

Dominique entertained Raleigh with her latest Peter story on their way to Detroit. Even as she told it, she realized how distant she felt from Peter sometimes—and the thought made her panic. She wanted him—wanted him forever, flaws and all. She would just have to work harder to keep him close.

Raleigh, not known for mincing words, had another perspective on the situation. "I'm very glad you didn't get those commercials," she said, frowning. "It would have been a bad career move. Get known as the orange juice queen and you're stuck with the image for life. You don't want to be Anita Bryant—you can do a lot better."

"Maybe," Dominique said. "But it was sweet of Peter to be so concerned."

"It wasn't sweet, it was totally self-centered. He's so involved with his own issues he doesn't have time to pay attention to yours."

"He'll learn."

"Maybe, maybe not." Raleigh motioned to the flight attendant to bring her another cup of coffee. "You're so wrapped up with him that you don't know what's best for you anymore. Maybe it's time you stopped being so loyal."

"No way," said Dominique heatedly. "It's baby time for me, and there are slim pickings out there for husband material. Haven't you read about the man shortage? Once I eliminate all the men in New York who aren't gay, married, over sixty, or twice divorced, I'm left with Peter."

"Bullshit. You're beautiful and smart, and you happen to be the sweetest woman in America. Men should be lining up at your door."

"Thanks for the confidence. But last Saturday night when Peter wasn't around, I was alone in my apartment taking a bubble bath. What were you doing?"

"None of your business," Raleigh said. She fingered the croissant next to her coffee cup, picked it up, then put it down again. "Actually, I don't mean to pick on Peter—I hardly know the guy. But it drives me crazy when you act like you're desperate."

"I *am* desperate. I'm the typical woman described in *Cosmo*—willing to put up with a man's foibles just to have a man."

"You've got yourself. That's all you need, and all you can rely on."

"Grim."

"But true." Raleigh sighed. "Doesn't Peter strike you as a tad narcissistic?"

"A tad?" Dominique asked with a fond smile on her face. "This is a man who owns the entire line of Clinique products for men. And uses all of it."

"I'm more worried about his using you. By the way, did you explain to him that orange juice commercials aren't the beginning and end of the world?"

"I tried," Dominique said lightly, "but he didn't have the

slightest idea what I meant. If he thinks people live and die by his ads, why should I disillusion him?"

"I don't know. I'm just afraid one of you has to be disillusioned eventually. But enough of this. We've got to get set for the interviews in Detroit." She pulled out her clipboard. "For the open, I thought you'd do a stand-up, straight to camera, and we'll have the robot cruise in, shake your hand, and lead you over to the technical-engineering manager. Good start?"

Dominique sat back and closed her eyes. Robots didn't really interest her. "I'm sure it will be wonderful. But I'm exhausted. Do you mind pulling it together?"

"Not at all," Raleigh said. "You rest, I'll write."

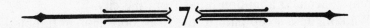

7

Jackie didn't see Julian for over a week. Their work schedules collided—when she wasn't traveling, she was getting in early, working all day; Julian got to his office later, worked through most of the evening. When he was ready to go to dinner at nine or ten o'clock, she was ready for bed. Julian was understanding —he knew she was getting to the studio at dawn, and also knew that dark circles under the eyes didn't photograph well—but he was accustomed to women being available when he needed them. Jackie wondered how much more of this crazy schedule he would tolerate before drifting away to a more comfortable match.

"You underestimate me and yourself," he told her on the phone, when she tentatively brought up the question. "I happen to think you're worth waiting for."

"That's good to hear," she said, "but even I have to admit that this is no way to run a relationship. I'm starting to forget what you look like."

"Fortunately, I have a better memory," said Julian. "But let's not test it any further. Why don't you come with me to Saddle River this weekend."

"You mean where wife and children are housed?"

"You got it. Marianne's going to the city, and it's my weekend with the kids."

"Then you'll probably want to spend it with them, not me."

"Jackie, the boys are teenagers. They're grateful if I have a diversion and don't bother them all weekend."

"I'm glad to be a diversion," she admitted.

They drove out on Saturday morning. Julian's house turned out to be a traditional English Tudor on the top of a winding hill, set far back from the road. As they drove up the long driveway, Jackie glimpsed a swimming pool and tennis court, and noticed a couple of bicycles casually parked against a tree. The family homestead, as it were, with its air of comfort and serenity, seemed a million miles from the city.

Walking up a steep path to the front door, Julian fumbled for his keys. The house seemed quiet.

"There was a time when my coming home brought two excited children and a Great Dane named Chipper to the front door," he said. "Now the boys are too cool to come greet me. Can you explain to me why teenagers think it's so terrific to be cool?"

Jackie laughed. "Being cool is the greatest defense known to adolescence. When you're cool, you don't express emotion, so nobody can hurt you. You're invulnerable. I, unfortunately, have never been cool in my life."

"What's the opposite of cool?"

"Passionate." Jackie grinned. "For example, I was the type of uncool girl who wrote a love sonnet to her ninth-grade boyfriend, thus putting her heart on the line. Needless to say, it was broken when he invited someone else to the Valentine's Day dance."

"Sad story," Julian said cheerfully.

"The worst part is that I didn't learn anything from it. By the way, has Chipper the Great Dane also grown into a cool teenager?"

"No, he's dead. He got diabetes and spent two weeks in the hospital before we finally decided to let him die with dignity. I'd never heard of a dog with diabetes before."

"Yours is a complicated family," said Jackie.

As they stepped inside, Jackie realized that the house bore no resemblance to Julian's apartment. The massive foyer was dominated by an antique armoire and two huge copper urns filled with flowers. It led to an enormous living room that had been divided into three separate seating areas—and decorated without a trace of glass or chrome. A cozy arrangement around the fireplace included several stately wing chairs, an oversize sofa in a pretty but faded chintz, and two imposing chests that were probably original Louis XVI—and had never been refinished. The room was comfortable and clearly lived-in.

Jackie was busy admiring the antique chests when a woman dressed in full riding attire burst in a side door.

"You're here," she said, looking at Julian. She strode over to him, kissed him on the cheek, and pulled off her riding cap. "I'm late. I was just at the stables, and had the best run you can imagine with Winchester. Herb says I should enter the show at the Garden with her next month. Come watch?"

"My pleasure," said Julian.

"Great. That would mean a lot to me." She pulled some pins out of her hair, and shook her head hard. A thick mass of honey-blonde hair came tumbling down.

"Everything well with you?" she asked.

"Of course."

"Good. Let's see, I should tell you what's up for the weekend, shouldn't I? Barney has permission to sleep over at a friend's house tonight. The phone number is on the refrigerator. Rick has a date with that cute blonde girl he's been talking about. He's been mooning about it for days, and I think he could use some fatherly advice on love and dating." She ruffled her fingers through her hair, found another pin that she hadn't removed, and pulled it out. "Which reminds me. Are you still crushed over the loss of what's-her-name? Or have you found a replacement?"

Julian looked slightly abashed, and glanced across the room at Jackie. The woman spun around.

"Oh," she said. "I didn't even see you. Forgive me." She walked over to Jackie, arm outstretched. "I'm Marianne. Marianne Beardsley."

"So I assumed," said Jackie. "I'm Jackie Rogers."

"Oh yes, I heard about you. You're the nice little girl on television. So you're Julian's new friend?"

Jackie looked at Julian, who seemed amused but didn't come to her rescue. "Yes," Jackie said through clenched teeth. "I guess I am."

"Well, good. There are lots of extra towels and things in the guest bathroom. If you need anything, please don't look for it in my bedroom. I'd hate to have to lock it." She turned back to Julian. "Have a nice weekend, dearest." She kissed him again. "If you need me, you know where I'll be."

She walked quickly out of the room and bounded up the stairs, her riding boots making a loud clacking against the wooden staircase. Jackie thought about bolting out the door before she could come back. Instead, she just said, "Let's go outside." Julian nodded and led her onto a patio, then across a walkway to a small greenhouse filled with fragrant roses, delicate orchids, and a variety of flowers that Jackie couldn't begin to recognize.

"Don't mind Marianne," said Julian. "She tends to get carried away, but she doesn't really mean anything by it."

"Of course she means something by it. I'm marching into her house and sleeping with her ex-husband. I guess I shouldn't have expected to see the welcome mat down."

Julian shrugged. "I can't imagine why it would bother her. There's nothing left for her to be jealous about."

"An impartial observer might say she wants you back. Or at least fantasizes about spending the weekend with you. In her bedroom, no doubt. She doesn't like seeing some other woman doing that instead."

"Good theory, but she's perfectly happy spending weekends in the city with her current lover."

"Who's that?"

"A young stud who needs to be housebroken, if you know what I mean. I can't imagine what she gets from him except good sex. Of course, this may be her way of getting back at me for my choice in women."

"I think you just put your foot in your mouth. What exactly is wrong with your choice in women?"

Julian grinned. "Absolutely nothing, from my point of view. Though there are others who might consider you too sexy for me."

"I'm not appeased."

"Sorry."

Jackie decided not to press the point. "Who is her young stud, anyway?"

"I thought you might have guessed by now."

"I haven't. But you know I'll find out."

"Cocky young reporters." Julian smiled. "Well, it's strictly confidential, but I'll tell you because you'll get a kick out of it. Marianne has been having a torrid affair with Feodor."

Jackie stared at him. "Feodor Zerkov? Our Feodor?"

"Is there another?"

"I don't know, but I think this may be the first time in my life that I'm speechless." Jackie stopped to sniff a flower, and for a moment she had the strange sensation of being out of her element, involved with people too sophisticated and fast-moving for her taste.

"You seem distracted," Julian said.

"Not really," said Jackie, recovering quickly. "But I thought I noticed a tennis court as we were coming in. Can we play?"

"Good idea."

As they meandered over to the tennis court, Jackie noticed Marianne pulling out of the driveway in her black BMW. Her window was down, and she waved to nobody in particular. Julian also noticed her going, and smiled.

"Funny, isn't it? When the kids were little, they used to stand at a window and wave whenever one of us went out. They'd be heartbroken if we didn't wave back, so Marianne got in the habit of waving to the house, even if she couldn't see a little face in one of the windows. I guess she never got over it."

"Charming," said Jackie. She wondered what else Marianne hadn't been able to get over. It was just possible that the expression about old habits dying hard applied to sleeping with an ex-husband.

They found rackets and balls, and began hitting easily. Jackie slammed a few shots past Julian, who didn't seem eager to run after anything.

"Want to play a game?" Jackie asked after she was warmed up.

"I'm up for it."

Julian came alive once they began keeping score, and Jackie had to struggle to keep up with him. They were surprisingly well-matched—Julian was stronger, but Jackie's strokes were smoother and more careful. They got to six-all and played a tiebreaker which Jackie won by a point. She tossed her racket up in the air, just as Rick—sixteen, lanky, dressed in cut-offs and a sweatshirt—came over to ask if he could play the winner of the next set.

He sat down to watch, and Jackie found herself concentrating harder, determined to win. She served two aces, and took the set 6–3. Julian dropped his racket in mock disgust.

"Women are supposed to know better than to beat men," he said. "Didn't your mother ever tell you that?"

"Nope. She said to fight for every point."

"I have to talk with her sometime." He handed his racket to Rick. "Teach her a thing or two, Rick. I'm going into the house to make some phone calls."

Rick nodded, and silently took his father's place on the court.

"Hit a few before we start?" Jackie asked.

"Not necessary," Rick said. "You serve first."

Jackie served and Rick smashed it back.

"Good shot," she called.

He nodded briefly, and got in place to receive the next serve.

Jackie laughed to herself, realizing that Rick was serious about avenging his father's honor.

He did it easily, trouncing her 6–1.

"I was definitely outclassed," she said, shaking his hand at the net.

"Uh-uh. You play well."

"You're generous."

Rick shoved his hands in his pockets and walked with her off the court.

"I saw you on television the other morning," he said as they headed toward the house. "Dad had told us about you, and Mom put your show on while we were eating breakfast. You were real good."

"That's nice to hear. It's always hard to judge yourself."

"What do you do next?"

"I'm not really sure. I'm a general reporter, so I do all different things. Any suggestions?"

"See if you can talk to Bruce Springsteen. God, that would be great."

Jackie laughed. "I doubt he's on my list. Or that I'm on his list, for that matter. But I'll certainly let you know if lightning strikes and I get to interview him."

When they went into the house, Julian was nowhere in sight. Rick looked around, as if he were hoping to conjure him from the ceiling. He'd obviously used up all the conversation with her that he was prepared for. Picking up her overnight bag, which was still sitting conspicuously in the foyer, Jackie said, "Thanks for the game. I won't bother you anymore, but maybe you can just show me where the guest room is?"

"Is that where you're staying?"

"I assume."

"Why don't you stay in Dad's room? You and Dad sleep together, don't you?" He looked at her innocently, cocking his head to the side.

She couldn't decide if he was being curious or hostile. "That is definitely something you should discuss with your dad, not me," she said.

He shrugged. "Okay with me."

She followed him up the stairs, carrying her own overnight bag and trying to remember if it had ever occurred to her when she was sixteen that her father slept with *anyone*.

The guest room was decorated with yards of pink-and-lilac Laura Ashley fabric on the walls and bed; an antique braided rug in the same colors was tossed casually on the floor. There were matching soaps in the bathroom and sweet-smelling sachets in the dresser drawers. Jackie grudgingly admitted to herself that whoever had decorated the house had a nice flair. She hated to think that it was Marianne.

About an hour later, as she sat reading the Thomas Mann novel she'd brought along, Julian finally knocked on the door. He came in and sat down on the edge of the bed.

"I hear you wouldn't talk to my son about sex," he said, a twinkle in his eye.

"What?" She put down the book.

Julian laughed. "We've just had one of those serious father-son talks. The young man has a date tonight, and he definitely has sex on the mind."

"I hope he wasn't insulted that I wouldn't answer his questions. But I can barely talk about sex with you, never mind your son." She paused. "Anyway, I thought we agreed that sex is for doing, not for talking about."

"It is," said Julian, "but not necessarily when you're sixteen."

She looked up, half-expecting him to come embrace her, but he didn't move. There was an awkward silence.

"I made a dinner reservation for us tonight at the Cloisters," he said. "It's a tiny French restaurant near here. You'll love it. The suburban version of Lutèce."

"Great. But I don't have anything dressy to wear."

"No problem," Julian said. "Just look through Marianne's closet." They both laughed, but Jackie didn't really think it was funny.

From outside, the Cloisters looked like another Tudor house, considerably smaller than Julian's. Inside, it was all wood paneling, white tablecloths, and candles.

The maître d' shook hands with Julian. "I have the table you requested, Monsieur Beardsley," he said with a heavy French accent. "You will be happy. Follow me."

They followed him past two tiny rooms, through a double archway, and into a room lit only by candles. The three tables in the room were almost hidden by baskets of flowers and greenery. He led them to a table tucked away in a corner.

"Enjoy your meal, *monsieur et mademoiselle.*"

Jackie sat down and reached for Julian's hand across the table. "What a wonderful hideaway," she said. "How did you ever find it?" She looked around, squinting in the dimness, then turned back to Julian in surprise. "I can't believe it. I think that's Bradley James sitting over there."

"I can't see a thing," said Julian. "But go over and say hello if you want. I don't mind."

"We're not exactly buddies. I'm sure he doesn't need me bothering him right now."

"You're right." Julian grinned. "Never disturb a man having a romantic meal unless you're willing to find out that the woman he's with isn't his wife."

"You're terrible. How can you even think something like that? Bradley James is a man dearly loved by the heartland of America."

"Do you have any idea what goes on in the heartland of America?"

"No. But what I was going to say before you started getting cute is that Bradley James barely knows who I am. He has ignored me since the day I arrived."

"I thought he was famous for being warm and personable."

"On the air, maybe. Off the air, he has an ego as large as

the network and treats most people like dirt. Particularly women."

"Then maybe I guessed right about his date."

"Meaning?"

"Men who have contempt for women usually screw around. They need women just so they can abuse them—intellectually, at least—and make themselves feel better. Don Juan was the classic misogynist."

Jackie would have commented, but was interrupted by the maître d', who came over to discuss what they would like to eat.

"We haven't seen menus yet," Jackie said.

"We have no menus, *mademoiselle*. We prepare what you desire. Tonight, may I recommend starting with escargots. The chef prepares them in a delicate tomato and cream sauce, with just a hint of basil."

Julian said that sounded wonderful, and Jackie tried hard not to wrinkle her nose. Nothing could make a snail seem edible to her.

"No escargots, *mademoiselle*? Then perhaps the gravlax, very subtly seasoned?"

"Actually, I prefer my food cooked."

Julian laughed heartily, and the maître d' tried to affect a small smile. "We have oysters tonight, very fresh. If you prefer them cooked, as you say, the chef can poach them for just a moment in white wine."

"Sold," said Jackie, and they discussed entrées.

After a lengthy discussion with Julian about the best wine to order, the maître d' brought out a chilled Puligny-Montrachet, and after exclaiming about the vintage, filled the crystal glasses. They were halfway through the bottle when Jackie's oysters, Julian's escargots, and America's Bradley James all arrived at the table.

"I was just going to make a phone call," Bradley said, "and I didn't want to pass by without saying hello."

"How nice," said Jackie. She noticed that Bradley was using his television voice and sounded as stiff as she felt. She introduced him to Julian, who stood up to shake hands.

"Julian Beardsley." Bradley gave him his favorite on-air look of contemplation. "Didn't I interview you once?"

"Yes, indeed," said Julian. "It was . . ."

"I've got it." Bradley snapped his fingers. "It was after the gold market went wild, and nobody knew what was happening. As I recall, the market acted exactly as you said it would."

"I get lucky sometimes."

"Well, next time I'm certainly going to follow your advice." Bradley asked a couple of questions about how gold was doing now, and whether or not Julian thought it was a good investment. Julian chatted amiably on the subject for a few minutes, then handed him a business card. "Our firm trades only on our own positions," said Julian, "but if you're serious, I'd be glad to give you some suggestions. Call anytime."

"That would be terrific." Bradley looked at Jackie with renewed respect. "I shouldn't be interrupting your dinner, but it was great to see you." He patted her shoulder. "Glad you're on our team."

As Bradley headed off to make his phone call, Jackie studied her oysters.

"It was nice of him to come over," Julian said.

"Lovely." She stabbed an oyster, sucked it into her mouth, and tried not to think about how slimy it was.

"You look annoyed," Julian said. "Anything wrong?"

"Nothing really." She put down her fork and tried to speak in an even voice. "Actually, there is something wrong. Two things, really. Number one is that you never told me you'd been on *A.M. Reports*, interviewed by Bradley James. And number two . . ." She paused, not sure she could explain why it bothered her to realize that Bradley James, one of the terrors of the industry, was going to be nice to her now that she had the whiff of money.

"I'm waiting," Julian said. "You were up to number two."

She took a sip of wine, realized that she couldn't explain that at all.

"Number two is that you never asked him if the blonde woman waiting expectantly at his table is his wife or not."

Julian laughed. "He actually seemed more interested in money than love. How much does he make?"

"The rumor is a million and a half a year, though I couldn't swear to it. From what I've heard, most of it is probably under his mattress. He's apparently saved the first dollar he ever earned."

"A talent I don't have," Julian said, tasting an escargot. "These are wonderful. Can I entice you to try one?"

"Not a chance." Jackie shuddered. "As far as I'm concerned, some things are better off left in the ground."

When Jackie arrived at work on Monday morning, she found a note from Steve Cawley stuck on her door: "See Jeff Garth. Re: Exercise series."

Well, that was promising. She wouldn't mind seeing Jeff Garth about anything. After their brief flirtation outside Darlie's dressing room, she had smiled at him in the hall a few times and talked with him briefly at various production meetings. But so far, they hadn't been assigned a shoot together. That was unfortunate, since Jeff was incredibly appealing—he was always charming and friendly, and had a reassuring air of confidence about him. He wasn't cocky, but he was unusually competent, and he had two Emmy Awards to prove it. They were on a shelf in his office, crammed in with his collection of autographed baseballs and footballs, remnants of his days as a sports producer.

After a brief detour to the ladies' room to comb her hair, Jackie headed to Jeff's office. She found him leaning back in a chair with his feet propped on his desk.

"Is that *Variety* you're reading?" she asked, as she walked in.

He looked up and smiled. "You bet. I try to keep the right image."

"You've done it—you look like a producer." An incredibly attractive producer, she thought. He was wearing a tweed jacket, knit tie and a flannel plaid shirt—the picture of what a man who peruses the L. L. Bean catalog would wear to the office. His slight stubble of beard suggested that he was too busy to pay attention to getting a good shave. But it was his eyes that were captivating—deep brown and piercing; she had seen them flash with such fierce determination that they seemed to belie his otherwise casual demeanor.

Now he took his feet down from the desk and motioned her to sit down. She did—folding her legs carefully, and smoothing her silk skirt around her knees.

"I take it you're here to talk about the incredibly fabulous series we're going to do together," he said.

"I don't know anything about it, since Cawley left me a very cryptic note. But I'm glad to hear that we really are going to be working together at last."

"Had enough of Raleigh?" Jeff asked.

"More or less. But I'm also just glad to be doing something with you. I've heard you're terrific."

"You have? Who's spreading those nasty rumors?" He put his feet back up on the desk. "Actually, this series could be terrific, even though its sole purpose is to attract viewers during sweeps week. You and I have been assigned the simple chore of getting America fit. It's a week-long series—yes, that's five full days, fans—of exercise, diet, and information, guaranteed to get you off your duff and on the road to the body you've always wanted. Your task, Ms. Rogers, is to be cheerleader, promoter and correspondent, sending out the message that it's time to *Get Fit, America.*"

"Not a bad idea," said Jackie.

"Thanks, but it wasn't mine."

"Whose, then?"

"Your good friend Raleigh—who, by the way, is pissed as hell. She couldn't do it because of scheduling problems, but she thought that at least Dominique should . . ." He stopped, looking momentarily embarrassed.

"She thought Dominique should do it instead of me," said Jackie, finishing his sentence.

"More or less," Jeff said lamely, "but don't be insulted. We've learned not to pay too much attention when Raleigh is on a Dominique kick."

Jackie wondered just what Raleigh had said about her. It was irritating to think that their personal battles were becoming public knowledge.

"I'm not sure why Raleigh and I haven't hit it off right," she said, hoping to defuse whatever bombs Raleigh had dropped. "I get the feeling that she wants me to fail, but is too professional to turn out anything but good stories—even if I happen to be in them. But you have no idea how unnerving it is to look up while you're doing an interview on camera and see your producer glaring at you."

"I promise not to glare," Jeff said. "Stare, maybe, but not glare."

"It's a deal."

Jeff clasped his hands behind his head and leaned back again. "Don't spend your time worrying about Raleigh—we have more important things to do. This series, for example. I've got one of the bookers looking for a couple of key experts to guide us through. And I thought we'd sex up the whole thing by putting you in a leotard to demonstrate some exercises."

"I'm afraid that wouldn't sex things up—it would only prove the point that most women are in bad shape."

He looked at her appraisingly, and she felt stripped bare. "You look okay to me, but I'll reserve judgment. You really won't wear a leotard on the air?"

"I really won't. Maybe if I lost ten pounds . . . no, that's not true, either. If I lost ten pounds I'd probably decide I'd do it if I lost ten *more* pounds. That, by the way, is a story in itself. Why most women have such a lousy body image."

"Do they?"

"Of course. Have you ever met a woman who was totally happy with her body? Every woman in the country wants to lose weight and have firmer thighs—so they'll watch this series, thinking we'll give it to them. Frankly, we'd be doing a greater service if we encouraged women to be more accepting of themselves, rather than giving them one more thing to feel guilty about."

"I'm game," said Jeff. "Go tell Cawley that we've changed the name of the series to '*Be Content, America!*'" He opened his top desk drawer, took out a large bag of popcorn, and began munching thoughtfully. He offered some to Jackie, who shook her head. "No thanks, I'm trying to lose ten pounds, remember?"

He tossed a piece of popcorn at her. "High-fiber, low-calorie," he said. "Just keep it unbuttered and unsalted."

She popped the kernel in her mouth. "Great tip for the series." She winked at him, noticed his piercing eyes were bright with interest.

"I didn't mean to be sarcastic before," he said. "I think you've really hit on something. If we focus on body image instead of just bodies, we'd be doing something a little different. I could see you doing some on-the-street interviews with normal, attractive ladies, who tell you how they feel about their bodies. If you're right—and I bet you are—we'll find some pretty women who'll tell us how ugly they feel."

"I like it. Then we have a psychiatrist in the studio to explain the whole thing."

"You got it. And it becomes easy to promote. *Don't make your body beautiful at the expense of your spirit! We'll teach you how to feel as good as you look.*"

"You missed your calling. You should be writing for *Vogue*."

"Sign me up." He scribbled a few things on a notepad. "I could get to like this. It may be the first series aimed at improving ratings that actually has some integrity to it."

"A word I like."

"I thought you might. You just don't hear it much around here."

"Was it better when you were producing sports?"

He looked at her in surprise. "You must be joking."

"I didn't mean to be. Weren't you at NBC in the glory days when Les Bresky ran the sports division?"

"You bet. But I guess you never heard the real Les Bresky stories."

"Tell me. I'm always the last to know gossip."

"It's juicy stuff, believe me." He took another handful of popcorn. "I won two Emmys for Les Bresky, broadcasting genius, and held his whole goddamn sports department together. Then he fired me."

"You're joking."

"Nope. The last show I produced was the Daytona 500. I thought Bresky was pleased with it, even though we had the normal shrieking back and forth over the remote phones. I went out for a couple of beers afterward, and when I got back to my hotel, I had a message—a message, mind you—that I was fired. He's one classy guy."

"What had you done wrong?"

"To this day I don't know. Les never talked to me again. But mine wasn't even the best story. Ever meet John Higgins, who produced football? He found out he'd been fired when he came back from covering the Pro Bowl and his office was all packed up. Bresky had left a note on his door that said 'Please leave address where boxes can be shipped.' "

Jackie shook her head. "At least Bresky didn't ask him to pay postage."

Jeff laughed. "Good point. But what can I tell you? Network television isn't such a nice business."

"Thanks for the information. I'll remember to read my phone messages more carefully from now on."

"You'll be fine. All you have to remember is that television is run by a bunch of bastards. There are a lot of superficial idiots on the air and a lot of political assholes behind the scenes."

"Well, as the newest superficial idiot, I'm pleased to be working with such a nice political asshole."

He grinned. "Now that that's taken care of, we can make some great television together."

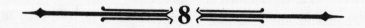

Jackie was sitting in her office poring over diet books and trying to decide whether or not she really needed to lose ten more pounds when the receptionist called to say she had a visitor at the front desk.

"Who is it?"

"Alden Taft."

"Tell him to come in. No, tell him I'm not here." She swallowed. "Forget it. Tell him I'll be right out."

The receptionist laughed. "I'll tell him."

Jackie took out a small mirror from her desk drawer, but immediately put it back. She felt flustered. What the hell was Alden doing at her office?

Pulling herself together, she took a deep breath and headed out to the front desk. You're a network television reporter, she told herself. Act like one.

Alden had his back to the glass doors, so Jackie saw him before he saw her and thought, say what you would about Alden Taft, he was still gorgeous. The receptionist was looking at him with cow's eyes, but he ignored her. He stood very straight, tapping his foot slightly. Jackie smiled to herself. That was Alden, all right. The man would never bite a fingernail or risk a frown line. All anxiety would be sublimated into the very slightest nervous tic.

Walking toward him, hoping she looked every inch the reporter, Jackie reached out to shake his hand.

"Alden, it's good to see you."

"Hello, Jackie. I hope I'm not interrupting anything, but I happened to be in New York seeing a client a block away from you, and I thought I'd stop in to say hello."

"You should have called."

He gave a small smile. "I didn't think it would do any good. You've never answered any of my messages."

The receptionist watched them curiously, making no effort to hide her interest.

"Why don't you come back to my office."

Alden followed her through the halls, and she sensed that he was being looked over carefully by everyone they passed. It wouldn't hurt her standing at the network to have Alden at her heels.

In her office, he walked over to the window to look out. "Nice view," he said. "I guess I don't have to ask if you're doing well."

"Every office here has a good view," she said. "We're on the thirty-sixth floor. How bad can the view be?"

Alden continued looking out the window. "You can actually see my client's office from here. It's a wonderful case I'm handling, by the way—a major tire company is trying to buy out a small bank. There've been a lot of jokes in our office about rubber checks, but I think the deal is going through."

"That's great."

He slipped his hands in his pockets and leaned back against the window, affecting a pose that would have worked nicely in *GQ*. "I've been very busy lately with mergers and buy-outs. Everyone's saying that the golden era for all that is over, but you could never tell from our experience. There's been almost no slowdown in the business, and just when you think there are no companies left to merge, you get involved in another big deal."

"Very interesting. But is that what you came by to talk to me about?" Jackie asked, impatiently.

Alden looked embarrassed. "Actually, I just stopped in to say hello and make sure you were doing all right. As I said, I was in the neighborhood."

"That was thoughtful of you. Sorry I never answered your messages—I've been busy."

"I'm sure." He sat down on the edge of the desk. It occurred to Jackie that she knew exactly what he wanted to say, but she decided not to help him say it. He missed her, wondered if she had any regrets, if too much water had passed under the bridge. She knew the questions, but she wasn't sure she knew the answers.

"Are you keeping busy in New York?" he asked.

"Very. There are a lot of interesting people around. I enjoy that, you know."

"I know." He stood up, and Jackie felt a pang—for his futile trip, for her hard-heartedness, for both of them. Turning around, he closed the office door and moved toward her. "You know, it's always bothered me that I never had the chance to kiss you good-bye. Maybe that's why I came up today." He touched her cheek and turned her face to his. "Should we try it now?"

With a chance to think about it, she might have said no, but instead, she found herself relenting as he wrapped his arms around her and held her close. He kissed her once gently and she pulled away, but then he found her lips again and let his embrace describe how he still wanted her. Though she wanted to collapse into his arms, she maintained herself firmly, yielding only slightly when his deep kisses announced his desire.

"I'd hate to think that this is a good-bye kiss," he whispered.

"Maybe just a good-bye for now."

"What does that mean?"

"I'm not sure." She took a step back. "We've had such a long history together that it's impossible to think of never seeing you again. But it doesn't work, Alden. You like the image, but not the real me. I hate to use the expression—but do you think we can be friends?"

"I hate to hear the expression." He smiled wanly. "As far as I know, women only want to be friends when they're in love with someone else. Is that it?"

She shrugged. "Not a fair comment, but yes, there is someone else."

"And does he understand the real Jackie Rogers, whoever she may be?"

"I don't know. But I hope so."

He picked up his briefcase and opened the door to leave. "I didn't plan to be kissing you today, but it was nice. Thank you."

"Nice for me, too."

"By the way, I'm staying at the U.N. Plaza Hotel tonight."

"Well, enjoy it," she said.

Getting in a cab after work, she gave Julian's address instead of the U.N. Plaza Hotel, surprised that she still felt any pull at all to Alden. It's just that he's safe, she told herself. She understood

everything about Alden and felt in control with him, while
Julian made her feel vulnerable, open to being hurt. He's worth
the risk, she thought as she arrived at his apartment. When
Vera, the Jamaican housekeeper, let her in, she told Jackie that
Julian wouldn't be home for at least an hour.

"I wonder why he told me to come right over after work," she
said, more to herself than to Vera.

"I can tell you," said Vera. "He likes to have someone here
when he gets home, and I'm leaving now." As she picked up her
pocketbook and raincoat, she gave a final look around the
apartment and nodded to Jackie. "Have a nice evening, honey.
I'm sure I'll see you in the morning. I get in early."

Vera swept out of the apartment and closed the door firmly
behind her. Jackie decided that she wouldn't mind having a talk
with Vera—she probably knew more about Julian than anyone
else. But propriety obviously wouldn't allow it. Wandering through
the apartment, marveling at the strange sensation of being there
alone, she wondered what it would be like to come home there
every night. She sat down on the sofa in the living room, trying
to decide if she was thinking about marrying Julian. Well, of
course you are, she told herself. He's your rich and powerful
teddy bear. What more could you want? She let the thought slip
out of her head as quickly as it had entered. She had told Julian
about the end of her affair with Alden, made it clear to him that
she wasn't looking for commitments right now. He liked that,
and she half-suspected that her lack of demands was a key to his
enchantment with her.

Vera had left a large platter of shrimp on the coffee table, and
Jackie nibbled some, thinking about the evening ahead. She had
finally told Julian about Dana, and Dana about Julian, and
everyone had agreed that it was time they met.

"Don't worry," Julian had said when they had settled on the
night. "I'll find someone terrific to fix her up with."

"Who do you have in mind?"

"I'll have to think about it. Is she just like you?"

"Depends how you mean that. We look nothing alike and we
have totally different careers, but as they used to say in the
seventies, we're soul sisters."

"Good. Can I introduce her to Sam Fredericks?"

"Your associate?"

"More properly the senior vice-president for planning and financial strategy at Beardsley Enterprises. And a man who needs a woman."

"Married?"

He smiled. "He's not married right now, but that could change at any moment. Sam believes in marriage. He's done it twice and is looking to make it three."

"Terrific. Dana is my best friend. I'll just call her up and ask her if she wants to go out with a piranha."

"You misinterpret. He's a man who has learned from his experiences. In fact, he's a sucker for women. The man makes a fortune, and anything that doesn't get sent to one of the first two wives is spent on roses for some girlfriend or other."

"How lovely. Anyway, I'll ask, but he doesn't sound like Dana's type."

Dana, however, had been interested, and now she walked in, prompt as usual, at the stroke of seven-thirty. After Jackie greeted her and gave her a quick tour of the apartment, she offered her some shrimp.

"Thanks," said Dana, settling down. "The apartment's nice, but tell me about the man. Are you desperately in love with him, or does Alden still have a chance?"

"Alden? What made you think of him?"

"He came to visit me this afternoon. Shortly after he left you, I understand."

"How tasteful of him. I thought we made it clear to all Harvard graduates that trying to screw both of us was unacceptable."

"He wasn't trying to screw me, dearest. Alden and I are pals, remember? And he came to me as a friend, to ask what was happening with you. He said he was concerned."

"Very sweet, but I suspect that the only thing he's really concerned about is his own ego, which has been slightly bruised by me."

Dana shrugged. "Well, the man was clearly upset about something. What did you tell him when he came to see you?"

"I didn't tell him anything. We kissed."

"That would explain it." Dana laughed. "You're shameless, Jackie. Seems to me you once accused me of being an . . . ahem . . . tease. How would you describe yourself?"

"A busy woman with the wisdom to keep her options open. By the way, speaking of options, I never asked you what happened on your trip to Chicago with his honor Mr. Osterfeld."

"Ah, dear Mr. Osterfeld. The perfect gentleman, by the way. We worked like crazy all day, at night he took me out to dinner, ordered a bottle of wine, then kissed me gently outside my hotel-room door. He never made a pass."

"I'm baffled."

"So am I. Either age has made him impotent or he's as much of a genius with women as he is with the Constitution. I'm now totally enamored of him and will follow him anywhere, with my tongue hanging out just slightly, until he'll have me."

Jackie grinned. "Doesn't sound like you. But at least you're not worried about being fired anymore, I take it?"

"No, but you shouldn't think I was totally off target in my previous assessment. As soon as we got back, he fired one of the other female associates, for reasons nobody can fathom. She had been a clerk to a Supreme Court justice, so let's just say she's not a dumb gal."

"Dare I say that it sounds like this man has a major problem with women?"

"Say it, I've already figured that out. Which is why I'm trying to end my mad crush and find others more suitable. Now, who's this man that I'm going out with tonight?"

Jackie described the little she knew about Sam, and a few minutes later he appeared, a smaller and slighter version of Julian, with considerable charm and a cool efficiency. He looked Dana over carefully, and immediately launched into an animated discussion of commodities law. Jackie was surprised by how much Dana knew on the subject, easily chatting with Sam about futures and options and risk arbitrage. When Julian finally arrived and joined the conversation, Jackie wondered how she had managed to be with Julian for so long and know so little about what he did. Her contribution to the discussion was to suggest that they continue it at Le Périgord, over dinner.

"Where did you get your education in commodities?" Jackie asked Dana, once they settled into the restaurant and began a second round of drinks.

"Our firm does a lot of commodities work," Dana said, "though I have to admit I'm not involved with most of it. Right now I'm working with Osterfeld, representing two of the stockbrokers being charged with insider trading."

"Are they guilty?" Jackie asked.

"Depends. You can't be a successful speculator without knowing what's going on—talking to people. And the people you talk to are all on Wall Street, too. Predicting prices is dinner-table conversation, and all the crackdowns in the world won't change that. Fortunately, it's not something these two gentlemen here have to worry about."

"Why not?" asked Jackie, surprised.

"There's no such thing as insider trading in commodities. Everyone is supposed to know what's going on."

"Anyway, we're not speculators," Sam said. "When you run a bullion company, you never try to predict prices on gold or any other commodity. We all sleep best at night if we know that all our positions are fully hedged."

"I hate hearing that," said Dana with considerable spirit. "Somehow commodities—which my dictionary says means things of value—have been turned into meaningless paper that gets shuffled back and forth for the sole purpose of making the shufflers rich."

"Not so," Sam said. "The whole purpose of hedging is to protect the people who need to use the commodities."

"Of course it is," said Dana. "But could you tell me the last time a farmer bought wheat futures in order to protect his financial interest in his crop? You know it doesn't work that way. The commodities exchanges live and die on speculators and financial insiders."

"You can't argue with her, Sam," Julian said with a chuckle. "What percentage of the futures deals done on the exchange actually end in delivery?"

"Not a lot."

Jackie sighed. "I hate to be obtuse, but could somebody explain to me what you're all talking about?"

"Ethics," said Dana.

"Money," said Sam.

"Well, that explains it all," said Jackie.

Julian put his arm around her. "Do you want a one-minute lecture on how Beardsley Enterprises works?"

"Shoot."

"It's relatively simple," Julian said. "We're brokers for bullion and precious metals—gold, silver, platinum, all that. If Tiffany's needs to buy gold to make into a necklace that Sam can give Dana, we sell it to them. That means we have to own the gold. But gold is expensive, and the market is volatile. When we buy it from the mine, the market might be at three hundred dollars an ounce—and when Tiffany's wants to buy it from us, the market might be down to two hundred dollars an ounce. We don't want to take losses like that."

"Don't you have to risk money to make money?" Jackie asked.

"That's what speculators do, but we're dealers. Businessmen. When Bradley James asks me on the air what's going to happen to the gold market, I'm glad to make a prediction, but I'm not risking my children's college money on the guess. We want to be neutral on prices, so no matter what happens—whether they go up, down, or sideways—we don't lose. If we buy gold to put in the warehouse tomorrow, we also hedge our bets by selling futures on gold. A future is a deal to buy gold at a specific price for some month in the future. A long position means you have a contract to buy down the road. A short position means you have a contract to sell. We make sure our positions even out. If the real gold we own decreases in price, the future increases, and we're even. That's what Dana meant about farmers. A farmer could protect himself in the futures market against declining prices, the same way we do."

"Understood," said Jackie. "But if you're perfectly hedged, how do you make any money?"

"Good question." Julian and Sam exchanged looks. "We charge a small markup, and when you're talking about sales that amount to billions of dollars a year, a tiny percentage is enough."

"Well explained," said Dana. "But I have a very hard time believing that the major function of Beardsley Enterprises is supplying metal to Tiffany's—or even to industrial customers. Are you going to tell me that you don't spend most of your time buying and selling paper gold?"

"I hate that expression," Julian said.

"So do I," Sam said, smiling at Dana. "But I have to admit that you cut through Julian's polished explanation very nicely."

"Is someone going to tell me what paper gold is, or should I just go sit at another table?" Jackie asked.

Julian laughed. "Don't do that."

"I'll try this one," said Sam. "Despite Julian's efforts to convince you that Beardsley Enterprises is a key cog in the industrial wheel, Dana happens to be right. Most of the gold and silver we buy and sell never moves from one place to another. It's not being used, it's just being traded. The classic image of a trader is a guy with a phone at each ear—he buys from one side and sells to the other, and never touches the stuff along the way. We might sell an ounce of silver for just five cents more than we bought it for—but if the contract is for one hundred thousand ounces of silver, and if we do it enough times, we make money."

"I wasn't worried about that," Jackie said dryly.

"Dana's point is well taken," Sam continued. "We work ourselves up into an incredible frenzy, do hundreds of millions of dollars' worth of trades in a week, and feel very important—when what we're basically doing is exchanging warehouse receipts with other dealers. If you'd like me to tell you what greater good we're serving, I'm afraid I can't."

Dana reached over and patted his hand. "I wasn't trying to force that confession, though I do take a secret pleasure in hearing people who are making phenomenal amounts of money admit that they don't deserve it."

"I didn't admit that at all," Sam said. "Making money is an art, and it happens we've perfected it. I just don't know that the world is better off because of it."

"The philosophical anguish of the intellectual businessman," said Julian. "Believe me, I go through it regularly. All I can say is that whether we believe in them or not, there are always going to be ways of measuring worth and exchanging value—whether it's dollar bills, gold, or rocks. People have a primal need to keep score and buy the things they need, whether it's bread or sex."

"Somehow, I knew you'd get around to sex," Sam said.

"Of course," Dana said, turning to Jackie, "these guys are trading czars. As far as they know, they can get anything they want, for the right price."

"Isn't that true in the real world?" Sam asked, putting his arm around Dana.

"Maybe, but people aren't always in the mood for negotiating."

"That doesn't bode well for your coming home with me tonight."

"Right," said Dana.

As they left the restaurant and went out into the cool autumn evening, Sam and Dana walked close together, but not touching, a few paces behind Jackie and Julian, who were holding hands. Jackie couldn't help thinking that there was a story in all this, if only she could find the right angle. Gold and silver trading had all the right elements for a piece on *A.M. Reports*—it was fast-paced, wild, and sexy. She loved the image of a trader talking into two telephones at once, spending millions of dollars for gold or silver he would never see. Julian had made it all sound so respectable, but Sam's explanation intrigued her. Millions of dollars were being made and lost every day on what was essentially a game. She'd like to know a little more about how Julian played it. Impulsively, she squeezed his hand and said, "Do you think I could do a story on you for *A.M. Reports*? Behind-the-scenes secrets of a commodities trader?"

"Definitely not," Julian said. "My secrets aren't for the air."

"Mmm, but you could tell them to me."

"Actually, I couldn't." His voice was unexpectedly severe. "Some of my dealings are pretty sensitive, Jackie. I want you in my bedroom, but I don't want an investigative reporter there."

Though Jackie didn't say anything, she pulled away slightly, discomfited by his reaction. What was she likely to find out if she used her reporting skills to investigate Beardsley Enterprises?

They said good night to Sam and Dana, then walked two blocks in silence. Stop being dramatic, Jackie told herself. Julian is just trying to separate business and pleasure. That's fair, isn't it? She snuggled closer to him, pleased that he responded by putting his arm around her shoulder and kissing the top of her head. Back at his apartment, she thought of reassuring him that she always left her reporter's notebook at the office, but didn't have the chance. As soon as he closed the door, he reached for her, pushing her gently against the wall and kissing her deeply, their bodies pressed tightly together. Feeling the stir that Julian's presence always evoked, she wanted him desperately. As they walked up the stairs, touching, anticipating, it flashed through her mind briefly that Julian didn't want her to get too close to his business because he was hiding something from her. But now was definitely not the time to pursue it.

Jackie expected to have a message from Dana when she got to work the next morning, but she hadn't called, so Jackie went directly into the sound studio to record a track for a story on teen suicide she'd shot with Raleigh a few days earlier. Raleigh listened to the track and announced that it was fine. Jackie sat in the edit room for a few minutes, watching Raleigh try to make good television out of a boring interview with a psychiatrist specializing in the problems of adolescents.

"Twenty-two minutes of tape, and I'll be lucky to get thirty decent seconds out of it," Raleigh muttered.

She pulled a question Jackie had asked at the beginning of the interview and an answer the psychiatrist had given at the end.

"Think you can make those work together?" she asked the tape editor, a bald, overweight engineer who was playing with the controls on the complicated console in front of him.

"Let me try it."

He made the edit on the machine, and they watched it— Jackie surprised, as always, that tampering with the interview didn't undermine the reality. If anything, it made it make more sense.

"Shit," said Raleigh.

"What's wrong?" Jackie asked.

"You recrossed your legs. Watch." The editor played the sequence again, and this time Jackie noticed the problem: when she was asking the question, her right leg was crossed over the left; when the psychiatrist answered it—twenty minutes later in real time, a split second later on the edited tape—her left leg was over her right.

"It's not real obvious," said the tape editor. "You're seeing her from behind in one shot, and by the time the brain registers the change in perspective, you forget to notice the mistake."

"Good try," said Raleigh, "but we can't use it. Let's find two shots that match."

They began searching through the footage. The interview had been shot with a single camera, focused on the psychiatrist.

When the interview was finished, the cameraman had spun around and turned the camera on Jackie, who had to ask her questions all over again so the final version could include her face on camera, too. "Good reversals. Now get some reaction shots," Raleigh had said then, so while the tape rolled, Jackie had to tried to look mournful, concerned, interested, and puzzled. It was Raleigh's job to take all the different pieces of tape—questions, answers, reaction shots—and cut them together, making it look as if it had all happened in a natural sequence. In the final version, Jackie would ask a question, and the psychiatrist would answer—but he might not be answering the question she had actually asked at the time.

After a few minutes, Jackie slipped out of the edit room, glad that putting it all together was Raleigh's problem, not hers. When she was just starting in television, she had worried about the editing process, sat through endless editing sessions to make sure that the integrity of her story wasn't damaged. Now she was convinced that it really *was* possible to capture the essence of a twenty-minute interview in thirty seconds, to change reality without distorting it.

Back in her office, Jackie shut the door firmly and called Dana.

"Just calling to see if you had a good time last night," she said, when she finally got through to her.

"It was fine. Sam was very pleasant."

"That sounds like you'll never go out with him again."

"Not true. I'd be glad to, but I think it will take him a few days to get over the fact that I didn't invite him in last night."

"I'm sure he'll recover." Jackie played with the telephone cord. "What did you think of Julian?"

"Also very pleasant, though I don't particularly trust a man who's that rich. I wouldn't have thought that he was your type."

"Why not?"

"Dearest, you're as far from a bimbo as any woman could be, but I have to believe that when you kiss Julian you taste gold."

"I'm not sure I'd recognize the flavor."

"Maybe not. The main thing in your favor is that you don't have the slightest idea just how powerful Julian really is."

"We'd never talked about his business before last night."

"So I gathered. Well, there's something to be said for the pure of heart."

When they hung up, Jackie felt restless. The problem with television was that you were either overwhelmed with work—and the panic of meeting an on-air deadline—or you were bored. Frankly, she liked the panic better than the boredom.

She wandered over to Jeff's office to ask what was happening with their series.

"Laurie's been booking it," he said. "If you're not too busy, we can go to the booking department and see what she's up to."

"Definitely not too busy," Jackie said.

They walked down the long hall together, and for some reason, Jackie was aware of Jeff's arm brushing against her own. She took a slight step away, thinking even as she did that it would be far pleasanter to move closer. There was a rough manliness about Jeff, an unself-conscious swagger as he walked, that intrigued her. It was going to be nice working together.

Laurie was on the phone when they got to her office—making calls was what bookers did most of the day—and she waved them in, mouthing that she'd be done in a minute. Jackie noticed that her desk was piled with clippings on diet and exercise, and she had two huge well-thumbed Rolodexes. A few baskets of flowers, in various stages of alertness, were scattered around the office, as were bottles of wine and champagne. Jackie wondered if Laurie had just had a birthday—then realized that they were probably gifts from people eager to be on the show. The bookers didn't make the final decisions on who would appear, that was up to the producers—Cawley, Jeff, and Raleigh—but the bookers made all the contacts. Authors, minor celebrities, and corporate representatives all clamored for the chance to be on the air, to promote something—whether a book, a movie, or themselves. The booker's job was to get bigger celebrities and experts, the kind who didn't need to promote themselves anymore and required subtler pressures to be convinced to appear. Jackie was sure that Laurie sent a lot more flowers than she got.

Laurie hung up the phone with a flourish and turned triumphantly to Jeff.

"You have perfect timing," she said. "You won't believe who I just got for the exercise series. Dick von Dickson."

"Is that good?" Jeff asked.

"Fabulous," said Laurie. "Every show has been after him. I had to pull out all the stops to get him." She smiled coyly at Jeff, making Jackie wonder just what stops she had pulled.

"Well, that's great then," said Jeff.

"I'm not so sure," said Jackie, trying to be diplomatic. "I have some problems with the guy."

Laurie's face contorted in amazement. "You must be joking. A problem with von Dickson? He's had two best-selling books on fitness and health. He was made for this series." Arrogantly dismissing Jackie, Laurie turned to Jeff and took his hand. "You can thank me for saving this series," she gushed.

Feeling a surge of annoyance, Jackie decided to stop being tactful. "Von Dickson is a fraud with no medical credentials. It just happens that I did a report on him when I was at the local show in Boston. He's popular, but his exercises are dangerous, his diets are unbalanced, and he's mostly full of shit. I'd never use him."

"Yes you will," said Laurie, still holding Jeff's hand. "I already told him that he'd be our primary consultant for the series."

"Then you can get out of it easily. Tell him we couldn't give him all he wanted."

"Hell I will," said Laurie, suddenly heated. "It's a great booking." She turned, simpering, to Jeff. "What do you think?"

"I know nothing about the guy. Why do you think he's so perfect?"

Laurie, clearly deciding to pretend that Jackie wasn't in the room, sat back in her chair, stroked Jeff's hand. "Well, dearest, as I said, he's had two best-sellers, and he has a diet plan that he'll do for us on the air. It guarantees you'll lose ten pounds a week. I'd make that the focus of the series. *Watch us every day this week, and you'll be ten pounds slimmer!*"

"It can't work," said Jackie bluntly.

Laurie raised an eyebrow. "Darlie told me she just went on his diet and lost twelve pounds this week. She thinks he's fabulous."

"Tell Darlie those twelve pounds won't stay off. It's water weight."

"That's what everyone says when they want to knock a diet, but it's not necessarily true."

"It is true. Want the simple arithmetic?" Sitting down on the edge of the desk, Jackie noticed Jeff discreetly pulling his hand away from Laurie. "A pound is thirty-five hundred calories, so to lose a pound of fat, you have to burn thirty-five hundred more calories than you take in. The average woman burns about fifteen hundred calories a day. Eat fifteen hundred calories a day, and you don't gain and you don't lose—you're even. A reasonably strict weight-loss diet—including von Dickson's—is about one thousand calories a day, which gives you a deficit of five hundred calories a day. What's five hundred times seven days?"

"Thirty-five hundred," offered Jeff.

"Thanks. That comes out to almost exactly a pound a week. Add some exercise and you're up to maybe two pounds of fat a week. That's it. All you can really lose. The rest is water, which will come right back."

"All I know is that Darlie looks great—and is telling everyone about this great diet," Laurie said stubbornly.

"Fine, and is she going to tell you next week or the week after when she stops the diet and immediately gains ten pounds back? Of course not, because she'll blame herself. She'll figure it's because she did something dramatically wrong, like eating an artichoke at the wrong time of the day, or something."

Jeff stroked his chin. "Is the guy good television?"

"Fabulous," said Laurie, her voice cooing again. "He's a good talker, real slick, and also very handsome. Trust me, Jeff, he'll work for us."

Jeff looked at Jackie. "I understand what you're saying, but is there any way we can tone down his claims and still use him?"

"I wouldn't," said Jackie angrily. "He's a pretender. He wants you to think he has some magic formula that nobody else knows. He's one of those who insists that food combinations are important—you know, grapes and oranges for breakfast, and artichokes and broccoli for lunch. No swapping, no substitutions. Whenever you see a diet like that, you know it's a lot of hocus-pocus that does nothing but prey on women's own insecurities. He does the same thing with exercise. He has the three perfect exercises that will get you in shape. That's crap. There are a million ways to get in shape. Women need information—

not one more plan that leaves them feeling guilty when they don't stick to it."

"I hear you," said Jeff.

"Oh, come off it," said Laurie, tossing her head. "Von Dickson is a great motivator and a great name. What more do you want?"

"I told Jackie we'd hold ourselves to a high standard on this series," said Jeff, almost apologetically. "We want to give women some confidence in themselves—in their own bodies and their own judgment. It doesn't sound like von Dickson is the guy to do it."

"You're making a huge mistake," Laurie said.

"Humor me," said Jeff. "Come up with a couple of other experts, and then we'll choose."

Laurie shook her head in disgust. "You know I wouldn't go to this trouble for anyone but you."

"Yup," said Jeff. "I know." He leaned over to kiss the top of Laurie's head, and Jackie felt a wave of jealousy. She wondered if Laurie had ever consummated her flirtation with Jeff, or if the dalliance was confined to the office. Either way, she felt unexpectedly irritated at the two of them. Laurie Spinner didn't deserve Jeff—and Jeff should have better taste.

Jackie convinced Dana to start exercising with her, on the grounds that before she could Get America Fit, she had to do something about her own thighs. She believed completely the premise she and Jeff had agreed on for the series—that women should stop worrying so much about what they look like and pay more attention to being healthy and fit. On the other hand, television was the land of the thin, and much as she didn't want to compete in the attractiveness sweepstakes, she didn't have much choice. Even Steve Cawley, who pretended to know better, spent half his time critiquing the way her hair looked on the air, before he remembered to tell her whether or not he liked the story. So it was three times a week to aerobics class and twice a week jogging around Central Park with Dana.

The search for new experts paid off. Jane Fonda agreed to come on and talk about why exercise was so important, but refused to demonstrate anything. A nutritionist from Harvard Medical School and an exercise physiologist from Stanford were signed up, in place of von Dickson. Craig Claiborne said he'd give some low-calorie recipes, and a soap-opera star named Holly Gotley was convinced to do all the exercise demonstrations. Laurie found five attractive women who agreed to have a rap session with a psychiatrist, talking about bad body image.

"It's going to be an incredibly good series," Jackie told Dana, as they jogged slowly around the Central Park reservoir. "I'm hosting the whole thing, and doing a field piece on how the rich get in shape. Tomorrow I go to the Golden Door for two days, with Jeff and a crew."

"How romantic," Dana said.

"Right. We'll eat rice cakes and tofu, and fight about whether or not I'll let Jeff shoot me taking an exercise class."

"Of course you will," Dana said. "And when he suggests at the last minute that you wear a leopardskin leotard, I suspect you'll do that, too. By the way, how does Julian feel about your traveling with another man?"

"Come off it. This is business. Anyway, I think Jeff is screwing around with a booker named Laurie Spinner. She's too cute for words, and has made it very clear that she'd do anything for Jeff."

"I wonder why sweet young things like screwing so much." Dana pulled back her shoulders and quickened her pace.

Jackie struggled to keep up. "By the way, Julian said you've been spending some time with Sam, but he has no details. How's it going?"

"Now there's a nice open-ended question. No wonder they pay you big bucks at the network." Dana tripped on a stone, but quickly regained her balance and her pace.

"And you earn big bucks as a lawyer, which explains why you didn't answer it."

"Well, dear, I'll tell you the truth. Sam has turned out to be very darling—even though I still don't trust rich men. He sends roses to my office every time we have a date. But if Julian wants the gory details on our screwing, we're not—though I can sense that it's getting to the point of put up or shut up. Or maybe I mean put *out*."

"By my tally, you like him, he's not married, and you're not a virgin. And you don't even have the career considerations you had with Osterfeld. Is there a new morality I don't know about?"

"No, but there's a new set of germs." Dana shuddered and slowed down again. "Every once in awhile, I think about all the guys I've been with, and it gives me the creeps. I heard an infectious-disease doctor on some talk show the other morning—it was probably yours, in fact—and he was saying that when you have sex with a man, you're not only having sex with him, you're having sex with all the people *he* had sex with for the last seven years . . . and all the people *those* people had sex with." She glanced at Jackie. "I suspect that somewhere in that vast chain of fucking even you and I have been in bed together."

"So send Sam a bouquet of flowers with condoms in it."

"Ah, safe sex," said Dana sarcastically. "I've thought of it, believe me. But there's something emotionally jarring about it.

When you have sex, you entrust a man with your body, your ego, and your soul. Shouldn't you also be able to trust that he doesn't have worms on his prick?"

"You're being disgusting."

"I'm making a point. It bothers me that I can't have an orgasm anymore without worrying about getting AIDS, syphilis, herpes, chlamydia, or crabs."

"Dana, this isn't a man you picked up on the street. He makes half a million dollars a year, at least. Don't you think he goes to a doctor once in a while?"

Dana pulled her sweatband across her brow. "I don't know what's the matter with me. I'm getting old and scared."

"Definitely not the Dana I used to know," said Jackie, "but I've gotten used to that. Anyway, you're just being cautious. Nothing wrong with that, I suppose."

They stopped talking for a minute, sprinting the last hundred yards to an invisible finish line, back at their starting point. Breathing hard, they walked out of the park and down Fifth Avenue. Dana stopped in front of Julian's building. "You going in here to shower?" she asked.

Jackie shook her head. "No way, I'm going home. We don't live together."

Dana laughed. "Oh, excuse me, but now who's being Little Miss Priss?"

"We all have our ways of protecting ourselves," said Jackie. "You can search Julian's apartment if you like—I haven't left so much as a toothbrush there."

"I wouldn't guess he was short on room."

"No, but he may be short on commitment," Jackie said.

The sex lives of personnel at *A.M. Reports* were outlined on a pink sheet of paper labeled "Morning Contact"—the result of a staff meeting at which Steve Cawley had announced that he didn't care who was sleeping with whom, but he did care that he had their phone numbers. "When news breaks overnight, I need to be able to reach everyone," he said. "It doesn't matter what number I'm dialing, as long as you're at the other end of it."

Jackie thought about it, and decided she wouldn't list Julian's number, after all. She went out and bought an answering machine, so she could leave a message on it the nights she wasn't in, saying where she could be reached. One hundred and forty-nine dollars' worth of discretion. It was worth it, since she noticed people poring over the phone list when it was distributed. Laurie Spinner listed only one number. Jeff Garth listed two, but one of them wasn't Laurie's. The record went to Dominique, who included five phone numbers. "My mother, my agent—who always knows where I am, Peter, the hotel in Atlantic City for nights I'm performing, and my apartment," she explained when someone teased her about the list at a production meeting.

Jackie didn't think Jeff was the type to scrutinize the list, but after their first night at the Golden Door, she wasn't so sure.

Late in the evening, after they finished eating dinner at a nearby restaurant, they stayed to go over interviews, scripts, and shooting schedules for the next day.

"We got some good footage today," Jeff said, sipping his second cup of espresso. "I have to say I'm surprised. I expected a spa full of fat, rich ladies getting massages, but they seem serious. I get the feeling they know what they're doing."

Jackie reached down to massage her left leg. "Trust me, that exercise class was serious. My muscles are aching. Too bad we're just visitors. I wouldn't mind going there for a week as a client. Think the network would finance a quick pick-me-up for the new correspondent?"

"Doubt it," Jeff said. "But I suspect you could find someone else to finance it."

Jackie wondered if that was an offhand joke or a grist from the rumor mills. She decided to ignore it.

"We should probably be getting back to the hotel. We have to be up for the break-of-dawn walk up the mountains, don't we?"

"Yeah, the crew loves that one," Jeff said, but he made no move to leave the table.

Jackie refolded her napkin and took a sip of water.

"How are you finding life on the road?" he asked.

"I don't mind it. There haven't been any long trips—mostly overnights. And I still enjoy seeing new places—you know, looking out the window at new scenery."

"Other ways to do it than being a reporter."

"I know, but something about traveling this way fits my

personality. I can get involved when I like, and be an observer the rest of the time. Even here—I'd probably never come to the Golden Door as a paying guest, but this way I come, take a few exercise classes, get a feel for the place, and still leave to go out to dinner. Be there and not be there at the same time."

"That's called having an uncommitted life."

"Maybe, but it's an interesting one."

"Anybody to rush home to?"

"Why do you ask?"

"Just curious."

"I've been going out with someone," Jackie said carefully, "but who knows? How about you?"

"Also who knows. My real love is a tiny cottage in Hillcrest—way upstate—where I escape whenever I have a couple of days off. A two-hour drive from Manhattan, and when I get there, I feel I've finally come home. Unfortunately, I've done all this traveling for longer than you have, and I don't even look out the windows anymore. Too much pressure all the time. I need a place to escape that's all mine."

"I can imagine," said Jackie. She wondered if the cottage was the second number on the phone list, decided it didn't matter. "It's really a shame, though—you have a job that a lot of people would kill for, and you're too pressured to enjoy it."

"You'd think I'd have learned my lesson when I was doing sports. It doesn't necessarily pay to care too much."

"But it's nice that you do."

They finally went back to the hotel. Their rooms were on the same floor, directly across from each other. Jackie felt a certain awkwardness as they fumbled for their keys, said good night, and opened their doors.

"I'll knock on your door at five tomorrow morning," Jeff said as he went into his room.

"I'll be up."

She found a message that Julian had called, and called him back.

"When are you coming home?" he asked after they had chatted for a few minutes.

"Tomorrow night. Can I come right over and slip into your bed?"

"I've got a better idea. Stay an extra night, and I'll meet you

Thursday morning at the L.A. airport. We'll fly together to Hong Kong."

"What exactly am I supposed to do in Hong Kong?"

"Keep me company. It's a long trip and an interesting city. I've got two or three days of business meetings, so you won't be away too long—but we can be together."

It was crazy, of course. No way she should go to Hong Kong when she was in the middle of a series and still new at her job. The only problem was that she wanted to.

"Can I let you know tomorrow?"

"I'll be hard to reach, but you can leave a message with my secretary. She'll arrange for your ticket and all."

"Where will you be?"

"Washington—testifying before the Commodities Futures Trading Commission. There's a new chairman who thinks that every time the price of silver goes up by a nickel, it means someone is trying to manipulate the market."

"Didn't that happen a few years ago?" She vaguely remembered the story about the Hunt brothers from Texas buying up billions of dollars' worth of silver with borrowed money, and almost precipitating an international financial crisis.

"Yup," said Julian. "It's no news that it can happen. But Travers—that's the new chairman of the CFTC—figures disaster is imminent. So I get to go down and reassure him."

"Could it? Happen again, I mean?"

"Easily. But Travers keeps getting excited about the wrong things. He's a political appointee—some academic out of Princeton with a very theoretical view of the market and no idea what the bullion business is really about."

"You mean he doesn't understand that when you want to manipulate the market, you go to Hong Kong to do it, not Washington?"

There was a brief silence on the phone. "That's not why I'm going to Hong Kong."

"I was only joking," Jackie said. "Anyway, let me see if I can figure out my schedule and get back to you."

She hung up and dialed the room across the hall.

"Jeff? It's Jackie. I'm not waking you up, am I?"

"Nope. I'm watching a Marx Brothers movie on cable. Anything wrong?"

"Got a question for you. Mind if I come by?"

When she opened her door, he was standing at his—barefoot, shirt unbuttoned, otherwise as she had left him. They walked into his room together. She perched on the edge of his bed and briefly outlined the situation, telling him that she had the chance to go to Hong Kong, wondered if there would be a problem in her disappearing for a few days.

"Let me guess," he said. "Your millionaire wants to whisk you away, and you can't decide if something as silly as your job should be in the way."

"That's not what I asked."

"It's not? Funny, sounded like it."

"Where do you get your information?"

"Dominique told me about the millionaire. The rest just seemed to follow."

"Playing coy at dinner, were you? You didn't say you knew."

"It didn't seem tactful."

"Neither was this."

"You're right. I'm sorry." He held out his hand. Their eyes met, suddenly intimate, and for an instant she thought he would lean forward to join more than eyes. But instead he said, "Friends?"

"Of course." She sighed and took his hand. "Let me ask you as a friend, then, instead of my producer—what do you think I should do?"

"Whatever your heart requires and your mind accepts."

"Poetic but not helpful."

He fiddled with a shirt button. "Okay, practical answer comes first. Sweeps start the week after next, and you'd better have your ass back in New York by then. You can do the voice-over on the spa story tomorrow—I don't need you in the studio in New York. Just about everything else in the series is going to be live, and Dominique should be able to handle any breaking stories that come up next week. So, yes, you can go."

"That's the practical answer. What's the impractical one?"

"I'm not sure I really know you well enough to say this, but here goes. You're being pulled in too many directions right now. You can't have a career like yours and be mistress to a millionaire."

"Colorful phrase, but that's not exactly how I see myself. Julian's a man I'm dating whom I happen to care about a lot."

"At dinner it was 'Who knows?' "

"Well that's right, too. We don't have any signed agreements. At the moment, we just like being with each other."

"Then go be with him and stop apologizing."

"It's a quick trip—I'll be back in the office by the end of next week."

"Plan on it, because if anything goes wrong and this series gets blown, I'll personally break both his legs. He may be richer, but I'll bet I'm stronger."

While he was talking, Jackie noticed that the skin showing under his open shirt was tanned, hirsute, and she decided she wouldn't mind running her hands across his chest. A puzzling reaction, she thought, since she was going to Hong Kong with Julian, and couldn't wait to be with him.

They finished shooting at the Golden Door at dinnertime the next day. Buoyed by the thought of seeing Julian, Jackie sprinted up the mountain during the dawn exercise to conduct spirited interviews with the spa director, a nutritionist, and two of the guests. Jeff was pleased, and he told her it was going to be a great series.

"If you still care," he said.

"Don't be like that. Of course I do."

"I know," said Jeff. As he kissed her good-bye on the cheek, she got an enticing whiff of his woodsy after-shave, and she hesitated a moment before she ran off.

Before dawn the next day, Jackie was on her way to meet Julian at the airport. He was coming in on the red-eye from New York; she was tired from too much work, tension, and not enough sleep. When they finally boarded their flight to Hong Kong, they reclined their first-class sleepers, talked briefly, and dozed off. Jackie awoke to find the cabin dark, a movie flickering on the screen. Next to her, Julian was reading by a small light. She reached over to him, pushed up the seat divider that separated them, kissed him. "Ever do it on a plane?" she whispered in his ear.

"The famous zipless fuck?" he asked.

"I think that was a train. Remember? *Fear of Flying.*"

"Great literary allusions." He reached for the blanket that was covering her, pulled it over both of them, and turned off his small light.

"Let me feel what happened to those leg muscles at the spa."

Beneath the blanket, he slipped his hand under her skirt to stroke her thigh.

"Firm?" she asked.

"Warm," he said. His thumb moved upward, drew circles, disappeared into her silky underwear.

"That's not my leg," she said.

"It's better." His thumb continued its circling, two fingers found a deeper mark. She groaned as his fingers vibrated in her.

"Anyone watching?" she asked.

"I hope so," said Julian.

She felt a slight shudder, an orgasm rippling through her body, her soul contracting at Julian's hand; she gasped, reached for him.

"You're easy to satisfy today," he whispered, pleased. "More?"

"Don't stop till we're in Hong Kong." Under the blanket, she struggled with his zipper, finally released his penis which was firm, ready. She held it in moist hands, gently rubbing. His body tensed, he pulled her closer.

"What happens if we get thrown off the plane?" she whispered, inching toward him, eager.

"We fly on our own."

They did just that, facing each other, moving with gentle thrusts and groping hands, searching for their satisfaction. Julian was silent, intent in his desire, finally grunting his relief, offering a gush of warmth. Jackie held him, closed her eyes as another orgasm flooded over her, and tried not to cry out.

A moment later they kissed, smiled at each other, and Jackie suppressed a giggle. "I feel like I'm in high school," she said. "How do we get out of this without having the stewardess come over?"

"She wouldn't dare," said Julian. He found Jackie's panties under the blanket, helped her put them on, pulled himself back together.

"Hope I wasn't too loud," Jackie said, slipping back to her own seat, smoothing her hair.

"I like hearing that you're happy. Even on a plane."

"Nothing excites you more than a risk, I suppose."

"You excite me."

"I'm flattered. Consider the compliment returned."

"I could tell it was."

She reached for his hand under the blanket, stroked it. "Something about you inspires me to do things I wouldn't normally dream of," she said. "Flying to Hong Kong on a moment's notice and copulating in the first-class section of the airplane."

"Nothing that's illegal," Julian said.

"Which reminds me—did everything go okay with your testifying in Washington yesterday?" Julian raised an eyebrow and Jackie blushed. "Sorry. I didn't mean there's anything illegal about your business. My mind just makes strange leaps."

"The testimony was fine," Julian said, ignoring her comment. "Travers' latest bug is that there are too many silver futures floating around with too little silver to back them. He's noticed that Beardsley Enterprises keeps taking delivery on our silver, instead of just turning over the futures when they're due. I pointed out that we're not speculators, we're bullion dealers. If we don't own the bullion, we're not in business."

"Sounds reasonable," Jackie said. "But why buy futures instead of buying the silver outright?"

"Leverage. I buy silver today, and I have to pay for it in full at today's price. I can buy a future on ten-percent margin—a hundred thousand dollars today means I can get a million dollars' worth of silver next March. The price of silver goes up, and my investment—which, by the way, the bank has probably lent me—stays the same, but the silver is now worth two million."

"And if the price goes down?"

"There are margin calls. You have to pay in full for the amount it's dropped. That's how people get wiped out."

"Sounds different from what you and Sam were describing that night at dinner—being fully hedged, taking no risks, all that. Doesn't this make you nervous?"

"Not really," Julian said, stretching his long legs on the sleeper seat. "You've got to figure that when I'm long in the market, it's not going to go down."

For the rest of the flight, they dozed, read, and ate the snacks that the flight attendants kept bringing by. Jackie stared out the window as they finally approached Hong Kong, and was surprised to discover that from the air it looked like New York—an island dense with skyscrapers, lights, and commerce, a feeling of bustling importance evident even at ten thousand feet.

"It's a good thing there are some signs around in Chinese," Jackie said after they had landed, passed through customs, and climbed into the car that was waiting for them. "Otherwise, I'd wonder where you'd taken me."

"The ultimate international city," Julian said. "Just wait, it's going to get better."

"Do we have time for some sightseeing now?"

Julian glanced at his watch. "No, unfortunately, I have a meeting in about an hour—in our hotel room, actually. Sorry I can't ask you to play hostess. It's not that kind of meeting."

"No problem. I'd probably spill the tea."

Julian smiled. "With this group, I think we'll serve something a little stronger than that. Or else considerably weaker. Anyway, hang around long enough to meet everyone, if you like—and then you can go exploring yourself. It'll be a long meeting. Should I keep the car and driver for you?"

"I wouldn't mind."

Half a dozen Rolls-Royces were parked in front of the Mandarin Hotel when they pulled up, and their driver joined the queue. He told them he'd be there whenever Miss Rogers was ready. Walking through the bustling lobby, Jackie ardently hoped that the driver would recognize her when she came out again—because she was going to have a hard time remembering which black Rolls was theirs.

They had a corner suite with an impressive view of the waterfront from two sides. The harbor was busy, far busier than any waterway she'd seen in New York. She wanted to have lunch and get outside. She checked the time. If she were in New York, she'd be going to sleep, and in Los Angeles she'd be having dinner. But in Hong Kong it was already tomorrow. Or maybe the day after. Since she wasn't particularly tired, she decided to wash up and change her clothes, feeling all the while the strange disorientation that long flights seemed to cause. Her own version of jet lag: her body arrived on schedule, but her mind couldn't move as quickly. It was less a question of crossing time zones than of changing herself, wondering if there had been a metamorphosis of her own identity somewhere over the Pacific. How else to explain going from the Golden Door to Hong Kong in twenty-four hours?

Julian was pacing in the living room—talking quickly into his Dictaphone, looking out the window, biting at the edge of his thumbnail.

"You seem hyperexcited," she said, taking a glass of orange juice from the bar that had been set up in the corner of the room.

"Just getting my thoughts in order," he said.

"You never really told me what these meetings are about. Who's coming?"

"Bullion dealers, speculators, people with thoughts about silver." He shrugged, looked at her meaningfully. "Nothing mysterious, you know."

Julian's guests were nothing if not prompt. As the beeper on Julian's watch sounded the hour, there was a polite knock on the door. Jackie stared in amazement as three Arabs, two dressed in traditional garb, one in a dark suit, walked in. Julian greeted them cordially, introducing them to Jackie. She was startled to hear that the first was Sheik Fahoud, but missed the other two names. When she extended her hand to the sheik, he looked pointedly away. Embarrassed, she went to answer the next knock on the door. It was Erwin. Jackie looked at him in surprise.

"What are you doing here?" she asked.

"Nice welcome. I was invited. How about you?"

"Same." She smiled. "I just wasn't expecting to find sheiks and Englishmen at the Mandarin Hotel in Hong Kong."

"You can find anything in Hong Kong."

"So I've heard, but I thought that meant cheap jade and luggage."

Erwin smiled. "Are you going out shopping?"

"I don't have any definite plans."

"You should go. Shopping, I mean. You won't believe what's available."

He stepped past her into the room to greet the Arabs. She felt uncomfortable and wanted to leave. Something about the presence of the Arabs was disquieting. Sheik Fahoud, with his white robe, small dark beard, and head covering, was standing slightly apart from his colleagues. He refused the small glass of juice that Julian offered and made no effort at conversation. Across the room, he caught Jackie's eye and stared at her suspiciously. He doesn't like having women around, she thought. I should probably just leave. She went into the bedroom to get the wrinkled linen blazer she had worn on the plane, put it on, and decided she would disappear from the meeting in a few more minutes. When she stepped back into the living room, one of the Arab businessmen, who was now talking to Erwin, glanced at her, then looked across to Sheik Fahoud. The sheik nodded, and the businessman said to her, "We thank you for your courtesy." Puzzled, Jackie looked from the businessman to Erwin.

"I think he means covering your arms," Erwin said. "Arab women always wear long sleeves as a sign of respect."

Jackie didn't bother explaining that she had gotten the jacket because she couldn't wait to leave—and whatever respect she might have had was diminishing. But she did wish that she owned a book on international business etiquette.

The final member of the group had arrived while she was getting her jacket. He appeared to be from Hong Kong, wore a dark suit and an unassuming manner. He bowed briefly when Julian introduced him to Jackie; his name was Lem Chen.

Have all these people come all this way just to see Julian? she wondered. Lem Chen was polite but as disinterested as the others in making small talk. He bowed again to Jackie, and a moment later was deep in conversation with Sheik Fahoud.

Wondering what strange dealings were about to take place in the room, Jackie looked curiously at Julian. Uncomfortable as she was, she suddenly longed to stay to find out what was going on. But Julian didn't look as if he would welcome her intrusions at the moment.

"Probably time for you to get going," Julian said quietly. "The car is waiting downstairs."

"I know." Jackie took a quick breath, unable to resist some inquiry. "You have interesting friends. How do you know them?"

"Now's not really the time to discuss it."

"Can we talk about it later?"

"I doubt it," he said. Aware of the sharpness in his answer, he tried to take the edge off it by adding, "We'll have more important things to do later." But she realized that he had no intention of letting her in on his business secrets.

She lingered for a moment, torn by conflicting thoughts. It was impossible to think of Julian being involved in anything not totally aboveboard, but there was something ominous about the scene. Why hold a business meeting in a Hong Kong hotel room unless driven by clandestine motives? Jackie swallowed, made her tone determinedly cheerful. "If you need a good secretary, I'll stay to serve coffee and take notes."

"Thank you, but we don't need anyone here," Julian said.

She left, squeezed into an elevator crowded with Chinese businessmen, walked outside to the row of chauffeured cars, and smiled in relief when her driver waved to her. As he opened the door for her, he asked where she was going.

"You tell me," she said. "I want to go shopping and get a taste of Hong Kong."

"Perhaps the Landmark," he said. "It's where I take most ladies like yourself. You can visit Hermès . . ." He shrugged, closed the door, and ran around the car to get in the driver's seat. "Forgive me," he said, looking at her now in the mirror. "I don't know the names of all the fancy designer shops. But there are many at the Landmark. Also many beautiful jewelry shops and art galleries."

"I'm sure it's beautiful, but how about taking me where your wife shops."

He turned around and grinned. "Yes, really?"

"Really."

"You know Li Yuen Street East?"

"No, but it sounds perfect."

"Just hold on tightly to your pocketbook."

She wandered through the crowded lanes where he dropped her off, marveling at the clothes, bags, and jewelry on display, and at the merchants hawking, negotiating, and making quick sales. People thronged through the market. Jackie paused at one rack, noticing a Calvin Klein outfit that she had in her closet at home. The price was a fraction of what she had paid. She remembered that a number of designers had factories in Hong Kong, and decided these must be factory overruns. In a short time, she selected three dresses, a stack of Ralph Lauren polo shirts, and went to pay for them.

The merchant, a lanky Chinese man wearing an oversize jacket and a rakish beret, took her money, gave her change. "Lady, you have nice taste." He leaned over, conspiratorial. "I have some special bargains I save for people like you. Come see?"

She knew she shouldn't, but couldn't resist. It was, after all, a crowded market, her driver was barely a street away. The merchant pulled aside a curtain, and she stepped back with him into a small, dark room thick with smoke. There were no windows, just a single lightbulb hanging from the ceiling and dozens of dirty cardboard boxes on the floor, overflowing with more clothes. In a shadowy corner in the back of the room, she saw three other Chinese men sitting around a rickety table. They stood up when she entered, stared at her with blazing eyes. She felt a wave of panic.

"You need an evening gown?" the first man asked. He pulled a long, glittery gown from a box, flashed it in front of her. "This is original from Givenchy. You've heard of him? Would cost thousands of dollars in New York or Paris. Here, one hundred."

It was pretty, all right, but she noticed a pile of spangles in the box from which he had taken it. Either the spangles were falling off, or someone had just finished gluing them on. I have to get out of here, she thought. She took a deep breath, trying to stay calm.

"Thank you, but I don't need anything so formal right now." She made a move for the curtain, but he grabbed her arm, pointed to another box.

"How about blue jeans, then? I have the best. Ralph Lauren, Oscar de la Renta, Yves St. Laurent. You pick. Ten dollars a pair. Buy five or six pair, yes?"

She thought she would buy anything just so he would let her leave. But as she reached for her bag, she noticed one of the shadowy figures in the back moving, taking a step toward her. Was this all an elaborate ruse so they could jump her, steal her money? She clutched her bag to her hip, edged toward the curtain. "St. Laurent doesn't make blue jeans," she said.

The merchant looked startled, then angry, pulled a pair of the jeans from the box and shook them in front of her. "What do you mean, doesn't make them? That's his label, right there."

"Yes, it looks like his." She pretended to lean forward, instead turned fast, backed out through the curtain, and ran out of the store into the crowd. It wasn't until she was at the end of the lane that she stopped, heart pounding, and started to laugh. She probably wasn't cut out for bargain hunting on Li Yuen Street.

When she told the story to Julian that night at dinner, she had him laughing at her fear.

"I thought you were going to tell me that you ended up in an opium den," he said. "Instead, you came across a hardworking capitalist. An entrepreneur. What's wrong with that?"

"Nothing, but I'd forgotten that Hong Kong was home to a thriving trade in counterfeit clothes. He probably sews all those blue jeans in the back room for fifty cents a pair, then sticks counterfeit labels on the rear end. I wish now I'd just shut up and bought a pair—I could have had the only pair of Yves St. Laurent dungarees in New York."

She tried to describe to Julian her sense of Hong Kong—how it vibrated, made New York seem positively laid back.

"It's true," Julian said thoughtfully. "Nobody thinks about the long term here. They want to make quick profits in business and in the market. In and out, take the money and run. Lem Chen told me that his company is open for trading twenty-four hours a day, playing the markets in London, New York—they just never stop."

"Don't tell me—you decided that sounded like a terrific model for Beardsley Enterprises." Pausing to taste the soup the waiter put in front of her, Jackie looked at Julian in surprise. "This is unbelievably good. What did you order for me?"

"Shark-fin soup. You like it?"

"It's incredible. Taste it."

He did, nodded appreciatively. "It is good. Care for a taste of mine? It's cockerel's testicles."

She looked at him in horror. "You're joking."

"Yup, but it was on the menu, next to boiled deer penis. Thought it might be a good aphrodisiac."

"You don't need one."

He reached under the table to rub her knee. "You're right. I'll stick with fried snake and chrysanthemum petals."

"I think you shouldn't get any more adventurous than eggroll. Tell me how your meeting went."

"Fine," said Julian, "though I must say you can change a subject with lightning speed."

"The result of never having more than three minutes on the air to talk. Anyway, I'd love to hear what the meeting was about, and who all those people were."

"Too complicated to explain right now," Julian said. "But they're coming by again tomorrow morning, so I'll understand if you want to go out early. I didn't really mean for you to get involved with them."

"It's all right. I'd never met a sheik before—not that he seemed particularly charmed or charming."

"I wouldn't worry about him," said Julian. "In fact, forget him."

Jackie looked at Julian curiously, surprised at the sharp tone in his voice. He was worried about something, but she wasn't sure what.

"By the way," he said, "I'll have some time tomorrow afternoon. Will you come with me to the jade market? We can look around, maybe buy something. You'll love it."

"Is this a bribe?"

"Absolutely," said Julian. "I'm buying your silence."

"It's not going to work. I haven't figured out what I'm supposed to be silent about."

"I know that," he said with a fond smile.

She thought of pushing him to explain what was going on, but decided he would just sidestep her inquiries and be annoyed by her persistence. The best she could do for the moment was watch and listen, and hope to make sense of it another time.

Meanwhile, she knew she'd like it if Julian bought her a gift. He'd never done that before, and frankly, she thought it was about time he did.

10

The phone rang in Dominique's apartment at seven-twenty A.M. and she woke up with a start, trying to shake off the dream she'd been having in which Peter was a turkey, running around the farmyard on the day before Thanksgiving while she was inside the farmhouse baking a cranberry pie. It means either that he needs me or that I'm going to kill him, she thought as she reached for the phone.

It would be her mother on the phone, of course—the one person who couldn't understand that Dominique liked to sleep late in the morning. Meaning to be sweet, her mother called every time Dominique had a spot on the air, to tell her how terrific she'd been. She just assumed that Dominique was up watching, and couldn't believe that she'd rather sleep than see herself on the air. Dominique had explained that the spots were on tape—sometimes shot a day before, sometimes a week before—and she could look at them whenever she wanted.

Once her mother had called to ask, "Did you see *People* magazine this week? There was a big article about your friend Darlie Hayes. It said she gets up at four every morning and has to be asleep by nine at night. So how come you can be on the show and still sleep?"

"She's on live, but I'm not."

Her mother sighed, a long hiss across the line from Nebraska to New York. "You have to explain it to me, dear. On the show yesterday, Darlie—on live, right?—asked you a question, and you answered it. How did you manage it if you were still sleeping?"

"The magic of editing, Mom. It's all scripted by the writers, so I know what question she'll ask, and a week before she actually asks it, I answer it on tape. On the actual show yester-

145

day, she said her line, and then the engineer put in the tape of me saying 'Good question, Darlie. But let me point out . . .' "

"Oh."

"You understand?"

"Not really." And her mother had emitted another sigh and hung up.

Dominique realized what a warped sense of reality television created: she could be curled up under a quilt in her cozy apartment while millions of people were convinced that she was standing in a rainstorm on the coast of Maine. Never mind that the rainstorm was two weeks ago. Nobody thought about that.

This morning, though, the voice on the phone wasn't her mother's at all, it was Jeff Garth's, telling her that the Italian ambassador would be unveiling some important sixteenth-century paintings that had just been donated to the Metropolitan Museum—and she should cover it.

"Doesn't sound like our kind of story," said Dominique sleepily.

"That's what I thought. But I just found out that the ambassador is engaged to Contessa de Vilado—you know, the Italian siren with all the jewels?—and she'll be there. Cawley thinks it's going to be glitzy. One of the biggest society parties of the year—the kind everyone loves to watch."

Dominique yawned. "Ambassadors and art. Sounds like a job for Jackie. Maybe she should cover it."

"She's in Hong Kong."

"Why?"

"Don't ask."

She laughed and agreed to pull herself together, stop by the office for some research, and meet him at the museum later.

"By the way, what time is this going on?"

"Starts early—seven o'clock tonight," Jeff said. "You should get there by five."

"Darling, that's fine, but why are you calling me at dawn with the news?"

"What?" Jeff sounded taken aback. Dominique imagined him looking at his watch. "Dear one, it's seven-thirty. I've been here three hours already."

"That's your problem," said Dominique. "I'm going back to sleep for a couple of hours."

Jeff laughed briefly. "Want a wake-up call at noon?"

"No," said Dominique. "But I want a job on the Midnight News instead of our show. I never liked worms, and I never wanted to be an early bird."

The research packet Dominique picked up at the office was all about art and Italy. She decided to ignore it and worry instead about what she should wear. Jeff said she could be as glamorous as she wanted. Studying her closet, she fingered the six glittery gowns she wore for her nightclub performances. Maybe the white sequins? She always heard gasps when she walked on stage wearing it in Atlantic City. It was really a skinny tube of lycra, covered in sequins, that she had to pour herself into. The top was totally bare, clung around her breasts, then dipped in a deep V almost to her waist. No, it was probably a little much for her television image. That was the problem: all her evening clothes looked like they belonged at a nightclub, not at a museum opening with the Italian ambassador. She'd have to borrow. The public-relations woman at Geoffrey Beene had been nice to her before—maybe she'd come to the rescue again. Dominique called.

An hour later, the public-relations woman, an assistant, a tailor, and three Geoffrey Beene evening couture samples were in Dominique's apartment. Everyone agreed that she looked fabulous in the orange-and-blue taffeta. "Sexy but classy," the p.r. woman said. It was strapless, a swatch of blue fabric from breasts to waist, a braided silk cummerbund, then flowing layers of blue and orange taffeta to the ground. Let Contessa de Vilado beat that.

The tailor didn't have to do a thing—Dominique fit into the sample as if it were made for her. "If you get tired of television, you could come to work for us as a model," he said.

It was too late to borrow jewelry, so Dominique put on what she had. She decided her huge rhinestone drop earrings were too much, and settled for small sapphire-and-diamond clips that had been a present from a brief affair she'd had before Peter. He had been rich, but old and impotent. The earrings were small, but at least they were real.

Dominique called a limousine to take her to the opening, assuming Jeff would find a place for it in his budget. When she pulled up, her favorite cameramen from *A.M. Reports* were setting up on the steps of the museum. One of them, Bek, was wearing a tuxedo jacket, ruffled shirt, and dungarees; the other cameraman, Rodney, had on tuxedo pants, patent-leather shoes, and a dungaree jacket. She giggled. There had been a network memorandum a few weeks earlier, saying that all behind-the-scenes personnel should dress properly when covering formal events, and giving men a forty-dollar allowance to rent a tuxedo each time. The problem was that in New York renting a tux cost more than twice that. The cameramen's union had officially protested, and Dominique suspected that the outfits Rodney and Bek were currently sporting were a subtler protest.

Jeff spotted her getting out of the limousine and came over to greet her. "My God, you're gorgeous."

"You're rather striking yourself," she said. In fact, he was almost irresistible in a classic black tuxedo with a crisply starched, pleated, wing-collared shirt. She took his arm, heard the rustle of her own taffeta, and felt pleased. It was going to be an interesting evening.

An hour later, Dominique was standing on top of the steps in front of the museum for her opening comment, reading the words Jeff had written for her about "this historic meeting of art, politics, and high society." The spotlight on her was bright; the cameras were rolling, and behind her, the gorgeous crowd was strolling into the museum.

The unveiling itself was a letdown: the ambassador pulled a curtain to reveal the pictures, and although there was a gasp from the crowd, the pictures looked dreary to Dominique—barely distinguishable images of angels, trees, and Jesus. The ambassador made a speech about the glories of Italy being shared with the United States, then an art critic from Princeton gave a talk about the artistic and historical importance of the pieces.

It didn't matter: Dominique had already noticed Jeff taking lots of close-ups of the contessa listening, and earlier, of the Vice-President arriving by limousine and shaking the ambassador's hand.

The art interlude over, the crowd meandered into the Temple of Dendur gallery for dinner.

"Hope you don't have hay fever," whispered Bek, the cameraman, as they walked in. The room had been turned into a giant garden, with huge sprays of exotic flowers everywhere. Fragrant baby orchids were scattered over the tables, and the center-pieces were elaborate porcelain urns, also filled with orchids. Jeff directed Rodney to shoot the hors d'oeuvre table, which ran down the middle of the room and was piled high with mounds of caviar, lobster tails, and tiny quiches of smoked salmon and truffles.

"Not the antipasto my Italian grandmother made," Rodney joked, moving in with his hand-held camera.

Jeff moved easily through the crowd, casually asking people if they would pause for a brief interview with Dominique. Every-one took one look at her and said yes. Dominique was in her glory. Jeff introduced her to the Vice-President, stepping back so that Bek could get an unobstructed shot of them chatting.

"Have you ever been to Italy, Mr. Vice-President?" she asked.

"I have, and our two great countries share a fine tradition of love of art and culture. It's a joy that we can share more of that now with all the American people."

It didn't mean anything, but it was perfect: a ten-second sound-bite from the Vice-President would certainly add class to the spot. A handsome young politician Jeff introduced as Sena-tor Tark from Massachusetts joined them then, and offered his comment before Dominique even had the chance to ask any-thing. When they finished, she thanked both men and turned around to find that the ambassador and Contessa de Vilado were waiting to be interviewed.

"Are you enjoying your stay in America?" Dominique asked the contessa.

"*Molto bene,*" she said. "But it's a new challenge for me. It may be the only place in the world where the journalists wear more beautiful clothes than the guests."

Dominique laughed, glanced at Jeff, who was making a thumbs-up sign. So he'd leave that comment in. It would be nice for her image to have a contessa complimenting her on the air.

After a few more interviews, she watched Jeff directing Bek to get some interesting shots of the room.

"Finished with the interviews?" someone asked behind her.

Dominique turned to see handsome Senator Tark standing close, smiling slightly at her.

"I think so. We got everything we need, and we really appreciated your comments."

"I'm glad. I wouldn't want to take you away from your work, but if you're finished, can I entice you to sit down and have a glass of champagne with me?"

She looked over at Jeff, then back to the senator. "My pleasure."

They found a small table, sat down with champagne and plates of hors d'oeuvres, and chatted pleasantly about the evening and the art. Dominique, struck by the senator's charm, found herself flirting easily with him. He was handsome, smart, and amusing, and when their eyes met, she could see that he was attracted to her. Several people stopped at the table to greet the senator, and he shook hands each time, then introduced her as "my good friend Dominique LaFarge." Although there were other seats at the table, he didn't invite anyone to join them.

"It's quite a life you lead," Dominique said to him after the chairman of the board of the museum had come and gone from their table. "Everyone in the world must want to meet you and get on your good side."

"I suspect you have the same problem."

"Not really." She smiled at him. "I can offer a few minutes of television time, but I'm not exactly a center of power."

"And not particularly impressed by power, either, I see."

"I grew up as a country girl, Senator. I was taught to be impressed with who people are, not what they are."

"An admirable distinction. Can I offer you more champagne?"

"Just a bit, please."

He clinked his glass softly against hers. "It's a real pleasure talking to you. I never expected to make a friend at an obligatory affair like this."

If we have an affair, it won't be obligatory, Dominique thought, feeling slightly heady from the champagne. She looked around for Jeff, and spotted him across the room. He seemed to be doing fine without her. Taking another sip of champagne, she tried to remember why Senator Tark's name was so familiar to her. Since she rarely handled political stories, it was unlikely that she had worked with him before.

"I just realized how I know you," she said, turning back to him. "You're Jackie's senator."

"Pardon?"

She laughed. "Jackie Rogers. She works with me now at *A.M. Reports*, but she was a political reporter in Boston. You once complimented her at a press conference, and she's always given you credit for helping her get to the network."

"Ah, yes, I remember Jackie," said the senator. "If she's as talented as you are, I'm glad she's doing well."

"Another example of the power of your position," said Dominique, smiling at him. "What's it like to know that your off-the-cuff comments can have such an impact?"

"Actually, it's the kind of thing that can become a problem. I say something casually and it becomes a headline in the Boston newspapers. The unfortunate result is that I become too guarded in what I say." The senator glanced at her, touched her bare shoulder lightly, and smiled. "I'll practice making an unguarded comment on you. That's an exquisite dress you're wearing. Or, more to the point, you look exquisite in it."

Dominique laughed. "Thank you. But you were right the first time—it's the dress."

"No, all the loveliness comes from you." He smiled warmly at her, but the comment was interrupted by the Vice-President, who had come over to exchange greetings with the senator.

An hour later, Jeff found Dominique, took her aside to say that he had all the footage he needed and was going back to edit. "Do you want to stay here or come?" he asked Dominique.

"Do you need me?"

"Everyone needs you. But I'm not sure I could edit with you next to me in that fabulous gown. Stay here where you'll be fully appreciated. At least by the senator, who hasn't taken his eyes off you for a minute. Is he falling in love?"

"Strictly professional, darling."

"Looks strictly personal to me."

She kissed him on the cheek. "Frankly, I hope you're right."

Dominique got back to her apartment well after one, dropped off by Senator Tark, who had insisted on taking her home in his limousine.

"You'll call me next time you're in Washington, won't you?" he asked.

"Unfortunately, the stories I cover for *A.M. Reports* don't usually take me in that direction," she said. But looking at his profile outlined against the car window—the strong jaw, straight nose, handsome smile—she wondered if she might find a reason to visit, after all.

In her apartment, she called Jeff before she got undressed, to make sure the editing was going all right and he didn't need her.

"Don't worry about a thing," he said. "The piece is going to be great, and I'm keeping it short. Three minutes of New York glitz and glamour. By the way, you look fantastic in every shot. Contessa de Vilado is going to go out and get a face lift when she sees how she looks next to you."

"She'll just buy another diamond bracelet. It'll make her feel better, I'm sure."

"Won't do any good. You're the one who glitters. And it comes from your eyes, not your diamonds."

"You're charming at one-thirty in the morning."

Jeff laughed. "I have to be, because I'm about to ask you to get four hours' sleep and come in to do thirty seconds live with Bradley. I'm ending the spot with you talking to the Vice-President and Senator Tark, and I'm sure Bradley's going to make some wisecrack about your being our new political correspondent. It would be cute if you were there to bat your eyes and say that politics was more fun than you'd realized."

Dominique was silent for a minute. "The bimbo strikes again, you mean?"

"I'm sorry." Jeff sounded embarrassed. "I didn't mean it that way at all."

"Don't apologize. I'll be there."

She couldn't tell if she'd feel better or worse going to sleep now. She wasn't really tired, but if she didn't sleep, she might be exhausted by the time she was on with Bradley. She unzipped the Geoffrey Beene, hung it up carefully, looked at her naked body in the mirror. Damn, she was good-looking. She ran her fingers down her slim body. Not much she'd want to change, really. Jeff and Jackie were planning that series about women's bodies, trying to give women body confidence; it was a good idea, but it was one kind of confidence she already had. Maybe her breasts should be a little smaller, since men seemed to assume an inverse correlation between breast size and brain size. But that was okay. Whatever people thought of her, she was doing just fine.

She put on a nightgown, got under the covers. It would have been nice to have Peter with her, because the night had made her feel randy. Sex just seemed to fit in with gorgeous clothes and television lights. She let her fingers roam her body, knew she could bring herself to the edge quickly. When she was young all her dates had ended with her being desirous but fearful, deciding that her Catholic God would be more likely to forgive her if she satisfied herself than if she allowed a man to do it. She closed her eyes now, let her fingers touch the concave smoothness of her cool, taut belly; then down to the pale, silky fringe that hid her deepest mysteries. Squeezing, rubbing gently, then harder and harder . . . the tenderness she demanded from a man didn't work when she was alone. She required a more forceful touch—her fingers probing her groin, her pelvis grinding hard, fast. Aroused, she reached to pinch a breast, the engorged nipple so tender that she cried out, moved by the ecstasy of crossing the fine line between excitement and pain. But only pain that was in her control, that was pure fantasy, never allowed in reality. She tried to conjure Peter's image, pretend it was his hands, his warmth, hovering over her, bringing her to the climax that she could scarcely hold off now. But instead, the face that appeared in front of her closed eyes was the senator's. She imagined him naked, lying on top of her now, his penis, firm and sure, disappearing into her. *Come on, Senator, more . . . faster . . . oh, God, that's good; deeper, come to me, fuck me forever when I need it . . . Oh, Senator . . .* she called into the empty room, again and again, until at last sated.

The fantasy had the unexpected effect of bringing a genuine blush to her face when Bradley asked the next morning on the air how she had enjoyed meeting the politicians.

"They're both fascinating men," she said. "And I truly appreciated their taking time to talk to me."

"Senator Tark isn't married, you know," Bradley teased.

"He's not?" Dominique had intended to raise her eyebrows coquettishly, but the blush crept up, and Bradley made a comment about power being a great aphrodisiac. Dominique recovered in time to laugh and say that the whole evening had been important as a salute to art and meaningful cooperation between two countries.

Bradley nodded. "Well said. And it's nice when all the stars get to dress up to cooperate."

"The only star missing from the crowd was you, Bradley."

"Next time. And thank you for your report." He gave a big smile, turned to camera two to lead into a commercial. The floor manager signaled that they were off the air, the red lights went off, and Dominique sighed as she shook out the tension that seemed to build in her shoulders anytime she was on live.

Bradley watched her. "Any scoop to give me on Senator Tark?"

"Afraid not," she said. "But I will say that Senator Tark is as charming as they come. I see why the female population voted for him. I had the feeling he wouldn't mind being on our show, by the way."

"Probably willing to do anything to get on—even if it means sleeping with the correspondent, I'll bet." Bradley winked at Dominique. "What a public servant the man is. Willing to put up with so much, just to get his views across to his constituency."

"I wish something really had happened," said Dominique. "Then I'd at least have the satisfaction of keeping it from you."

Bradley laughed, crossed his long legs. "I hope you know that you've been getting better and better lately. It's good working with you."

"Thanks, Bradley. That's dear of you."

It was like Bradley James to pay a compliment, have an intimate conversation, in the middle of the studio while two or three dozen people raced around him, taking the commercial break to set up the next spot. Bradley used his time wisely, had a knack for turning a fleeting moment into a memorable meeting. It occurred to Dominique what a fine politician he would be. He could shake a hand, kiss a baby, and make a friend for life. Unlike Darlie, Bradley gave you his full attention when you were with him. He was one of the only interviewers on television who actually listened—on the air and off.

Bradley asked her a few more questions about her meeting with Senator Tark and the Vice-President, seemed genuinely interested. Dominique marveled at his cool. He had another on-air interview coming up in a minute and a half, but he appeared in no hurry to move on. He was all personality, relied on others to take care of details like time.

The floor manager, Chico, came over to tell Bradley to move into the living-room set for the next spot. It was a live interview with a young woman who had been an alcoholic, reformed, and was now an executive at a major company. Bradley had read his research the night before and was ready.

"Don't forget to show the book she's written," said Chico. He was a heavyset man in his late thirties, totally unflappable. He handed Bradley a slim volume, and Dominique glanced at the title: *From the Barroom to the Boardroom.*

"Looks fascinating," Dominique said, meaning to be sarcastic. The floor manager rolled his eyes in agreement, but Bradley opened the book and flipped the pages, as eager and ingenuous as a ten-year-old.

"This book is incredibly inspiring," he said. "I read the whole thing last night—and it's the kind of story we all need to hear. We sometimes forget that our lives are under our own control, and no matter how low we've sunk, we're still our own masters. When we want to change our destiny, we can."

"You're absolutely right," Chico said. "And your lovely guest is already sitting down, if you'd like to go join her. We're out of commercial in thirty seconds." Bradley moved over to the living-room set. Chico glanced back at Dominique and shrugged his shoulders. They tended to forget that Bradley was Mr. Sincerity. It didn't matter how much he earned—he was the average guy, enthralled by celebrities, politicians, and real people who had made good.

"See you later, Bradley," Dominique called, but he ignored her, already thoroughly involved in the story of his next guest.

Bradley James was a cipher, Dominique decided, a made-for-television special who didn't really exist outside his electronic persona. When people found out where she worked, they invariably asked what Bradley James was really like—and her standard answer was absolutely true: "He's the same in person as he is on the air." He was an actor who had turned his television role into his life. She thought of him as the ultimate chameleon, able to take on the character he was expected to be in the fifteen seconds it took to walk from the newsroom set to the living-room area. On the air with her, he had been a nice mix of devilish, charming, and lecherous; now he'd spend the next four minutes with the reformed alcoholic as a deeply concerned, highly moral humanist. Bradley took his image of the moment to heart, adopted it to the depths of his soul.

As Dominique wandered out to the green room, she noticed the young actor Robbie Baker—this week's hottest star—sitting alone, waiting for his chance to go on the air. The day's other guests were buzzing around the green room, but Robbie ignored them and sat staring at the closed-circuit television that hovered above the room like an icon. His eyes looked blank, and Domi-nique wondered if he were tired or stoned. She smiled at him pleasantly as she walked in, and in response, Robbie looked at her dolefully and asked, "Does it help?"

"Does what help?"

"Telling your story on the air." He motioned toward the television, where the reformed alcoholic was talking passionately.

"Of course it does," Dominique said. "When people watching at home have the same problem, they realize they're not alone. It gives them hope."

"Then I'm going to do it." He sat back again, his face drawn in pain.

"You're going to do what?"

Robbie didn't say anything; his eyes seemed to sink deeper into his tense face.

"Are you all right?" Dominique asked, trying again.

Robbie nodded slightly, but didn't look up again.

One of the young pages—a pretty college girl who worked for no pay, just to have television experience—came in and said, "Mr. Baker, I'll take you into the studio now."

Dominique continued down a maze of corridors to the control room—the real guts of the show. The room was packed with the director, producers, production assistants, engineers, and tech-nicians, all talking and moving at once. Pandemonium. It was hard to believe that the frantic screaming and running around that took place behind the scenes resulted in the calm, smooth show that went out over the air.

When she walked in, Steve Cawley swiveled around in his seat, called out, "Nice spot," and then turned back to the monitors. There wasn't much time for reflection in live television. You were either good or bad, a hero or a dog. She was always glad to hear that she had done all right, because there was no sense of history at *A.M. Reports*—do ten great pieces and then one bad one, and everyone would be as unforgiving as if you had been bumbling for months. You were only as good as your last spot.

The tension in the control room seemed to be at a higher pitch than usual, and Dominique quickly realized the source of the current crisis: Bradley had gone overtime on his spot with the alcoholic, and so, during the commercial break, the schedule for the rest of the half-hour had to be readjusted.

There was no time for expansion in television. Steve Cawley had a sign in his office that said "A Half-Hour Is Eighteen Minutes, No Matter How You Slice It." With commercials, station breaks, and local updates, that's all that was left for the live portion of *A.M. Reports*. Each second was carefully scheduled, but Bradley had a tendency to disregard time use; when he ignored the stage manager's signal to wrap up a spot, there was nothing anyone in the control room could do except curse, wait for him to finish, and cut some time out of the next interview—which was usually Darlie's.

Cawley was pacing around the room now, yelling at production assistants.

"Don't tell me we've got *about* four minutes for Darlie," he shouted. "There are no fucking *abouts* on this show."

"I'll have it in a second," called the production assistant. Cawley walked over, looking like he was ready to strangle him. The assistant, who couldn't have been more than twenty-five, continued scribbling numbers on a pad, trying to avoid the threatening presence behind him.

"Got it," he said, triumphantly. "Dominique's spot was three seconds over. The spot with the drunk was forty-three seconds long. Kill credits and the update at the end of the show, and Darlie can go four-twenty-six with Robbie Baker."

"It's goddamn about time," said Cawley. He grabbed a red microphone that connected directly to Darlie's headset and, suddenly calm, told her how long the interview should run.

"Fine," Darlie said from the set. Dominique watched her curiously on the closed-circuit monitor, saw her lick her lips, touch her hair, glance at the sheet of questions on her lap.

Cawley turned off the microphone and sat back.

"Fifteen seconds to commercial end," called one of the production assistants. In the front of the room, Joe Banks, the director, tensed visibly, getting ready again for live air.

As far as Dominique was concerned, Joe was the real genius on the show. Smart, solemn, and intense, he directed the show every morning without missing a beat. In front of him were at least a dozen monitors—one for each of the three cameras on the set, others that showed tape being rolled in, graphics that were available, preview screens . . . At each moment, he had to see everything, and decide which image would be sent over the airwaves. He never flinched, never raised his voice, and never made a mistake. While the show was on live, he talked continuously into the headsets that Chico and the three cameramen wore—directing the cameras, giving stage cues and time counts. Dominique was convinced that Joe Banks was an automaton—a small machine with a dark furry beard and darting black eyes.

"Mike check from Darlie," called Joe Banks.

"Three-two-one," Darlie said from the set.

"Darlie opens to camera three," Joe Banks said.

In the monitor, Dominique noticed Darlie turn slightly, present her best profile and sweetest smile to the camera.

"Music up," Banks called.

The theme song for *A.M. Reports* filled the room. Darlie turned her big blue eyes to the camera.

"*Welcome back,*" she said, reading easily from the teleprompter. "*I'm thrilled to introduce our next guest, since he's probably this season's hottest star. Handsome and charming, Robbie Baker began his career at three, when he starred in a diaper commercial. While he hasn't bared quite that much to the camera since then, he's had a lot of exposure in movies and on television. He's starred in five movies in the last two years, and his latest promises to be a box-office smash. Good morning, Robbie. Thank you for joining us this morning.*"

In the monitor for camera two, Dominique could see Robbie Baker, slouched in the chair across from Darlie, a day's growth of stubble on his face, his hands shoved into his pockets.

"It's so good to see you," Darlie said brightly to Robbie and everyone watching *A.M. Reports*. "Before we talk, I want to show a clip from your latest movie, *Dangerous Love*."

"Roll tape," Banks said.

Darlie, who didn't bother turning her head enough to see the clip, smiled at Robbie when it was over.

"You're a wonderful actor," she said, "but you're also very young. What's it been like for you dealing with this sudden fame?"

Instead of answering, Robbie Baker just stared dully at Darlie.

"What the hell's the matter with him?" Cawley asked.

"Could you repeat the question?" Robbie asked Darlie.

"Oh, shit," Cawley said.

Darlie repeated the question, and Robbie seemed to slouch deeper into his chair.

"I know what you expect me to say," Robbie finally said, "but the truth is that I haven't dealt with the fame very well at all. All of a sudden I've got girls hanging on me, and money and everything. To be perfectly honest, I started using drugs, cocaine, all the stuff I said I'd never do. I've licked the coke problem now, but it wasn't easy. I'd like to do something so that other kids never get started."

There was an audible gasp in the control room.

"What a scoop!" Cawley shouted. "Go to it, Darlie." He tossed his script down, knowing that Darlie was going to have to wing it now, handle this interview herself.

Dominique found herself wishing she were out there to prod Robbie gently, to get him to tell this story, which he had obviously never told before. She wondered why he was coming out with it now. He was incredibly intense and uneasy.

On camera, Darlie wrinkled her eyebrows briefly, said, "That's interesting, Robbie," then looked back down at her prepared questions. "Mary Tyler Moore plays your mother in this movie," she said. "What was it like working with her?"

Cawley sank into the chair next to Dominique. "Jesus fucking

Christ!" he screamed at the monitor. "This isn't a time to stick to the script. Didn't you hear what the kid said?"

"She never hears," Dominique whispered.

"Oh, crap." Cawley threw a pen at the monitor.

Robbie mentioned drugs twice more in the interview, and Darlie ignored him. After four minutes and twenty-three seconds, Darlie thanked Robbie Baker and turned enticingly to the camera. *"Please stay with us while we pause for some important messages."* The red light went off.

"Three minute break for commercials," the assistant said.

Just then the door to the control room swung open, and Bradley James, a white sheet of fury masking his face, stormed in.

"Cawley!" It came out as a bark, a command.

Steve Cawley turned around, his angry eyes locked with Bradley's.

"Cawley, I want that woman out of here. Off this show!" Bradley's voice was quiet but seething with controlled anger.

"You won't get a fight from me," Cawley said.

"I don't want a fight, I want a change," Bradley said, almost shaking, visibly trying to keep himself in control. "Get rid of her, Cawley, or you won't be seeing me here for much longer. It's Darlie or me at this point. She's just made a mockery of everything we try to do here."

"What do you want me to say, Bradley?" Cawley asked. "I'm as furious as you are. We had a teen idol admitting he had a drug problem, and Darlie asked about Mary Tyler Moore. The woman has styrofoam for a brain."

"She's destroying this program."

Dominique noticed Bradley's hands were clenched in tight fists; she thought he was going to hit someone.

Joe Banks, the calm in the storm, turned around briefly. "Relax, Bradley. You'll talk about it later. You have a show to finish this morning."

"There's nothing to talk about. I've said what I have to."

"We're back in thirty seconds," the production assistant said.

"Better get out to the set," Joe Banks told Bradley.

When he left, Dominique decided it was time for her to slip

out, too. She felt a sick churning in her stomach. Not that she
had much respect for Darlie—she had never liked the woman,
and had to admit that her performance with Robbie was disgraceful. What *had* Darlie been thinking? Maybe it just hadn't
registered with her what Robbie was saying. The bright lights,
the tension of live television, could addle your mind. I could
have done something just as stupid, Dominique thought.

Stepping into the hallway between the control room and the
green room, she noticed Robbie Baker standing by a door,
looking confused.

" 'Scuse me, do you know how I get out of here?" he asked.
"Looking for the front door."

"No problem," Dominique said. "Follow me."

He put his head down, followed close behind her. Dominique
wondered why he was alone, without the entourage—agent,
press reps, managers—that usually accompanied a star to the
show.

"Thanks for your advice in the green room," Robbie said, as
they ambled through the narrow corridors. "I needed some
encouragement. You're a correspondent on the show, aren't
you?"

"Sure am."

"I saw the spot you did this morning. It was neat."

"Thank you." It struck Dominique that Robbie Baker, for all
his fans and millions, was still nineteen and awkward.

"Well, I saw yours, did you see mine?" asked Robbie.

"Beg pardon?"

"My interview, I mean."

"Of course."

"Like it?"

Dominique thought of the scene she'd just witnessed in the
control room, then looked at Robbie, lonely, anxious, bleary-
eyed.

"You were fine," she said.

"That woman who interviewed me was kind of strange. I felt
like we were on different planets."

"Darlie can be like that. By the way, I thought what you said
about the coke was very brave." She looked at him carefully.
"Unless it was a cry for help."

"Nope, I'm done with the stuff. But I had a big fight about it with my agent last night. I told him I wanted to talk about drugs, and he said it was bad for my image. 'Course, he was the one who got me started on the coke, so I guess he's not real eager to hear any great confessions on the air. I know this sounds like a line, but if I could keep other kids away from it, I'd feel better about this whole business."

"Doesn't sound like a line. Sounds like you mean it."

"Yeah, well, I wish you'd interviewed me, then. I felt a little stupid. I mean, I stayed up all night worrying about whether or not I was going to say this, and when I did, it went over like a lead balloon. That woman—what's her name, Darlie?—looked at me like I was dropping my pants in front of a hot camera."

Dominique laughed. "You were, more or less. But I admit that Darlie did a pretty rotten job with the interview. Which doesn't mean that this is the last you'll hear of it. I'll bet your agent's phone is ringing off the hook right now."

"He's not my agent anymore. He already told me that first time I talked about coke in public, I was off his list."

"He'll change his mind."

They got to the big wooden door that led to the street, Dominique nodded to the guard, opened the door a crack, peeked out, and turned back to Robbie.

"You should know that your morning's not over. There are three or four paparazzi on the sidewalk, and a couple of women who look like reporters. They always hang out here, hoping to get a story on a star like you." She smiled at him. "But take heart—there are also about two dozen teenage girls who I'd say are waiting to get your autograph."

He looked miserable. "This is the part I hate. Maybe you should have me on the show again, and I'll announce that I'm gay. Get the girls away from me."

Dominique laughed. "I'll suggest it." She looked out the door again. "A couple of the girls are kind of cute. Maybe they've got brothers."

For the first time all morning, Robbie smiled. "I like your attitude."

"Thanks."

Robbie's smile disappeared, and he gestured to the door.

"Any suggestions on how I get past the waiting horde? I'm just not up for it. Maybe my agent was right—I never should have said that stuff about the coke."

"Don't second-guess yourself. You did the right thing." Surprised at how protective she felt toward Robbie—he seemed so young and vulnerable—Dominique peeked out the door again. "The good news is that we have a limousine waiting to take you home. How much damage can the photographers do between the door and the limousine?"

"A lot." He looked at her. "Any chance you need a lift somewhere? I'd love to have you come with me."

Dominique raised her eyebrows, then grinned. "I see. You get to distract attention from what you said, and I get my picture on the front page of the *National Enquirer*."

"Would you mind?"

"Not a bit. But if we're going to do it, let's do it right." She sidled over to him, and he put his arm around her. When the guard opened the door for them, the flashbulbs began popping, and Dominique planted a big kiss on Robbie Baker's cheek.

11

"How was Hong Kong?" Jeff asked on Tuesday morning when he saw Jackie.

"Terrific. Great food, fabulous shopping, and a fascinating city. I owe you one for letting me go." The trip had left her exhilarated rather than tired, and though she had arrived in New York late Monday night, she got up in time to arrive at the control room as Tuesday morning's show was ending.

Jeff looked at her through half-closed eyes. "Was it romantic?"

She raised an eyebrow, not sure if he were teasing or truly interested. "We had dinner out last night in a Chinese pavilion that floats in a miniature lake. Soft music, flowers everywhere—and at midnight there's an incredible fireworks display. Will that do?"

Jeff shrugged. "Not impressed. If you wanted to see fireworks, you should have stayed here."

"What happened?"

"Darlie made an ass of herself on the show yesterday, and Bradley stormed into the control room and announced to the world in general that she should be fired. Here, look at this." Jeff reached under his pile of scripts and papers, pulled out the morning's *Washington Post.* The paper, frayed from having been passed around the control room all morning, was crumpled, coffee-stained, and already open to the TV page. Jackie glanced at it. The *Post* critic had picked up the story, reporting first on Darlie's performance. *"An unprofessional and embarrassing interview,"* the reporter called it. *"An example of what happens when you put a wind-up doll in the anchor's chair."*

"Ouch," said Jackie. "How did Darlie face the cameras this morning?"

Jeff shrugged. "I don't think she even read it. Look what he says about Bradley, though."

"Behind the scenes, things were just as bad," the article continued, *"with Bradley James offering another display of his famous temper."*

"Funny," Jackie said, "I've never seen Bradley get angry. I think of him as Mr. Cool-as-a-Cucumber."

"He is. God knows where his reputation for having a temper came from, but you can bet it will be reported forever. The truth is that Bradley was furious about Darlie, but he never even raised his voice in here. Just ice-cold anger."

"Was the *Post* guy in the control room?"

"No, and I don't know who his spy is. Probably not even someone who was there. It's a little like the kids' game of telephone. Someone whispers it to someone who whispers it to someone else, and eventually it winds up in the newspaper as fact. Nonetheless, Cawley is devastated."

She could just imagine. Steve Cawley, like a lot of people in television, had a print complex. If the newspapers said something, it must be true. Never mind that millions more people got their news and ideas from the television network than from a single newspaper.

Jackie glanced at the column again. It was the kind of story newspaper critics loved to run with, since it made television reporters look stupid. "They know how to get us," she said to Jeff, sighing. "We hate print reporters because we think they're smarter than we are, and they hate us because we're richer. Not exactly a mutual-admiration society."

"The only consolation is we did a good show this morning, and Bradley even managed to smile at Darlie when they were saying their eight-o'clock hellos. The man's a good actor." Jeff took the newspaper back and shoved it under his pile of papers. "I say we all try to forget it and head back to work."

Jackie returned to her office, thinking about Jeff and fiddling with the new ring on her finger. The fact that Jeff hadn't even noticed it was a sign of how upset he was. The big opal in the center glimmered, the diamonds around it caught the light, shot it out in dazzling patterns. A friendship ring, Julian had called it. Something about Hong Kong had put him in a mood for giving. First the glorious jade pendant they had bought together at the market; then the ring he slipped on her finger the next evening. She sighed a happy sigh and thought: Back to work.

She stayed in the office all morning putting finishing touches on the fitness series. She stopped by the research office to pick up the statistics she had requested on exercise and obesity, then took them over to the art department where a graphic designer named Raoul looked them over carefully. He made a face when Jackie suggested putting the important statistics into a full-screen chart. Too boring. He ran his ink-stained fingers through his curly hair.

"Is it important that people remember the exact numbers, or the general concept?"

"The concept, of course."

He sketched, crossed out a few things, then sat back and snapped his fingers. "How about animating it?" he asked.

"Donald Duck talks about obesity? Doesn't seem right."

He laughed. "Different kind of animation." He peered again at the statistics she'd given him. "Look, you want to show here that if you walk two or three miles a day, you can lose half a pound a week, or almost twenty-five pounds a year." He drew quickly on a sketchpad. "The screen represents a year. We animate a woman walking across, getting slimmer as she goes. Under her, a man rowing, same point. Then we spin the screen, show it for"—he glanced at the script—"whatever else you have. A woman bicycling and a couple playing tennis."

"I love it." She was impressed and pleased.

"Good. I'll play with it. Come back late this afternoon, and I'll see if I can make it work."

Jackie was aware that while everything appeared to be business-as-usual, there was a hum in the air, the feeling that comes after the first crack of thunder, when everyone stares at the sky, wondering if the storm will pass or if there'll be lightning, blackouts, and a downpour. Small clusters of people huddled in the corridors, talking quietly, speculating.

While the clouds gathered, Julian called to complain about her having left so early.

"I'm still in bed and can't believe you're not next to me," he said. "Don't you believe in jet lag?"

"I was feeling great this morning. Couldn't wait to get to work again. But wait until you hear what I came back to."

She told him briefly.

"Does this put you in line for Darlie's job?" he asked.

It was just like Julian to say what she had decided not to think.

"Of course not. I'm much too new. If Darlie really leaves—and I'm not sure that's going to happen—I'd say Dominique would get the nod."

On her way to bringing her finished scripts to Jeff, Jackie peeked in Dominique's office and saw Raleigh there, leaning against the window, a lit cigarette in one hand, a cup of coffee in the other. She decided to go right by, but Dominique called out to her.

"Hey, don't you say hello?"

Jackie backed up, walked in.

"Good trip?" Dominique asked, getting up to give her a welcome-back kiss.

"The best."

"I can see." Dominique spotted the ring immediately. "From Julian?"

"Yup, but don't get any ideas." Jackie tried to keep her voice light. "It's just a friendship ring."

Dominique laughed, her throaty, silvery laugh. "You're too much, Jackie." She turned to Raleigh. "Raleigh, darling, you're supposed to be my friend, but do I have a ring like that to show for it?"

"Someday," Raleigh said, as she stubbed out her cigarette and reached into her shirt pocket for another one.

Dominique turned back to Jackie. "Did you hear about what happened while you were gone?"

"You mean Bradley and Darlie? It's the only thing anyone around here is talking about this morning."

"Should be," Raleigh said, cupping her hands to light the cigarette. "The *Post* hates us, Cawley's hiding out in his office, and the rumor is that Darlie's leaving is a *fait accompli*. Smart money says Dominique LaFarge will be Bradley James's new co-host within the month."

Dominique bit her lip, glanced at Jackie.

"Don't believe it. Darlie's been attacked before, and she always ends up on her feet. I don't see why this time should be any different."

"It *is* different." Raleigh was impatient. "Darlie has been hanging on by the tips of her red fingernails, and she's about to take a fall. The newspapers are going to run with this, and things are going to get too hot for Darlie to handle. Could be the Dotson-Webb debacle all over again."

"What was that?"

"Don't you remember? A few years ago, when Phyllis George was co-hosting the *CBS Morning News* for a mere million bucks a year, there was one of those sensation-of-the-day stories about a midwestern woman named Cathy Webb who had accused a guy called Gary Dotson of raping her. He was in jail for a bunch of years, and she decided to change her mind, say he never did it after all. After he was free, they made the talk-show circuit. One boring interview after another until Phyllis asked them to shake hands on the air, and they did. Then she asked them to hug."

Dominique laughed. "I do remember it. Everyone acted as if Phyllis had asked him to rape Cathy Webb again."

"So it was bye-bye million-dollar Phyllis. Driven out by a stupid mistake."

Dominique got up again and walked over to the window. "If Darlie leaves, and I still don't think she will, I'm not the obvious choice. You don't replace one bimbo with another."

"Cut it out," Raleigh said, harshly. "That joke's not even funny anymore. You've got as many brains as anyone else around here." She tossed a nasty look at Jackie, started to say something, and then changed her mind. Jackie muttered that she needed to get back to work and walked out of the office.

Safely back in the corridor, she felt as if she'd just left a viper's den.

She and Jeff went over the final scripts for the fitness series and then she asked to see the spot they'd done on the Golden Door.

"You'll love it," he said. He pulled a tape off his shelf, popped it in his VCR. The screen flickered, then revealed a long shot of a mountain at dawn. The camera made a slow pan across the mountain, then moved in to show half a dozen small figures walking steadily up the mountain. Jeff had laid in the upbeat sounds of a jazz guitar. A quick cut to the women at the top of the mountain, music down, and Jackie's voice: *"A visit to a spa can teach you about exercise, about nutrition, and about the best ways to diet. But most important is what it teaches you about yourself."* Another cut, this one to a close-up of Jackie sitting at the edge of a mat after an exercise class, the sweat running down her face. Then a montage of Jackie running, exercising, diving into a pool—and a cut to her interviewing the director of the spa, who explained the goals of the Golden Door.

The piece went on for close to five minutes, and Jackie watched, almost stunned. When it was over, Jeff asked, "What do you think?"

She turned around, looked at him. "I don't know what to say."

"You don't like it?" He looked shocked. "Cawley says it's fabulous. Even Raleigh screened it and announced that it had its moments."

"Of course I like it. You did an incredible job. But I'm embarrassed."

"Why?"

"I don't know. I didn't expect you'd focus so much on me."

"It's my ode to you," said Jeff, lightly. "Someday when you're married to that rich old man, you'll turn on this tape and think: Gosh, I wonder what life would have been like if I'd paid more attention to that handsome producer."

She laughed. "Handsome, *talented* producer."

"Thanks. If you want to use this as the lead piece in your Jackie-for-co-host audition tape, you have my blessings."

"I wasn't planning on making one."

"No? What a shame. Raleigh is already selling ringside seats to the Dominique-versus-Jackie catfight. May the best fighter land in the co-anchor's chair."

"I hate to disappoint, but there's not going to be a fight—catty or otherwise. One, I happen to like Dominique, and two, I'm not campaigning for Darlie's job."

"Any special reason why not?"

She smiled. "Probably because I don't think I'd get it anyway."

Jeff took the cassette out of the machine. "I don't think anybody's going to get it."

"Meaning Darlie can ride out the storm?"

Jeff shrugged. "The newspaper critics might care about Darlie's stupidity, but I can guarantee most of our audience doesn't. We might get a few viewer letters about this, but do you know the only time Darlie really gets deluged with mail?"

"I give up."

"When she changes her hairdo. *That's* what people care about."

Jackie laughed. "I always figured that Reuven the hairdresser was the most important person on the show. Darlie lets him follow her around like a puppy dog. But you don't think the incident with Robbie Baker will destroy Darlie's credibility as an interviewer?"

Jeff shrugged. "Nobody watches Darlie because she's smart or does brilliant interviews." He fiddled with the knob on his television set, turned it to the all-news cable channel with the volume off, and sat down in his chair. "Want the Jeff Garth theory of morning television?"

"Shoot."

"The first thing you have to understand is that all the morning shows are the same. People watch one or another because they've always watched, and they come to think of all you folks on the air as part of the family. Know how many pairs of hand-knit booties Joan Lunden got when she had her babies? Same with Jane Pauley. Consistency is the key. People like to see a familiar face in the morning. They want to know who's going to be with them in their bedrooms when they wake up."

"What wonderful respect you have for us," Jackie said. "I suddenly feel like a fat old woman whose husband is used to having her around—even though she wears curlers and cold cream to bed."

Jeff winked at her. "I bet you look great in bed, even with curlers and cold cream."

Jackie tossed her head. "I never wear either."

"Ah, then I'll fantasize about what you do wear. Or don't."

She laughed. "If I were with you, I definitely wouldn't wear anything."

Jeff sauntered over to his office door and clicked it shut. He moved close to Jackie and put both hands on her shoulders. "I have a warning for you. Don't flirt with me unless you mean it."

"I thought flirting was the style around here."

"It is, but it's different coming from you."

"Why?"

He leaned forward and kissed her firmly on the lips, then pulled back. "I happen to be wild about you, in case that's not obvious. At the first sign that you feel the same way, I intend to

throw you to the ground and have my way with you—just to
make my intentions very clear. I wouldn't want to do this
mistakenly."

Jackie stood very still, surprised by the sudden pounding of
her heart. "You know how much I like you," she said quietly.

"Mmm. I'm glad. I also know that there's another man and
you're a woman of honor. I'm not asking for anything, I just
wanted to let you know that I'm excited about more than your
work."

Resisting the urge to throw her arms around him and let loose
the suppressed passion behind their kiss, Jackie squeezed his
arm, and walked quickly out of the office.

Dana was the only person Jackie knew who actually lived in a
loft in SoHo. A converted warehouse just off Spring Street, it
had been hers since she had first arrived in New York to attend
Columbia Law School. Her classmates at Columbia thought it
strange that Dana would live so far downtown and take the long
subway ride to classes each day. But Dana didn't mind the
subway, and far preferred the young working artists who were
her neighbors in SoHo to the professional grinds she met at
Columbia and later at the law firm.

When Dana first moved into the building, it was strictly an
artists' haven, a mostly down-at-the-heels building where the
front door rarely locked, the staircase was shaky, and the plumb-
ing temperamental. But the lofts were large sun-filled spaces
with high ceilings and room to breathe. Going off to work some
mornings, Dana would encounter neighbors just returning from
their evening out. While they looked suspiciously at her brief-
cases, she looked admiringly at their offbeat clothes and hairstyles, and the oversize canvases they dragged into the huge
elevator. Eventually, they got to know each other. Dana helped
her neighbors with the legal problems they encountered—mostly
exploitative contracts from local galleries and art dealers—and
took her remuneration in paintings, watercolors, and sculptures.
Then SoHo became chic, and uptown lawyers, stockbrokers and
advertising executives turned the building into a co-op, sending
the prices of the lofts soaring. All her artist neighbors moved to
Hoboken and points west, and the professionals she had been
trying to escape moved in. The rickety staircase was repaired,

the lobby spiffed up, and Dana, in dismay, discovered that her loft was too valuable now to leave.

Jackie visited Dana at the loft a few nights after she got back from Hong Kong. She and Dana tried to get together every week or so, realizing that female friendships were too often dropped in the onslaught of work, lovers, and city living.

Jackie gave Dana the jade-and-gold bracelet she'd bought for her in Hong Kong.

"It's gorgeous, darling. Thank you." Dana hugged her in thanks.

"Don't get too excited. It cost twelve dollars in an outdoor market. Actually, Julian spotted it and said it was worth about ten times that."

Dana studied the bracelet. "I hate to compliment him, but the man definitely has a good eye." She slipped on the bracelet. "How was the rest of your trip?"

"Terrific. Julian was as loving as I've ever seen him."

"Mmm, sounds good." Dana winked at her. "Don't tell me details. I don't have time to be horny this week. By the way, what was Julian doing in Hong Kong?"

Jackie recrossed her legs, trying to get comfortable in the steel-and-leather sculptured chair. It had clearly been made for Dana's long legs, not Jackie's more compact form. "I don't know why he was there, but the business stuff made me a little paranoid." She described the scene in the hotel room with the Arabs, Lem Chen, and Erwin, telling Dana how she obviously wasn't welcome at the meeting. "It might have been my *faux pas* with the short sleeves, or the fact that I was a woman, or I don't know what. But anyway, they all came back early the following morning, and I left before we could have a repeat."

Dana played idly with the bracelet on her wrist, her face creased in a deep frown. "You don't have any idea what Julian's up to?"

"Specifically? No. Just some big deal to make the rich richer, I suppose."

Dana bit reflectively on her bottom lip, leaving a round smudge in her glossy red lipstick. "I don't think you're being paranoid at all. Julian and a roomful of Arabs can't be up to any good."

Jackie hesitated, torn between defending Julian to her best friend and admitting that the meetings had seemed very strange to her, as if there were some covert agenda. "You're just suspicious of Julian in general," Jackie said lightly. "Haven't we already determined that you don't trust men that rich?"

"Of course, but it's more than that. I'd be willing to bet, dollars to doughnuts, that . . . No, forget it." Dana bit the other side of her lip. "Here, try this. Tell Julian you're thinking of investing in silver. Ask him if it's a good time."

Jackie shook her head, felt herself bristling at Dana's comment. "Dammit, Dana, we're talking about a man I care about—in case you've forgotten. Just what are you trying to trick him into saying?"

"Nothing." Dana looked abashed. "Oh, hell, I am trying to say something, but it's rude and accusatory, and I'm too nice for that."

Jackie burst out laughing. "I like it when you're rude and accusatory. It's better than beating around the bush—which drives me crazy."

"Then I'll tell you. It's pure speculation on my part, but I'll tell you. It strikes me that Julian is trying to corner the market on silver." Dana sat back. "There. I said it."

Jackie looked at her curiously. "Well, say more. What's that supposed to mean, and what's your source?"

Dana shrugged. "No particular source. I've heard a few things from Sam and a few things from you, and after that, it's been a matter of putting two and two together and getting four. As opposed to five, which is what the rest of you seem to get."

Jackie sighed. "I'm afraid there's a synapse missing in my brain that keeps me from understanding anything to do with finance. Want to explain this to me?"

"It's not really that complicated. The first thing is that everyone in the business has noticed that Julian is buying unusual amounts of silver lately. Buying enough maybe to drive up the price. If he has buddies—like a rich Arab—doing the same thing, they could totally skew the market."

"Buy more so what they have becomes worth more?"

"Something like that. But point two—and this is the information from Sam—is that Julian is deeper into the futures market than ever. Sam noticed that Julian was perfectly hedged on the books, but all his personal long positions are due in three months and his shorts are due in four months."

Jackie looked at her blankly.

"Come on," Dana said, slightly exasperated. "When you're long, you have a contract to buy; short, the contract is to sell, remember?"

Jackie nodded. "So in three months, he can buy a lot of silver. What's the point?"

"Let's say the Arabs and Lem Chen have done the same thing—a lot of long positions due at the same time. It's usually a paper transaction. But if they demand delivery, and there's not enough silver in the warehouses, all hell breaks loose. They can demand any amount they want from the guys holding short positions they can't meet. Companies could go bankrupt. The whole economy could spiral."

Jackie scratched her forehead. "Okay, I understand the theory, but you don't know Julian. He'd never do that."

"Famous last words, said by an innocent."

Jackie smiled slightly. "That did sound innocent, didn't it? Let me try again. I don't see Julian as someone who'd dance on the edges of the law for more money. I mean, what the hell would he do with more money, anyway? He has that incredible apartment and all, but he doesn't really seem to care about *things*."

"I know what you mean," Dana said, "but he cares about the game. And to these guys, making money is all a game. It's like football—they want to score the most points, not so they can win the Super Bowl or get the championship rings. They want to score for the sake of scoring."

The next night, sitting in Julian's study drinking cognac, Jackie thought about Dana's remark: *He wants to score for the sake of scoring.* She had seen that side of Julian only once, late on a Sunday night when they were lying naked in bed, watching *The Sting* on cable television. Jackie wasn't paying much attention to the movie, she was more interested in the gentle massage she was giving Julian, her fingers playing on his chest, making patterns down to his thighs . . .

"I can't stand it anymore," he said finally, sitting upright in bed.

Jackie felt stricken. "I'm sorry. Was I hurting you?"

He looked at her, surprised, then leaned over, genius grin intact, to kiss her. "*That* part was great. It's the movie. They're all making money and I'm not."

He picked up one of the phones by the bed, dialed Hong Kong where, because of the time difference, it was already a workday, and made two quick deals—one to buy silver futures, the other to sell gold short. Overhearing the orders, Jackie realized he had just put half a million dollars on the line, just for fun.

"Hate being out of the action," he said, putting down the phone. There was a sparkle in his eye as he returned to bed and, reaching for her, ran his strong hands across her bare breasts. He rolled on top of her, lusty and aroused.

"Shouldn't we wait until the end of the movie?" she asked, giggling.

"I've seen it."

He began to make love to her, fast and forcefully, and she felt subsumed by his energy and power. Burying her face in his chest, it occurred to her that he was probably consummating his deal more than his love for her—but in a moment she was overcome by his desire, felt her own peaking, and in the panting pleasure of their mutual orgasm, forgot all else.

Now, as Julian got up from his chair to answer the telephone, Jackie recalled her own suspicions about Julian's business. Could Dana's theory possibly be right? At first blush, it sounded more like the jealousy that went on in any business—attack the man who was constantly successful. Julian had an unpredictable, brilliant mind—that much everyone knew. Was she being naive, thinking she understood the depths of the man?

Julian finished his phone call, sighed, and stretched. "Did Dana like the bracelet?" he asked.

"Loved it." The opening seemed appropriate so she decided to report her conversation with Dana to get his reaction.

Julian looked thoughtful when Jackie was finished. "Dana should come to work for me," he said. "She has good ideas. But did she tell you what we're supposed to do with the silver after we drive the price up?"

"Sell it, I assume, and escape with your billions."

"And how exactly do we sell it without sending the price down?"

"I don't understand."

He sighed. "Look, cornering the market isn't a new idea. You buy enough silver—or have a consortium buying enough—to drive the price artificially high. It's a self-adjusting market, you know. Demand outstrips supply, so the price goes up. The problem comes at the other end. You want to take your profits, so you start selling the silver. What happens? The supply goes up, so the market price plummets. You had a lot of paper profits, but there's no way to turn them into real profits."

"You mean to tell me the free market actually works?"

Julian grinned. "Unfortunately, it does. That's point one. Point two is the old saying that when you're playing the market, the bulls make money and the bears make money—but the pigs lose. And trying to manipulate a market is the ultimate in being piggish."

Jackie laughed. "So Dana is wrong on strictly practical grounds. I'm waiting to hear your ethical objections."

"You're the one who told me that it's easy to be ethical when nobody's trying to corrupt you. In my case, it doesn't work to be corrupt."

"Well, I'm glad to know you aren't."

"It would have been nice if you knew without asking."

He said it kindly, but Jackie felt a blush rising, knew what he meant. Your lover was supposed to trust you and support you, not listen to vague rumors or speculation and assume the worst.

"I'm sorry. You wanted Maureen Dean and you got Judas Iscariot instead."

Julian smiled. "You'd make a terrible Maureen Dean. I can't see you as the loyal little wife."

"That's not fair," Jackie said, only half-joking. "Asking questions isn't a sign of disloyalty, is it?"

"I guess not. Anyway, I don't worry about your loyalty when you're sitting next to me. I only worry about it when you're off on your business trips—or shoots, or whatever you call them. Different kind of loyalty I'm talking about, but I get concerned when you're away overnight."

Jackie looked at him in surprise, and realizing that he was serious, felt slightly annoyed. "You don't have much to worry about," she said. "The only one I've been sleeping with lately on business trips is Thomas Mann, and that was at your urging. When I can't get up for him, I go to bed with Agatha Christie or P. D. James. I like women writers."

Julian grinned. "Anything kinky go on?"

"Nothing you'd enjoy." She looked at him, half-expecting an apology. He understood.

"I wasn't accusing you of anything. It's just that however old-fashioned or chauvinistic it may sound, I don't want to share you. Can you understand that?"

Jackie nodded. "I don't particularly want to share you either, honey. But I don't know if that's a commitment you're ready to make."

"Why not?"

"What's the expression about sauce for the goose and sauce for the gander? If you want a pledge of loyalty, you have to give one."

"Fine."

She looked at him sharply. "You mean it?"

"Of course. Sounds like a fair deal."

Cupping her chin in her hand, she studied him, trying to decide what was behind the pact. "Forgive me, but I'm not as practiced in making deals as you are. I tend to look at the implications and wonder what you mean when you make that commitment."

"Are you asking if I love you?"

"No, I didn't ask that at all." But she felt a slight tremble in her body, and the anxiety she had felt a moment earlier drained to her toes. Julian leaned forward, picked up the cognac glass and rolled it between the palms of his hands. "Okay, you don't have to ask anything. It's just time I told you that I love you." He put down the cognac glass and reached for her hands. "I do, you know, and it feels good to say it. I love you."

"I love you, too." She was surprised at how easily the words came out, surprised also to realize how deeply she felt them. She kissed him, wondering what it would be like never again to kiss anyone but Julian.

"Ready for bed?" he asked.

She smiled. "Ready. But after that declaration, don't expect me to let you sleep."

12

"Are you distributing the ratings?" Jackie asked when Cawley's secretary, Isabel, appeared at her office door with a stack of papers.

"Nope. Just a note."

"Why aren't the ratings up?" Cawley usually posted the ratings for the morning shows on Thursday, right after they arrived on his desk. But though it was the Thursday after the first week of sweeps, the bulletin board outside his office remained conspicuously blank.

Isabel just shrugged and handed Jackie one of the sheets she was holding. It was signed by Cawley and said: "All-staff meeting. Conference room 1 P.M. today. Be there."

"Good news or bad?" Jackie asked.

"I'm not supposed to tell," Isabel said.

Jackie got to the conference room on the dot of one, and noticed everyone else streaming in then, too. One advantage of working in television was that everyone understood the importance of being on time.

By three past one, there were close to fifty people packed into the conference room. Jackie pulled up a chair next to Dominique and looked around, wondering what they all did.

A moment later Steve Cawley walked in, flanked by Bradley James, and a portly and somewhat unpleasant-looking man wearing a gray striped suit and Gucci loafers. Jackie tried to place him, then realized it was Winston Axminster, the vice-president of daytime programming.

"Oh, God," Dominique whispered. "What's he doing here?"

"Isn't he nominally in charge of the show?"

"He's too much of a fool to be in charge of his own shoe-

178

laces." But Jackie noticed that Dominique's whole body tensed in what seemed like anger, and the color drained from her face.

Meanwhile, Bradley James and Axminster sat down in the front of the room, and Cawley nodded at them, then faced the staff. The room fell quiet.

"I have news that I felt I should bring you in person," Cawley said.

Jackie wondered if they were all being fired.

"The ratings came out for last week. The first week of sweeps, as you all know." He stopped, and the tension in the room was palpable. Jackie sensed that Cawley was enjoying keeping them all on edge.

He pulled out a piece of paper and glanced at it. "Anyone want to guess what the ratings were?"

There was silence. Then someone from the back called out, "I'm sure we won."

"You mean we beat the *Today* show?" Cawley asked.

"Right," said the same person.

"Wrong."

More silence. Then Cawley grinned at Axminster and announced, "We didn't beat them, we *killed* them!"

The room broke out in cheers.

Cawley let the cheering continue, then raised his voice to continue. "We beat the bastards by one and a half points. The biggest margin in a couple of years. I called this meeting to celebrate, so let's do it!"

Isabel walked into the room pushing a cart loaded high with boxes of pizza and six-packs of beer and soda. Cawley reached for a beer can and yanked at the tab, letting froth spill over the edge onto his hand. "To my winning staff!" he said, lifting it up high. He tossed his head back and chugged down the can of beer—and the staff descended on the cart as if no one had eaten in weeks.

After everyone had pizza, Bradley James stood up and in his booming, authoritarian voice asked for attention. There was an immediate hush.

"Just a few words," Bradley said.

He started off by thanking Cawley and Axminster for the party, Darlie, Jackie, and Dominique for being such a terrific "on-air family" . . . and on and on until Jackie figured that he was practicing his thank-yous in case he ever won an Emmy.

"In closing," Bradley said, after he had finished sending out accolades, "let me point out that while it's nice to win—and win big—what really matters is that we're the best. We have the best and hardest-working staff. Producers committed to honesty and quality, and an overall dedication to integrity."

He stopped to take a sip from the glass in front of him.

"Winning by so much doesn't surprise me a bit," he went on. "People all over America who care what's going on in the world *have* to watch us. They need the reliable information and insights we provide. As long as we keep providing that, we'll keep winning, and we'll never have to worry about ratings."

Bradley sat down, and Jackie joined everyone else in applauding. She couldn't decide how much of what Bradley said was sincere. Probably most of it, since Bradley honestly believed in *A.M. Reports.*

"If that speech doesn't make it to one of the media columns tomorrow, I'll eat my hat," Dominique whispered as they continued to applaud. Jackie noticed Kalina, a stately older woman who handled public relations for the show, rushing out of the conference room, and knew that Dominique was right. Kalina would call up every reporter she knew to "leak" Bradley's private, and very gracious, comments to his staff.

"Hope nobody wants to know what Darlie said," Jackie whispered.

"Don't you think Kalina will tell the truth?" Dominique said. "Darlie has a standing appointment for a manicure at one o'clock and certainly wouldn't give that up. Priorities, darling."

Winston Axminster stood up next to offer "my personal support and thanks to this fine staff." He seemed stiff and very managerial, and received only polite applause.

"You could forget his personal support if we weren't making money for the network," Dominique told Jackie.

The speeches over, Cawley called out, "Have more beer and pizza, everyone! This is a party." As the pizzas and beer disappeared, the level of carousing started to rise.

Jackie noticed Cawley talking to Axminster. After a minute, Cawley looked around the room, caught Jackie's eye, and motioned for her to come over with Dominique.

"I think Cawley wants us," Jackie said.

"Go ahead," Dominique said. "Tell them I had an important phone call waiting in my office."

"What's wrong?"

"Tell you another time, darling. But Winston Axminster isn't a man I choose to be seen with in public." She turned abruptly and left.

Jackie wended her way across the conference room, shook hands with Axminster, whom she had met when she was first hired. "Winston here just wanted to congratulate you on a fine series," Cawley told her. "I was telling him that I thought your fitness series helped pull in viewers this week, and so did the one I came up with for Darlie to do on Hollywood homes."

"That was a clever idea," Jackie said, trying to be noncommittal. The Hollywood series was the kind she hated, but it had been Cawley's idea, and he seemed to want to get some credit for it in front of Axminster. The series had involved Darlie's traipsing through half a dozen houses owned by movie stars, talking knowledgeably about Mies van der Rohe chairs, elegant eighteenth-century antiques, and postmodernist decorating. It was taped and tightly scripted, and viewer reaction was terrific. Jeff had apparently been right: only the critics cared when Darlie made a major *faux pas* like the Robbie Baker interview. The audience just wanted to see her walking down a sweeping spiral staircase in a Hollywood mansion, pausing to admire a two-hundred-thousand-dollar crystal chandelier, "the only one of its kind."

"I think it accomplished what we set out to do." Cawley looked meaningfully at Axminster, and Jackie wondered if that meant Darlie's job was secure again.

Raleigh came over to join them, shook hands warmly with Axminster.

"So nice to see you again," she said. "I've been dying to hear what you thought of the spots I did during sweeps. I really think they made a difference."

Excusing herself, Jackie walked away, not interested in hearing Raleigh trying to prove that she had been personally responsible for the high ratings. Jackie wondered if the entire staff was going to line up in front of Axminster to try to get a few brownie points. Well, of course they were. Jackie felt a surge of anger.

She wasn't much good at self-promotion; she assumed her work would get the credit it deserved without her clamoring for it. But by the end of the day, Axminster might have forgotten how important "Get Fit, America!" really was. Had anybody told him about the response they'd already gotten? Jeff had come up with the idea of letting viewers write in for a two-page synopsis of the week's diet and fitness information, and there were eight huge mailbags, filled with requests, piled in an enormous heap outside his office.

Spotting Jeff across the conference room, Jackie started over to him. But Laurie Spinner got there first.

"I can't begin to imagine how many thousands of letters are inside each of those mailbags," Laurie said in a voice loud enough for Jackie to hear. "You did a great job with the series, and it makes me so happy to know that all my hard work in booking it paid off. You and I are a great team."

"It all worked out well," Jeff agreed.

Jackie wondered why Laurie's cooing didn't make Jeff want to throw up. She noticed Laurie leaning close to Jeff, letting her cashmere sweater graze against him. She caught Jackie's eye, then stood on tiptoe to whisper something in Jeff's ear. They both laughed.

Jackie decided she'd had enough celebrating and slipped out the back door of the conference room. As she pulled the door shut, she felt a resistance from the other side.

"Are we playing tug-of-war, or didn't you know I was following you?" Jeff asked, getting the door open and joining her in the hall.

"I didn't mean to make an obvious departure."

"It's okay. When we have high ratings, everyone is too happy to notice anything. The guys in advertising are happy because the rates go up. Bookers are happy because it's easier to get guests when you're number one. And talent—as we so fondly call you on-air stars—are allowed to raise their smugness quotient by one notch."

"Really? From what I just overheard, I had nothing to do with the ratings—or even the series. The debt of gratitude belongs to Laurie Spinner."

Jeff stopped walking, turned to look at her with a small smile. "Is that bitchiness I hear? I never expected it of you."

"Sorry. I was just fuming at Laurie's selective memory. As long as everything worked out, she was glad to take full credit and forget about Dick von Dickson. I can just imagine how different it would be if the series had bombed."

"At least Laurie was bragging to me, and not to Axminster."

"You noticed the lineup too? I thought the man was going to have to give out numbers."

"He probably would have if he knew how to count." Jeff shook his head. "Axminster is a total jerk. He wouldn't know a good television show from a dinosaur."

"How did he get to be where he is, then?"

"Come on, Jackie, you've been around here long enough. Do you think talent or knowledge has anything to do with success in this business?"

"I don't know what it has to do with anymore, and I'll try not to take the question personally." She turned from Jeff, started walking toward her office again. He fell into step beside her.

"I noticed Dominique left without a word to Axminster," he said. "Think she's embarrassed about the publicity she's been getting?"

"She should be, but knowing Dominique, she's probably delighted."

The big story about Dominique had broken the first day of sweeps, when the *Star* tabloid came out with a front-page headline—"TV REPORTER IN LOVE WITH TEEN IDOL"—and a half-page picture of Dominique kissing Robbie Baker. As soon as she saw the paper, Jackie dashed over to Dominique's office. She expected to find Dominique in tears, but instead, she seemed thrilled. Jackie, sure that Dominique was just putting up a good front, asked how the paper had possibly gotten the false story and picture.

"I planted it."

"You what?"

"Not really." Dominique laughed, pushed her thick hair away from her eyes. "I knew there were a few photographers on the sidewalk, and I figured the guy who hangs out by the studio door all the time and sells to the *National Enquirer* was around. Ever see him? Tall skinny black guy who always wears a shirt and tie? Anyway, he wasn't there for some reason, but one of the others got it to the *Star*. Really just as good."

Jackie stared at her. "You mean it's true? You're dating Robbie Baker? What happened to Peter?"

Dominique laughed again. "No, darling, it's not true, and Peter is still my only beloved. But dating him isn't going to get me much publicity, is it?"

She told Jackie about her unexpected meeting with Robbie, their brief but interesting conversation. She hadn't heard from him again until an hour ago, when two dozen roses arrived on her desk.

"Look at the note." She handed a small florist's card to Jackie, who read it and grinned. *If they're saying we are, maybe we should. You're a good sport. Love, Robbie.*

Jackie handed it back to her. "I wouldn't show that to Peter."

"Of course I'll show it to Peter. Anything to encourage the man to action."

Glancing at Jeff now, Jackie decided that she wouldn't share that conversation with him. She felt a certain allegiance to Dominique. No allegiance to Jeff yet: but a bond was developing. How could she explain the overwhelming pang of attraction? Stop it, she told herself. You just made a pledge of loyalty to Julian.

"Listen, everyone will be at the party for a while longer," Jeff said. "Feel like going out and grabbing a cup of coffee? Give us a chance to talk a little."

Jackie nodded, and they headed toward the elevators.

Which brought them face-to-face with Laurie Spinner, again.

"I've been looking for you everywhere," said Laurie, grabbing Jeff's hand. "Where have you been?"

He shrugged. "What's up, Laurie?"

"I have a story idea that I need to go over with you." She looked at Jackie, back to Jeff. "Right now."

"Can it wait an hour?"

"No way," said Laurie. "If I don't get started on it, we'll lose it."

Jeff opened his mouth to say something, but Jackie interrupted. "Go ahead, I'll see you guys later. I've got to get back to work."

As Laurie dragged Jeff off, Jackie realized that her sense of a lost moment was surpassed only by her intense dislike for Laurie Spinner.

*   *   *

When Jackie and Julian arrived at the Benefactors Gala for the New York Public Library later that night, they nearly stumbled over Norman Mailer in close conversation with two other men and a tall, beautiful woman dressed in red silk. Then Jackie spotted Tom Wolfe across the room and smiled at him. He nodded pleasantly in recognition.

"Old boyfriend?" Julian asked, catching the silent exchange.

"I wish, honey. That's Tom Wolfe. I interviewed him when I was in Boston. You know who he is, don't you? *Bonfire of the Vanities, The Right Stuff* and all that?"

"The book was better than the movie," said Julian.

Jackie laughed. "Just what you're supposed to say in this crowd."

It hadn't occurred to Jackie that the literati would be assembled tonight, but of course it made sense. She let her eyes wander across the room, wondered if the older man with the lined face and the intelligent eyes could possibly be Saul Bellow. She asked Julian.

"I don't think so," said Julian. "But whoever it is has just turned around, and he's looking at you like lunch."

Jackie grinned. "Well, for future reference, you should know that if Saul Bellow asks me to sleep with him, our deal of loyalty and exclusivity is off. It would be my literary duty to see if he's as good in bed as he is on the page."

"Typical Radcliffe girl," Julian said. "Takes a Nobel prize to arouse you." He slipped his arm around Jackie's waist, stroked her sensuous silk dress. "Feels good," he said.

"Thank you. You, by the way, look wonderful in a tuxedo." She twiddled with one of his studs, which were solid gold with large diamond centers.

"The only reason to put on a tuxedo is to get to see you this way. You're very sexy."

"What do you have against tuxedos?"

"They remind me of Marianne, who judged the success or failure of her life by how many black-tie dinners we attended in a week. After we split up, I vowed to send large donations to various charities and never go to their affairs."

"But this is different," said Jackie. She knew that Julian had supported the library even before it became a *cause célèbre* for the glamour crowd. He thought of the public library the way other people thought of home and family—it had nurtured him in his youth, and he felt he owed it a perpetual debt of gratitude. This year, Julian wasn't just attending the dinner, he was being honored. Jackie wondered how much you had to donate over the years before the library invited you to a Gala and hung a gold medal around your neck.

Julian looked around the room at the elegant crowd. "You're by far the sexiest woman here."

"You're biased."

"Maybe, but every time I look at you, I get bedroom thoughts and wonder when this will be over."

Jackie smiled. She *did* look her best tonight. After obsessing for days about what to wear, she had consulted Dominique.

"If you're going to be wearing it on the air, you can always borrow from a designer," Dominique told her. "But since this is private, maybe you should try wholesale." She said she knew two or three designers who were always happy to have her come to their showrooms and buy their evening dresses at cost.

Dominique set up the appointments, and promised to come along. "I love shopping," she insisted when Jackie said she didn't want to take her out of her way. "But at the moment I don't really need anything for myself. Of course, if I just happen to see something while I'm with you . . ." She giggled, and Jackie joined her—and the high spirits continued throughout the expedition.

They met in the late morning at the Bill Blass showroom, and agreed that the clothes were too tony for them.

"You need to be older, richer, and taller than I am to wear something like this," Dominique said when the director of the showroom showed her a sophisticated dress of navy jersey with a high collar and long sleeves.

They went next to the Carolyn Roehm showroom, where Dominique found a dazzling gown to wear for her next show in Atlantic City, but decided that the price, even at cost, was too steep.

"It may be pricey, but it's worth it," said Evon, the young man in the showroom who was helping them. "All of the beading is hand-sewn, and the fabric is exquisite. In fact, Ms. Roehm wore the sample to a dinner party she had last week in her apartment."

Dominique laughed. "Well, I'm afraid she's the only one who can afford it. It's probably this dress, or one of the Old Masters hanging on her wall."

Jackie fell in love with a pale gray wool suit. She could wear it on the air and use it as a tax deduction.

Dominique sent her a warning glance. "Don't do it," she finally whispered, when Evon disappeared into the racks.

"Why not?"

"The little fur collar. It's darling, but you're going to get letters from conservationists who will tell you that the entire seal population has been wiped out because of women like you."

Jackie looked at her in surprise. "It's not seal, it's curly lamb. All they had to do was sheer the critter. Little Lolly Lamb is probably still alive if she hasn't been made into a lamb chop."

"I know, but do you want to have to explain that in three dozen letters?"

Jackie agreed that she didn't, and took off the suit, stroking the collar regretfully. Dominique was right, of course. In television, it wasn't reality that mattered, it was appearances. No sense raising the ire of even a handful of viewers over something so unimportant.

They left the showroom, walked back out onto Seventh Avenue.

"Cheer up," Dominique said. "I know the next one will be a winner."

At the next showroom, Dominique convinced her to try on a slim black silk dress that looked to Jackie like a long slip. It had spaghetti straps and a scalloped border of lace above the breasts, then fell in a straight line almost to the floor.

"I'm not sure I can wear this out in public," Jackie said, standing in front of the mirror in the showroom. "It looks like I should wear something over it."

"That's the whole idea," Dominique pointed out. "It's fabulously sexy. Julian will know you're wearing an expensive designer gown, and he'll wonder why it seems so naughty."

When she tried it on again alone in her apartment, she decided it would be just right. She wanted to make sure that Julian's eyes stayed on her the whole evening and didn't wander across to wherever Marianne would be sitting.

Jackie hadn't seen Marianne since her visit to Saddle River, and she wasn't eager for another encounter. But she wasn't going to be able to avoid it. For one thing, Julian had given many gifts to the library while he was still married, and they came from "Marianne and Julian Beardsley." The library officials felt that Marianne's name belonged among the benefactors, and had even talked about giving her one of the evening's gold medals. Fortunately, Marianne hadn't wanted that. But she had wanted to be there.

Standing in her glorious dress, with Julian's arm around her, Jackie was grateful that she hadn't seen Marianne yet tonight. Dana and Sam came over to say hello, and there were hugs all around. The men went off to get drinks, and Jackie, tucking her arm through Dana's, told her about Marianne.

"Do you think she's coming out of goodwill or to be a thorn in his side?" Dana asked.

"From what I've heard, she wants to see Julian being honored," Jackie said. "According to Julian, the marriage is over, but they're still family, and they like to be around for each other's big moments."

Jackie knew Julian had gone to watch Marianne compete in the horse show at Madison Square Garden, but he'd had the good taste not to invite Jackie to come along.

"I think it's a sign of good character," Dana said. "He's not trying to pretend that all those years of his life didn't exist. He was loyal to her, and now he'll be loyal to you."

Jackie made a face. "What about *your* loyalty? As my friend, you're supposed to say that she's a slimeball who won't let Julian out of her clutches. And you don't understand why she can't accept their divorce as final."

"Sorry I got my lines wrong, but you're the one who used to say that just because you stop being lovers doesn't mean you should stop being friends. I think it's healthy that they can let go of the marriage and still care about each other as people. Remember, they've also got two teenage kids to think about."

"You would have made a great social worker," Jackie said. "Why don't you stick around a few minutes and meet Marianne? I'm sure you two will have a lot to talk about."

"Don't be nasty, I'm just being reasonable."

"When I want reasonable I'll talk to Julian. From you I expect support."

A few minutes later, standing alone with Julian again, Jackie finally caught sight of Marianne. Never one for understatement, Marianne was wearing a short bouffant dress in a bold floral print. She had spike-heeled pumps in the same print, and was carrying a jeweled evening bag in the shape of a frog. Feodor Zerkov was walking with her, his arm loosely around her shoulders. So their affair was public now.

Julian caught Jackie's gaze, put his arm around her and stroked her bare shoulder. "Promise me you won't let Marianne spoil your evening?"

"Of course she won't."

"Let's go say hello and get it over with," he said. But they didn't have to bother, because a moment later, Marianne and Feodor appeared in front of them.

Marianne, looking quickly at Jackie, didn't bother to say anything, but turned to kiss Julian warmly. She tucked her arm through his. "I have so many things to talk to you about, Julie, and I haven't seen you in weeks. Let me have you for five minutes." She glanced at Jackie, then turned back to Julian. "Your girl won't mind, will she?"

"Really, Marianne!" Julian said.

"Don't worry," Jackie said icily, "I would have been shocked if the gay divorcee was anything but rude."

Turning quickly, Jackie headed over to the bar. She could have used vodka, but she would settle for white wine.

She didn't realize that Feodor had followed her until she got her drink, tried to back away from the crowd, and found herself in his arms.

"Feodor!" She jumped back in surprise and the wine sloshed precariously in the glass but didn't spill.

"My little pet. You are so busy with your Julian that you have no time for your old love, Feodor?"

She looked at him in amazement. "What are you talking about?"

"I have missed you, my darling. But tell me, you are happy?"

"I'm shocked, Feodor. All the conversations we had when I first met Julian, and you never told me about Marianne. Or you and Marianne."

"What could I say? It didn't seem important to my dear little Jackie, so happy with Julian. And think of poor Feodor, with so many loyalties." He came closer, his head next to hers, cooing his Russian-accented words in her ear. "Marianne and I have something . . . special. But I love my Jackie, and what greater loyalty can I have than to my friend Julian?"

"Some friendship. Sleeping with his ex-wife."

"Yes, it is very special," said Feodor, purposely misconstruing the remark. "But you know what is lucky? That you and I never . . ." He rubbed his hands, making a suggestive, almost obscene gesture. "Julian would not have liked that. And Marianne— well, she knows I am a man of the world. But she has one rule for me. I must stay away from Julian's girls."

"How difficult for you," said Jackie. She was starting to feel annoyed by the conversation.

"Yes, I understand it, but it makes me sad. I have had everyone except the woman I want."

At least Feodor hadn't changed.

"I admire you, Feodor," she said, handing him her empty glass. "It can't be easy trying to seduce everything that walks."

The cocktail hour was mercifully short, and when the doors opened for dinner, Jackie was relieved to see Marianne and Feodor sitting at a table near the back. Julian's table was in a prominent position at the front. Dana and Sam and Dominique and Peter—whom Julian had invited at the last minute—were already sitting down, immersed in cheerful conversation. Dominique's unmistakable laugh punctuated the discussion, and Jackie ambled over to join them.

Meeting Marianne and Feodor wasn't going to spoil her evening, after all.

13

Jackie and Julian got home from the benefit sometime after two in the morning, Julian resplendent in the gold medal he'd been awarded. Jackie had switched from white wine to vodka shortly before midnight, and was already feeling it. She had no intention of getting to the office anytime before noon.

So when Julian's phone rang at five A.M., it took her awhile to decide that it was probably for her, and she should answer it. Her tongue was almost too thick to talk, and her eyes felt blurred and swollen. It was Cawley, shouting that he needed her in right away because he had a fucking hole in the show. He had lost a live interview with the two Texans who had witnessed a terrorist shoot-out on the West Bank of Israel the previous evening. The director of the Mid-East bureau, who had been trailing them for nine hours since the incident, had apparently just called to say that there was nothing he could do. The Texans had decided they didn't want to be on television after all, and they were boarding a plane for Dallas.

"I spent three thousand goddamned dollars for a satellite from the Mid-East, and my goddamned bureau chief can't keep two lousy Texans in sight until showtime," Cawley yelled, losing his temper for what was obviously not the first time this morning.

"What can I do?" Jackie asked.

"Get your ass over here. Now."

It was no time to argue. She took an almost-cold shower, drank two cups of coffee, and prayed that Barry the makeup man hadn't forgotten how to get rid of black circles under the eyes.

Cawley was calmer when she got to the studio. "I have terrific footage of some big Italian designer's bathing-suit show," he said when she walked through the door. "Happened yesterday.

Raleigh shot it and said it's great. One of the models is topless. Or bottomless. I can't remember. It's silent, so if I have Raleigh cut a montage, can you give me a two-minute narration?"

She hesitated. "I imagine so. But you're using that to replace a story on a terrorist shoot-out?"

He glared at her. "What would you like me to do? Terrorism in the Middle East isn't exactly news anymore. The only angle here was that two Americans were witnesses. If I don't have the Americans, I don't have a goddamned story."

"You want two minutes on bathing suits I've never seen?"

"Go see them if you want. Raleigh's editing. But I see it more as a think piece."

Her narration was written by seven-thirty, a think piece that she'd thought about for barely an hour. She discussed the changing tastes of women and fashion, questioned how much of a woman's body should be shown on public beaches, and wondered why European women bared more breast than Americans. Cawley glanced at it and pronounced it brilliant. At seven-forty-nine, adrenalin rushing, she was on the air.

The spot was clever, and Jackie's narration worked perfectly with the tape. Jackie wondered whether any viewer who knew what story was originally scheduled for seven-forty-nine, and what finally ran, would really have cared. Afterward, for the first time in a long while, Jackie thought of the millions of sets across the country, tuned to *A.M. Reports,* watching whatever was presented. Terrorism or bathing suits, it was all entertainment to them.

Feeling exhausted, Jackie went back to her own apartment and slept until almost dinnertime. Cawley had scheduled her to be on live for the next two mornings, so she had to get used to the early risings.

A thought intruded, making her sit bolt upright in bed. Why was Cawley suddenly putting her on live in the mornings, testing her on short notice? The immediate crisis with Darlie had blown over, just as Jeff had predicted, but Darlie's contract was up soon, and there was great speculation about whether it would be renewed. The most persistent rumor was that Bradley was pushing to have Dominique in the co-anchor's chair, and his opinion would obviously hold considerable weight. Jeff had hinted once that others thought Jackie was the obvious choice to replace

Darlie. She still didn't think it could happen, wouldn't even discuss the possibility with Julian on the few occasions when he brought it up. But her reaction was a defensive one. In her heart of hearts, she had to admit that she would do almost anything to get that job. Fortunately, that didn't include stepping on Dominique, with whom she had become close friends.

"Television believes in type casting and you and I are very different types," Dominique had told Jackie wisely some time ago. "You stand for smart and serious and I stand for dumb and sexy. They're going to pick a type, not a person, to be co-anchor. So we can tell everyone to stop thinking of us as competitors."

"Believe me, I've tried," Jackie said. She thought about it for a moment. "You're probably right about type casting, even though it's total bullshit. It makes you feel a little helpless, doesn't it?"

Dominique shrugged. "I'm used to it. But there's a danger when you go against type, and I may do that. Cook my own goose, as they say. I'm supposed to be a pin-up girl, and all I really want to do right now is to be a frumpy married lady with lots of babies."

"Definitely not the Dominique the world knows and loves. Does this mean Peter has finally proposed?"

"Darling, Peter will never propose. But he's been talking about babies and commitments lately. All the dear man needs is a little push, which I'm happy to provide."

"Do you think you'll get married?"

"I think we'll do everything. And soon."

Jackie hugged her. "You deserve it."

A few weeks later, on a Saturday afternoon, Dominique called Jackie, sounding a little desperate. Julian was in Washington, and Jackie was sitting in her living room listening to Mozart piano concertos and rereading *Portrait of a Lady,* her favorite book.

"I have to talk to you," Dominique said, her voice trembling slightly. "What are you doing right now?"

"Nothing that can't be interrupted," Jackie said.

"Can you come over here? I don't feel like going out."

"Fine." For some reason, she had never been to Dominique's apartment, so asked for the address.

"I'm at Seventy-second street, East Side, near the river." As she started to give the exact address, Jackie thought she heard Dominique's voice crack. "Give me a half-hour to pull myself together."

Jackie took a cab to her favorite food shop at Seventy-second and Lexington Avenue, bought a big tin of Amaretto cookies for Dominique, and after she'd paid for them, went back to buy another tin for Julian. Then she began to walk to Dominique's, but after a few blocks realized that the address wasn't just near the river, it was practically in it. Her feet hurt from the pavement and the damn tins of cookies kept slamming into her legs.

Jackie was in a foul mood when she arrived, but nothing to compare to Dominique's. Her eyes were red and puffy, her mouth was set in a tight, angry grimace, and her hair was tied back in an unflattering knot.

Jackie felt her own distress immediately disappear. She decided not to ask what was wrong right away, just handed Dominique the cookies and stepped into the living room.

"Make yourself comfortable," Dominique said. Jackie looked around. There was a big picture window with a river view. The room looked as if it had been done by *House and Garden* for an article on cozy New York living. Lots of plants, a peach-and-cream sofa, overstuffed chairs covered in peach chintz, and a soft, fluffy cream-colored rug.

"What a gorgeous apartment," Jackie said. "You clearly have a better contract at the show than I do."

"Don't believe it. This place was furnished by two pudding commercials, my Saturday-night shows at Atlantic City, and my latest record."

"Go ahead. Tell me that in two hours singing in Atlantic City you make as much as you do in a month at our show."

"More or less."

Jackie sighed. "I wish I could sing. My parents told me to get into television for the money. So I got into television, but Bradley James seems to be the only one to get the money."

Dominique offered a feeble smile, and the angry lines around her mouth softened slightly. Then she looked up at Jackie, and her eyes filled with tears.

"Come on." Jackie took her arm and led her over to the peaches-and-cream sofa. "Tell me what's happened."

"It's Peter," she said. "He . . ." She lifted a hand to her mouth, as if to hold back the sobs, but it didn't work, and she buried her head in her hands, crying silently. Jackie put an arm around the shaking shoulders. Dominique lifted her head, tears still streaming down her face. "I'm pregnant," she said. "I don't know how else to tell you."

For a moment, Jackie was too stunned to say anything. But she realized that no words were necessary, because Dominique was leaning on her, sobbing and shaking.

"It's okay, Dominique," Jackie said finally, softly, hugging Dominique, holding her like a child. "It'll be okay."

The sobs finally subsided and Dominique stood up abruptly, sniffled, and walked to the window.

"I just feel like such a fool now. That's the worst of it. Feeling like a fool."

"Come on, Dominique. It happens. Mistakes happen."

Dominique's lips curled slightly. "It wasn't really a mistake," she said. "Peter's told me a million times that he wants to be a father someday, so I thought he'd be thrilled when I told him."

"He wasn't?"

"Right."

"What did he say?"

Dominique sat down on the sofa again, stared straight ahead. "I'd tell you, but I'll start to cry again."

Jackie didn't say anything, just watched her try to pull herself together. Finally Dominique cleared her throat and spoke in a whispery voice. "Peter said he does want children, but not right now. He was very sympathetic. And he gave me the name of a friend of his who's a gynecologist and does abortions."

"Not great."

"No." She reached into her pocket and pulled out a folded piece of paper. "Here's the name he gave me. I've decided to save it. Maybe I'll make it the first page of Junior's baby book."

Jackie swallowed. "You want to have the baby?"

Dominique looked as if she might start to cry again, but instead her eyes just glistened for a moment. "Of course I want the baby. I thought I wanted to have Peter and the baby, but that's not going to happen. Why should I lose everything? I want a baby, and I'm too old to wait any longer."

"Thirty-two is hardly old."

"Unfortunately, I'm not even close to thirty-two except in my press release."

Jackie wondered why things like that never occurred to her.

"There are other reasons, too," Dominique continued. "Believe me, I've done nothing but think about it all day. I want this baby, Jackie. And I'm too Catholic in my heart to dream of having an abortion. The Church doesn't believe in it."

"I don't mean to be rude, but the Church doesn't believe in premarital sex, either."

"I think there's a difference."

Jackie shrugged. "Ultimately, you have to justify your decisions to yourself, not the Pope."

"Spoken like a good Protestant." Dominique smiled slightly.

"Okay," Jackie said, "let's assume you're doing this for yourself, not the Pope. The real question is whether you can handle the pressures of being a single mother."

Dominique took a deep breath. "I finally figured out that it's not going to be easy without Peter. Jackie, I need a friend right now. That's why I called you. I can't talk to Raleigh about this, because all she'll think about is my career. Her career. And she'll try to talk me out of it. I couldn't bear that."

"I'm glad to be a friend, and I'm not trying to convince you of anything. I'm just trying to be practical."

"Good." She seemed to brighten. "I want this baby, Jackie, I really do." She patted her very flat stomach. "Strange to think that there's something in there. Do you think I can keep my job at the show?"

"What do you mean?"

"Will they fire me for being—what's the expression?—an unwed mother?"

"Don't be silly. It's not the 1950's anymore. These things are common now."

"Not in televisionland, I'm afraid. And not in the world Bradley James lives in. Do you know he made his wife quit her job as soon as they got married? He told her that with his salary, they didn't need her paltry thirty-five thousand a year."

"I've heard that he can be a bit rigid. But Bradley James also loves children. So he should be delighted with the whole thing. Actually, the only problem I can imagine is with Darlie's job. I think this is going to spoil your chance to replace her."

"Oh, God, that's the last thing I care about," Dominique said. "At this point my life seems a lot more important than television." She rubbed at her eyes. "Don't get me wrong, I want to keep my job. You're supposed to be a good writer. Can you help me come up with a story?"

"What kind of story?"

"I don't know." She waved her hand vaguely. "Like saying I was about to get married but my fiancé died in a car crash. Or that I'm secretly married. Something that will make this whole thing more . . . respectable. So I don't think people are whispering about me."

"The proverbial war widow?"

"What do you mean?"

"Isn't that the story women in the 1940's told when they got pregnant? That the husband was killed in the war. But these days, I'm afraid you'd have to claim a fatality in Nicaragua. Or maybe El Salvador. And that would require too much explaining. Of course, there are always plane hijackings and terrorism in Lebanon."

Dominique looked at her unhappily. "I called on you for help. Why are you being so nasty?"

"I'm sorry"—Jackie's voice softened—"I'm just trying to make a point, Dominique. You're the most open and honest person in the whole world. Everyone loves you for that. But it means that you've hardly kept Peter a secret. For a phony man to materialize —and disappear—in your life would sound ridiculous. To Bradley James and everyone else."

"So what do you suggest?"

"Tell the truth. Or some version of it. You decided you wanted to be a mother, but you haven't decided yet about marriage. That's that."

"I'll get fired within the week."

"You won't. I don't mean to be rude, but this won't be the first time you've broken the rules that good little girls are supposed to follow. And it didn't hurt you before."

A dark blush swept over Dominique's cheeks. "You mean the story of how I got hired in the first place?"

Jackie nodded, instantly sorry that she had brought it up.

"Want to hear the real story?"

"It's not necessary."

"I don't mind. I was singing in Las Vegas—the opening act to Henny Youngman. George McGill, the senior vice-president of the network, was there with his wife, and we all became good friends. Yes, he brought me to New York, but I never slept with him. Ever."

Jackie tried not to look skeptical. "It doesn't matter. You're pregnant. You don't have to prove your virginity anymore."

Dominique stood up angrily. "It *does* matter, because I've trusted you with the biggest secret of my life, and you're not even willing to believe me about something that happened half a dozen years ago."

"You're right. I'm sorry. Please sit down."

Dominique walked around the room, looked out the window again, and came back to the sofa. "Do you believe me?"

"Of course I believe you. It's just that according to the stories I've heard, you two were a big item in all the gossip columns."

"God, you're an innocent. You've been in this business too long to still believe what you read in newspaper columns. You should hardly believe most of the stuff that's on our show every morning, respectable as we try to be. Journalists make up their own reality. You must know that."

"What would George McGill—is that his name?—say was the reality about you two?"

Dominique smiled. "He'd say that I'm an awful flirt, and he loved every minute of it." She stretched. "One thing feminists should learn is that you can still get pretty far by flirting."

"And you did."

Dominique's face suddenly darkened, and Jackie noticed the knuckles on her clasped hands getting white. "George was never anything but sweet and helpful to me. It's the rest of the story that nobody knows or gossips about that's awful." Jackie waited, watched the emotion crossing Dominique's face. "George quit and moved out to L.A. He's running a movie studio or something now, and Winston Axminster got promoted into his job. Slimy bastard. He started taking me out for lunches and dinners and made it very clear that if I wanted to keep my job, I'd better sleep with him."

"You're joking."

"I wish. I won't say he raped me, but it was damned close."

She looked at Jackie, pain and anguish in her eyes. Jackie reached over and took Dominique's hand. "That's awful!"

Dominique nodded. "Axminster finally backed off, but it sickens me to think that he still has control over my career."

"You think he'll intervene?"

"Not really." Dominique held her hand more tightly. "Jackie, I'm just scared. I'm scared about being pregnant, and I'm scared about what people will say. Doesn't that sound ridiculous? It's the kind of thing your mother would say."

"Well, you're going to be a mother, so apparently you get to say things like that. But I know what you mean, since I just proved how hurtful people can be."

"No, you've been great. I needed an injection of reality."

Jackie sighed. "Listen, as far as what people are going to say, there's nothing either of us can do about that. You're just going to have to be strong and not read gossip columns. But as far as being scared about the pregnancy, I don't know. I've never been pregnant. But I admire you, and I'll do everything I can to be there for you."

"Thanks, Jackie. That's what I really needed."

Dominique sat on the sofa for a long time after Jackie left, rubbing her stomach and looking out at the city lights twinkling their reflections in the East River. She wasn't sure why she had decided to pour out her heart to Jackie, but a few hours ago she had been feeling desperate and alone, and she couldn't think of anyone else to call. It had worked out fine. She smiled slightly to herself. Female friendships based on shopping together seemed a lot more stable than relationships with a man based on fucking.

She had sworn Jackie to absolute secrecy, except for Julian. Jackie seemed surprised that Dominique would even consider that she would tell anyone.

Dominique got up to pour herself a glass of wine, but remembering some of the warnings she had read about pregnancy, she took a glass of orange juice instead. So this was it. She was pregnant. She had thought there'd be more to it. A little while ago, she had felt as if she would never stop crying, but now a certain calm was returning. Peter was going to abandon her, that much she knew, and it didn't really matter anymore. She had been foolish to think that getting pregnant would change anything between them. When she had broken the news to him last night, he had responded by coming up with the name of his local abortionist. Then, this afternoon, he had stopped by her apartment, looking pale and shaken.

"Why aren't you at work?" she had asked, opening the door for him.

"I was too distracted." Peter pulled off his Armani suede jacket and tossed it on the sofa. "By the way, announcing this pregnancy was incredibly bad timing on your part. I have a presentation for that new coffee account tomorrow."

"I'm sorry. I thought I was sharing good news."

He shoved his hands in his pockets, paced around her apartment, hit the remote control for the television set and then quickly turned it off again.

"You did this on purpose, didn't you?"

"Did what on purpose?"

"Got pregnant. It's the oldest ploy around. A guy doesn't propose marriage fast enough so the girl says she'll take care of the contraception, and the next thing you know, this happens."

"That's not fair." Yes, she had wanted a baby and hadn't been particularly careful about her diaphragm, but he was the one who seemed to get his kicks out of screwing at unexpected times, when she couldn't possibly be prepared.

"You expect me to be responsible for this baby, don't you? Well, listen, Dominique, this isn't the time, and you know it. I've told you we'll get married someday, but too many things are happening in my job right now. It needs my full attention, and it's not right of you to try to distract me."

"What about my job?"

"That's not my problem."

She looked at him, suddenly seeing him for the self-centered individual that he was. Raleigh had been right about Peter: he couldn't see beyond his own needs and never would.

"None of this is your problem, Peter. It's my baby."

He looked relieved, then seemed to put up his guard again.

"Have you changed your mind about keeping it?"

"No."

"Then what do you want from me? Should I give you some money?"

"I don't want anything from you that you're capable of giving," she said softly. "Leave and go back to work. It's where you belong."

Unbelievably, that's what he had done, and that's when her tears had started.

She had spared Jackie the details of Peter's insensitivity. Hearing it again would have made it impossible for her to explain, even to herself, how she could have been in love with the man. Or thought she was in love. Could real love end so abruptly, come crashing to the ground with such a deadening thud?

It was curious that she had told Jackie about Winston Axminster. She hadn't planned to, but she wanted Jackie to know how horrible men were. Sometimes, looking back on her life, she felt it had been little more than a series of abuses at the hands of men.

But she had never been a victim.

She was suddenly aware of that, as surely as if someone had flashed a sign in front of her face. She went along just so far, and then some unexpected strength appeared, her independence reared up, and she was saved. She had hidden reserves. Just like her mother, she supposed. They were farm girls, and so maybe more trusting than they should be. But from her mother she had learned that all you have, in the end, is yourself. Your own strength and courage. That was the legacy she would pass on to this baby someday.

It was funny that when Jackie had mentioned Darlie's job it seemed so unimportant to her. It would be nice if Jackie got it, though she probably didn't realize what it would entail. Jackie would be fine on the air, probably handle it better than Darlie. But she'd lose Julian in the process. Jackie was a lot younger than thirty-two in real life, never mind press releases, so there was no way to tell her that. Jackie probably still had the notion that she could do everything, didn't understand that men like Julian got distracted if the lover of the moment wasn't in front of them. They didn't mean to destroy relationships, it just happened.

Dominique was beginning to understand why Raleigh had run away, burying herself in her work and in her female lover's cunt. She had been disappointed too many times by men.

"It's not their cocks I don't like," she had told Dominique one day after they shot a story in Houston and went into a bar for a drink. The men there, with their loud voices, expensive

cowboy boots, and aggressive swaggers, were particularly obnoxious. "I just get tired of all the shit that men bring to a
relationship. I want love and equality and they want a power
struggle. It's not worth it."

Raleigh's solution was a long-standing affair with Sandra Ste-
vens, an aging television actress who lived in Hollywood and
was mostly seen doing guest appearances on TV serials. Dominique had met her once and thought she was smart, sharp-
tongued, and forceful. Just like Raleigh. The two women liked
each other, but obviously didn't need each other. They kept
their relationship well under wraps, taking vacations together,
occasionally spending a week or two in the other's home.

"Nobody really needs a full-time relationship," Raleigh had
said. "What you want is for someone to be there when you need
them. Whether for sex or support."

Dominique didn't really believe that.

Oh God, did she still want Peter?

She supposed she wanted what Peter stood for, the security
and love and *normalcy*. But she wasn't going to have that.

She was going to have a baby, though, and that was just fine.

Jackie didn't tell Julian about Dominique for the simple reason that she wasn't seeing very much of him. She was constantly busy with the show—Cawley had her taking short trips to shoot stories and do interviews, then rushing back to be on live several mornings a week. The rumor began to spread that Cawley was trying to increase Jackie's visibility, prove that she was the right choice to take over for Darlie. Dominique, meanwhile, was being handed big interviews arranged by Bradley, getting extra air-time on live spots, because Bradley seemed to find everything she said enthralling. Jackie had never felt more like a pawn. Cawley and Bradley each had a girl, but it was the men who were competing.

Jackie realized that there was no real edge to the competition, because Dominique had taken a step back from the daily grind. She just wasn't interested anymore in fourteen-hour days. Nobody else seemed to notice the change until Darlie announced she was taking a week's vacation and Dominique decided that she didn't want to fill in for her.

"I don't think I could stand coming in early every morning," Dominique told Jackie, in the closed-door chat they had almost every morning now in the office. "I have awful morning sickness. Do you think it's all psychosomatic?"

"I used to think so," admitted Jackie, "but there are incredible chemical changes going on in your body during pregnancy. The least that happens is they make you a little nauseated."

"I read that if you're nauseated in the morning, you should eat saltine crackers before you get out of bed. I tried it, and threw them up twenty minutes later."

Jackie laughed. "Another one of the joys of being a woman. The nausea ends, though, doesn't it?"

"It's supposed to. But getting up early kills me right now. I was in at five the other morning to do that voice-over for Raleigh, and I went to the bathroom three times to throw up. Raleigh couldn't figure out why I kept disappearing."

"How long are you going to keep this a secret?"

"As long as I can. It's making me miserable, but I have the feeling I'll be more miserable once everyone knows."

"The way you look, you probably won't have to announce it until your eighth month." Dominique insisted that her waistline was getting thick, but it was impossible for Jackie to tell.

"Well, I'm going to tell Cawley that I can't fill in for Darlie that week. I'll come up with some excuse. Will you do it, instead?"

"I don't know if he'll ask me."

"Of course he will."

Cawley asked Jackie almost immediately, and she was thrilled. Co-host of *A.M. Reports,* even for a week! It was a dream come true. She found herself watching Darlie carefully for clues on how to be a successful anchor. Dominique told her that filling in was a snap. Nobody expected you to be any good, so if you managed to remember your name, you were already a winner.

Jackie's first morning as substitute host of *A.M. Reports* was easier than she expected. She felt a charge of excitement when she sat down in Darlie's chair, a sense of being center-stage. She had almost nothing to do in the first half-hour since Bradley handled all the news interviews. Filling in for Darlie meant she had all the fluff spots on the show, including two celebrities, an interview with a woman who had written a book on divorce, and a demonstration spot on making festive drinks without alcohol. For that, Jackie donned an apron and made light banter on the kitchen set with the young cook who was demonstrating the recipes.

The show was tightly scripted, so virtually every word she had to say was on the teleprompter. The writers for the show gave her the introductions and questions for every guest, though she tried to make the interviews her own by changing them around a bit. She was less adept than Darlie at reading from the prompter, and preferred to follow her own instincts whenever she could.

The two hours went unbelievably fast. She made a mistake once in announcing the time on the air. "Actually, it's not eight-thirty-nine, it's eight-forty-one," Bradley said good-naturedly, correcting her. She shrugged and rolled her eyes, and the moment passed. Other than that, everything went smoothly.

Immediately after the show, Julian sent her two dozen roses with a note: "You're fabulous! And I love you!"

She suspected that Julian had arranged for the flowers before seeing the show, but it didn't matter. She *had* been good, that she knew.

The shows on Tuesday and Wednesday also went well, and Jackie was starting to think that it was going to be awfully hard giving up the seat at the end of the week. She was getting into a rhythm—asleep by ten at night in her own bed, up at four-thirty, at the studio at five. After the show, she would work in her office until noon.

In the early afternoon on Wednesday, just as she was getting ready to leave, all hell broke loose.

The bells rang on the AP and UPI machines, which meant that an urgent message was being sent. But that wasn't unusual. The wire services considered a fair number of stories worthy of urgent attention. One of the researchers ambled over to the machines, just to check the news.

"Holy shit!" he yelled. "An American plane has been hijacked and is landing in Russia. There are at least two hundred passengers on board."

Jackie, halfway out the door, realized that she wasn't going anyplace. Tomorrow's show was going to have to change dramatically. She went back to her office, flicked on her television to the all-news cable network. The anchor there was just making the same brief announcement that had come over the wire service, but promised that more details would follow.

Jackie felt a sudden shift around the office, a gearing up for crisis. Most of the staff had been around long enough to remember similar incidents, to know what was going to happen. They would wait for the story to unfold, try to book guests for the morning who could shed new light on it. The bookers at every one of the networks would be trying to get the same people, and in getting guests, it helped to be the top-ranked show. Sometimes in the middle of the night there would be a new development, and another scramble for guests. Unbook the ones they already had, get new ones. They also needed to have a whole back-up show, because if the crisis ended before air time, with nobody hurt, it became a simple news story. You didn't need experts then to analyze the situation—you just needed to report the story and move on to something else.

By four in the afternoon, it was clear that the crisis wasn't going to end quickly. Soviet officials were refusing to comment. There were suggestions that the Soviet government was involved and that it wasn't a hijacking at all but an inexplicable act of aggression. The downed plane was a DC-10, on its way from New York to Helsinki. It had stopped in Greenland for refueling, then somewhere over the Bering Sea the hijackers had made themselves known, demanding that the plane be diverted to Leningrad. They claimed to be holding hand grenades. The pilot had radioed his intentions, then complied with the demand. Details out of Leningrad were otherwise sketchy.

Cawley held an informal meeting in his office. Jeff was perched on the radiator, Raleigh on the sofa, and various writers and bookers sprawled around on the office furniture. They would, of course, find an expert in American-Soviet relations to comment on the possible implications of the event. Cawley wanted the Secretary of State, and a call was put in to his office, but it seemed unlikely that he'd agree. "We've got to get some good human interest on this one," Cawley said. He had already managed to get the passenger list from the airline, and about sixty percent of those on board had American passports. He handed the list to Laurie Spinner. "Start making calls," he said. "I want concerned family members, at least three of them. The best stories you can find. Maybe there's an old couple who was taking their first trip to Europe, and we'll get a friend to comment. Or someone who was going to visit family in Finland. I wouldn't mind a gorgeous Scandinavian girl who's worried about her husband on the plane."

Laurie looked pale, scanned the list. "If it's all right, I'll go right now and get started."

"Go," said Cawley.

The meeting went on, with people drifting in and out. An hour later there was a report that a seventy-year-old man on the plane had suffered a heart attack and had been released. He was being rushed to a Soviet hospital, but it didn't look as if he would live. The man was identified as Sven Jorgensen from

Miami, Florida. One of the other bookers, Danny Marks, was dispatched to get an interview with the family.

Danny came back a little while later. "The younger Jorgensens, whose names are Jonas and Lila, were very polite, but said they're not interested in talking to anybody," he reported. "Sven is Jonas' father. He's lived with them in Miami for many years, and he was flying back to Finland to see his sister, who's apparently in the hospital right now. A lot of crises at once. They said they want to be alone right now."

Cawley raised his eyebrows, and everyone in the room knew what he was thinking. *We have to get the Jorgensens.* Theirs was the kind of personal story that made a crisis real, made it strike the hearts of everyone watching. *It could be your father on that plane.* People might not remember the measured statements of the Secretary of State, but they'd remember the pained eyes of a young man whose father had been involved in a hijacking.

"If you can't convince them on the phone, you'll have to do it in person," Cawley said. "Be on the next flight to Miami."

Danny nodded, didn't even look surprised. It wasn't the first time he had been sent to stake out potential guests, use charm, pressure, and lies to get them to appear on the air at the moments in their lives when they least wanted to. Arthur, the transportation coordinator, hurried out, came back a moment later saying that Danny was confirmed on a flight leaving in an hour and a half. He could pick up tickets at the airport.

"You don't have time to stop at home," Cawley said, "so take five hundred dollars from the business office and go. Call when you arrive, we'll have a hotel room for you. But you'll probably be better off camping out outside the Jorgensens'."

"Not a problem," said Danny. "I'll do everything I can to get them."

"I'm sure you will," Cawley said. "Because if they're on any other show tomorrow morning and not ours, don't bother to come back here. You're fired."

Danny walked quickly out of the room, and Jackie felt ill, less for the pressure being put on Danny than for the Jorgensens, who were about to find out what it meant to be wanted by the media. Jackie had seen it happen many times before, when a personal tragedy became public property. If Cawley thought they were such a good story, so would every other network producer and news editor in New York. The Jorgensens would be all but helpless to fight back. They would be wrung limp at a time in their lives when they were most vulnerable, made to cry on the air a few times, then, when public interest waned and another tragedy became news, they'd be abandoned. Jackie suspected that Danny would get the Jorgensens to appear by promising them that sharing their story might help the other passengers, still on the plane. It wasn't true, of course. The only reason for having them on was that people loved to watch misery. The cliché was that viewers liked to see other people worse off than they were, but Jackie thought it was more subtle than that. People just wanted to be made to feel something— some emotion, whatever it was.

By seven o'clock in the evening, not one spot on the show had been firmly booked for the next day. Jackie wandered over to Cawley's office again to see what was going on. Cawley seemed to notice her for the first time all day.

"What are you still doing here? Go home."

"I've just been trying to follow the story so I'll be ready for tomorrow."

"By tomorrow it will be a different story. Come back early. Around four. We'll be making final decisions then."

She stayed awhile longer before she finally decided to leave. Tomorrow was going to be a real test of her skills, and she had to be awake for it.

But sleeping turned out to be impossible. Danny called her at close to midnight to brief her on the spot with the Jorgensens. They had agreed to be on the show, but wouldn't speak to a writer for the standard pre-interview. "I can fill you in on the background and suggest some questions," Danny said.

As Jackie took notes, she tried to put aside her earlier reservations about having them on the air, but she couldn't convince herself that this was anything but exploitation. Jonas Jorgensen, the son, was thirty-five, had moved to the United States to get married. His parents hadn't been happy about it. About a year ago, the mother died and the father came to visit them and make peace. He stayed on, since he had no other family in Finland except the sister, who was now sick.

"One heartbreak after another," Danny said happily. "Great human stuff. I know you'll do a fabulous interview with it. By the way, I almost didn't get them, because they were going to try to get permission to go to Leningrad to be with the dad. But he died a couple of hours ago. You heard that, didn't you?"

"No. I'm sorry."

"So were they. But at least they're staying around. And I made a deal with the booker from the *Today* show that she could have them as soon as we're done. She said okay, but I don't trust her. I think she's going to try to steal them in the morning to get them first. She's clever. She once went in a limo to a guest I'd booked, told him she was from *A.M. Reports,* and took him to the *Today* show. He was on the air before he figured out what had happened."

"Well, hang in there, Danny." She hung up, reflecting on how excited Danny sounded. To the bookers—in fact, to most of the media—these weren't people, they were A Story. And it was the story that mattered. She wasn't sure why it was so important who got a guest or story on the air first, but it was. News careers were made or broken on that basis.

She had trouble getting back to sleep, but finally dozed off, only to be wakened what seemed minutes later by her alarm clock. She shook off her grogginess and rushed to the studio. Cawley was in the same clothes he'd been in the day before, as were several other people on the staff. Jackie looked at the rundown for the show. She was interviewing the Jorgensens, the panel of worried relatives and friends that Laurie Spinner had put together, and an expert on Soviet foreign policy. She took the scripts that were ready, went to the makeup room, and tried to catch up on the story while Reuben and Barry got her hair and makeup ready for the air.

The show went smoothly, and Jackie had the heady sense of being in the midst of important world events. This is why people get involved in news reporting, she thought in a flash, while she sat out of camera range watching Bradley interview someone from the State Department. You feel that you are the news, not just reporting it.

Her interview with the Jorgensens went well. Jackie hated herself for manipulating them, but was surprised at how easy it was. She began to feel like a master surgeon, so skilled at handling a knife that she could get to the core of the problem in a few deft strokes. After just two questions, the lovely Mrs. Jorgensen had tears glistening in her eyes, and her husband reached over to take her hand. It was the kind of warm moment that would definitely play in Peoria.

That day in the office was a repeat of the previous one. Nobody dared leave, for fear that something would break suddenly. They scurried for guests and information. The Soviets still hadn't issued a statement condemning the hijacking, and there were more and more indications that it was the work of a Soviet agent. Reports claimed that the Soviets were expressing sympathy for the hijacker, willing to give him amnesty. At the end of the day, Jackie saw a sign on Danny Marks' office: "Day #2, Bookers Held Hostage." At least they were keeping a sense of humor.

Again Jackie slept little, forgot even to call Julian. She was so tired she was on a high, as if she had been sniffing cocaine for the last two days. But it was simply her own body keeping up a constant surging of adrenalin. By four on Friday morning she was in the studio, reading updated reports and preparing for the show.

"You're taking this seriously," Bradley said as they sat down for the opening shot, a few moments before seven.

She looked at him in surprise. "How else could I handle it? It's serious stuff."

"There are those who would just take their scripts and leave it at that."

The decision had been made to devote the entire show again to the hostage crisis. Jackie wondered briefly if television had the power to enlarge a crisis—at least in people's minds—by focusing on it so intently. Is this all anybody is talking about, or all we're talking about? she wondered. Cawley had cynically said that it was a good time for a crisis—there hadn't been one in a while, and people were hungry for a big story. The overnight ratings for the show had been high, so whatever their motives, people were watching.

Their expert on Soviet foreign policy returned, and Jackie was to interview him again to get his latest reactions. It wasn't easy unraveling this puzzle.

At eight-forty-five in the morning, halfway through her interview, the show was interrupted for a special news bulletin. They cut live to Tom Haskell, the network news correspondent stationed in Russia. He was wearing a trench coat, standing on the edge of the airport runway. *"The hijacking drama appears to be at an end,"* he said excitedly. *"Soviet officials agreed about an hour ago to meet with the hijacker. When he opened the door to let them on the plane, sharpshooters opened fire, apparently killing the hijacker. No word of any casualties among the passengers. Soviet officials now report that they condemn the hijacking and that it was apparently the work of a crazed man acting alone. There's pandemonium at the scene."*

Jackie listened to the news report, tried to decide what it meant. "We're cutting back to you and your guest," said Cawley's voice in her earphone. "Can you handle it?"

"I'll try."

The red light on camera two flashed on, and she knew she was back on the air.

"Mr. Seratov, we're lucky that you're still with us now, to help us understand that report," Jackie said to her guest. "Should we gather from this that earlier suggestions that the Soviets were in sympathy with the hijacker were simply a way of tricking him?"

Her guest, Mr. Seratov, a portly and erudite man, chuckled. "Very smart observation, Ms. Rogers. Like you, I would assume the Soviets used their powerful propaganda machine to convince the hijacker of their sympathy. If this now ends quickly and smoothly—as it appears it may—world opinion will certainly be with them."

She asked several more questions, then, at a signal from the stage manager, thanked her guest and said good-bye. They broke for commercial, and Jackie heard Cawley's voice in her ear again. "You were fabulous, kid. Some interview. We're going to skip the last segment, and have you and Bradley sit together for . . . wait . . . four minutes, eight seconds, summing up what's happened the last two days."

Bradley appeared almost immediately, sat down next to her on the sofa. She tried to gather her thoughts. Four minutes was an eternity of air time. Especially when it was unscripted. What were they going to say?

Bradley began by recapping the events of the last forty-eight hours, the political puzzles that were just now beginning to be answered. Jackie spent a moment dwelling on the human side.

"What is so frightening is how easily any of us can become pawns of a world situation," she said, looking straight into the camera and the bright lights. "Most of us may breathe easier now, knowing that this was the work of a lone, crazed individual and not a sign of imminent global unrest. But I'm not sure that means much to the Jorgensens, the family we met yesterday. World politics may go on now, but their life as a family is forever changed. As are the lives of the two hundred people who sat on that plane, unsure if they would be alive or dead this morning."

Bradley looked at her sagely, nodded. "Our lives are also changed."

"We're more tired than we were forty-eight hours ago," Jackie agreed, lightly.

"And maybe more understanding of Soviet-American politics."

The stage manager signaled thirty seconds left.

"I'm glad you were with me this week, Jackie. I can't think of a better partner to have in a crisis."

"It was my pleasure." She smiled at Bradley, hoping camera two would catch her good profile.

They previewed events and interviews scheduled for the following week, and the big overhead lights dimmed as credits rolled. Off the air. Bradley kissed Jackie, congratulating her on a show well done. Cawley raced out of the control room and did the same. There was a lot of back-patting and chatter, but then, in a few minutes, the studio was almost empty.

Jackie looked around, suddenly aware of her fatigue. She felt a curious emptiness. Her week as co-host was over, and she had been nothing short of stellar. But what did that mean? Nobody was handing her a contract for Darlie's job, and she hadn't really been expecting that they would. What she needed to do now was sleep, and sort it through when she was more alert.

A limo was waiting for her, as there had been all week. The small advantages of being a star. Nice to have my own limo instead of Julian's, she thought sliding into the seat. Julian. She had missed him this week. There was a chance he hadn't left for work yet this morning. Even if he had, she could just sleep the day away there, let him find her, sleeping naked in his bed, when he came home at night. She smiled to herself. It would be a nice way to end the week.

She gave the limo driver Julian's address, and when he pulled into the huge circular driveway, the doorman was at her door immediately.

"We've all been watching you this week, Miss Rogers," he said. "It certainly brightens the morning."

"That's very nice of you, thank you." She wondered if Bradley and Darlie still enjoyed hearing compliments, or if they had been at their jobs long enough to be jaded about them.

Vera opened the door to Julian's apartment. "You just missed him," she said. "He left about fifteen minutes ago to go to his office."

"Oh well," said Jackie. For some reason, Vera seemed to be planted in the doorway, not welcoming her in. "If you don't mind, I think I'll come in and make myself a cup of coffee. I don't have the energy to head home right now."

"Suit yourself. Not up to me to mind." Vera looked worried and walked away before Jackie had quite closed the door. Jackie ambled into the kitchen, and suddenly understood Vera's discomfort. Marianne was sitting at the breakfast table, wearing a violet Bill Blass robe and smoking a cigarette. *The New York Times* was propped open in front of her, and she was holding a half-empty mug of coffee. Jackie stopped, stunned. She didn't have time to compose her face before Marianne looked up. Her hair was a tumble of uncombed curls, and she had the slightly bleary-eyed look of someone who has just woken up. She took a deep puff on her cigarette and carefully blew the smoke away from Jackie.

"You're certainly the glowing young professional this morning," Marianne said.

Jackie wondered how she could be glowing when she felt as if all the blood had been drained from her body. "I was on the air this morning," she said, irritated that she was bothering to explain herself.

"How lovely for you." The venom Marianne had exuded in her previous meetings with Jackie was gone, replaced by a contemptuous calm. Marianne stubbed out her cigarette, a disdainful smile on her face. "You must be very committed to your work."

"I am," Jackie snapped.

"That's good, I suppose. But it means you miss a lot. Think of poor Julian. You can't really expect to leave him alone, can you?"

Jackie heard what Marianne was trying to tell her. She wanted to leave, but felt immobilized. "How's Feodor?" she asked, for lack of any other tack to take.

Marianne lit another cigarette. "He's fabulous. But having one man is like having one orgasm, isn't it? Just not enough."

Jackie felt a wave of revulsion, and a wild anger rising. "What are you doing here, anyway?" she asked, practically screaming, unable to control herself.

Marianne laughed, a shrill staccato laugh, and tightened her bathrobe around her very apparent cleavage. "Really, dear, use your imagination."

Then Jackie did leave, quickly, with a mumbled good-bye. Marianne called after her, "Sure you can't stay for coffee?" but she didn't bother to answer, just ran out, letting Marianne finish her coffee in triumph.

Jackie tried to calm down in the cab home, but she couldn't—she was shaking with anger and fatigue, reliving the scene, thinking what she should have said to puncture Marianne's disdain. But it wouldn't have mattered, because the point wasn't Marianne, it was Julian.

Jackie paid the cab driver and stumbled up to her apartment. She undressed quickly, then spent a long time washing her face, hoping the fragrant suds from the rose soap she kept in her bathroom would be comforting. As she splashed warm water on her face, she was surprised that she didn't even feel like crying. Maybe she was too tired, or maybe the thrill of the week on the air was still supporting her ego. God was always making unfair deals with her. *You can be co-host of a network television show for a week, but the man you love is going to screw his ex-wife at the end of it, okay?* No, not okay. She toweled off her face, wondering if she would have taken the deal, had it been offered ahead of time. Damn, this wasn't fair. Too reminiscent of Alden. Love shouldn't need your total attention to work.

She lay down on her bed, trying to think it through. Of course, there were explanations other than the one Marianne implied. Julian's apartment had half a dozen bedrooms—so there was no particular reason to think that Julian and Marianne had been in the same one. Julian often stayed—innocently—at Saddle River, so why couldn't Marianne visit the penthouse? Perhaps she'd been on a date last night in the city—not with Feodor or she would have stayed with him—and decided it was too late to go home. Julian was generous, they were still cordial to one another, so why not use a room in his apartment?

A comforting theory, but simply not true. She knew that with a conviction she simply couldn't explain. Marianne had been gloating when Jackie walked in. She was delighted to be caught fresh from Julian's bed, the scent of passion still clinging to her thighs.

It didn't make sense. Julian was the one who had brought up loyalty and commitment, convinced her that their relationship should be exclusive. It was what *he* wanted, insisted upon. So what had happened now? Was he just recoiling from having made that commitment, reacting with typically male fear that she would get too close?

She closed her eyes, but knew she wasn't going to sleep. She stared at the ceiling, thinking about Julian, trying to find the scenario that fit all the pieces together. There wasn't one. The puzzle remained in a million pieces.

She jumped off the bed, called Julian, and asked if they could have lunch. He seemed surprised, but agreed.

"Everything okay?" he asked.

"Fine. But there are a couple of things I need to talk about, and I'll probably be too tired by tonight."

"Come to my office whenever you want. I'll have lunch sent up."

Beardsley Enterprises was on the eighty-ninth floor of the World Trade Center, and the elevator ride up made Jackie feel sick. It occurred to her that Julian spent most of his time on one lofty perch or another, looking down on the rest of the world. His feet almost never touched the ground. She watched the numbers on the elevator click relentlessly upward, and realized that Julian didn't play by anyone else's rules. He didn't have to, and she probably wouldn't be as enthralled with him if he did. It was a classic situation; she had fallen in love with him because he was an original, had his own spirit and sense of morality. And now that very spirit was upsetting her. She felt a little like the women who write to Ann Landers: *I married him because he has a sense of adventure, and now it drives me crazy that he can't remember to pick up his socks.*

She found Julian in the trading room, presiding over the noise and chaos of two dozen traders, each screaming into two telephones, furiously punching numbers into the computers on their desks and shouting instructions to one another across the room. It looked more like a control room at NASA than a center of business. Julian waved when he saw Jackie, patted one of the traders on the back, and walked over to her. His hair was wild, and his eyes were gleaming behind the glasses he sometimes wore. It suddenly seemed childish to take him away from this financial orgy in order to discuss whether or not he had slept with his ex-wife.

As they walked into his office, Jackie decided to be direct—telling Julian she had gone to his apartment after the show and been greeted by a contemptuous Marianne. It was embarrassing, and she wanted to know where she stood.

"Where you stand?" Julian looked genuinely puzzled. "You know I love you. What else can I possibly tell you?"

"Whether you slept with Marianne last night."

"That was blunt." Julian laughed, and went over to stroke her head. "I'll be glad to answer you, but what difference does it make? I was married to the woman for seventeen years. We've had two children together. It must have occurred to you before this that we slept together."

"But you're divorced now." She sounded petulant even to herself.

"Of course we are. But we're still family. We've got ties that don't break that easily."

"Sexual ones?"

"Those are the least important."

Jackie stood up, walked over to the window. She wondered what it would be like to jump from the eighty-ninth floor. Would you die before you hit ground, or would you have the long trip down to reconsider, knowing it was too late to do anything but feel the earth's doom rushing up to meet you? Shaking herself, she turned back to Julian. "I don't understand what you're telling me. That you're still in love with Marianne?"

"I'm trying to tell you that my relationship with Marianne has nothing to do with my relationship with you. You might as well be jealous of my business as of Marianne. They're both staples in my life, and they won't go away. I've always considered you very special because you seemed to understand that. You don't want to give up everything else in your life for a relationship—no matter how important it is—and I don't think you expect me to either."

"Of course I don't, Julian. But I felt like the little cutie in all those thirties movies, coming up against Tallulah Bankhead. I'd just like to know whether or not she had the right to be so arrogant this morning."

"Nobody has the right to be arrogant, but Marianne has made an art of it."

"For Christ's sake, just give me an answer. Whose bed was she in last night?"

"Mine."

"Thank you."

There was silence for a moment. Jackie felt her lower lip starting to quiver, but bit it hard. She was not going to cry. Julian came over, kissed the corner of her lip, cupped his hands around her face. "You understand that it doesn't mean anything. Nothing has changed between you and me. I love you."

"You have a lousy way of showing it."

"You're not in competition with Marianne."

Jackie pulled away, slammed her hand against the back of a chair. "Goddamn it, Julian, you slept with another woman after you promised you wouldn't. I don't care that she's your ex-wife, I'm hurt. It was a rotten thing to do."

"You're taking this more personally than you should," he said, still calm.

"I consider sex rather personal, don't you?" She knew her eyes were blazing, her voice seething with contempt.

Julian shrugged. "I'm puzzled, Jackie. You're my liberal, liberated woman. You want to have a tough career and play by a whole set of new rules. I thought you'd just laugh about Marianne."

Jackie glared at him, felt her fists tightening at her sides, tried to control her anger. "That's nothing but stupidity, Julian. What does my career have to do with your lying? Being liberated doesn't mean being abused—it means you don't have to stand around and take crap from a man anymore." She turned on her heel and walked quickly out of his office, resisting the urge to slam the door.

15

Jackie finally slept: Friday night and half of Saturday, alone in her apartment. When she woke up, it was close to noon, and she went out to the kitchen, made some toast, cut up a grapefruit, and brought them back to her bed. She ate slowly, flipping through an old copy of *Town & Country* that was on her night table, and tried to decide what to do for the rest of the day, other than think angrily about Julian.

She didn't know whether his bedding Marianne had been an aberration, a single unexpected night of falling back into old habits, or standard fare for them. She didn't much care. It wasn't the sex that rankled as much as the embarrassment. Infidelity was a secret that wasn't shared, an exclusion of trust. It meant your lover kept part of his soul to himself. Instead of being central to Julian's life, she was on the outside looking in. Her faith in their bond was shattered.

She lay back down in bed and let herself drift off to sleep again, but her dreams were filled with anxiety. She woke up once or twice and willed herself back to sleep. All in all, her dreams were better than her thoughts.

She was finally awakened for good in the late afternoon by the persistent ringing of the doorbell.

"Who is it?" she asked grumpily.

"Dana. Can I come in?"

Pulling on a robe, she wondered why the doorman hadn't called first. Typical of Dana, she had probably just smiled and sauntered past him. Jackie opened the door, and Dana hurried into the apartment. "Are you okay?" she asked.

"Of course."

"You had me worried." Dana sank into the Eames chair by

218

the window. "Your phone's been busy all day, and I finally had an operator confirm it was off the hook."

"I took it off the hook to get a little sleep. Thanks for the concern, but I'm fine."

Dana looked at her carefully. "Then why are you in a bathrobe at four in the afternoon?"

"I had a big week. Just resting."

"Save the bullshit for Julian," said Dana. "Your eyes are red, your face is puffy, and you look like hell. And the only reason you'd ever take your phone off the hook would be to avoid someone's call. What's going on?"

Jackie started to contradict her then bit her lip. She needed to tell. "Ready for an awful story?"

"Of course."

She relayed the tale of Julian and Marianne, and was surprised by her own lack of emotion in the telling. As soon as she finished, she felt an enormous sense of relief, as if the story couldn't hurt her anymore, once it was shared with her best friend.

Dana didn't say anything when Jackie stopped talking, just came over and hugged her tightly. "That's awful," she said finally. "I know you're being calm and noble, but you must feel like stringing him up by his balls."

"Such thoughts have crossed my mind."

"What are you going to do?"

"That's the whole thing—what *can* I do? It's not as if I've lost him. I have as much of him as anyone is likely to get. But he's a man of appetites, Dana. He gets his thrills from handling millions of dollars and making hundreds of trades, and he doesn't understand boundaries. He wants endless money and endless sex and no limits on anything."

Dana frowned. "Brilliant analysis, Jackie, but he was the one who wanted loyalty and faithfulness, as I recall—and the fact is, the relationship isn't going to be the same anymore. Either you'll sleep with someone else to get back at him, or you'll break the whole thing off. You need some constructive way of getting rid of the anger. Then you can get on with your life, with or without him."

"What constructive activity did you have in mind—racquetball?"

Dana laughed, disappeared into the kitchen for a moment and

came back with two Diet Cokes. "Are you up for discussing Julian's manipulative brain as well as his wandering pelvis?"

"Mmm. What's going on?"

"A lot. And since I found today's *Times* sitting unopened outside your door, I suspect you don't know that the price of silver went up six dollars an ounce yesterday."

"Is that significant?"

Dana stared at her. "You amaze me. The price of silver usually fluctuates by pennies. A dollar is drama. A six-dollar rise, on top of the three dollars that occurred the day before, is major stuff. Millions—no, probably billions—are being made and lost, and nobody outside the market is really paying attention."

Jackie nodded, trying to understand the full implications of what Dana was saying. A six-dollar rise yesterday, when she had interrupted Julian in the trading room to discuss Marianne. Well, he had seemed to be on a particular business high.

Dana sipped her soda, put it down carefully. "Shall I spell it out for you?"

"Please."

"Something is up in the silver market, as I've hinted before. May I suggest you do an investigative report for *A.M. Reports* on just what that is? Look, if the stock market doubled, and the Dow Jones average went from two thousand points to four thousand points in a couple of days, the media would be going crazy. Virtually the same thing is happening in the silver market, but you newsies don't really understand silver, so it gets ignored." Dana cleared her throat. "I'm sure Julian wouldn't object. I mean, he cares about your career, and a good investigative piece would surely help you get the Darlie Hayes job, wouldn't it?"

"Not necessarily, but I hear what you're saying. Is this what you're recommending for my anger instead of racquetball?"

"You have to admit, it would be more fun."

"Of course it would. I hate racquetball."

Jackie arrived in El Paso, Texas, the cowboy-boot capital of the world, on what she decided was the hottest day of the year. She felt a burst of irritation at Cawley for having sent her.

"It will be a great spot for the fashion-week series," he had said, sending her off. "Boots with rhinestones. The most expensive boots in the world. That kind of thing. People love to see it."

Darlie, meanwhile, was off doing interviews with Calvin Klein and Ralph Lauren. Jackie made it quite clear to Cawley that the boot assignment was a mistake—and she would be better than Darlie at handling the big interviews.

"Should I guess that you enjoyed sitting in that co-anchor chair last week?" Cawley asked.

"Very much so. And I think I did a good job of it."

"You did, and you know I'd like you to be there permanently. But that's off the record. On the record, Darlie is still in contract negotiations with Axminster and company. They're the ones who are going to make the decisions, not me."

Jeff had arrived in El Paso the day before to scout locations, and in the cab going to the hotel, Jackie admitted to herself that being with him would be the only saving grace of the trip. A young Mexican man checked her into the tacky hotel, and the moment she saw her room, she rushed back to the front desk. "I was supposed to have a suite," she said. "Could you please send someone up to help me change rooms?"

"You have a suite, ma'am," said the young Mexican receptionist. "Room 724 is the best room in the hotel."

"A suite usually has two rooms."

"Yes, ma'am. The second room is on the other side of the bathroom. Perhaps you didn't see it."

She'd seen it, all right, but thought it was a walk-in closet. Realizing that there was no sense arguing, she shrugged and walked away. She was hanging up her clothes in the tiny closet when Jeff knocked on her door. "Everything okay?" he asked, coming in.

"Oh, wonderful. My air conditioner knocks, my shower is big enough for a Barbie doll, and I have a view of smokestacks."

Jeff walked over to the window. "Actually, I think that's a view of Mexico."

"So I have a view of Mexican smokestacks. Culturally enriching."

"You bet." He glanced at her and smiled. "I suppose if I say something like, 'You're beautiful when you're angry,' I'll get thrown out?"

"Immediately." Jackie laughed, felt her annoyance seeping away. Being around Jeff made her feel calm and happy lately. She sighed. "What am I doing wrong? I'm trying to be a prima donna, but my temper tantrums don't seem to last long enough. I have a feeling that if Darlie were here, she'd get a new hotel built for the night."

Jeff grinned. "Think of me, here for twenty-four hours already, and I don't even have a suite. But I've been to five boot factories and eight stores. Would you like to know the differences between Tony Lama, Larry Manhan, and Justine boots?"

"Only if I have to."

"Oh, you'll have to. According to my schedule, we're due at the Tony Lama factory in twenty minutes to get some background beauty shots and talk to the guy you'll be interviewing on the live spot tomorrow. Are you ready?"

"If you're taking me, I'm ready."

"I won't leave you for a minute."

"Just what I like to hear."

Jeff put his arm around her, kissed her on the cheek. "Didn't I warn you once about flirting with me?"

"Maybe I've decided I like the consequences."

They went downstairs, climbed into the car Jeff had rented—a red Ford with a small dent in the side. "Nothing nicer was available in El Paso," he said, "but at least it has air conditioning." The temperature was over a hundred degrees and the sun beat down unrelenting from the cloudless sky. Jackie, looking out the window as Jeff drove, noticed scraggly cactuses growing, and teenagers on dune bikes zipping by on the sandy hills along one side of the road. The sand flew from beneath their tires, making dusty arcs on the road.

"That's got to be dangerous as all hell," Jackie said, pointing the teenagers out to Jeff, "but I guess there's not much else to do in El Paso."

They stopped at the boot store Jeff had picked as the location for the remote. It was perfect: boxes of boots everywhere, garish displays of exotic and brightly colored styles. The man Jackie would be interviewing was waiting for them at the door, dressed in western shirt, string tie, and pointy-toed black alligator boots. He offered a hearty handshake, and Jackie tried not to smile when he introduced himself as Tex. He gave them a tour of the store, explaining the different boot styles on display. Jackie decided there wasn't one she would ever wear.

"I just figured out why Texas men always seem so tall." Jackie picked up a man's tan ostrich boot and turned it over. "Those boots have big heels, much higher than eastern men would wear."

Tex, who must have been a foot taller than Jackie, beamed down at her. "Well, now, that's right. But the boots just give an extra inch or two to the fine work God already created."

He showed her a pair of boots intricately sewn with diamonds and rubies and explained they'd had dozens of offers to buy them—but they weren't for sale.

Despite her intentions, Jackie found herself getting involved in the story. As usual, Cawley's instincts had been right. People would step out of the bathroom while they were brushing their teeth in the morning to check out a pair of cowboy boots that were worth tens of thousands of dollars.

Jackie worked all afternoon, interviewing, collecting information, finding the high points in the story. Jeff was busy with the technical angles, deciding where the shadows from the sun would be in the morning, and whether the clickety-clacking from fifteen men and women modeling cowboy boots would disturb the audio feed.

When they were finished, they made arrangements to meet Tex before dawn the next day and escaped quickly from the store.

"That man is an unbearable example of that long-forgotten term, male chauvinist," said Jackie when they were rolling back to the hotel in Jeff's car. "He's arrogant—and not even good-looking."

"Would his chauvinism be more acceptable if he were handsome?"

"I might not notice it so much."

"This from my favorite feminist?"

"Nobody said feminists are blind."

Jeff tossed back his head and laughed, and a minute later, without explanation, turned off the main road, drove down a dirt street, and pulled to a stop.

"What are we doing?"

"Out of the car, as they say in westerns."

He got out and Jackie followed, stepping carefully through the cactus plants. Jeff sat down in the sand, looked up at the sky. "I was watching the sunset through my rear window and decided it was worth our full attention."

Jackie, following his gaze, caught her breath in amazement. The sky was a blaze of color, perfect lines of orange, purple, red. Like the fire in a Turner picture, she thought. Maybe Julian's son should come here.

Shaking her head to clear the thought, she sat down next to Jeff in companionable silence. "Amazing to just watch the sky," she murmured several minutes later. "What a show."

Jeff, sitting inches away, nodded, his face still turned to the sky. She thought how pleasant it would be to lean over and kiss his sensuous mouth, put her arms around his broad shoulders. Turning from the fire show in the sky, Jeff smiled at her. "A sunset like this really puts me in awe of nature," he said. "I start thinking about my small place in the world."

"Small but important."

"We're only important to the people we love, I'm afraid."

On the way back to the car, they discussed dinner. Jeff was in favor of going to Juárez, Mexico, across the border over the Rio Grande, about twenty minutes away. The town Jackie could see from her hotel window.

"Not a chance," she said. "I want to do my whole spot tomorrow morning without any signs of *turista*. I don't look good in green."

"And I suppose it's my job as producer to keep roses in your cheeks?"

"One of your most important jobs."

They went to a local Tex-Mex restaurant that had a romantic fountain splashing water. A wandering guitarist regaled them with two songs in Spanish. "Think you'd get that in Juárez?" Jackie asked when the guitarist walked away.

"You're right," said Jeff. "Romance is more important than food. At least when I'm with you." He reached his hand across the table, and Jackie covered it with her own—a small gesture, but as Jeff looked at her, she felt her heart pounding against her chest. He squeezed her hand, then pulled his own away, and Jackie was amazed at the flood of desire that he unleashed in her.

The frozen margaritas were heavy with tequila, the glasses frosted in salt. Jackie licked the salt from the rim, sipped the thick drink thoughtfully. They dug into the piles of fajitas and chimichangas and guacamole the waiter kept putting in front of them. The food was good and authentic, and Jackie noticed that there were no refried beans on the plate. She smiled to herself, recalling Dana's refusal to eat at Mexican restaurants in Manhattan on the grounds that a Wall Street lawyer shouldn't have to eat peasant food. "Like those beans that they cook half a dozen times," she once explained.

They finished the meal, Jeff picked up the bill, and laughed. "All we ate, and the whole thing was twenty-eight dollars. We'll have to make up for that on our next stop."

"What's that?"

"L.A. But I wasn't supposed to tell you until after your live spot."

"Fine. I don't really want to know."

They drove back to the hotel, Jackie awed by the dry heat and clear evening. She was quiet in the car, trying to think about her spot the next morning. But she kept glancing over at Jeff. The sky was flooded with stars, and she decided to wish on one, as she used to when she was a child. *Please let me know what to do,* she offered to the sky, more prayer than wish.

At the hotel, they took the elevator together to the fifth floor. Outside their doors, each fumbled for a key. Jackie turned around first, key in hand. "Come in for awhile?" she asked quietly.

Jeff nodded, pocketing his own key as she opened her door. Closing it firmly behind them, Jackie stood awkwardly by the door, thought of mentioning tomorrow's spot, making this a business meeting, but knew it wasn't.

Jeff noticed her embarrassment and smiled. "Should we have a nightcap?" he asked.

She laughed. "Ah, yes. That's what I'm supposed to offer you. Let's see, I have a warm bottle of seltzer, and I noticed a vending machine down the hall. What can I get you?"

"Nothing really." Jeff sat down on the sofa. "I'm just trying to figure out why it feels so improper being in your room tonight."

"Maybe it's the margaritas. Or maybe you have a sixth sense.

I . . ." She stopped, realizing that what she was going to say wasn't quite true, but decided to say it anyway. "Julian and I broke up." Jeff raised his eyebrows, and she decided to amend the comment. "At least we're having some hard times. I'm not sure we're going to stay together."

"I'm sorry."

"Don't be." She sat down next to him. "It just means I'm not sure of the ground rules with you anymore, and it's making me nervous."

Jeff reached over and stroked her cheek. "Don't be nervous. Just tell me what you want to do."

"I don't really know. But I don't want you to leave."

"That's good, because I don't want to. Let's try one step at a time." He kissed her lightly on the lips, then got up and turned down the air conditioner, which was clattering loudly and blowing drafts of frigid air. Jackie flipped on the television, changing channels until she found an old Fred Astaire movie. Jeff sat down again, and she curled up next to him. The movie would calm her down, ease the tension. She closed her eyes briefly. She was tired, after all.

A loud alarm clock woke her, and she sat up abruptly. Next to her in bed, Jeff was also stirring, looking bleary-eyed. The digital clock showed three-forty-five A.M., in red neon. It was the only light in the room. She was wearing a sleeveless silk nightgown; Jeff had slept in his jeans.

"Good morning," Jeff said. "Ready to rock-and-roll?"

"I'm ready to sleep."

"You've done that. For at least four hours."

She remembered their kissing the night before, deciding to watch the movie in bed. She had changed out of her clothes— but all she could remember after that was falling asleep.

"I think I missed the end of the movie," Jackie said.

"I know. And I couldn't bear to leave you. Anybody ever tell you how beautiful you are when you're sleeping?"

"Nobody. Anything happen I should know about?"

"In the movie or with us?"

"Either."

"Nothing. I stayed just to look at you."

"Tell the truth. You were afraid I'd never get up at this

ungodly hour if you weren't next to me." She kissed him on the cheek. "Sorry if it wasn't much fun sleeping with me."

"*Au contraire.* Just because I didn't take off my pants doesn't mean I didn't enjoy it."

Jeff went to his own room to change, promising to be back in twenty minutes. She showered and dressed quickly. A limousine— the only one in El Paso?—was waiting for them downstairs. They drove through the dark, silent streets. Jackie, feeling a deep sense of calm, reached over to hold Jeff's hand.

"You look pretty this morning," he said.

"It's too dark to see. But I'd say you put the roses back in my cheeks."

"Mmm. Wait until you see what I do next time."

It bothered Jackie that doing a live remote was beginning to be so mundane. Even this morning, when nothing seemed to be right. The hairdresser, a local woman they'd hired for the morning, had a curling iron but no blow dryer. Jackie thanked her, said she would do her own hair. The makeup man never showed, which Jackie decided was probably for the best. All the New York crews had been busy, so this one was from the network affiliate in Amarillo. Jackie watched Jeff showing them how to set up. He was clearly exasperated, but stayed calm. A few minutes before the live spot, she did a standard mike check, heard Joe Banks through her earphones. "Garth, I can't hear the mike. Double-check the mike setup." It turned out to be simple. The audio man hadn't plugged in his equipment.

They got through the spot, which seemed to go well, no apparent hitches. The models showed off their boots, Tex chatted amiably, and she talked glibly about Texas boot-mania. At the end, Jackie took off her earphones, thanked Tex and the others who had been on with her. They congratulated each other, filled with the high spirits that come once the tension of a live television appearance is over. It was a moment of glory, and nobody wanted to leave. Jackie finally excused herself to join Jeff, who had walked in from the control truck. He had his arms crossed over his chest and looked angry.

"Everything all right?" Jackie asked.

"Some technical errors with the tape we rolled in."

"I didn't have a monitor so I didn't see. What happened?"

"When I called for the tape, the idiot on the panel hit the wrong button, and it came on with fast forward."

"Oh God." She shrugged. "How long was it, five seconds of screw-up?"

"Worse." He grimaced. "You won't believe it when I tell you that he then made it rewind—on the air—to start it again from the top."

"Shit." Jackie rubbed her eyes. "Well, at least it wasn't your fault. You had this inexperienced crew to deal with."

"Tell me something I don't know. But do you expect Cawley to call up this kid from Amarillo and tell him never to work for us again? I take the shit for this, and it was already flying after the spot. Surprised you didn't hear it."

"I took off my earphones." Her high spirits plummeted when she realized that she would be tainted by the error, too. The general feeling would be that there had been a screw-up in the spot from El Paso. She hadn't done anything wrong, but her spot had been an embarrassment. You didn't always get the reflected glory in this business, but you always got the reflected disaster.

Jackie looked around at the crew members, who were busy unplugging wires and taking down lights. "Do you have to stay around while they finish, or can we get out of here?"

"Let's go," said Jeff. They said their good-byes to the various people in the boot store, walked out into the El Paso morning. It was barely seven o'clock El Paso time. The spot they had just done had already been seen on the East Coast, wouldn't be seen until eight-twenty A.M. local time. Jackie felt she'd already done a day's work, though the sky was barely light.

They took the limousine to a local diner for breakfast. The waitress recognized them at once from a spot about the network's visit that had been on the previous evening's local news. She told them breakfast was on the house, and brought them a huge pile of greasy doughnuts and watery eggs.

"So is it really on to L.A.?" Jackie asked, after eyeing the food and pushing it away.

"Yup. Cawley didn't have the heart to break it to you. Coming up next: An interview with Keesha Havens on how to put together the perfect wardrobe. It's on the day after tomorrow, as the wrap-up to fashion week."

"Forgive me if I don't know who Keesha Havens is."

"Don't you watch television? She's the sexy blonde on . . . Damn, I forget the name of it. One of those nighttime soaps."

"Ah, yes." Jackie grimaced. "Is there any real point to the spot, other than the obvious one of having Keesha wiggle around in various seductive outfits?"

"None." Jeff laughed, sipped at the coffee and made a face. "This is really rotten stuff. Let's get out of here."

They drove to the airport, grateful to leave El Paso. Jeff fell asleep on the plane at once; Jackie, sitting next to him, spent most of the flight to L.A. thumbing through *Newsweek* and staring out the window. Jeff would leave her at the airport, since he was meeting a crew and shooting some tape of Rodeo Drive, background shots he would feed to Cawley to be used as promos for the continuing fashion week.

"At least it's an L.A. crew," Jackie said cheerfully as they prepared to part at the airport. But Jeff looked glum; the morning's failure still rankled.

Jackie took a limo to the hotel where they were staying, an elegant place called L'Hermitage. It was slightly off the main track in Beverly Hills, but Jackie sensed the air of wealth as soon as she walked in. The small, decorous lobby was not a place to see and be seen—no meetings "taken" there. Her room was huge, with a fully stocked bar, elegant mirrored bathroom, and a large sitting area. The size compared favorably with most New York apartments she'd seen. Jackie grinned as she looked around the room, and decided that the expensive hotel, on the relatively quiet street, was the perfect hideaway for rich married men and their lovers. She flicked on the lights, noticed that one of the switches turned on the electric fire in the fireplace, laughed to herself, and turned it off. Truly a room made for romance.

There was a knock on her door, and a bellboy brought in a bottle of wine on a silver tray—"a small welcome from management," he said—and a large bouquet of roses. As soon as he left, she looked curiously at the attached card: "Thinking of you and missing you. Love, Julian." She wanted to feel moved, but all she could think about was the number of phone calls his secretary must have made to track her down at the hotel.

It bothered her that she hadn't been totally honest with Julian, and promised herself that she'd have a serious talk with him as soon as she got back to New York. She'd just have to figure out what she wanted to say—and even more, what she needed to hear. She still loved Julian, but she was becoming more and more involved with Jeff. Maybe she should try to back away from Jeff until she understood her motives better.

Jackie went up to the rooftop pool to swim, and stopped to look out over the L.A. hills from poolside. As she accepted a fluffy towel from a handsome, bronzed pool attendant, she noticed that there were no deck chairs in the open around the pool—they were all discreetly tucked into the enclosed private cabanas. She dived into the water and swam rapidly up and down the empty pool, wondering what illicit lovers were peeking out at her from their sunning cubicles.

She didn't see Jeff again until later that afternoon, and was glad that he seemed more cheerful than earlier in the day. They headed out to Keesha Havens' house in the black Porsche he'd rented. Quite a change from El Paso.

"Sparing no expense, are you?" Jackie asked.

"We're the number-one show, we can afford it. Besides, I think Cawley should see that you get treated like a star."

Keesha greeted them at the door wearing a very short dungaree skirt and a tight-fitting sleeveless black turtleneck. Her blonde hair tumbled down her back and her skin seemed to be made of porcelain. She was stunning, Jackie had to admit; maybe not a good actress, but a gorgeous one. Jackie, well-dressed and carefully made-up, felt suddenly frumpy in her presence.

The maid brought them herbal tea and crackers, and they all sat in the beachfront living room for a few minutes, chatting about the wardrobe tips that Keesha should offer.

"All Keesha knows about putting together a wardrobe is that you hire someone to do it," Jackie whispered to Jeff, when Keesha went off to the bathroom. "Thank God for Amy." Amy Davies, one of the writers on the show, had sent a suggested outline for the spot to Keesha. Jeff gave a copy to Jackie, but Keesha had already memorized it, was spouting the information as her own.

"At least she read it," Jeff whispered back. "But she seems really tense, and that means she won't be cooperative. We've got to get her to let down her guard."

When Keesha came back in, they continued their discussion, and Jackie noticed that Jeff was gently flirting with the actress. She responded, seemed to relax, and agreed to show them around the house to select sites for shooting. As soon as Keesha's back was turned, Jeff glanced at Jackie, rolled his eyes.

"Actually, I don't mind this spot at all," he said when they were back in the Porsche an hour later. "It's going to be fun."

"Fun for you," Jackie said. "You not only get to look at Keesha Havens, you get to flirt with her."

"Strictly a professional ploy."

"I realize that, but it worked. Something you use often?"

Jeff grinned. "Only in desperate circumstances. Any other questions?"

"Just one. Why did you agree to hire Jose Eber?" Before they'd left, Keesha had asked to have her own favorite hairdresser and makeup person on hand in the morning, and to Jackie's surprise, Jeff had agreed—even after he'd casually asked how much they charged and learned it was over a thousand dollars for each.

"Jose, the hairdresser to the stars? I thought it would be fun for you to have your hair done by him. Don't women like that kind of thing?"

Jackie laughed. "You sound ridiculous saying macho things, but yes, I'd love to see what Jose can do for me."

The red message light was on when Jackie got back to her room; Julian had called, left a message that he'd call later in the evening. What am I doing? she wondered, taking off her clothes and turning on the water in the tub. Dana was right, of course— maybe her anger at Julian was repressed, but it was still there, bubbling dangerously close to the surface. There was a reason she had always made herself invulnerable to men, kept away from commitments; she was not good at accepting hurt, had no way to deal with it except to run away. And what better place to run than Jeff's welcoming arms? she thought. No, that wasn't fair. Her feelings for Jeff were deeper than that. She wasn't looking for vengeance, she was looking for love, and Julian's actions made her realize that she might have been looking in the wrong direction.

Was Jeff the right direction? The longing in her chest said he was. Meanwhile, Jeff had suggested dinner at Ma Maison, and she was looking forward to it.

Lowering herself into the warm water, she reached for the fragrant soap that the hotel provided. The phone rang, and she noticed that she didn't have to get out of the tub to answer; there was an extension within arm's reach. True luxury.

"I've a better idea for dinner." It was Jeff on the other end, sounding cheerful.

"What's that?"

"Room service."

She giggled. "I usually get room service at breakfast."

"We'll do that, too."

"Let's go out, it's safer."

Jeff let out an audible sigh. "I don't know what to do about you, Jackie. Can I come to your room and talk it out?"

"I'm in the bath at the moment."

"All the better. I'll join you." He hung up quickly, and Jackie smiled into the phone, then jumped out of the tub, dried off, and put on the thick terry bathrobe that the hotel had left in her dressing room. A minute later, she opened the door to Jeff.

He had changed into khaki pants and a Lacoste T-shirt, and looked every inch the handsome L.A. producer. His hands were stuffed in his pockets.

"So tell me, am I being improper?"

"What do you mean?"

"Are you going to file a sexual-harassment charge against me for having stayed in your bed the other night, albeit fully clothed, or do you secretly like having your producer sleep with you?"

She laughed. "You get right to the point."

"A sign only of an undeceptive mind. I'm lousy at games, and if I know what you're thinking, I can't make any mistakes."

"That's fair. The answer is that I loved having you in my bed. Even though we didn't exactly sleep together in the colloquial sense."

"Ah, yes. I noticed that. And I'd be glad to make up for it. But I don't want you to feel like I'm pushing, moving in on you when Julian's body is still warm."

"Very warm," Jackie admitted. "I'm sorry if I'm sending mixed signals. It's just that my head is a little mixed, too."

"Understood," Jeff said. "I take it you're looking for no-strings affection?"

"Mmm. Is that awful?"

"Not a bit. I could use some myself, frankly—lots of affection and kindness but no expectations."

"And nobody getting hurt."

"Got it. Now, just tell me if I can kiss you right this minute. You look very dewy and seductive when you come out of a bath."

For an answer, she took a step closer, turned her face toward his. He wrapped his arms around her, drew her close. They kissed deeply and languorously, holding each other tightly. His kiss was different from what she would have expected, softer and more sensual, and she felt herself yielding to him, wanting him desperately. They seemed to have been kissing forever when his hands finally disappeared under her bathrobe, and his firm touch on her bare, moist skin made her tremble.

"This body feels wonderful," he murmured, his hands moving slowly across her torso, exploring breasts and waist.

She closed her eyes, sighed. "I've dreamed about what this would be like."

"So have I," Jeff said. "Now it's real."

He took her hand, led her to the bed. As she lay back, he sat close, fully clothed, gently caressing her. "You're exquisite," he said. "Just let me look at you."

"I'd rather have you hold me."

"Mmm, in time. But first I want to feel these breasts, so firm, your nipples so beautiful . . ." He touched them lightly, both hands gliding over her, admiring. "Then your tiny waist, this flat, flat stomach, and this right here—ah, the glorious curve of your hip." As he stroked her hip he added, "I want to know every inch of this body."

"It's yours to know."

"Good. I'll take my time making its acquaintance."

He stretched out beside her and she unbuttoned his shirt, ran her fingers across his strong chest. He moved on top of her, their bodies touching at every point. From under his khakis, she felt the rising power of his seduction and reached to unbuckle his belt.

"Not yet," he said. "I want to delight in you first." He slipped the opened robe off her shoulders, then reached down to stroke her thighs, kiss the backs of her knees until she felt devoured by his attention. He moved slowly and sensuously, and an ache of wanting built in her body. She murmured for him to come to her, but he persisted in his tantalizing devotion, bringing her to the brink of pleasure over and over, until finally her desire overwhelmed both of them and her body exploded in pleasure. Her legs wrapped around him, she rocked uncontrollably, calling his name, clutching him. When finally the rapture slowed, he held her tightly, whispering the bliss he felt with her. The intoxication of his words aroused her again, and now when she asked, he let her slowly remove his belt, his pants. She was amazed by the glory of his body, uttered a sharp intake of breath. He grinned and lay down next to her, pulling her closer and closer until the division between them was gone and she felt him a part of her, deep inside. She moaned, felt her pleasure rising, and this time her release was at one with his, made all the more powerful by the intensity of sharing.

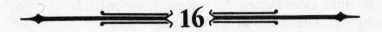

16

Moving carefully, Dominique carried a cup of weak tea into her living room and let her newly heavy body sink into the sofa. The heft of pregnancy made her feel unbalanced, and some of the tea sloshed into the saucer as she sat down, a few drops splattering onto the silk sofa. Dominique decided not to get up to clean it; these would be the first drops of her new lifestyle. In a few months, she imagined, there would be baby bottles and spittle all over her peach-and-cream apartment. Was it time to start thinking about slipcovers?

As she sipped the tea, she tried to decide if the day had been better or worse than she had expected. Probably both, since it had been a roller coaster from the start. Jackie had kept Dominique's secret well for these many weeks, and Dominique was grateful. But yesterday Jackie had suggested that it was time to admit the truth, face the world, and Dominique knew she was right. Her skirts were all being held together by safety pins and a prayer. She had gained slightly more weight than she'd planned, but she didn't really mind. There was a fullness about her body that matched her spirit, a sense of wholeness she'd gathered ever since she made the decision to accept the baby. She would have been happy to keep the baby as her secret forever, but Jackie quietly told her that people around the studio were already beginning to notice the change in her appearance. She thought she was hiding it well by wearing fuller tops and shorter skirts; a fine deception, but apparently it was no longer enough.

She'd been turning down assignments in a way she had never dreamed she could, starting with the decision of three months ago not to fill in for Darlie. Then the rumor started that Darlie wasn't being given a new contract—the network refused to meet her demands—and Jackie had come over to her apartment to discuss it with her.

"From what my agent says, they want you for co-anchor," Jackie told Dominique, "but nobody understands why you're becoming less and less of a presence."

"They'll understand soon enough."

Jackie insisted that the co-anchor spot could still go to Dominique, would go to Dominique, if the baby situation, as she called it, were handled well.

"I don't want it," Dominique said. "It's the wrong time in my life." She smiled at Jackie. "Take it when it's offered, and don't feel guilty."

It was hard to understand that the tiny being in her tummy could change her whole perspective on life. Change her priorities, anyway. She still wanted to work, wanted her career, but some of the driving edge was gone.

So this morning she had asked Steve Cawley if he had a minute to talk. Jackie had advised her to be positive, not apologetic, and that's exactly what she was.

"I've got good news," she told him, smiling brightly.

Behind his desk, looking typically rumpled and bedraggled, he had looked up. "I could use some." She had wanted to change the subject, ask him if something was wrong, see how she could help. Stick to the point, she told herself.

"I'm pregnant," she said, trying to keep a broad smile on her face. "I'm due in about four months, and I expect to work right to the end." She took a deep breath. *Keep going and he can't interrupt.* "I'd like six weeks of maternity leave, and then I'll be back. I hope we can work it out so there's not much interruption in my presence on the air."

She sat back, looked at Cawley's shocked face. His surprise was almost palpable. "Well, congratulations," he said finally. He stood up, rubbed the back of his head with his palm. "It's not exactly the great news I was expecting, but . . . you're happy?"

"Very much so."

"It's funny—someone in the control room the other day was complaining about the clothes you've been wearing lately. Saying you don't look as sexy as you used to. I guess that's the reason."

Dominique smiled feebly. "I guess. I thought I could get away with wearing loose tops without anyone noticing. But it's getting to that point."

"Well, I wish you luck," said Cawley. He was nearly white with restraint, trying not to ask the obvious questions about the father and marriage. Finally, he cleared his throat and said, "I don't see any problem with the maternity leave and all that. In fact, I'll personally clear it. Have you thought about how you want to make the public announcement?"

"I haven't really. Any suggestions?"

"Nope. I'll ask Kalina what she thinks."

"Thanks." She stood up. "I appreciate your support."

"Have you told Bradley yet?"

"No, he's my next stop." She winked at him. "You've given me courage, and I appreciate it."

She was practically flying when she left Cawley's office, thrilled that he hadn't pressed about any personal issues, hadn't made a big deal about it at all. Maybe she had built it up more than anyone else would. Kalina would handle it, make the announcement, and life would go on.

But Dominique's comfort was short-lived. She told Bradley James as cheerfully as she had told Cawley, but Bradley just stared and asked who the father was.

"I'm not really discussing that," she said, trying to keep her tone light.

"Are you getting married?"

"Not at the moment." Don't be defensive, she told herself, but it didn't matter. Bradley's eyes had already narrowed; he looked like an angry minister preaching about evil to his flock.

"You don't expect to stay on the air, I assume."

"Actually, I was hoping to. Cawley didn't think there'd be a problem, and neither does my doctor."

"There is a problem. Very much of one." His voice was angry and he moved to the front of his desk, sat down on the edge, looming over her. "You're not married, and you are pregnant— and that's not something we can condone on this show. We do spots all the time about having responsible sex. Preventing teenage pregnancy. Keeping you on the air would be totally hypocritical."

"This isn't exactly a teenage pregnancy," Dominique said. But the feeble joke didn't get any measure of a smile. Bradley just moved behind his desk again, sat down in his chair. "I'm sorry I can't support you on this, Dominique. You know I've always liked you personally. But this is bigger than a personal issue, and I'm not sure you've thought about that."

"There's been a lot to think about."

Bradley drummed his fingers on the desk, his face creased in a deep frown. "God dammit, Dominique, this was a stupid thing to do. Frankly, I feel personally hurt by it. I've been pushing for you and your career. In case you weren't aware of it, I've been behind you all the way to replace Darlie Hayes. Now you make it impossible."

She couldn't believe that Bradley was taking her pregnancy as a personal affront. She tried to change the tone, tell him how pleased she was about becoming a mother, that she knew it would be everything his wife, Lacy, had always said. But there was no way to break through his narcissistic anger.

"I'm disappointed in you, Dominique, that's all I can say. Very disappointed."

She walked quickly out of his office, trying not to feel like a naughty sixteen-year-old caught losing her virginity. She went immediately to Raleigh's office, totally obsessed now with telling everyone, collecting all the reactions. Raleigh, hurt that she hadn't confided in her sooner, told Dominique that she had guessed her secret weeks ago.

"It's what you get for screwing around with men," Raleigh said. "I've been trying to tell you to stay clear."

"I didn't listen," Dominique said, laughing. "And I don't regret it. I just regret not listening to you when you tried to tell me how callow Peter really is."

"You learned the hard way?"

Dominique nodded.

Raleigh stepped behind her, leaned down to rub Dominique's shoulders. "Don't regret anything, sweetheart. He's the father of your child, and you should always think well of him because of that."

"You surprise me."

"I shouldn't. I've always wanted what's best for you. Peter wasn't best, but maybe the baby is."

"I think so, too." She looked at Raleigh, feeling a glow return to her cheeks. "What am I going to do about Bradley the bastard?"

"Fight him. Because God knows he's going to fight you."

Bradley, in fact, hadn't wasted any time. By the end of the day, Dominique had a call from her agent reporting that Bradley was demanding her immediate resignation. Dominique was startled that he could turn against her so quickly, from her greatest supporter to her archenemy in the course of one conversation. He was trying to distance himself from her totally, and announced that he didn't want her pregnancy made public while she was still associated with the show. Her agent advised her to give in. "If you do, nobody will make a fuss about it, the whole thing will blow over. You'll have the kid, and if you want to go back to television afterward, I'll find you something. Guaranteed. Everyone loves you."

"What if I stay?"

"Bradley will draw blood. It ain't worth it, Dominique, trust me. Want my suggestion? Take a few months to yourself. Relax. When this is all over, you'll be back in Atlantic City, and back on TV, the same glamorous gal you've always been. But right now, get out of the storm."

Sitting in her apartment now, she tried to sort through the conflicting advice. Her agent's idea made sense; in fact, it was very tempting. She didn't particularly feel like being on the air these days; her attention was elsewhere.

But she also wasn't going to quit just because she was pregnant. And just because Bradley James told her to.

She finished her tea, sat back with her hands over her stomach. It was such a natural position; almost like holding the tiny being inside, comforting her in her darkness. There was a little girl in her stomach, she'd known that for weeks now, ever since the first tests came back confirming that all was well as far as medicine and genetics could determine. She was secretly grateful that it was a daughter; it would make her feel less guilty about not having a second parent, a male role model for the child. But it distressed her that it was going to be just as hard for her little girl growing up, trying to build a career, as it had been for her. Nothing had really changed. Men like Bradley James

still reviled women, tried to destroy them whenever they didn't
fill the tiny circumscribed role the men had in mind for them.
There were double standards, discrimination . . . all the things
that the bold feminist rhetoric had tried to alter seemed as
firmly entrenched as ever. Her future and her career were going
to be determined by the likes of Bradley James and Winston
Axminster.

It made a certain amount of sense to quit now, step out of the
fray for a little while. She had plenty of money, and she didn't
really feel like fighting. But she had a sense of obligation now
that she'd never really felt before, a need to stand firm. Yes,
Bradley James would try to draw blood, but if she gave in, the
blood would be drawn anyway, a slow leeching that would
continue into the next generation.

What would they do if she stayed, call her a slut, a whore?
One lesson she'd learned years ago: a woman's morals didn't
really matter, it was how men chose to interpret them. When
she was eighteen, pure and pretty, men assumed she was a slut,
because that was the only way they knew to deal with her. She
had always kept her private integrity, let the public image be
whatever satisfied the men in power. Well, now it would be
different. Privately, she *had* screwed up, more by trusting Peter
than by straying from the straight and narrow; but she would
insist in her public voice that she had a right to her own life, her
own decisions.

It was going to be tricky, a fine line. She'd love to spit back at
Bradley, make his adulteries public. But it wasn't in her to do
that. She hoped none of this would get too nasty—but she had
the sinking feeling that it might.

The minute Dominique arrived at work the next morning,
Cawley called her into his office and shut the door.

"How are you feeling?" he asked.

"Good, actually. I can't get used to gaining weight, but at
least I know it's temporary."

Cawley nodded. He shuffled some papers on his desk, then
looked at her, a picture of misery. "Listen, I'm not going to beat
around the bush. Bradley is going to the mat on this. He's met
with Axminster and the president of the network, and they're all
in agreement. They want you to resign."

Dominique sat back, trying to stay composed. It wasn't much of a surprise, really; she was taken aback only by the speed with which things had moved. "And if I don't resign?"

Cawley shrugged. "It doesn't make sense not to, Dominique. Bradley will make sure that your life here is miserable. Or, frankly, he might go farther, and see that you're fired."

"Isn't that illegal? Firing someone for getting pregnant?"

"I don't know, but it doesn't really matter. There's always a way around those things. Listen, Dominique, I stood up for you, but I didn't have a chance. You have another fourteen months on your contract. The best I could do was get them to agree to pay you in full if you resign immediately." He looked at her expectantly, hoping for a quick agreement, a chance to get the whole thing over with right away.

"Yesterday you didn't foresee any problems."

"Don't make me feel worse than I already do. I was wrong."

She left his office with a promise to think things over and get back to him as soon as possible. She needed someone to talk to. Jackie was in Paris, a two-day trip covering an economic summit meeting. She found Raleigh in an edit room, asked her if she had a few minutes to talk.

"Let's take a ten-minute break," Raleigh said to the editor, following Dominique back to her office.

When Dominique told her the latest events, Raleigh's face tightened in anger.

"Doesn't anybody get tired of Bradley playing God?" Dominique asked.

"He's not playing God, he's playing husband. All women follow his rules or they're expendable. Darlie makes a mistake and it's good-bye Darlie. You get out of line, and he'll find a pretty replacement. Wonder what he would do if you were carrying *his* baby."

Dominique winced. "An unpleasant thought. But that's the whole point, isn't it? They threaten to fire me, and I'll be glad to give a list of all the men at this network who've gotten women they're not married to pregnant. It's just easier to tell when I've done it."

Raleigh raised her eyebrows. "Does this mean you're not giving in?"

Dominique nodded slowly. "I think it does mean that. If I walk out of here, it's saying I did something wrong. And I don't see how deciding to have a child and love it is wrong."

"You don't have to convince me," Raleigh said. "Half the people in any industry, including television, have something in their private lives to hide. You haven't exactly seen me be forthcoming about where I spend weekends. You're right to fight. This is pure bullshit. The only problem is that Bradley has friends in high places."

"So do I."

Back in her office, Dominique sat down at her desk, stared at her phone for a few moments, screwing up her courage. Senator Tark. *Call me anytime I can be of assistance,* he had said to her that night at the Gala. That had been months ago, though, and they hadn't really managed to see one another since. But it was worth a try.

She spoke to two secretaries and three aides, identifying herself as Dominique LaFarge from *A.M. Reports,* but making it very clear that she was calling on a personal matter. The last aide said he would make sure that the senator got the message, and five minutes later, the aide called back.

"Miss LaFarge? I have Senator Tark on the line for you."

"Thank you." She felt her heart beating as the aide clicked off, transferring the call to the senator. She imagined him sitting in a huge suite in the Executive Office Building. Would he be furious to discover what she wanted? Calling for favors had never been one of her strong points.

The senator got on the line, all heartiness and good cheer, told her how delighted he was to hear from her. "I've thought about you a lot since the evening we met," he said. "I just never had the chance to call and tell you what a pleasure it was. I enjoyed the story the next day."

"Well, thank you, Senator, I enjoyed doing it."

"Come now, please call me Harris."

"I can't," she said with a little laugh, "because I'm calling on business."

"What a shame. The message said it was a personal matter."

"A personal matter for me, but business for you." She took a deep breath. "I'm calling about the Family Support Bill that I know you're sponsoring. I thought we might be able to help each other out."

He laughed. "You might be the only one in the country who knows that I'm sponsoring it. Nobody's paying it a nickel's worth of attention, even though I happen to think it's one of the most important domestic bills in front of Congress right now. Excuse me, please." She heard him cover the phone, tell someone who had just walked in to ask Senator Dole to wait outside a moment. He picked up the phone again. "How do you happen to know about the bill? As I said, it hasn't gotten much publicity."

"I'm a reporter, Senator. I try to keep up on what's happening in Washington." It wasn't totally correct, but she didn't feel like mentioning that since she had met him, she had tried to keep up on what *he* was doing in Washington.

"I guess that's true," he said. "Now, tell me how we can help each other."

She told him she was pregnant and about to be fired, but she wasn't going down without a lot of noise. "And in this business, that means publicity. I'd like to use my position as evidence of why we need your bill, give you the publicity you need so the bill gets some attention. In exchange, I'd like to know I have your personal support while I'm fighting the network."

"Interesting." He paused, buying time, she supposed. "The philosophy behind the bill is that families come in all shapes and forms. We as a country can't pretend to support families and then not give women the backing they need to have careers and children, too."

"My point exactly."

"Just what kind of personal support do you need?"

"Nothing specific. I'd just like to be able to use your name, know you're in my corner."

"Listen, Dominique, let me think about it and talk to the aide who helped me draft the bill. I think we just might be able to work out something."

She went back to Cawley's office to tell him that she had no intention of resigning.

"I have a question for you. Or really for Bradley, but you can pass it along. If I had an abortion, and didn't announce this to anyone, could I keep my job?"

Cawley looked almost hopeful. "I can't imagine why not," he said.

"You think that would be Bradley's position?"

"Of course. If nobody knows, nobody cares."

"Well, you tell Bradley that he better think about whether he has the right to make getting an abortion a condition for employment here."

Cawley, putting his chin on his fleshy palm, shook his head slightly. "Don't do this, Dominique. Don't make things nasty."

"I'd hardly say that I'm the one doing that," she snapped, getting up with all the grace she could muster and making a decisive exit.

Telling people that she was pregnant must have sent some strange signal to her body, because within the next week Dominique gained ten pounds and found her breasts growing unbelievably tender. She was also randy, her hormones raging. She wanted Peter to stop by, just so she could seduce him, get him back into her bed. But she knew he wouldn't, and in truth it didn't really matter, since, even hungry for sex, she wasn't sure she could tolerate him.

But she had to do something to make herself stop thinking about Senator Harrison Tark.

The senator had called her back to say he'd be happy to work with her in getting publicity for her problem, and for his bill. They both acknowledged the need for discretion, and even over the phone, she felt the chemistry that had held them the night they met. After that, he called several times, at first to talk about the bill, very soon just to laugh and talk with her. She sensed a subtle change—the calls were no longer put through by his assistant.

"I can be in New York next week," he told her one day, at the end of a typically long conversation. "What's your schedule?"

"I'll make time whenever you'll be here," she said.

"Good—then we both feel the same way. I kept all my appointments tentative until I knew if I could see you."

He asked where they could meet unobtrusively, and she

laughed. "The senator from Massachusetts and the pregnant television reporter aren't exactly an unobtrusive pair," she said. "Anything other than my apartment would probably be as private as Yankee Stadium."

"Isn't there supposed to be anonymity in crowds?"

"Not for us, I'm afraid."

"Then your apartment it is. Though I have to admit that since the Gary Hart fiasco, I avoid the homes of beautiful women."

She laughed. "As far as I know, no newspaper reporters have me staked out. And anyway, I'm not inviting you to stay overnight."

"What a shame," he said, and Dominique realized that there was a serious streak to his teasing.

The senator appeared at her apartment in the late afternoon, wearing sunglasses, had the doorman announce only that "Harris" was coming up.

"I feel as if I'm undermining national security by seeing you," she said, opening the door for him.

"Not at all," he said, stepping into the apartment and taking off his glasses. "A senator is best able to govern when he's happy." He took both her hands in his, looked at her carefully and smiled. "And I'm very happy to see you."

She had worried that he would be startled by the physical change in her, his dignified spirit offended by her new appearance. But instead, he sat down comfortably with the tea she offered, seemed fascinated by her pregnancy; he even touched her rounding tummy as if she were a goddess of fertility.

They chatted easily, and a closeness quickly developed between them. There was something cozy and illicit about their meeting, a sense that if they stepped outside, a camera would flash, announcing the affair they had never had. When it got dark, Dominique moved through the apartment, closing the curtains, turning on lights. She felt the senator's eyes on her, but instead of being discomforting, his gaze was warming.

"I can't tell you how lovely it's been to see you," he said, getting up from the sofa. "Given my druthers, I'd stay here all evening, but I have some dreary function that I must attend."

She felt a pang of disappointment.

To ease his departure, he said, "I'm in and out of New York a lot for the next few weeks. May I see you again?"

"I'd be terribly disappointed if you didn't."

He came again the following afternoon, bringing a box of Perugina chocolates. The next evening, he asked her to go out with him to dinner. "I don't want to keep you locked in here," he said. "There's nothing wrong with our being together, and I don't want to make it seem as if there is."

Touched by his graciousness, she smiled, but said, "Let's not cause any scandals at the moment. That's not the kind of publicity you need for your bill."

He agreed to send out for Chinese food, and when it arrived, Dominique took it into the dining room, quickly set out her best Rosenthal china and Baccarat crystal. She displayed the food on silver serving dishes and lit the candles in the Tiffany candlesticks on the sideboard. Harris came in, and putting his arm around her, said, "You're the only woman I know who can make Chinese food seem elegant."

At the table, Dominique sensed a new closeness: the senator touched her hand lightly when making a point in a story, sat forward close to her, talking in low tones. When they finished the meal, he leaned over and asked, "May I?" and Dominique nodded, felt his smooth skin on her cheeks as he kissed her.

Senator Harrison Tark definitely knew how to kiss. His lips lingered, found hers, moved softly. He didn't seem to want to do anything more than kiss, and that was fine, because neither did she. For the next few months, her body belonged to her baby.

They moved back to the living room, discussed the plan Dominique had devised for getting the Family Support Bill on *A.M. Reports.*

"Will I see you in Washington when you're doing the story?"

"No, I'm staying as far away from it as possible. Jackie Rogers will probably interview you."

"Then this is good-bye for a couple of weeks. My schedule is so packed I don't see how I'll get back right away."

"I'll miss you. And I hate to think what my body will look like next time I see you."

He looked at her as he were trying to decide whether or not to say what he was thinking, took the plunge.

"I love your body. Pregnant or not, it's perfect." He moved

his hand from her shoulder down to her breast, touched her gently, and when she started to speak, removed his hand quickly, touched his finger to her mouth. "I know. No physical advances right now. I wouldn't dream of it. But I just wanted you to know how I feel about you."

He left soon after that, and once alone in her apartment, Dominique closed her eyes for a moment, thinking how comforting it would be to slip into bed with Harris right now. Her body needed to be touched, hungered for a man's strong, soothing hands to relieve the throbbing. But she had never allowed herself to be ruled by her body, and she wasn't going to start now.

17

Jackie confided to Dana that she was having an affair with Jeff, waited for Dana to tell her how foolishly she was behaving, but got, instead, a wry smile.

"Are you doing this just to prove me right?"

"I'm doing it because . . . I don't know why. Pure sex, I guess."

"Oh, Jackie. How can you be my best friend and be so totally lacking in insight? It's pure revenge. If you're smart, you'll just tell Julian about it, have your tit-for-tat, and then you two can kiss and make up."

"Why should you want me to do that? I thought you didn't like Julian."

Dana tossed her head. "Thinking he's a manipulative businessman doesn't mean I don't like him. Anyway, darling, you're too obviously in love with Julian. I hate to see you screw things up."

"What would you like me to do?"

"Talk to him. For God's sake, if you can't talk to him, you might as well go back to Alden."

Jackie wrinkled her nose. "Very funny."

"I'm not being funny. I seem to remember you left Alden in part because he wouldn't talk to you. What are you doing to Julian?"

"Giving him time to think."

"Bullshit. The only thing he's been thinking about lately is getting richer. At least I assume he is. The price of silver went up another two dollars and forty cents yesterday."

"I haven't been keeping track."

"I have—and I keep watching *A.M. Reports* to find out more about this intriguing story. Alas, I never do."

Jackie sighed. "What can I tell you? I haven't discussed silver with Julian. I haven't discussed Marianne with Julian. And I certainly haven't discussed Jeff with Julian."

"In silence comes peace?"

"No, misery."

Dana looked at her sympathetically. "I know what you're going through."

"Personal experience?"

"Actually, yes. I have an affair to confide, too. His Honor Mr. Osterfeld and I have finally consummated our flirtation."

"I can't believe it. I thought he was all gentle kisses and nothing more."

"He decided he wanted more, and who was I to say no?"

"You haven't mentioned this to Sam, have you?"

"Of course I have." She sighed, looked pensive for a moment. "Darling Sam. I wonder why I can't just appreciate him. He said he's not particularly pleased about it, but he understands that I'm pursuing my great passion, and he'll still be there for me when the bubble bursts."

"The woman who has everything. Tell me how you feel with Osterfeld."

"That I've finally done it—entered the inner circle! I'm in love."

"You're joking."

"No, I finally understand what it is about you and Julian. These powerful old guys have some magical effect on us, Jackie. They manipulate and get what they want, and for some reason, we love it." She grinned. "And I do love it. Every minute of it."

"Where are the guilt and anxiety I would have expected? The torment about your career and your principles and all that?"

"I've given up on that, decided to stop wallowing in angst, as it were. We did that in college, remember? Made ourselves miserable over things that really didn't matter. I seem to remember your all but throwing yourself from a bridge when you got a B on your senior thesis, which meant you graduated *magna cum laude* instead of *summa*. And I managed to create my own hysteria about similarly vital issues of the moment. Now I look back and I think: Why didn't I just appreciate all the *good* things that were going on?"

Jackie raised her eyebrows. "We did appreciate the good things, didn't we? We just recognized the problems, too."

"Maybe," Dana said, "but I sometimes think it's hard for people like us to admit that we're happy. We're reasonably complex people, you and I, and it seems so *shallow* to be happy. But maybe in ten years or so life won't be so perfect, and we'll look back and wonder why we didn't just enjoy ourselves while we could." She grinned. "Remember Andrew Marvell? 'Gather ye rosebuds while ye may, Old Time is still a-flying.' "

Jackie smiled. "I get the point, but that was Robert Herrick. Marvell was *To His Coy Mistress*."

"Forgive me. I get my seventeenth-century poets mixed up."

"I can't imagine why. Shall I recite?" Jackie cleared her throat. " 'Had we but world enough, and time, This coyness, lady, were no crime . . .' "

" 'But at my back I always hear Time's winged chariot hurrying near . . .' " intoned Dana, joining along. They both stopped reciting and started to giggle. "What's next?" asked Dana.

" 'And yonder all before us lie Deserts of vast eternity.' " Jackie smiled. "I remember being thoroughly convinced by Marvell that you should screw before you were too old to enjoy it. If only I'd lived in the seventeenth century."

"It still makes sense now, darling. Marvell would probably say we should just go ahead and enjoy our men and our screwing. Stop whipping up all this internal anguish. *Carpe diem* and all that."

"It's not a bad theory of life."

"I can't think of a better one."

Jackie expected that rumors about her relationship with Jeff would rip through *A.M. Reports*, but for some reason that didn't happen.

"Maybe because nothing has really changed between us," Jeff said. This was two weeks after their trip to L.A., and they were flying to Washington for the day to do interviews at the Environmental Defense Fund for a spot Jeff had suggested on dioxins.

"Nothing has changed?" Jackie asked. "You mean we always held hands on the D.C. shuttle? Funny, I don't remember that."

Jeff let go of her hand. "You're impossible. What I meant is that we were friends before, and we're still friends. That's the relationship everyone sees. We're not trying to get anything out of each other."

"True enough," said Jackie. "Though how did you manage to convince Cawley that a spot on dioxins required two days of shooting, and one night at the Hay Adams Hotel? It's my favorite in Washington, by the way."

"I'm glad," said Jeff. "But this happens to be an important piece. And frankly, I figured that you needed some strong piece to do after all the fluff you've been getting. You're not going to get Darlie's job by out-fluffing her."

Jackie didn't say anything. Darlie's job had become the golden ring—probably unattainable, but always out there, enticing her. Jeff felt that since Dominique's pregnancy, Bradley was going to be forced to make a decision between supporting Darlie and giving in to Cawley's unstated plan of replacing her with Jackie. But this wasn't the time to pursue the discussion.

"The only thing that's changed between us is that I know I won't get any sleep when I go on a shoot with you," Jackie said. "I never seem to get my own bed."

"You're lucky you got your own bed when you went with Raleigh."

"Nasty." Jackie had heard the rumors about Raleigh and her female lover in Los Angeles. Funny how that was accepted in the general scheme of things—a topic for gossip, but not particularly of distaste—while Dominique's pregnancy wasn't sanctioned at all.

"I guess the best thing about Dominique's getting pregnant was that it ended the rumors about her and Raleigh," Jeff said, picking up on Jackie's train of thought.

Jackie looked at him, surprised. "Dominique and Raleigh? Come off it. Who would have said anything like that?"

Jeff shrugged. "It wasn't true, I suppose, but Raleigh always took a lot of interest in Dominique."

"Maybe she thought she was talented. Poor Dominique. Why does everyone assume that she can't cross the street without screwing the person who'll help her across?"

"I don't know, but the biggest irony is that as long as she had the reputation for being—what's that lovely expression?—a loose woman, Bradley loved her. Now that she's becoming a mother, Bradley thinks she's immoral."

They did the interviews at the Environmental Defense Fund, Jackie struggling to comprehend the vastness of the subject, grateful that Jeff had it under control. A woman toxicologist named Hester Silver told her that there were forty thousand chemicals released into the air each year, and nobody really cared very much about their long-term effects. Hester explained dioxins in simple terms: as the by-products created when other chemicals were made. "They're not used for anything," she said. "And that is what is so foolish. This government is spending vast sums of money trying to determine how to dispose of hazardous waste, when there's no reason for it to be generated in the first place."

Jackie nodded, then asked all the right questions about what could be done and why this had been allowed to continue. Hester was terrific—low-keyed but forceful. Jackie thanked her and went to join Jeff, who was already setting up for the next interview.

"Great stuff," she told him.

"You're handling it well." He seemed relieved, and it occurred to Jackie how trying it must sometimes be for a producer to have a good idea and then stand helplessly by as the on-air talent mangled it.

When they finished, they wandered out to Dupont Circle, then down to Joe and Charlie's for lunch. It was crowded with Washington politicos, but the maître d' recognized Jackie after some prompting from Jeff, and seated them quickly.

"I have a confession to make," Jeff said, his hand on Jackie's knee under the table. "I brought you to Washington for ulterior motives."

"You intend to drag me back to the hotel, strip off my clothes, and make passionate love to me for the rest of the afternoon."

"Don't tempt me."

"Why not?" She took a sip of water, felt in high spirits. "If you don't want to drag me back, I'll go willingly. Very willingly."

He grinned and squeezed her knee. "So would I. Unfortunately, I've made other plans for this afternoon. We have a meeting with Senator Harrison Tark."

She wrinkled her eyebrows. "For the environment story? I never heard that he was involved in this."

Jeff sighed. "He's not, but I got myself in the middle of a deal he made with Dominique. They met at some bash we did a spot on months ago, and they're apparently pals. Anyway, he has agreed to support Dominique if she gets thrown out of the show on her very lovely ass, and, in exchange, she's promised to get him as much publicity as she can on his Family Support Bill."

Surprised that Dominique hadn't mentioned the deal or the senator to her, Jackie just nodded. "Are he and Dominique . . . involved?"

"Who knows? I assume so, though to go back to our previous conversation on the subject, maybe they just have a good deal of respect for each other."

"How did you get in the middle?"

"Dominique came to me off the record about doing a piece for *A.M. Reports* on the Family Support Bill." Jeff shrugged. "I like Dominique and I think she's getting a bum deal. So I came up with a legitimate story and sold it to Cawley. A spot on families in crisis—in which the loyal senator will be prominently featured. You, of course, will be the correspondent."

"Won't you get screwed if Cawley ever finds out what's behind it?"

"Yup. I'd probably be out on my not-so-lovely ass. But it seems to me that it's time to rally 'round Dominique, and job security be damned."

Jackie agreed with him, but wondered what she would do if her job and her morals were on the line. She wanted to help Dominique, but she wasn't eager to lose her edge on the show, risk the position she had so carefully built.

"Why the meeting with Senator Tark?" she asked.

"He requested it, actually. I guess the whole thing is pretty touchy for him, and he wants to make sure that it's handled properly. From our perspective, whatever my loyalty to Dominique, I want to make sure we have a story before we come down with a crew."

After lunch, they took a cab over to the Senate Office Building. There were several aides in Senator Tark's outer office, all of them looking harried. One of them broke away from the telephone she was on long enough to bring Jackie and Jeff into the inner sanctum, where Senator Tark stood up from behind his large antique desk to greet them.

"Jackie Rogers," he said, shaking her hand, "are you still offering brilliant comments at press conferences?"

Jackie laughed. "I try, Senator. Funny that circumstances have brought us together again."

He looked at her quickly, as if struck by the sharp tone in her voice. "I understand you're looking for some background on my Family Support Bill," he said. "Tell me what you need to know."

Jeff intervened then, asking questions about the direction the story might take, the key issues the senator wanted to get across. The senator answered easily, elaborating on his concerns about families in America. As he spoke, Jackie found herself being won over, convinced that even if they weren't doing Dominique a favor, they had hit upon an important man and a good story.

When he finished, Jackie and Jeff exchanged looks, and Jeff stood up. "Thank you, Senator. This is exactly what we're looking for. We'll plan to be back in a week or two with a camera crew."

Senator Tark nodded, looked at Jackie. "You'll be doing the interview, I hope?"

"Absolutely." She smiled at him, unable to resist adding, "The only other correspondent who could do this is Dominique LaFarge, and I don't think she'd be right for it."

"No," said the senator, nodding slightly, "I don't think it would be a good idea."

When the story on dioxins aired—and created a minor stir— Jackie got a scribbled note from Cawley: "Only you could have pulled this one off. Good stuff. We need more like it." It was the closest thing to an outright compliment Cawley would ever give, and Jackie tucked it into her top desk drawer. She felt slightly guilty, knowing that the credit really belonged to Jeff. Still, it was nice to be appreciated, and she had the feeling that Cawley was appreciating her more and more each day. She certainly didn't mind that he had begun to count on her to handle late-breaking news stories as well as important features. The more she succeeded, the more he relied on her.

So a few mornings later, when Jackie's phone rang at a quarter to four, she was sure it would be Cawley needing her in right away for some breaking story, and half-consciously she began deciding what to wear on the air.

But instead of hearing Cawley's bark when she picked up the phone, Jackie heard a shaky woman's voice that sounded very far away.

"Is this Jackie Rogers?"

"It is."

"I hope I didn't wake you."

"Of course you woke me. It's four in the morning."

"I'm sorry." Suddenly the voice broke, and all she could hear was sobbing. Jackie waited a moment, trying to wake up, figure out what was going on.

"Jackie, this is Cynthia Hall. D-Dana's mother." She stuttered, began sobbing again. Jackie had met Mrs. Hall once, at college graduation. She was a small, cheerfully competent woman, as tough in many ways as Dana. Jackie vaguely remembered that Dana's father had walked out on the family when Dana was very small.

"Mrs. Hall. Where are you?"

She heard Mrs. Hall swallow, trying to control her voice. "I'm at home in Minnesota, but I just got a call from a hospital in New York. Dana was in a car accident. Hit by a drunk driver. They said . . ." She stopped again, blew her nose away from the phone. "They said she's been very badly hurt."

"Where is she?"

Jackie heard a paper rustling, and Mrs. Hall read her the name of a hospital. "Have you ever heard of it?"

"I think it's on Long Island," Jackie said. "I'll go right out there, Mrs. Hall, and find out what's happening."

"Thank you. I . . . I didn't know who else to call. The hospital called me. My name was still in Dana's wallet under who to call in an emergency." She began to cry softly at that, moved by the thought that her daughter, grown up and in New York, still needed her mother in Minnesota if something went wrong. And when it did go wrong, there was nothing she could do.

Jackie hung up and called the hospital. She told them who she was—giving first her connection as a friend of the family, which yielded no information, and then snapping that she was a reporter for *A.M. Reports* and needed to speak to someone in charge immediately. She felt her anger and anxiety rising, her temper about to burst. She was switched to three different people, and finally spoke to a Dr. Stein.

"I'll be perfectly honest, Ms. Rogers," he said. "We don't think she's going to make it. Maybe you should get over here as soon as you can."

She barely changed, got in a cab and went. One hour later, in a cold and brightly lit hospital room on the north shore of Long Island, Dr. Stein told her that her best friend in the whole world was dead.

"That can't be." Jackie heard her voice rising and felt gripped by panic. "You have to save her." She wanted him to run out of the room and attend to Dana, but instead he just stood there.

"I'm sorry. We did everything. She was brought in shortly before midnight. We've been trying to resuscitate her ever since." He wouldn't look at her, instead stared down at his shoes, which were splattered with dark brown spots. Jackie, wondering if it was blood, felt an overwhelming urge to slap this despicable doctor.

"Dana can't be dead." She sounded hysterical even to herself, and saw her own hands shaking. But she had to stay in control, save Dana. "Should we call in doctors from Manhattan? A surgeon? Tell me who you need. I have connections, I can get anyone."

"There's nothing anyone can do, Ms. Rogers. Nothing anyone could have done." His voice was low, calm. "The team here was totally competent—even heroic. Your friend was probably killed on impact, but once she got here, we tried everything we know to get her back. Frankly, I kept the team trying long after . . ." Dr. Stein stopped and let his eyes wander again. He was young, intense, obviously exhausted—and she abhorred him.

He pointed to a chair in the corner of the room. "I know this is shocking. Why don't you sit down for a moment."

"Don't tell me what to do." She felt her eyes flashing anger at him. "You let Dana die. How can you stand there and call yourself a doctor?"

He pursed his lips for a moment as he rocked back and forth on his heels.

"At least tell me what happened, who brought her here."

"Certainly." He seemed relieved to be dealing with facts again. "The police said a drunk driver jumped the median strip on the Long Island Expressway, going about ninety-five miles an hour. She never had a chance. The car was a total wreck. We had no identification until the police brought in her handbag much later. We called her mother immediately."

Jackie wanted to scream, but suppressed the impulse with a sudden surge of hope. "Maybe it's not Dana. Maybe someone stole her bag or got it mixed up or . . ." She buried her face in her hands, feeling her own choking sobs. She saw Dr. Stein standing there, unmoving, listening to her gasping cries.

"I guess you don't really care, do you?" she shouted at him, tears streaming down her face, her eyes burning. "Just one more body to you, isn't it?"

"An accident like this is a horror for everyone." He seemed stolid, unaffected.

"Dana didn't deserve this. Don't you realize what you've done?" she cried. Her body was tensed, her hands in tight fists, ready to kill this man who had killed Dana.

"The police have the drunk driver in custody," said Dr. Stein quietly. "As so often happens, he was scarcely hurt. Believe me, all of us here will support you in any action you want to take against him."

His meaning somehow pierced her hysteria, her sobs, and redirected her anger. *A drunk driver killed Dana.* That was the person who deserved to be dead—not Dana, not the doctor. Of course he had tried to save her. She suddenly felt chilled to the bone and began to shake. "Could I see . . . I mean, maybe I'm right, and it isn't Dana."

The doctor nodded. "We do need an identification. But maybe you'd like to wait a few minutes until you're a little calmer."

"I'm fine. I want to do it now."

"All right, then." He took her elbow, led her through a maze of corridors, people. Then, in the cold nightmare of the emergency room, she saw Dana lying on a bed in the corner. Whatever tubes had been connected during the resuscitation attempt were gone; she looked white and bruised, but calm. Jackie stumbled, whispered her friend's name. "It's Dana, but she's not dead. I know she's not." She felt dizzy for a moment, the room rushing around her, and wondered if she would faint. Dr. Stein tightened his hold on her arm, then led her firmly away.

Now, feeling suddenly drained, unable to fight, she finally sat down in the chair he offered.

"What's next?" she asked, her voice rasping.

"I'd like to notify the family. How well do you know them?"

"Not very well. From what I remember, Mrs. Hall lives alone, but her oldest son is married and lives nearby." She huddled in the chair, her arms crossed in front of her chest, fighting off her chills. "I'll do the calling, if you think it's easier to hear it from a familiar voice."

Dr. Stein nodded. "I was going to call the local police department there and have someone go to the house with the news. But your plan is fine."

They went to a quiet room with a phone. Jackie called Mrs. Hall, who answered on one ring. Jackie told her the news briefly, her voice cracking as she spoke. "I knew it when they first called," said Mrs. Hall, sobbing. "But I couldn't believe it. I can't." Dr. Stein got on the phone, and spent a long time explaining exactly what had happened, and what they had done. He got the phone number of her son and gave her his own phone number at the hospital. "I can always be reached," he said. "Call me back and let me help."

He hung up and put his head in his hands.

"You can't help," Jackie said, her voice low, trembling. "You may want to, but you can't."

"I do whatever's possible," he said. "The pain is that you can't always do enough."

Jackie wondered how many times a day Dr. Stein watched a patient die. But she didn't care, really. This wasn't just any patient, it was Dana.

She dialed Mark Hall and repeated the information. There was a baby laughing in the background, and after Mark's cry of "Oh my God!" Jackie could hear Mark's wife asking what had happened. This time when Dr. Stein took the phone, he explained that there was no rush to do anything except decide what they wanted to do with the body. Mark said he would call his mother and call them back.

Dr. Stein left, and Jackie sat huddled by the phone. She had a strange sense of unreality now, a numbing throughout her body. *This isn't really happening. It can't be.* She wanted to take some action, prove that she was still in control, but instead she sat, almost immobile, until Mark Hall called back and said they wanted Dana buried in Minnesota.

"I'll take care of it," Jackie said. She hung up and stared at the phone. Action was required now, but she wasn't capable of it, couldn't move. A young nurse walked into the room and asked Jackie if she needed anything. Jackie told her Mark's request and the nurse nodded briskly. "Would you like me to make the arrangements?"

"Can you?"

"Not personally, but I'll see that it's done."

"That would lift an enormous burden. Thank you."

The nurse took down the necessary information, and walked out of the room. Jackie stared after her, amazed. She remembered when she had been in the hospital several years back with appendicitis and could never get a nurse to answer her call to bring a glass of water. Were hospitals that much better at dealing with the dead than the living?

Jackie paced aimlessly around the small room, not wanting to leave, not wanting to abandon Dana here and now, as if there was still a shred of hope to cling to.

Dr. Stein came back. "Would you like to call someone to see you home?"

"No. Just a cab." She was glad that her words were rational, even if her heart wasn't.

She got home, closed the door to her apartment, and heard the silence echo. *Dana. Dead.* She couldn't put the words together and make them mean anything. It didn't seem possible that Dana wouldn't be back, wouldn't call her in a few minutes to say what a peach Dr. Stein was, and really wouldn't it be just too perfect if she started dating a Jewish doctor?

Jackie heard her own sobs coursing through the room, almost foreign to her, as if a strange animal had burst in the window and grabbed her by the neck. Falling on the sofa, she cried into the pillow, banged her fists, wanted someone to come hug her, tell her that everything would be all right. But it wouldn't happen.

She stumbled to the bathroom, turned on the shower and let the room fill with steam. She took off her clothes—the dungarees and sweater she had tossed on to go to the hospital—and stepped under the scorching shower, hoping the sharp pelts of hot water would drive the anguish from her body. *How could the world be so random?* A drunk driver swerving at the exact moment Dana was riding by. What were the odds against that—a million to one? A zillion to one? She thought of all the public-service spots done on *A.M. Reports* about drunk driving. In the end, what good did it do? There was still another drunk, driving a car, killing Dana.

She felt woozy from the heat and despair, stepped out of the shower, trying to think what she should do now, could do now, for Dana. Out of habit, she turned on the television and watched the end of *A.M. Reports,* but the show and everyone on it seemed totally unconnected to her life, to anything that mattered in the world. At a little after nine, she turned off the television, called Dana's work number, and asked for Herman Osterfeld. An officious secretary got on the line and announced that Mr. Osterfeld was in a meeting.

"Is there any way you could interrupt him?" Jackie asked. "This is extremely important."

"Absolutely not. But if you give your number and tell me what this is about, I'll see if he can call you back this afternoon."

"This afternoon is too late. Please tell him it's Jackie Rogers from *A.M. Reports.* It's quite urgent."

"If you're looking for an interview, I'll need to tell him what the topic is," said the secretary, persisting.

"I'm not looking for an interview."

There was silence. "Mr. Osterfeld is a very busy man."

"Tell him he's going to be even busier," said Jackie, exploding. "Dana Hall is dead."

She slammed down the receiver and stormed into the kitchen to make a cup of tea to calm herself. But finding the kettle and boiling the water seemed too complicated at the moment.

The phone rang, and she picked it up.

"Ms. Rogers, please."

She'd never heard the voice before, but she knew who it was at once.

"Mr. Osterfeld?"

"Yes. You were trying to reach me earlier?"

"I was, and I assume you got the message. Dana Hall was killed in a car crash just before midnight. Hit by a drunk driver on the Long Island Expressway."

"My God."

"I thought you should know. She spoke of you often. By the way, I wondered if you happen to know what she was doing on the expressway at that hour alone in a rented car."

"She was coming back from a meeting. We'd been there together all evening. We normally travel together, but she left before I did." He stopped, the lawyerly instinct telling him that he'd already said too much.

"I just wondered."

"This is quite shocking, isn't it? Is there anything I can do? For the family perhaps?"

"Her family knows. The funeral will be in Minnesota." Owl Creek, thought Jackie. It ends where it begins.

"That's too bad. I know there are many people, myself included, who would like to be able to say good-bye to her."

Jackie felt the tears starting again. Nobody wanted to say good-bye to Dana, they all wanted to say hello, keep her around forever. Or at least a few more days. "Perhaps we could have a memorial service in New York."

"An excellent idea." All business, he began planning the service, suggesting places where it could be held and people who could speak. Jackie found herself only half-listening, agreeing to have the service at a church near Wall Street. "I think it would be appropriate," said Mr. Osterfeld, "because in many ways Wall Street really was her home."

He sounded to Jackie like someone already preparing the eulogy that he would give, and since she didn't want to hear it, she ended the conversation quickly and hung up.

Early the next morning, still in a daze, Jackie got on a plane to Minnesota. At the airport, she rented a car and drove the nearly two hours it took to get to Mark Hall's house. The young woman in blue jeans and a sweatshirt who opened the door introduced herself as Linda, Mark's wife. "Mark is over with his mom," she explained. "I'm staying with the baby."

"It's nice to meet you," said Jackie. "I remember Dana telling me that her baby brother and sister-in-law were having a baby." She didn't add that she understood exactly what Dana had meant. Linda couldn't have been much more than twenty-two—far too young in Dana's scheme of things to have a child.

Linda took Jackie's bag and led her into a small den. "I hope you won't mind sleeping here. It's not very comfortable, but it's the best we have."

"It's perfect. It was kind of you to let me stay."

"Can I get you coffee or a soda—or would you like to go right over and see Mrs. Hall?"

Jackie hesitated. "What do you think? Will they want to be alone now?"

Linda shook her head. "Frankly, I think they could use someone to get things in control. Answer the phone and all that."

"Then I'll go right away. But I could use some coffee first."

She followed Linda into a snug kitchen, surprised to see the sun streaming in. How could the sun be shining on such a day? Linda made coffee for both of them, and they sat glumly at the cheery table, hard-pressed to make small talk. A few minutes later, the baby gurgled loudly from the next room, and Linda's face brightened as she dashed out of the kitchen. Jackie heard her cooing and giggling, and in a minute Linda was back, holding a smiling, bright-eyed bundle wrapped in pink.

"She looks awfully happy," said Jackie.

"She's just five months old," Linda said almost apologetically. "This is the first tragedy she's ever known. Unless you count a wet diaper."

Linda looked at her baby and hugged her tightly. Jackie thought briefly what it would be like to embrace a baby, in all her hope and promise, knowing that someday all the joy might be replaced by despair. Was Mrs. Hall right now looking at mental pictures of baby Dana, wondering how a life could end so abruptly, wanting her baby back?

Leaving Linda and the baby, Jackie drove the short way to Mrs. Hall's house. The shades were pulled, and there seemed to be no activity in the house. Maybe they had objected to the bright sunshine in the same way she had. Mark let her in and thanked her for coming, and then Mrs. Hall came out, hugged her tightly. "I still can't believe this happened," she whispered in a voice hoarse from crying.

"I know," said Jackie. "We all love Dana too much to lose her." She was aware how hollow the words sounded, how impossible it was to offer sympathy, or even express the pain that she was truly feeling. Any emotion seemed too puny in the face of death.

Jackie did what Linda had suggested—answered the phone, which seemed to be ringing constantly, made tea for Mrs. Hall, turned away the dozens of friends and neighbors who kept stopping by. Everyone in the small town seemed to want to help, and it was easier for Jackie than it was for Mark to accept the casseroles they had made and firmly shut the door.

"They really shouldn't be alone," one old lady said, after handing Jackie a tin filled with brownies.

"It's what they want," Jackie said. "At least until after the funeral."

She opened the door at least twenty times in the course of the day and felt a great sense of relief only when she opened it in the early evening and found Sam Fredericks on the other side. She had called Sam right after phoning Osterfeld, and Sam had been as devastated and disbelieving as she. Now he introduced himself to the Halls and made the appropriate comments. Meeting at a funeral instead of a wedding, thought Jackie, seeing him shake hands with Mrs. Hall.

They left the house and drove through the dark suburban streets until they found a diner where they could eat.

"Hard to imagine that this is really where Dana is from," Sam said as they drove.

They had dinner, then went out again to take a walk in the cold Minnesota night.

"I need to talk to you about the night Dana died," Sam said quietly, "and I don't quite know how to begin." Jackie swallowed, unable to imagine what he was about to say. In the dark, she saw him shove his hands in his pockets, look straight ahead. "Maybe I have no right to ask this, but did you know that Dana and Osterfeld were having an affair?"

"Yes, I knew. I don't think it had been going on for very long."

"No, but Dana was enamored. Recklessly in love, you might say. I was hurt, but I had a sense of what was going to happen."

"She told me that you were always there for her, and I know she appreciated it. But what does this have to do with the night she died?"

"She had been at a meeting with Osterfeld. You told me that, but I already knew it, because she called me from there. She was sobbing, and said she was walking out of the meeting because she couldn't stand to be in the same room with him anymore. Unfortunately, he had chosen that evening to tell her that she was deluding herself about their affair. He was sleeping with one of the other associates." Sam pulled a handkerchief out of his pocket, blew his nose hard, and put it back. "I told her to come right over when she got back to the city."

Jackie felt a familiar wave of despair sweeping through her as she imagined how Dana had felt that night—humiliated, embarrassed to the bone. *Like the day I found out about Marianne.* At least Dana was able to turn to Sam. But Jackie had a sudden image of Dana driving back to the city, alone with her tears, probably unable to focus on anything except the headlights that finally killed her.

Sam shivered, seemed even colder than Jackie. "I keep wondering if Dana was more upset than I realized on the phone—if there was something else I should have done."

Jackie suddenly realized why he was telling her this and what he needed to know. She stopped walking and turned to look at him. "The doctor at the hospital told the police that there were absolutely no drugs or alcohol in her body. And she was driving in her own lane, Sam. No way had Osterfeld made Dana suicidal. Maybe she was blinded by tears, but she couldn't have kept a drunk driver from jumping the median strip, no matter how she felt."

Sam nodded through the darkness, and Jackie wondered whether she really wanted to know the story Sam had just told her. *Carpe diem,* Dana had said. It would be nice to think that in seizing the day, she had been joyous before her death. Frightening to think otherwise.

Dana's funeral was attended by nearly everyone in Owl Creek. Jackie thought of the acerbic comments Dana would have made, had she been able to see her hometown coming to pay its respects. Jackie left right after the burial, and as soon as she got home she began to plan the memorial service, scheduled for two days later. The morning of the service, she was startled to find the church on Wall Street packed. As she walked in, she noticed Sam in one pew, Alden Taft in another. Alden got up when he saw her, hugged her tightly, and Jackie felt her eyes getting wet. *Nothing left but memories.*

She went all the way to the front pew, which was empty, sat down, and opened the hymn book. A few minutes later the minister appeared at the pulpit, and a choir began to sing behind him. As they finished, he nodded to Jackie, and she walked to the pulpit to join him. Dry-eyed, she delivered her eulogy to Dana. She heard her own voice, strong and firm, reading the words on the page, and though she had written them carefully and practiced them several times, she had no idea as she spoke what she was saying. *Dana is dead and I don't want her to be dead. What more is there to say?*

Jackie noticed several people in the church crying when she finished. She returned to her seat as Sam went to the podium. He was followed by the minister, some other business associates, and several college friends. Jackie had asked Osterfeld the day before not to speak at the service, suggesting the honor be given to the managing partner at the firm. He had agreed, with no further discussion. The minister was eloquent, though Jackie wasn't sure whether he had actually known Dana. Still, Jackie felt the church was rocked by sorrow for Dana, and not just anguish at a tragedy, which was what she had sensed at the Owl Creek funeral.

When the service was over, Jackie walked slowly from the church. *So that's the end. Nothing more.* She noticed Alden leaving with a group of their friends who now worked on Wall Street, and she wondered bitterly if that was why he had come to New York for the service in the first place. *The grave's a fine and private place, But none, I think, do there embrace.* Funny that the last time she had been with Dana, they had recited Andrew Marvell. With a stabbing pain, it occurred to Jackie that there would probably never again be anyone with whom she could do that.

A slight drizzle began as they stepped outside the church—the weather finally matching her mood—and she paused, trying to decide what to do with the rest of the day. She couldn't go back to work, not yet. She noticed Sam standing on the sidewalk, also hesitating. "A lovely service," he said when he saw Jackie. "I think Dana would have approved." Jackie nodded, not trusting her voice to speak. Sam walked away, and Jackie stood alone on the sidewalk, shivers coursing through her body. She pulled up the collar of her Burberry trench coat, suddenly felt faint and reached for the banister on the stairs in front of the church. She managed to hail a cab and stumble into it.

Later in the day, pacing restlessly through her apartment, she remembered to look at her schedule for the rest of the week. She was supposed to leave with Jeff the next day to shoot the series on families in crisis. Well, she would do it. The story was important, and she intended to focus on things that made a difference now. Life was too brief and chancy to be wasted. She had a profound need to make sure that her life mattered, that her work and love added up to something.

That meant resolving the questions she had about Julian.

Dana had once mentioned the hold these powerful older men had on them, and Dana, of course, was right. It was time to release herself from that, put herself on equal footing with Julian. Maybe that required finding out what was really going on at Beardsley Enterprises. Dana had suggested doing an investigative story out of vengeance, but that wasn't the point anymore—now the point was for Jackie to know what she was dealing with so that she could get on with life.

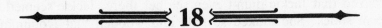

18

Dominique couldn't wait for her pregnancy to be over so she could give up the role of expectant mother and become a real one. She read several books on childbirth, resented the emphasis they placed on the actual moment of birth. Why was it that pregnant women seemed to focus all their attention on learning how to go through labor rather than learning how to be good mothers? It was a concept she resisted. The important part of having a baby wasn't the delivery, but all that came afterward.

She was beginning to look longingly at the slim dresses and sexy gowns in her closet, wondering if she'd ever fit into them again. It was a strange feeling, having her body out of her control. It wasn't just the weight, though that was bad enough, but the fact that she couldn't even put on a pair of high heels without making her back hurt or feeling as if she would tip over. Fortunately, she was still energetic and hadn't slipped into the lethargy that so many women described in their last trimester.

Dominique wondered if married men found their wives unbearably sexy during pregnancy, or if there was something else going on, attracting men to her right now. Funny that when she had been desperate for a man, the only one around was Peter. Or maybe he was just the only one she could see. Now she was feeling independent and full of herself, not wanting or needing anyone, and she felt a bit like a junior-high prom queen.

She was wearing her pregnancy well now, she knew that. Her skin had never been smoother, her hair was unusually thick and shiny. Though her face was just slightly fuller, her legs had remained slim, and she dressed to emphasize them. She looked hugely pregnant to herself, but realized her size wasn't obvious to everyone else. She didn't look sexy—that, clearly, was too much to expect when you were pregnant—but she was still attractive.

Dominique had gone to the memorial service for Dana, but realized that Jackie didn't even see her there. Jackie seemed to be in shock. She looked so pale and wooden that Dominique doubted she would be able to do the story on families in crisis later that week. But Jackie surprised her by appearing at the office the next day totally composed. Jackie had thought about the story and had some striking ideas. Dominique wanted to be involved, but knew it wasn't appropriate. She was grateful, a few days later, when Jackie and Jeff told her that they had finished shooting and invited her to join them in the edit room to look at the raw footage.

"Hope you've got some time," Jeff said, showing her a stack of tapes.

Dominique looked in surprise from the tapes to Jeff. He normally shot tightly, didn't waste any tape. But he had eight thirty-minute cassettes in front of him.

"I'm afraid I went a little long on some of the interviews," Jackie explained apologetically.

"Not true," Jeff said. "It wasn't overshot at all. There was just a lot of good stuff."

They ran through some of it—the background shots, the setups—on fast forward, stopped to listen to the moving interviews Jackie had done with women whose husbands had deserted them; poor families struggling to survive on two incomes with no adequate child care; middle-class working mothers who found that they were abandoned by bigger interests and left to deal with child-care issues on their own. The last cassette was Jackie's extensive interview with the senator, who was clearly going to come across as the hero of the piece, "the only man in America who understood the true dimensions of the problem."

"More than half the women in this country with children under the age of six work outside their homes," Jackie said during one stand-up. *"Yet we have no national policy on pregnancy or maternity leave, and the one senator who has tried to make us focus on the issue has been ignored—despite the brilliance of his proposals. If we as a nation love our children, why do we make it so difficult to be a parent?"*

"I'm sorry, but I didn't hear all of that," Dominique said,

trying to pay attention to the small screen while the tape editor answered a telephone call.

"Rewind to the top of the stand-up," Jeff said to the tape editor.

"No, that's all right, just keep going and I'll listen to the second take."

"With Jackie?" Jeff asked with a laugh. "You must be kidding. Jackie doesn't know about doing second takes."

Dominique listened to it again, nodded her head. Jeff had shot the stand-up in a playground, with some tiny children playing in a big sandbox behind Jackie. One of the children was crying, and there were no mothers in sight.

"It's terrific footage," Dominique said to Jackie as Jeff sped through the end. "But your stand-up makes me nervous. Do you think you're making the senator's halo a little too bright?"

"I like the guy, remember?" Jackie grinned. "If I've overdone it, everyone will just assume I'm hot for him."

Jeff shook his head. "Nobody's overdone it, because it happens that Tark's terrific. He knows what's going on, and he talks about it perfectly."

"I just don't want you to get in trouble for doing this," Dominique whispered.

Jeff shrugged, patted her hand. "Forget it. The story stands on its own, and so does your friend the senator. I put the deal you made with him totally out of my mind. Doing the story at all was my favor to you, but once I take on a story, I do it right."

"You think it's good?"

"I think Jackie's going to win an Emmy for it."

Jackie smiled. "If I do, it goes on Dominique's shelf."

Dominique hugged them both. "You guys have both been wonderful. How do I thank you?"

"Keep fighting, have a healthy baby, and introduce Bradley James to the fact that this is the twentieth century," Jeff suggested.

Dominique thought that the finished pieces were incredibly beautiful and moving. There was, of course, nothing about Dominique in any of them, but a quick blurb in the television gossip column of the *Daily News* made the connection. *"Congratulations to* A.M. Reports *for its brilliant three-parter of families in crisis,"* said the article. *"But shouldn't the network listen to its own advice on how to treat pregnant women? Word is*

that Dominique LaFarge has been all but thrown out since she
announced her pregnancy. We miss her."

Dominique smiled to herself when she saw the paper, pleased
that she had finally learned how to use gossip columns to her
own advantage. Someone had to feed the columnists the information they printed, and it might as well be her. She half-
expected Jackie to come dashing by, as baffled as she had been
when Dominique and Robbie's picture had appeared in the *Star*.
But Jackie didn't say anything to her about it. Maybe she was
developing a little savvy of her own, after all.

Dominique knew that newspapers and television fed off each
other. If *A.M. Reports* was devoting a lot of attention to pregnancy and families, it must be a big story, something they should
all do. There was a constant fear of being scooped, missing the
big one. And if there was a glamorous angle to exploit, so much
the better. So Dominique wasn't the slightest bit surprised when
Entertainment Tonight called the next day, asking to do an
interview with her. An editor from *People* magazine stopped by
a few days later, and after that, staffers from two women's
magazines.

Dominique told each of them the same story. The network
had backed down and decided not to fire her, obviously fearing
a discrimination suit. But they were also refusing to use her on
the air. She made it very clear that she got paid according to the
number of stories she did on the air, so it wasn't just her pride
that was suffering.

Each journalist who interviewed her was thrilled to discover
that Dominique was able to arrange an additional interview with
Senator Harrison Tark to discuss the greater dimensions of the
problem.

Though Dominique had been around television a long time,
she could not recall ever having seen the television publicity
machine grind quite so effectively.

"Before this is over, our pictures are going to be running side
by side in half the women's magazines in America," Dominique
told the senator when he came to her apartment one evening for
one of the cozy dinners that had become a tradition for them
whenever he was in New York.

"I'm delighted," Harris said. "I never imagined you could

really prompt such a flood of publicity for this bill. Everybody had been ignoring it."

"Well, it deserves attention."

Harris reached for her hand. "Is anybody going to figure out that our pictures are running side by side because that's how we like to be?"

"Somebody's going to figure it out eventually," said Dominique, feeling a stab of anxiety. "Does that bother you?"

He shrugged. "The timing wouldn't be wonderful, but it would be a certain relief for me. I hate keeping you a secret."

"Actually, I don't mind at all. I like having our own little world that nobody can touch."

"Unfortunately, you are being touched. Manhandled, I'd say, by the chauvinists in your office." Harris walked over to his briefcase and pulled out a sheaf of papers. "I told you that one of my staff is investigating whether there are any laws to protect you from what's happening right now, and whether our bill would do it better. But apparently I didn't give her enough details to go on."

Dominique smiled. "I gave you all the information yesterday."

"I know," said the senator, "but I was so busy looking at you that I forgot to pay attention."

"Write it down this time," Dominique said, laughing. "I still have an office, and I get my base salary—but I don't get assigned any stories. Since the real money I make comes from appearance fees, I'm not getting much in the way of paychecks."

"That's lousy. As far as I'm concerned, it's no different from firing you."

"I agree. Fortunately, I don't have to worry about the money, but what about principles, Harris? Can women be abused at will?"

"On this issue, yes." He put his arms around her. "At least, most women can be. Anybody who tries to abuse you is going to have to fight me all the way." They kissed sweetly, then pulled apart. Harris got up to go back to his hotel. Holding hands as they walked to the door, Dominique thought how pleasant it was that their chasteness had never become an issue. Their affection was growing nicely without any sexual involvement. Dominique thought of it as a classic courtship—with the twist that she was already pregnant.

"I'm seeing you tomorrow for *Donahue,* right?" Harris asked at the door.

"You bet."

He kissed her again. "I'll be thinking about you until then," he said as he left.

Dominique was looking forward to the next day. She had been pleased when the producer from the Phil Donahue show called, asking if she would like to appear. She agreed, but explained that she and Senator Tark had already made some other television talk-show commitments.

"You have to do *Donahue* first," said the producer. "We can't have you on local shows, and then here. It looks bad."

Dominique understood, and they reached a compromise—her hour on *Donahue* would be slated for the following week, and she would cancel any shows scheduled before that.

The next morning, when Dominique and Harris met in the green room of the *Donahue* show, they shared a smile as they shook hands.

"I'm nervous," admitted Dominique. "This is the first time I'm putting my life on the line in front of an audience."

"You'll be terrific," predicted Harris.

He was right. Dominique was used to hearing applause when she was on stage, but the cheering she heard regularly in nightclubs had never been as heartening as what she experienced on the *Donahue* set. There was something about the approving roar of this audience, comprised mostly of housewives, that brought tears to her eyes. Bradley James could say what he wanted, the real people of the world were on her side.

Harris sat next to her, of course, and the audience was equally approving of him. He spoke eloquently about his Family Support Bill, and Phil Donahue nodded vigorously, asked a lot of questions, and finally said, "Senator, we need more people in Congress like you!" He then popped the microphone in front of one audience member after another, and Dominique found herself beaming as each found a new way to tell the senator how terrific he was. In the interests of balance, Donahue had invited a personnel manager from a big corporation to represent the other side. His main point seemed to be that personal life and professional life had to be kept apart, because corporations weren't able to take care of individual needs. He was roundly booed at first, then just ignored.

Dominique had decided to speak honestly to everyone about the father of her child, hoping people would identify with her situation and respond with sympathy. She never mentioned Peter's name, just said he was a man she had been hoping to marry, who had unexpectedly backed off. When she said that on the show, Donahue adjusted his glasses, stroked the back of his gray hair. "I can't imagine anyone deciding not to marry you," he said. There was a ripple of laughter from the audience, and Dominique smiled sweetly.

"You really know how to handle yourself," Harris said to Dominique as they hurried from the Donahue studios to a waiting limousine.

"Thanks. But I sometimes wonder if I'll ever work in television again after speaking out this way."

"We're going to make sure you do," Harris said. "I can't think of anything that will make me happier than seeing the network back down and admit that there's nothing disgraceful about motherhood and pregnancy."

"Even on terms that Bradley James doesn't understand?"

Harris laughed. "I meant to tell you—my office got a call from him."

Dominique looked at Harris, surprised. "What was that about?"

"Something to the effect that he wanted to tell me personally how important my Family Support Bill is, and how pleased he is that his show was able to devote so much attention to it."

Dominique laughed. "The man plays all the angles, doesn't he? Takes credit for something even when he had nothing to do with it."

The senator shrugged. "As I understand it, he's always been a champion of the family. The traditional family, admittedly, but still the family. He must be a bit baffled now, because somehow he came out on the wrong side of the issue this time."

"Oh, come on, Harris, he doesn't really support the family, he supports his own vision of the world. You—and your bill—support the family as an entity, whatever shape or form it comes in."

He smiled at her. "You've been listening to my rhetoric for too long."

"Probably. But I happen to believe it. And I suspect you do, too."

"Actually I do." He sat back comfortably in the limousine, and they exchanged a warm look. "How many more of these joint television appearances do we have coming up?"

"A lot, Harris, but don't worry, there are no local shows. I made sure that it's all network or syndicated programs."

He laughed. "A distinction I never would have thought to make."

"At least we'll know each other's lines pretty well by the end of this."

"And hopefully a lot more about each other, too." He shifted in his seat. "Any way I can entice you to come to Washington for a few days when we finish?"

"You could probably entice me to do anything. But for what?"

"To do some lobbying for the bill. Your name will be associated with it enough that it would make sense—and I think your direct influence might make a difference."

"It would be my pleasure." She smiled. "Any other reason you'd like me to visit?"

Harris looked fondly at her. "Of course there is. I'd like you to see a little of my world—meet some of my friends in Washington and see what you think."

"Introduce me to the power and glory? I'd love it."

"There's a certain amount of power in my life, I'll admit," Harris said with a smile. "But you're the only glory."

Most of the anxiety Dominique had expected from being alone during pregnancy just didn't appear.

"I admire you for taking on the responsibility for another human being all by yourself," Harris told Dominique one day when they went out for tea after another television appearance together.

Dominique smiled. "Thank you, but I don't think I can take too much credit for having a baby. Even by myself. Sixteen-year-old girls in the ghetto do it, too."

"Unfortunately, I know that. But this is different. You have so much in your life, but you're willing to show that another life is as important as your own."

Dominique nodded. "The only thing that sometimes bothers

me is that my pregnancy has become politicized. I wanted a child, and I seem to be having a principle instead."

Senator Tark laughed and hugged her surreptitiously. "You're having both. But you see what I mean about your pregnancy not being the simple matter you like to pretend."

The idea of going through labor alone was the only thing about her solo pregnancy that worried her. However much she decided to look beyond the delivery date, it hovered—an unavoidable obstacle. Her doctor, an understanding older man, had said it would be fine for her to have a friend at her side. "We'll treat the person like we would a husband," he said. "He or she will be your coach." Dominique liked the idea but couldn't decide whom to ask. Her mother had volunteered to come after the baby was born, to help out, and Dominique had happily agreed. But asking her to come early and wait for labor to begin seemed excessive. Dominique considered Raleigh, who she knew would be glad to do it, but decided it would make her uncomfortable. The obvious person was Jackie, who had been a confidante throughout the pregnancy. The only problem was that Jackie seemed distracted these days, sorting out her own life.

Dominique agonized about it for a few days before broaching the subject to Jackie, who seemed genuinely delighted.

"Coaching you through delivery would be the greatest honor of my life," Jackie said, as soon as Dominique suggested it. "How do we get started? What do we have to do?"

Dominique laughed. "Don't get so excited. Your job, as I understand it, is to keep me calm."

"I know that." Jackie smiled. "As with everything else in my life, I've done a story on it, even if I haven't lived it. Can I come with you to Lamaze classes?"

"I'm not taking them. I couldn't bear the thought of going to a class and sharing my feelings about pregnancy. My feelings are my own, thank you."

"Aren't you supposed to learn how to breathe, or something like that?"

"I know how to breathe. I do it every day."

Jackie thumped the eraser end of a pencil against her chin. "Maybe we could have a Lamaze teacher come to your apartment one night for a couple of hours. Just to run through what we can expect during the delivery, get both of us prepared."

"I guess that would be all right. In fact, my obstetrician's nurse is a Lamaze teacher, and I know she'd do it. You wouldn't mind?"

"I'd love it." Jackie pulled out her calendar, looked at the crammed pages and frowned. "Why is it that my days are never my own?" She flicked the pages back and forth. "Next Tuesday night sound okay?"

"I'll see if she can make it."

"Great." Jackie closed the calendar. "I'm so pleased you asked me to do this."

"I'm grateful. How are things going with you and Julian, by the way?"

"Difficult. We're both very busy."

"A lousy excuse."

"I know that." Jackie sighed. "Since Dana died, I seem to be a walking cliché, trying to figure out the meaning of life. I'm not sure how much meaning Julian contributes." She brightened. "But having a baby—well, there's no doubt about that, it *is* meaningful."

Dominique wondered why it was that smart people like Jackie and Senator Tark were so enthralled by the powerful simplicity of human reproduction. "You could have a baby, too, you know," she said.

Jackie blanched. "Thanks, but at the moment, I'd rather coach."

19

Julian invited Jackie to come to London with him for a few days—"just to get away from everything and be together," he said. He had business, of course, which he didn't expect would take very long. They would fly the Concorde both ways, and then hop over to Paris for a romantic weekend before returning home.

"I'm filling in as co-anchor for two days next week," Jackie said. "It wouldn't work out."

"I'll have you back by Monday."

"Thank you, but no."

There must have been a firmness in her voice that wasn't usually there, because for the first time, he didn't try to convince her otherwise.

She spent the weekend alone, thinking of Julian and Paris, glad she was at home. She felt a sudden dull regret for the trips she had taken with Julian—they had been exciting and romantic, but there was something fundamentally wrong; they had put the relationship on the wrong footing. Was it really Jackie Rogers, not so very long ago, who had left in the middle of an assignment to fly off to Hong Kong? Julian had beckoned and she had gone. If she were to be cruelly honest, she had to admit that she had been swept away by Julian's apparent ability to control the world.

Which wasn't to say she didn't love him.

But she had to separate the love from all the other elements muddying it. Funny that she and Dana, both allegedly bright, independent women, could turn so irrational when confronted with powerful men. Each could see the mistake in the other, but not in herself. What was Dana's fascination with Osterfeld, if not that of a strong woman who nonetheless felt she needed a man to bring her into the real circles of power and success? Maybe in every woman's collective unconscious she was still a secretary. Or a showgirl. Curious that Dominique was the only one who had shaken free of that and found her own power. Who was the bimbo now?

Jackie went to the office on Monday morning in time for the daily production meeting at eleven o'clock—the one time of the day when those who worked early in the morning and those who worked until late into the night were all there. The meeting was usually part technical and part editorial, a time for the various department heads to get together and grouse about that morning's show and prepare for the next. Cawley would distribute the next day's show rundown, discuss the holes they still had to fill, and hear a report from the booking department on what was pending. Then Joe Banks would decide how the show would flow, and where each live spot would be shot. Chyrons and bumpers—the ten-second previews leading in and out of each commercial—were discussed with the graphics department. On-air talent almost never came to the meetings, but Jackie liked them, thought they gave her a feel for the texture of the show. Since she was substitute co-anchor for the next two days she didn't want any surprises.

Jackie arrived in the conference room, sat down next to Joe Banks, and listened to the conversation that had already started around the table. The head writer, Nate Burrows, a large bearish man with a red beard and a gruff manner, seemed upset.

"What the hell happened on the milk story this morning?" he asked.

Cawley grimaced. "Not the way you wrote it?"

"Not the way anybody would have written it," Nate said. "I know you're trying to get Darlie to pay more attention and be more spontaneous during interviews, but that was shit."

'I didn't see it. What happened?" Jackie asked.

"Two kids died in Philadelphia over the weekend," Cawley explained. "Everyone thinks it's from contaminated milk. We got the head honcho at the FDA—what the hell's his name . . . changes every week—in the seven-thirty half-hour to talk about what could have caused it and how concerned the rest of us should be. You know the questions."

"Sounds pretty standard," said Jackie.

"Except all Darlie wanted to talk about was non-dairy creamer," Nate said.

There was snickering around the table.

"What would you put in your coffee, Mr. FDA?" Nate asked in a mocking falsetto. "Should we drink our coffee black? Is non-dairy creamer still safe?"

Jackie laughed. "What got her onto that?"

"Unfortunately, I can tell you," said Joe Banks, "because I heard the whole thing over headphones during commercial. The stage manager was taking her to the home-base set before the spot and reminding her who the next guest was. Darlie was holding her normal cup of light coffee, and he looked at it and said, 'Sure you want to drink that?' Little joke, you know. Darlie said, 'You think there could be a problem?' and he said, 'Ask your expert.' "

"Tell your stage managers that they're not writers," said Nate.

"Shit, Nate, it was banter. He didn't expect her really to ask."

"Well, she wasted a good three minutes on it. And this was an important story. People are going to be worried about it."

"Should we do something on it again tomorrow?"

"I don't think so," Cawley said. "It's old news by then. But the booking department should stay on top of it in case something dramatic happens."

The show rundown was basically unchanged when Jackie left that evening, but when she arrived at the studio at five the next morning, she found Laurie Spinner already there, just getting off the phone.

"Cawley's putting in another milk spot at eight-oh-seven," Laurie told her, without bothering to say hello. "Replaces the piece you were supposed to do on the lawsuits against the tobacco companies, so I guess you'll be doing this one. Bradley's handling all the Iran stuff in the first half-hour, so it would be too unbalanced if you don't get this."

"Why another milk spot? What's happened?" Jackie asked.

"Four more kids in Philadelphia died. But the really scary news is that two kids in Virginia are seriously ill, and there's a suspicion that it may also be from milk."

"Wow. Who'd you get?"

"An epidemiologist from the Centers for Disease Control is on his way to the Atlanta affiliate. He'll be on live from there. You'll have a pediatrician from Philadelphia with you in the studio. The limo's picking him up right now. Oh yes, Nate's on his way in to write the spot for you."

"How'd you get the guests at five in the morning?"

Laurie gave her a sour look. "I found them yesterday and booked them. Of course, I didn't tell Cawley that. If nothing happened and he didn't need the spot, I would have just called to cancel them."

"Doesn't sound quite ethical."

"Neither is losing my job because there's a hole in the show at five in the morning and I don't have anybody to fill it."

"What happens to the tobacco story?"

Laurie shrugged. "The experts all flew in last night, so I'll call them at the hotel in a little while to tell them they've been bumped. They'll get a nice breakfast and a limo back to the airport. Should keep them happy in case we ever want to get them again."

Jackie walked to the makeup room thinking how unconcerned Laurie was about rearranging people's lives to fit the whims of the television show. Did people understand? Were they really so honored at having the chance to be on national television that they were willing to put up with any inconvenience?

Nate handed Jackie a script for the milk story a few minutes before seven, and she looked at it quickly before heading down to the studio. She'd have plenty of time during commercials and news breaks to study it and get prepared. It wasn't her favorite way of handling an interview, but there was obviously no choice.

The epidemiologist turned out to be a good television guest, the pediatrician was dull—but neither of them had specific answers to why the children had died.

"What about the children in Virginia who are sick? How likely is it that the same contaminant would accidentally appear in two different places at the same time?" Jackie asked, moving from the script for a moment during the interview.

"Very unlikely," said the epidemiologist. "If you're suggesting that there may be foul play involved, believe me, we haven't ruled that out."

After the show, Jackie went back to the office and watched

the wires. She wasn't surprised when, in the course of the day, there were three more deaths reported in Philadelphia, all assumed to be associated with the same milk contamination. The story wasn't going away.

"We're playing this big tomorrow," Cawley told Jackie. "I want you to keep handling it." On Wednesday's show, she interviewed the epidemiologist again, along with the local health commissioner. After a commercial break, there was an interview with the head of the dairy farm that produced the milk. Jackie was surprised that Cawley had decided to devote two spots to the story. That was rare.

By Wednesday afternoon, Cawley's instinct that this was a big story had turned out, as usual, to be right. Eight more children and two adults were dead—and the problem was spreading. Three of the deaths occurred in Florida. The two children in Virginia had recovered, but others were sick.

"There's about to be a panic," said Cawley. "It's random, unexplained deaths at this point, and rumors are starting to go like crazy that it might be sabotage or who the hell knows what. We'll give it the whole eight-o'clock half-hour tomorrow. Laurie's got the surgeon general, and we're working on some others."

"I wish I could stick with the story," Jackie said, "but Darlie's back tomorrow, right?"

"Maybe," Cawley said. "Do me a favor, and go home early tonight and go to bed."

Jackie was already in bed reading at nine o'clock when Cawley called to say that they needed her to fill in again for Darlie the next day.

"I'm delighted, but why?"

"Darlie's continuing her vacation," Cawley said grimly.

"I didn't know that."

"Neither does she. But as usual, we can't reach her, and I'm not having her float in here tomorrow morning and fuck up another big story. She doesn't have any research and she hasn't been briefed. Going on unprepared is her favorite trick lately, but it's not going to work this time."

"Hold on a second and I'll grab a pencil to get briefed," Jackie said.

Cawley transferred Jackie to Nate, who had written the next morning's milk-story interviews.

"The guy from Centers for Disease Control says it's a deadly bacteria that's actually very rare, and it's almost impossible for them to think of a natural way for it to be in milk," Nate explained.

"So someone must have put it there?"

"That's the guess. You got him to mention possible foul play the first time you interviewed him, which was smart, because nobody else was talking about it then. But you're going to have to be delicate now, because if you ask it outright, he'll skirt it."

"Got it."

They talked for about twenty minutes about the details of the interviews, until Jackie felt comfortable with them. It was strange having someone else write her scripts for her, but given the number of interviews lined up, it would be impossible to write all of them herself. Still, she was determined to put her own stamp on them. That meant understanding the stories and having full information on her guests, so she could wander from the scripts confidently.

When the limo picked her up in the morning, there was a New York *Times* waiting on the seat for her, and she saw the big headline on the front page almost before she got into the car. Seven more children were dead. Cawley was right. The story was snowballing. It was going to be all anybody would talk about.

Jackie was so preoccupied with what she'd read in the paper that when she got to her makeshift dressing room, it took a moment for her to register the shouting match going on next door in Darlie's dressing room.

Darlie and Cawley were talking in angry, raised voices. It didn't take Jackie long to get the gist of the fight. Darlie's limo driver had arrived at the usual time that morning, but when Darlie got into the car, he gave her the message that her vacation was being extended by two days.

"How dare you treat me that way?" shouted Darlie. "Sending a peon in a chauffeur's cap to give me a message like that."

"Nobody knew where you were last night," Cawley said. "You didn't even bother to call in to get briefed on the show. Exactly how would you have liked me to get a message to you?"

"What kind of bullshit is this? You know I don't always call in. I've been on this show long enough that I can get a script in the morning and handle it cold."

"You can't, and I've told you that before. This time I'm acting on it."

"Well, fuck it, Cawley, let's get to the bottom line right now. I'm tired of being jerked around. You guys have been dancing around in contract negotiations for months. Only way I stay off the air today is if you're throwing me off for good."

She doesn't think he'll do it, Jackie thought, looking into the mirror. Her face looked white and she saw her large eyes staring back at her, filled with anxiety.

"Don't try that," said Cawley. "You're off the air today, and that's that. We'll settle the long-term later."

"No, let's settle it right now. Who do we need, Axminster? Get him over here. Bradley James? Come on, Cawley, he wants me off because I'm getting my own following on the show. You're smarter than that. Why are you trying to shake things up when we're number one?"

"Because we can be better, and we would be if you cared a little more."

"What you mean is that Bradley would be happier if he had someone sitting next to him who kisses his ass, and I don't do that anymore. Who are you getting to replace me this morning— the little girl with the rich boyfriend?"

There was a moment of silence.

"I won't go on with this conversation," Cawley said quietly. "You're not on this morning, Darlie, because you're not pre- pared. That's it."

"Then fuck you all. You don't make somebody a star, Caw- ley, then treat her like shit."

Jackie heard the door to Darlie's dressing room slam, and a moment later Darlie stormed past Jackie's open door. Seeing Jackie, she stopped in the doorway, hands on her hips, glaring.

"Feeling smug?" Darlie asked.

"Not at all."

"Well, you were certainly standing there listening to every word, weren't you?"

"This happens to be my dressing room today."

"Lucky you. By the way, I've got to congratulate you. I

understand your boyfriend has made Bradley a fortune in the silver market. It's all he can talk about lately."

Jackie tried to think what Darlie was talking about. She remembered Julian's telling her that Bradley had followed up their meeting at the Cloisters and called for investment advice. "Julian gave Bradley some business advice, I suppose. I don't know much about it, but I'm glad it worked out."

"You bet you are. Guess you had a choice of fucking Bradley or buying him. Buying him's got to be more pleasant."

"Cut it out, Darlie. Their business deals have nothing to do with me."

Darlie raised her eyebrows. "Really? I thought Julian gave advice in exchange for making his little girlfriend a star."

Darlie turned on her heel and walked off before Jackie could say anything. Jackie sat down on the small stool in the dressing room, shaking in anger. She had to control herself. This wasn't the best way she could think of to prepare for a show.

Jackie handled the show smoothly, but she hurried to the control room afterward to find Jeff. He was sitting in his usual position by the monitors, but his feet were up and he was flipping through the newspaper, letting the tension of the show ease away.

"Have a few minutes to talk to me?" Jackie asked.

"Sure, after promos," Jeff said. "By the way, you did a nice show. Good job in the eight-o'clock half-hour with all the information on the milk story. Just the voice of calm reason and intelligent thinking Cawley was hoping for."

"I'll say." Cawley came over, rubbed her shoulders. "If I had you as my co-anchor already, I'd start running ads right now showing you interviewing the surgeon general, with a kicker: *When You Don't Know Where to Turn, Turn to Us.*"

"I like it," said Jeff.

In the monitors, Jackie saw the crew beginning to filter back in. She sat in the back of the control room for the twenty or so minutes it took for Bradley to do and redo the promos, wondering, as always, why the efficiency that was so evident during the live show always disappeared once they were on tape.

Finally Joe called, "That's a wrap, thank you, everybody," and Jeff stood up and stretched. He turned around to smile at

Jackie. "Where should we go to talk?" he asked, walking over to her.

"You name it."

He grinned. "My place."

"Tempting, but name something else."

"Your place."

"You'd be welcome, but my bed's not made."

"All the better."

She laughed. "I said I needed to *talk*. I'm giving you one more chance."

"Stiles Coffee Shop."

"Sold."

Stiles Coffee Shop was tiny, smoky, and always overheated, but since it was within five blocks of the studio, network head-quarters, and most of the news offices, Jackie always assumed that some of the biggest television deals were cut there. The waiters and countermen were so used to seeing television stars sitting in the grimy booths that they rarely bothered to look up, no matter who walked in.

"So what's up?" Jeff asked, once they were settled into a snug booth so close to the grill that they could hear the bacon sizzling.

Jackie sighed, covered her face with her hands for a moment, then looked up at Jeff again. "It was a good show, but it's been a bad morning. I need advice." She told him about the fight she'd heard between Darlie and Cawley, and then what Darlie had said to her.

"You're not paying attention to that nonsense, are you?"

"Of course not, but I have a desperate urge to prove to Darlie that I'm not kissing Bradley's ass, no matter what she thinks."

Jeff reached across the table for her hand. "You're so sweet. You didn't understand what happened last night, did you?"

"What do you mean?"

"Why Darlie wasn't on."

Jackie felt her cheeks getting red, assumed it was the heat from the grill. "She wasn't prepared to handle the milk story, and Cawley wanted me to continue with it."

"Sure. And you did a great job. But it was also something of a tactic, keeping Darlie off because she wasn't properly pre-pared. Gives ammunition to Cawley's argument that they shouldn't renew her contract because she's a detriment to the show. If everyone begins thinking that, one, Darlie doesn't care, and that, two, she's going to make a fool of herself every time there's a big story, he has a reason to stand firm in insisting that she goes."

"And Bradley?"

"Come on, Jackie, you know Bradley originally wanted Dominique. It's no secret that he likes his co-anchor to be docile and under his thumb. You're a little too smart for his taste. On the other hand, he really does care about the show, and he's sick of Darlie screwing up. Cawley's showing him that you're the reasonable alternative. That's what's winning him over. Not Julian."

"Though Darlie's not totally wrong. My association with Julian hasn't hurt in his eyes."

"It's a more complicated game than that."

"And I'm a pawn."

"A pawn who's about to become the queen." He squeezed her hand, then let it go. "Forgive me if the analogy doesn't work, I don't play chess. But since you're facing the grill and I'm facing the door, I should tell you that the strategy may have already worked, since Bradley and Axminster have just walked in and are about to sit in a small booth in the corner."

"Which means?"

"Expect a call from your agent this afternoon."

Darlie's extended vacation continued through Friday, for reasons that Cawley didn't explain, and Jackie didn't ask. They planned to lead the show with the milk story, though there were no new developments.

At a few minutes after five in the morning, Cawley burst into the makeup room where Jackie was sitting.

"We've got a problem," he said. "New chief of the FBI, Frank Mannoli, is having a press conference at eleven this morning to announce a breakthrough in the milk case."

"No way we can get a preliminary briefing?"

"We've got better than that," said Laurie, who was right behind Cawley. "We can get a morning show exclusive with Mannoli, a little after seven."

Jackie sat back. "What's the problem, then?"

"One, he won't tell us what he's going to say. Two, he'll only do the interview with Dominique."

Jackie, startled, looked from Cawley to Laurie and back again. "Why is that?"

Laurie shrugged. "We don't really know. Dominique's in Washington this week, and Mannoli apparently met her through Senator Tark. According to Mannoli's assistant, he has no reason to give an exclusive unless it's, quote, to benefit someone he admires, unquote."

"What does Bradley say?"

"He's furious but he hasn't said anything—he's trying to get Mannoli on the phone right now to see if he'll give him the exclusive."

Ten minutes later, Bradley called them into his dressing room and announced through clenched teeth that it was either Dominique or no interview. "I'm willing to make the deal and let Dominique do it for the good of the show," Bradley said. "But it's been your story, Jackie."

"No problem as far as I'm concerned," Jackie said.

On the air, at a few minutes after seven, Bradley gave an update on the milk deaths, then tensely announced, "Our correspondent Dominique LaFarge has an exclusive interview this morning—she's live in Washington, D.C., with FBI chief Frank Mannoli." Jackie noticed that everyone in the studio was riveted to the monitor. Dominique's first appearance on the show in months. In the Washington studio, Dominique appeared comfortable and in control. Since she was sitting down, her pregnancy wasn't obvious, and she looked as beautiful as ever.

"Go to it," Jackie murmured under her breath.

For the next six minutes, Dominique did just that, getting Frank Mannoli to reveal that the FBI had tracked down a brilliant young scientist whom they suspected of being involved in the milk crisis. The anomalous bacteria that had killed the children was found growing in his laboratory. As yet, they had no motive. Dominique listened carefully, asked the right questions. Mannoli pointed out that the intrigue wasn't over, but the panic was.

At the end of the interview, Dominique said, "Mr. Mannoli, what would you advise pregnant women and mothers of infants to do until the milk crisis is totally settled?"

After the FBI chief answered, Dominique smiled and said,

"Thank you. Since I'm pregnant, I know how important that information can be."

She tossed back to Bradley, who looked shocked but thanked her and quickly threw to commercial. It occurred to Jackie that Dominique had just won the round, and there wasn't a damn thing Bradley James could do about it.

Dominique's interview with the FBI chief was reported on all the morning news programs at eight o'clock. Around the studio, the feeling was that her interview had been superb, and her personalizing the information at the end made it even better. Bradley seemed intent on ignoring the whole thing. It had been good for the show, and he wasn't going to get involved.

After the show, Bradley was in no hurry to leave. He sat at the home-base set, drinking his cup of coffee, long after he'd said good-bye and the lights had dimmed. Jackie played with her script, in no rush to leave.

Bradley made a brief comment about Dominique, then said, "It's nice working with you, Jackie. You made this show easy for me."

"I feel the same. It gets easier every time I do this."

"It shows. Any special plans for the weekend?"

Jackie looked at him in surprise. "I'll probably just catch my breath and sleep."

"Good. Why don't you and Julian come over for dinner on Saturday night?"

"How nice." Jackie realized that she hadn't spoken to Julian all week, and certainly hadn't made any plans to be together for the weekend. "I'm just not sure what Julian's doing."

"Why don't you find out?" He sipped the coffee. "Did he mention that we live practically around the corner from him in Saddle River? I never realized it before. Of course, if he's not going to be up there seeing the kids this weekend, Lacy and I can come into the city and meet you there. But let's all get together one way or another."

"Sounds good." Jackie promised to leave a message with Bradley's secretary later in the day, after she'd spoken with Julian. What does Bradley know about Julian's kids? she wondered as she left the set. And how about Marianne? She wondered just how close Bradley and Julian had really become.

Jackie walked the few blocks back to her office and got a big smile from the receptionist when she came in. Jackie waved, signed in with the guard, and headed to her office. Her own agenda for the day was crowded, and the first order of business was to call Julian.

When she opened her office door, she gave a startled gasp at finding a man standing by her window. It took Jackie barely a moment to realize that it was Feodor.

He turned around eagerly when she came in. "My darling! I didn't mean to scare you." She took a deep breath, trying to regain her composure. Feodor strode over to her, kissed her lightly on the lips. "You are surprised, my darling, yes?"

"Yes, Feodor, I'm surprised. What the hell are you doing here?"

"I came to see my little one. Give you my congratulations in person. I turn on the television this week, and there is my Jackie, the host of the show. Did Feodor not always say that you would be a big star?"

"I was just filling in, but thank you." She flung her bag down on the sofa. "How did you get in? The receptionist isn't supposed to let anyone through without calling."

He shrugged. "I told the young lady who tried to keep me from you that I am your dearest and oldest friend. She understood that I wanted to surprise you." He winked. "She agreed to be part of my little surprise and helped me get by the guard. I will thank her when I leave and tell her how happy you were."

Jackie was irritated, but laughed despite herself. Feodor could get through any obstacle, as long as it was female and succumbed to flirtation.

Jackie tossed the morning's script on her desk and sat down on the sofa. "So, Feodor, now that you're here, what can I do for you?"

"Do for me, my darling? Nothing. I am here to congratulate you, as I said. I would have brought champagne, but not in the morning, I don't think."

"No, not in the morning." She sat back on the sofa, waiting for him to leave. Instead he sighed. "Ah, how my little Jackie knows me. There is an additional reason for my visit. My heart is broken, and I thought: who better to heal it than my sweet Jackie."

"Why is your heart broken?"

"Marianne. She has left me."

Jackie felt a pang in her own heart, looked up sharply at Feodor. "Has she gone back to Julian?"

Now Feodor looked surprised. "Julian? Of course not, darling. But she has begun dating some wealthy old man, and she says he would not approve of me. So that is all between us. Poof. Over."

"I'm sorry to hear it, Feodor." He seemed genuinely upset. "Tell me about the man. Who is it?"

"Pfft. Who cares?" He flicked his hands in the air. "Just another like Julian, I think. Too rich for his own good. The president of a bank, an investment bank, she calls it, on Wall Street. What does she need him for? She has all the money she could want. In me she has everything else."

"Maybe she likes him."

"Ah, Jackie." He slouched in his chair. "You don't know personally, my darling, but no man is better or more giving than I am. No woman who is with me needs sex elsewhere. How could she leave?"

"I don't really know the answer. But there are other things than sex, you know. Not to be rude, but maybe she was tired of supporting you."

"Money and sex go together, darling. Give and take. Besides, I honestly thought she liked our agreement. A woman like Marianne needs virility in her life. She will be sorry, Jackie. She will miss me."

Jackie stood up from the sofa, walked around to her desk. "Well, I'm sorry it didn't work out, Feodor. I'm sure you'll find someone else." It was meant to be dismissive, but he didn't move.

"It's strange, darling, yes? I have troubles with Marianne, you have troubles with Julian. As if God wants you and me to be together, after all."

"I doubt that."

He leaned his elbows on her desk. "What's happening with you and Julian, darling? The perfect couple, I think. Is there— what's the expression—trouble in paradise?"

Jackie grimaced. "It sounds like you already know what's going on."

"Only that Julian told me he misses you. Doesn't see you enough anymore. He thinks you are unhappy with him, and doesn't know why."

"Did he ask you to mention this to me?"

"Goodness, no. I went to him about my sadness over Marianne. He sympathized by talking about you. And since I first brought you two together, I feel responsible."

"You're not." She leaned back in her chair, suddenly wanting Feodor out of her office and out of her life. "Feodor, I hate to be the one to tell you this, but Marianne was screwing around long before this banker."

"No." There was a look of horror on his face. "It's not true, why do you say that?"

"She and Julian were getting together."

The horror disappeared, and he tossed his head back and laughed. "My darling, they were married for seventeen years."

"But they were sleeping together a few weeks ago, despite your virility." She wanted to be hurtful, but he just laughed again.

"It means nothing. Only that the past crept into the present. You cannot be disloyal to your present lover with your past husband, no matter what you do." He stopped laughing and peered at her. "Little Jackie, could it be that bothered you? Is that the trouble in the paradise?"

She stood up, annoyed at the turn the conversation had taken. She hadn't meant to give herself away to Feodor. "Feodor, I hate to throw you out of my office, but I've got a stack of work to do, and I've been up since four. Thank you for coming by. And I'm sorry about Marianne."

"If ever you want me, darling, I am yours."

It took twenty minutes after he left for Jackie to feel sufficiently calm to call Julian. He wasn't in the office, but he called her back moments later from his car phone. He thought having dinner with Bradley James sounded like a terrific idea, and asked Jackie if she would spend the weekend with him in Saddle River. She said she was too busy to get away, and couldn't they just have dinner in the city?

"Of course we can," Julian said, a slight edge to his voice, "but we've got to talk sometime. I know you're busy. I'm busy, too. But I want a weekend with you so we can sort out what the hell's going on."

She swallowed. Julian was right. Enough avoidance. "A weekend to talk sounds fine, but Saddle River isn't exactly the place to do it, is it?" She knew she wasn't doing much of a job of keeping the hardness out of her voice. "You've got children and an ex-wife there who need your attention."

"I guarantee you won't see Marianne. She's in Florida for the week with her new boyfriend. Barney is spending the weekend in the city at his grandmother's apartment, and Rick is going on some school trip, no doubt accompanied by Brynne. The proverbial coast is clear."

"Were you planning on spending the weekend in an empty house?"

"What do you think, I'm having an affair with the maid? For God's sake, Jackie, what is the problem? I was going to stay in the city, but the combination of Bradley's invitation and the possibility of getting you to talk to me for ten minutes straight has caused this change in plan. Spur-of-the-moment."

She took a deep breath, glanced at her watch. "Want to pick me up at my apartment about six?"

"It would be my pleasure."

20

When they arrived at Saddle River that night, Jackie felt a difference in mood from the previous visit: there were no bicycles parked against the trees, no feeling of activity around the house. One thing hadn't changed though: Julian was coming home, but she wasn't.

Julian picked up her overnight bag when they got inside and headed upstairs immediately to his room. Jackie followed. At least there would be no discussion of guest bedrooms this time.

"I know how tired you must be," Julian said. "Should we hold talking for tomorrow?"

"I'm not that tired. Supper revived me a bit." They had stopped for a light meal on the way up and chatted pleasantly for most of the ride about Jackie's week on the air. But there were more pressing issues at hand, and they both knew that.

"Good," said Julian, sitting down on the bed, "because I have a few things to say that can't wait. The first is that I miss you. The second is that I've already apologized for the night with Marianne, but I have a feeling you've never accepted the apology. The third is that I sense something else wrong, and I don't know what it is."

Jackie smiled, sat down next to him. "Dear clearheaded Julian. Maybe I should wait until morning after all, because if I try to respond to all that I'll just sound muddled."

"You're never muddled."

Jackie sighed. "There is something else wrong, and I was going to tell you that it's all leftover sadness from Dana, but that wouldn't be fair. Dana's death was shattering, but partly because it made me wonder why you and I are really together, what we get from each other. Dana always seemed to be the most centered woman I knew, but when it came right down to

293

it, she was always the outsider, struggling to make it in the old
boys' network. I think she saw Osterfeld as her entrée, and
that's why she fell in love with him."

"I'm missing the connection to us."

"You've been my entrée to a world that's not quite mine
either. Hong Kong. London. High rollers and high finance.
Young Jackie Rogers has been in awe."

"Young Jackie Rogers is a network correspondent on the
highest-rated morning show on television. You don't need anyone opening doors for you."

"But you've still tried and I've followed along. I always feel
that your life is more important than mine. That doesn't fit your
image of me, and it doesn't fit my own, but it's what happens."

"I was attracted to you because you're smart and strong and
not dependent at all. You're the most self-assured woman I
know. Nobody can control you."

"Not professionally, maybe, but I still have the heart of a
woman. I see what happens when I'm with you, Julian. Our
needs get entangled. And then I get hurt when you lock me out.
I sometimes suspect that no matter how close we get, there's a
barrier, as if you haven't let me into the secret side of your life
so our souls could click."

Julian got up from the bed, strolled around the room with his
hands in his pockets. "I don't buy it," he said at last. "And I
don't really think you do either. There's something else going
on."

"Of course there are other things going on, Julian, but what I
just said *is* true. In my mind it's the basis for everything else."

"Will you tell me the everything else?" He sat down on the
bed again, reached to hold both her hands in his. Not for the
first time, she was aware of how overpowering Julian could
sometimes be. Even his hands were large, smothered hers.

She bit her lip, looked right at him. "I'll be honest. I've
gotten involved with another man."

Julian didn't let go of her hands, just dropped his head to
them, rubbed her thumbs gently against his lips. He closed his
eyes and she could tell he was thinking, gathering his breath. He
picked his head up again.

"Lust for him or anger at me?" he asked.

"A funny question. Are those the only possibilities?"

"The only ones I can bear to think of."

"There might be another reason," she said, but her voice was small. How could she tell Julian that she was in love with Jeff?

Julian sighed. "I'm not a forgiving man, but you somehow bring it out in me. Do we get to say that all is forgiven and start again?"

"I'm not sure it's possible."

"Of course it is. Let's at least take this weekend to rediscover each other. Give the relationship a chance."

"I'll try," she said.

When they woke up together on Saturday morning, Jackie asked Julian about Bradley James, and Julian admitted that they'd spoken often, but not about her. Yes, Julian had suggested that Bradley invest in silver futures, which he'd done and made a fair amount of money. Julian admitted he liked Bradley James.

"Weren't you taking a risk telling him to invest in silver?"

"Why?"

"It could have gone down."

"I don't guarantee my advice. I expect people to understand that any investment is a risk." When she nodded, he added, "You're obsessed with silver, aren't you?"

"Just curious. It's a mysterious world to me. Would you help me if I decided to do a story on the silver market?"

"Of course. Would that clear the air between us? Make you less suspicious?"

"It would help."

They both worked for much of the afternoon, and in the early evening, Jackie dressed carefully for dinner, slightly discomfited at the thought of socializing with Bradley James. Giving credence to Darlie's theory, she thought.

Arriving at Bradley James' address, Jackie was surprised to see a very modern house, distinctly unlike Julian's. It was large but undistinguished. They were greeted at the door by Lacy James—a small blonde in her mid-thirties who chatted easily and looked adoringly at Bradley whenever he spoke. His ideal woman, thought Jackie as Lacy gave her a tour of the house, which was expensively but unimaginatively decorated.

Bradley was far more congenial than Jackie had ever seen him, and the conversation at the dinner table was filled with unexpected warmth—though Jackie noticed that the men seemed to be doing most of the talking; she and Lacy listened and laughed and exchanged friendly looks. Directed by Lacy, two young women in starched white aprons carefully served and cleared, arousing Bradley's annoyance only once, when his water glass wasn't refilled quickly enough.

The dinner itself was excellent, laced with expensive French wine and cognac. After a glorious dessert that Lacy had baked, Bradley popped the cork on a bottle of Perrier Jouet champagne, instructed one of the aproned young women to pour it into the fluted champagne glasses. "None for me," Jackie said, covering her glass.

"But you must," said Bradley. "Just a sip. I have a toast to offer in your honor."

Jackie moved her hand, and watched the champagne bubble into her glass.

Bradley winked, raised his glass. "To this lovely foursome," he said. "I suspect we'll all be spending more time together, and I know that Lacy and Julian will understand that Jackie and I are about to begin a very public affair. You can watch it every morning from now on from seven to nine."

Jackie felt the blood drain from her face, put down her glass. "I . . . I don't understand," she said.

"My dear, unless agents and lawyers get in the way, you're going to be the new co-anchor of *A.M. Reports.*"

Everyone at the table was grinning at her, and Jackie felt her head beginning to spin. "How—when—did this happen?" she asked.

"It's been under discussion for some time," Bradley said, "and the way you handled yourself this past week clinched it."

"I'm thrilled." For some reason, the words stuck in her throat, seemed inadequate, but Bradley didn't appear to notice.

"We're all thrilled," he said. "We could probably have drifted along with Darlie for awhile without the ratings going down, but I'll tell you, eventually you have to pay the piper. Cawley knows that, too—and on those rare occasions when Cawley and I agree, network brass know enough to let us have our way. Contract negotiations with Darlie have been terminated, and

Axminster will have an initial offer to your agent in a day or two. Congratulations."

Jackie smiled weakly. "All I can say is thanks. Contract negotiations aren't going to be too tough. I'll admit it—I want this job."

"And you'll be great at it," Julian said. He leaned over to kiss her, realized he couldn't reach across the large table, and stood up. In a minute, everyone was standing, hugging each other, offering social pecks of congratulations on the cheeks. They moved to the living room, where the conviviality continued. The good cheer was in her honor, but Jackie felt curiously detached from it. This isn't how I was supposed to get the job, she thought at one point, looking over at Bradley and Julian, talking animatedly. According to Bradley, Darlie wouldn't be back the next week, so until contracts were signed, Jackie would continue as temporary co-anchor.

Well after midnight, Julian, noticing Jackie's fatigue, said solicitously, "We'd better get home or neither of you will be able to get up on Monday morning." Saying their good-byes at the door, Jackie wondered just how dramatically this evening was going to change her life.

She was tired, and grateful that the ride back to Julian's house was short.

"Are you elated?" Julian asked Jackie as they took off their clothes and climbed into bed.

"It's what I've wanted," admitted Jackie.

"Aren't you glad you gave this weekend a chance?" he asked, stroking her hair as they lay down. She nodded, and he said softly, "I want you, Jackie. Give up your affair if you haven't already. Let us really be together."

When she didn't say anything, he said, "We could have many more weekends like this one. Should we make a deal to try?"

"Deal," she said softly. He reached for her, and they made love quickly, Jackie wondering if Julian's orgasm was as passionless as her own.

He fell asleep at once, his deep breathing filling the room. Jackie lay quietly beside him, stroking his chest, replaying the evening and the weekend. What a fine couple she and Julian were now: the businessman and the television star. The image was right.

But maybe the couple wasn't.

Jackie turned over in bed, snuggled against the pillow. She was going to give their relationship a chance, just as Julian had requested—and that meant disregarding the persistent feeling that something fundamental had changed in her attitude toward him. It wasn't just Marianne anymore. Somehow Jeff had insinuated himself into her heart; the real reason for her involvement with him wasn't lust or anger at all, but an honest delight in who he was, their easygoing encounters and very real love.

But she wasn't going to think about it. She had made a deal with Julian, and for the time, she was willing to try. This wasn't the time to rock her personal life and risk her career.

She woke up late on Sunday morning. Julian had already brought up breakfast trays and was sitting next to her, sipping orange juice and reading the Sunday *Times*.

"Is the world still with us?" she asked, yawning.

"More or less."

"You're frowning," she said. "Shouldn't you be happy waking up next to me?"

He put down the paper and kissed her. "I am. It's the stock market that has me worried."

Jackie groaned. "I'm just beginning to understand the slightest bit about the commodities markets. Are you switching allegiance now?"

"Not at all. I was just noticing that Kodak stock has gone down significantly."

"You own a lot?"

"None. But Kodak is the biggest industrial consumer of silver, and I suspect that the stock is going down because the price of silver is going up. It just means that broad-based repercussions from the silver market are beginning."

Jackie sat up, pulled the sheet to her shoulders, and took a muffin from his breakfast tray. "What else is going to happen, that they'll understand in Iowa, as we like to say."

Julian shrugged. "Short supply and high price mean that silver becomes worth so much by weight that it pays to sell family heirlooms and melt them down for the bullion. Last time silver skyrocketed, bullion dealers were setting up shops on street corners to buy silver. Everyone had a horror story about the beautifully engraved antiques that were consigned to the smelter."

"Is that happening now?"

"I don't think so," Julian said slowly. "The price hasn't really gone crazy. There was a big jump last week, to almost thirty dollars an ounce, but my bet is that it's not going much higher."

"I've got to do something on this story now, then. I've been ignoring it."

"Do it," said Julian. "You're a woman obsessed. But as long as you're my woman, I don't mind."

Jackie found Jeff after the show on Monday and asked if they could go back to Stiles Coffee Shop.

"Something important to discuss?" he asked as they settled into a booth and were served large cups of steaming coffee.

"Very. I want to do a story on the silver market. Cawley has agreed that I can still do the occasional investigative piece if I want to, and I really want to do this one. The market is spiraling—it's gone from six dollars an ounce a couple of months ago to nearly thirty dollars an ounce now. I don't think these things happen on their own anymore, and I'd like to look at who or what might be behind it."

Jeff crossed his arms, looked thoughtful. "Your happy millionaire is in the commodities business, isn't he?"

"He is, but what does that have to do with it?"

"If this is a favor to him, I'm going to say no—not because I hate the man, which of course I do, but because I think that's a very different favor from the one I did for Dominique. I refuse to use my clout at *A.M. Reports* to influence financial markets."

Jackie looked at him despairingly. "You've got it wrong. One hundred percent wrong. I'd never ask you to do something like that. In fact, this is quite the opposite."

"Ah, you're worried that the millionaire is involved in something illegal, and you're using me to find out what he's up to."

"I'm not *using* you."

"Okay, what if you find that Julian's involved in something you don't like? Find some impurities in his dealings?"

Jackie took a deep breath. "Frankly, I expect to."

Jeff raised his eyebrows. "Am I allowed the faint twinge of hope that things are finally over between you two?"

Jackie shook her head, felt unexpected tears stinging at her eyes as she told him about the weekend, her agreement with

Julian that their renewed attempt at being together demanded her loyalty. "It's hard for me to tell you this," she said, looking at him imploringly.

"But not so hard that you can't do it."

She put down her coffee. "What am I supposed to say?" she asked softly. "You know I always tell you the truth."

"It's not what you should say to me, it's what you should say to that old bastard who's pulling your strings. For God's sake, Jackie, you're not in love with him anymore. Why are you still there?"

"I'm giving it a chance. We've had a long enough relationship that it deserves that."

"Bullshit, you're giving it a chance." Jeff's voice started to rise, but he noticed people at other tables turning around and brought his voice carefully under control again. "You're afraid of him, Jackie. And goddammit, Darlie was right—you feel beholden to him for your job. To all the world, you look like the tough lady reporter, but underneath, you secretly believe that if you break up with Julian Beardsley, your career will fall apart."

"That's an awful thing to say."

"Awful because it's true." He slammed his coffee cup on the table and sat back, glowering at her. "Why else would you still be with a man you've stopped loving?"

Her voice was trembling, and she was afraid she would burst into tears as she whispered, "I'm not sure."

Jeff shook his head. "I happen to love you, Jackie, and even if we're not going to be together, I care about what happens to you. Julian is the wrong thing to happen to you, and you know it."

"And you're the right thing?"

"I'm a helluva lot better than he is." Jeff pushed back his chair, slapped five dollars on the table to pay for the coffee and muffins, and walked angrily out of the coffee shop. Feeling tears splashing down her face, Jackie wiped them off quickly as she wondered what she could do about the fact that Jeff was right.

The announcement that Jackie was the new co-anchor of *A.M. Reports* was made exactly nine days later at a press conference at Tavern on the Green. The room was mobbed with reporters, network executives, and photographers. Dominique came, once Jackie convinced her that she belonged—"not because you work there, but because you're my friend."

As Jackie had promised Bradley, her own negotiations with the network had gone quickly, largely because she was happy to accept what they offered.

"You have to remember that they want you as much as you want them," Dominique said when Jackie told her how undemanding she had decided to be.

"No way," laughed Jackie. "I'd pay them for the job, and they know it. My agent is ready to kill me."

"He should."

The press conference was full of back-patting and mutual admiration. Jackie made a brief speech about how pleased she was to be working with Bradley James, the best anchor in the business. Bradley responded by calling Jackie the smartest woman on television. Nobody mentioned Darlie Hayes. Jackie felt it unfair that Darlie had been so thoroughly crucified in the press. Somehow—Jackie thought she was beginning to understand how—the papers had discovered that Darlie was off the air that Thursday and Friday because she didn't give a damn about the show anymore and hadn't bothered to be prepared. Cawley was quoted as saying how lucky they were to have Jackie, who was always an ace in a crisis. Jackie realized that whether it was true or not, that would be her reputation for a long time.

After the speeches at the press conference, Jackie and Bradley posed—arms around each other and smiling—for endless photographs. When they finished, Jackie went to find Dominique.

"Thanks for coming. I hope it hasn't been too painful."

"Not painful at all. I just hated hearing you say nice things about Bradley."

"All I said was that he's a good anchor, which he is. I didn't say he's a nice person." She looked inquisitively at Dominique. "But what do you want from the man, anyway? He backed down, didn't he? You had a big story on the air and announced your pregnancy. You won."

"Only because I had a story he needed. Interesting, isn't it? Bradley sold out his moral standards for the sake of the ratings. If you like, I'll take the microphone now and mention that he's a self-centered, two-faced hypocrite."

Jackie grinned. "Thanks, I'll let it go."

"Actually, I'd better leave before I irrevocably damage your fine reputation. Winston Axminster is already sending steely glances our way. I'm pleased to report that he and I now share an intense dislike of each other."

Jackie laughed, and Dominique nibbled at one of the cheese sticks from the trays put out for the assembled press. "One last thing, sweetie: you should know that two of the men in your life have apparently hit it off. Bradley and Julian are standing over there, talking like the best of friends."

Jackie looked over in surprise. She hadn't seen Julian come in. "Actually, they do like each other very much," she said. "It surprises me how well-suited they are to each other." She had never told Dominique about the evening with Bradley James—it seemed too humiliating to admit how she had been told about her job.

"Ah, dear Bradley," said Dominique. "Certainly knows how to cultivate friendships that suit his image. If he's got to have a woman co-anchor, it might as well look to the world like she got there because he's drinking buddies with her boyfriend."

Jackie felt her face tighten. Dominique, suddenly white with embarrassment, said, "Forget I said that. And please go be pleasant to the two tall men in the English-tailored suits."

Jackie kissed her on the cheek. "I'll call you later. Don't go into labor before I get home."

Dominique promised, and when she left to get her coat, Jackie headed over to where Bradley and Julian stood talking.

Jeff stopped her briefly to say, "Nice going. And here's my official apology for the outburst at Stiles the other morning." He kissed her on the cheek. "Are we still colleagues and friends?"

She nodded, suppressing the overwhelming urge she felt to hug Jeff, tell him how much she still liked him.

"I assume this new position means we put the silver story on hold for ten years?" he asked.

"Wrong. The last week has been frantic, but I'm ready to go to it now."

He looked surprised, but just squeezed her hand and said, walking away, "I'm yours when you need me."

When she finally got to Julian, he hugged her tightly and gave her a generous kiss. Bradley smiled at them, and the several photographers who were standing nearby began snapping pictures of the three of them. Jackie realized that most of them didn't know who Julian was, but he had his arm around her as if it belonged there, and she was making no effort to shake it away. She just hoped that Jeff was elsewhere.

Jackie's new office at *A.M. Reports* seemed embarrassingly large to her—a corner suite with a small outer office for her assistant, a private bathroom, and an S-shaped conference room that separated her office from Bradley's. Darlie had decorated the office in shades of gray and beige, with a comfortable suede chair behind the desk and two Helen Frankenthaler lithographs on the walls. It showed far better taste than Jackie thought Darlie possessed.

Darlie, who disappeared quickly before Jackie's press conference, surfaced a week later in Los Angeles with a new half-million-dollar contract to be host of a syndicated entertainment show. Jackie listened to the news ruefully, wondering if she had made a mistake signing her own contract for $250,000. But it didn't matter. She had the job, and she'd know better next year.

Jackie had imagined what her first day as co-anchor of *A.M. Reports* would be like, but Darlie's quick move meant that she never really had a first day. Darlie left, officially on vacation, and Jackie filled in for her. Darlie was supposed to come back for a final week on the air, but she never bothered. One afternoon, Cawley stopped by Jackie's office and plopped a slightly wilted rose on her desk.

"For the new co-anchor," he said. "You're official as of tomorrow. Darlie's contract has been terminated, and your agent wants yours to start immediately."

"Nice of him to tell me." She grinned. "Well, thanks for the good news. Do I automatically become smarter, prettier, and more talented as of tomorrow, too?"

"Sometimes I think the opposite." Cawley stirred the rose around in the vase like a swizzle stick. "Bradley's going to make a short announcement to welcome you at the top of the show tomorrow, and again after the eight-o'clock news. Kalina will send out announcements to the press, but that's about it."

"Fine. I can't think of any reason to make a big fuss."

"I can't either. You're already on, and the ratings last week were strong. I don't believe in rocking boats."

Jackie agreed, but she still felt a certain excitement in the pit of her stomach as she walked to her chair on the set the next morning. *Her* chair. She half-expected it to have changed color or grown an extra leg overnight, but everything was as usual. Word of the transition had gotten out to the crew, and the stage manager gave her an extra squeeze on the arm when she came in, and the sound engineer said, "Congratulations. We're all really happy you're gonna be here," when he hooked up her microphone. It was enough. On the air, she listened to Bradley's official welcome, which was short but gracious, smiled happily, and thanked him. The transition made, they got on with the show. One of her first guests was Robbie Baker, who was on to discuss his new movie. Jackie assumed it was just coincidence that he was booked for this particular day, but she couldn't help smiling at the irony. In contrast to his last appearance, he was alert and charming, and Jackie made sure that she listened very carefully to all his answers.

Jackie was slightly surprised to find people in the office becoming more and more deferential to her. She realized they were responding to her position, not her personality. She began to understand what it meant to grow into a job—even if you didn't change, people assumed you did. The role was larger than the person filling it. Jackie quickly realized that it was going to take time to put her own mark on the show. However unhappy the staff had been with Darlie, she had been co-anchor of the number-one morning show, and everyone assumed that her style would live on, even if she didn't. Besides, no one was eager for major changes. Most of the staff members were veterans of other shows, other networks, and knew that any job in television was tenuous—jobs were lost when a show got cancelled, a format or star or executive producer changed. Jackie sensed a collective sigh of relief from the staff when she was able to take over the co-anchor spot unobtrusively.

The ratings went down one-tenth of a point the first week she was co-anchor, then went back up two-tenths of a point the next week. She was pleased. Everyone expected to lose part of the audience with a new anchor and have to work hard to build it back slowly. The relative stability was surprising.

"Maybe nobody has noticed that Darlie's gone," Jackie said to Bradley at one meeting when the ratings were being discussed. "After all, you're still here. That's what matters." It sounded cloying as she said it, but she knew that Bradley expected everyone to be deferential, and that seemed to apply to Jackie too, when Julian wasn't around.

"It's true that I've been around a long time, and people feel comfortable with me," Bradley said pompously, "but you should be pleased that we're not losing viewers. You're doing well."

"It's starting to feel more natural. I was so nervous at the beginning that it's all just a blur."

"Different being here full-time than just filling in, isn't it?"

"I'll say. I suspect it's the difference between baby sitting and having your own baby."

However gentle the transition had been, there were some changes she wanted to make in her role on the show. She promptly invited Nate Burrows, the head writer, to a meeting in her office. She asked how the writers would feel about consulting with her on each interview before committing it to paper. "That way we can work out the questions and introductions together," she said, "and I'll feel a little more comfortable about what I'm saying."

Nate looked at her skeptically. "It's a nice idea, Jackie, but it's our job to write the interviews and brief the talent. Your job to do them on the air."

Jackie had a feeling that she was treading on carefully staked-out territory. "I don't mean to upset the status quo, but the truth is that I'm not very good at being a puppet."

"Did you do all your own writing on the road?" Nate asked.

"More or less."

"There were some nice pieces."

"Thanks." She realized that it was a big concession coming from Nate, wondered how many different anchors he had written for in the course of his career. Despite the thick red beard, he was probably close to fifty, and had been putting the words in other people's mouths for a long time.

"Listen," said Jackie, "I figured out a long time ago that it's the writers on this show who make the talent look good or bad.

I think you guys are the most important and least-appreciated people on the show. I'm determined to stay on your good side."

Nate laughed and lit a cigarette, and Jackie felt some of the tension in the room ease. "Nice to hear you say that since there are some anchors who don't think writers *have* a good side."

"Trust me, I know how dependent we are on you."

He nodded, leaned back in his chair. "Actually, your plan is fine," he said. "The only problem I anticipate is that we often don't have a chance to pre-interview guests until late in the afternoon. You might not want to be around then."

"Depends how late. If it's before, say, five o'clock, the writers can just stop in. I'll probably be around, and we can work out the scripts together."

Nate raised his eyebrows. "You'll be here until five? That will be a change. Darlie was always gone by noon."

"That's because she had to spend her time decorating this office," said Jackie with a grin. "Now that it's all decorated, I won't have anything to do in the afternoons."

Nate chuckled. "Then we've got a deal."

They chatted amiably for a few more minutes, and when he got up to leave, Jackie followed him to the door. Nate hung back for a moment. "It's going to be good working with you," he said. "You're smart. Just make sure you don't start stepping on too many toes."

"Things change with each anchor. I'm sure you've seen that before."

He nodded, glanced at the woman sitting in the outer office. "When's Melba leaving?"

"She's not. I convinced her to stay on."

"Really? Good for you."

Jackie walked slowly back to her desk. She had been sincere in telling Nate that she thought the writers were important. The only problem was that they were also arrogant.

She was glad that Nate at least approved of her assistant, because Melba was the one person in Darlie's entourage that Jackie had been determined to keep. An outspoken black woman in her early forties, Melba had been Darlie's assistant for two months. She had just submitted a resignation, giving two weeks' notice, when it was announced that Darlie was leaving. Jackie immediately asked Melba if she would reconsider and stay on as her assistant, and she agreed. "It wasn't the job I didn't like, it was Darlie," admitted Melba. "She thinks the whole world should revolve around her because she's a star. Trust me, she's not as big as she thinks she is."

Melba's first task as Jackie's assistant was finding a replacement for Reuven the hairdresser, who left the show to follow Darlie to L.A. "He's the only person who actually liked Darlie," mused Melba. "Very strange relationship, if you ask me." For a replacement, she recommended Angelica, a wide-eyed, wild-haired woman who was currently doing the hairstyles on one of the afternoon soap operas.

"The only problem is that she's a woman," Melba said.

"That's a problem?" Jackie asked.

Melba shrugged. "Darlie couldn't stand having a woman doing hair or makeup. She liked being handled by men."

"If Angelica's good, you can hire her. What's her last name?"

"Hairdressers don't have last names, Jackie. It's just Angelica."

Melba was also well-versed in the arts of making on-air clothes schedules, finding manicurists, and arranging for dry cleaning. They were details that Jackie knew made a difference, but didn't want to handle. She was genuinely grateful to have Melba, and at the end of the week, she had the network florist deliver a big bouquet of flowers to Melba's apartment with a note that said, "Thanks for getting me through."

Jackie didn't find it very hard getting used to the new early-morning schedule: up at four-thirty, a limousine waiting outside her building to get her to the studio by five. In her dressing room, she studied scripts, put on the clothes Melba laid out for her the night before, spent nearly an hour getting hair and makeup ready. Jackie had asked that Darlie's dressing room be redesigned for her. Most of the clothes shelves and open closets were ripped out, replaced with a large desk and bookshelves. "It's a dressing room, not a study," Cawley reminded her, so she reluctantly left up the large mirrors, one wall of clothes racks.

Jackie quickly got in the habit of going back to her dressing room after the show, nibbling at breakfast, and turning on the closed-circuit television to watch the West Coast feed of *A.M. Reports*. She watched the show critically, alternately pleased and embarrassed by her performance. It was hard knowing she wouldn't get another chance if she goofed. They would only do a new, live feed to the West Coast if there was a major crisis.

Jackie tried to take a nap after the show a few times, but found she was too keyed-up to sleep. She decided that exercise would be as good as sleep, and asked Melba to set up a schedule so she could swim, jog, or go to the health club after the show. With all of it, she could still be back in the office well before noon, to start preparing for the next day's show.

The only problem with the routine, as far as Jackie could see, was that it all but eliminated a personal life. Her public image was becoming more glamorous, but she was sleeping alone. Don't blame it on the show, she thought. It's your own decision.

She told Julian that she was trying to make their relationship work, and on some level she was. But she needed time for her new job and didn't want anything to interfere with it. As always, Julian was so busy with his own life that they could be together only when she rearranged her time to fit his. She wasn't willing to do that right now. Let Bradley think of her and Julian as a pair, if it made him happy. She could be as manipulative as they were.

While Julian pressed, Jeff stepped back, seemed to be waiting for a cue from her. They chatted in the control room when Jeff was around and shared meaningful glances across the conference table at production meetings. But Jeff was on the road much of the time, and she wasn't with him. The new field correspondent was a handsome Californian named Douglas Smith who had a deep tan, burnished blond hair, and a perfect swimmer's body: wide shoulders, strong chest, slim hips.

"Where did they find him?" Jackie asked Jeff when he came up to her dressing room after one show.

"On the beach, modeling a Speedo bathing suit that showed off his buns to unusual advantage."

"Come on, really."

"He won a medal a couple of Olympics back—I think it was in backstroke. Maybe breaststroke. Anyway, the network's been using him to do color on some sports specials ever since. Nice guy, but he should have stayed in his bathing suit."

"I suspect you're not giving him a fair chance."

"He doesn't need a chance—he needs some talent. I shot my

first spot with him a couple of days ago—about some kids in Harlem who cut a record that's zooming on the charts. It took eighteen takes before he got the stand-up right, which, by the way, was all of two sentences. Do you know what it's like to stand on a street corner in Harlem while a pretty blond boy does eighteen takes?"

"I can imagine." She laughed. "That spot's on the rundown for tomorrow, isn't it?"

"It is, and it's a good spot, but I spent all night editing it. Eighteen takes was the fastest Mr. Smith managed to do anything."

"Strange to think that he's my replacement."

"Actually, I think he's unofficially replacing Dominique. They're looking for someone smart and beautiful to replace you—which, of course, is impossible."

"You're sweet."

"No, I'm lonely." Jeff stalked around the dressing room, picked up one of the perfume bottles on her dressing table and put it down again. "I've been the perfect gentleman since you told me about your ridiculous loyalty to Julian, but the truth is that I miss working with you and talking with you and getting everything in the can in the first take. I also miss having every story I shoot turn out terrific because you've had a hand in it."

"Thank you. I miss our time on the road, too."

"Funny, I was thinking about the fact that we've almost never been together in New York. Ours is—or should I say was?—a relationship based on hotel rooms." He reached for her hand. "Did I mention that I also feel deprived not having your sexy, warm body around?"

"No, you definitely didn't."

"Well, let me mention it." He clicked the lock on her dressing-room door, came over and draped his arms around her shoulders. She saw the embrace reflected in the mirror, saw him notice it, too. He kissed her once, then let go. "Something about this just doesn't feel right."

She laughed. "You object to mirrors?"

"I thought they were supposed to be on the ceiling. Anyway, who are we kidding? You broke up with me a week or so ago, and we're now friends and professional colleagues. Besides, the stage manager is going to be calling for you in five minutes to do promos, and I have to be on a plane to Toronto in a couple of hours, with the young hunk beside me."

Jackie laughed, changed the subject. "Did you get the silver story cleared with Cawley?"

"I did—he says to go ahead."

"I'll start today. I'll have the groundwork done and we can shoot as soon as you're back. Time is of the essence, I think."

"I'll be back from Toronto at the end of the week, and either I'll have three great stories in the can, or Doug Smith will have three black eyes. Either way, I'll be ready to shoot with you."

"Be good. Do they have *A.M. Reports* in Toronto?"

"I don't have the faintest idea. If not, I'll see you in my dreams."

"Trite. Very trite."

"But true. By the way, are you still being loyal to the millionaire?"

Jackie shrugged. "I guess so."

Jeff fiddled with the door handle. "Ah, Jackie, you're a woman divided. I just wish I didn't love every one of those divisions quite so much."

After he left, Jackie thought about the fact that they had shied away from any connection to each other at home, confined their passion to the road. She imagined talking about it with Dana. Dana would say that it was their unconscious way of limiting the commitment and keeping the affair unreal. What happened when you were off shooting a story wasn't part of your day-to-day existence, it was a fantasy life come true. Jackie bit hard on her bottom lip. She didn't want her time with Jeff to be unreal.

Back in the studio doing the promos, Jackie found herself distracted by the conversation with Jeff. She stumbled over words, redid one promo four times. When they were finally finished, she hurried back to her dressing room, took off the leather skirt and silk blouse that she'd been wearing on the air and kicked off her high heels. She'd have to remember to tell Melba that she didn't want to wear leather on the air anymore. It wasn't comfortable, and it wasn't her style. That was the nice thing about having her on-air clothes provided by the manufacturers now. She could wear them once and send them back.

She changed into her own clothes and left the studio. Her

limo driver, David, was waiting by the front door. "Where are you going this morning, Miss Rogers?"

"Just back to the office. I think I'll walk."

"Don't be silly. I'll take you."

She got into the car, let him drive her the three and a half blocks from the studio to her office. It seemed foolish, but it was sometimes easier to do what was expected than protest too much.

21

Jackie answered a few phone calls when she got to the office, then went over to the research department and asked if she could use the files.

For the next several hours, she pored through the files on the silver market and read the endless articles called up on the computer. After awhile, she understood everything that the popular publications could explain and began to study the denser articles in *Euromoney* and *Barron's*. She read a few of the articles twice, including one that had been written by Erwin Sewall two years earlier called "Commodities Trading: Where Are We Heading?" She was beginning to understand the intricacies of Julian's world.

She took copious notes and wrote lists of questions on a yellow legal pad. Back in her own office, she called Julian and told him that she was pursuing the silver story, if it was still all right with him.

"Of course it is, sweetheart. You need help?"

"Do you have time for a few questions?"

"I always have time for you."

She smiled into the phone, pulled out her notepad. "Okay, this isn't being taped, it's just for my own background. Let's start with the basics. Why, in your opinion, is the silver market going wild all of a sudden?"

"Probably the standard reasons that silver always rises—precious metals are a hedge against inflation. When the dollar's weak, as it is now, people fear that their money will start to be worth less. So they change their dollars into hard currency, traditionally gold or silver, that seems to have a more stable value than paper money."

"Does it really?"

"What do you mean?"

"As far as I can tell, silver is worth whatever anyone will pay for it—whether the buyer is an industrial user or a speculator."

"True enough, but the supply of silver is limited. The government can always decide to print more dollars, making them worth less. You can't mint more silver. There's a finite supply."

"How much is there?"

"Good question. Probably not more than eight hundred million ounces in the world. Less than sixty million ounces in the Comex warehouses—you know, the commodities exchange in New York."

"Yes, I know. What's it worth?"

"It changes every day, of course. Maybe six or seven billion."

"Maybe I should be more impressed, but as I understand it, most silver is bought on credit." She glanced at her notes. "When silver was at ten dollars an ounce awhile ago, you could put up two thousand dollars in margin and have a contract for five thousand ounces of silver worth fifty thousand dollars."

"Sounds right."

"My math's lousy . . . wait a second." She pulled out a calculator, played with the numbers. "So it would take only forty thousand dollars to control a million dollars' worth of silver. And—is this right?—if you have a million dollars to play with, you can control twenty-five million dollars' worth of silver."

"I suppose. But you're starting to talk about an awfully risky game."

"Okay, bear with me. I also learned about variation margin. If the price goes up a dollar, a speculator who has a short position has to cover the entire loss on the contract that day. On the original fifty-thousand-dollar contract, that would be five thousand dollars. The money goes to the account of a speculator holding the correct long position. Vice versa if the market is going down."

"You got it. You can easily end up owing more in a day than you paid at the beginning. If you're at the right end of the speculation, though, you can use the gain to buy more contracts, without putting up any more money. It's called pyramiding."

"So someone with a few million dollars and very good timing could end up with a fair chunk of the silver market."

"It would take more than a few million dollars, sweetheart, but that's the idea."

"And if one takes delivery of some of the silver?"

"What about it?"

"I remember when we were flying to Hong Kong, you told me that Chairman Travers at the CFTC was worried about your taking delivery on so much silver. I know it was all legal, but why was he worried?"

"Just for the reason you've been getting at. If too much silver is hoarded and taken out of circulation, it becomes easier to squeeze the market when the price is going up, and put pressure on the speculators who own the short positions. They start to worry that the longs will demand delivery, and they have no place to get the silver."

Jackie held on to the phone for a moment while she flipped through her notes. "Something doesn't make sense," she said finally. "You said before that gold and silver are the traditional hedges against inflation. But gold has been virtually unchanged recently while silver soars. How do you explain that?"

"It's probably a matter of emotional investing. Silver's lower price makes it more accessible. Silver also has daily uses—film for your camera, fillings for your teeth, flatwear for your dinner table. So the price is affected by users as well as speculators."

"Understood. One more question." Jackie took a deep breath, felt her heart pounding. "Is there any way in which you or anyone you know could be—wittingly or unwittingly—squeezing the silver market and driving the price up?"

"Absolutely not. It's a free market, and the market adjusts to existing conditions. That's what's happening now. There'll be winners and losers, but there's no duplicity."

Ask him again. Jackie noticed her hands trembling slightly.

"What would you say to someone who claimed that the price *is* being driven up artificially?"

"They're wrong. Period."

"I hear you," said Jackie. "Thanks for the help."

"My pleasure. I'm impressed. You've really got a good grasp on the market."

"It's a big story. I'll be using the information you gave me when I call other people. Anyone you'd like me to stay away from?"

"Not at all. Get your story."

When she hung up she realized that she was sweating and her

blouse was sticking to her back. She decided to ignore it, and put in a call to Chairman Martin Travers at the Commodities Futures Trading Commission. His secretary said he would get back to her. While she waited, she called Sam Fredericks. Telling him that she had *carte blanche* from Julian to pursue the story on silver, she asked to interview him. He seemed surprised, but agreed to answer any questions.

"Would it be easier if we got together?" he asked.

"Yes, it would, but unfortunately I don't have time. Instead of pounding the pavements as a good investigative reporter should, I'm pounding the telephone lines."

He laughed, and Jackie pulled out the sheet of questions she had prepared for him. They talked for forty-five minutes, and she filled half a dozen pages in her notebook.

"Do you know about Hong Kong?" he asked carefully at one point.

Jackie swallowed. "Of course, Sam, I was there with him, remember?"

"Yes, I do remember, which is the only reason I'd bring it up." He seemed to be considering what to say next, and Jackie decided to propose her own conclusions as fact.

"As I understand it, Sam, even Julian Beardsley doesn't have enough money to move the silver market himself, so he found a partner in Lem Chen—and they've been working the market together. I think they also have some Arab money at their disposal."

"So you do know." Sam sounded relieved. "What more do you need from me?"

Without asking too directly, she managed to get some information on the specifics of the deals Julian and Lem Chen had made.

By the time she hung up, her guilt at her own manipulation was replaced with a sense of triumph. She had a grip on the story now. After that, she called Erwin Sewall in London, who was pleasant but far more circumspect than Sam. When Chairman Travers got back to her, she told him what she was doing and asked if he had time to talk.

"We're not really sharing our information with the press at the moment," he said. "But I'll certainly let you know when we're ready."

"Maybe we could just make this an off-the-record exchange of information," she said, persisting.

"Ms. Rogers, we have several investigators involved already. I doubt you could provide us with any information we're lacking."

"I'm not so sure, Mr. Chairman." She swallowed hard, and decided to continue. "Perhaps you'd be interested in knowing that I attended a meeting in Hong Kong with Julian Beardsley and several international businessmen."

"Really?" His tone changed, the governmental arrogance gone. "I'm sorry, Ms. Rogers, I just realized who you are. I hadn't placed the name properly before. I've heard Mr. Beardsley speak of you."

She didn't say anything.

"If you'd like to come to my office tomorrow, you're certainly welcome. But I'll have to stand by the provision that everything be off-the-record."

"I'll catch the eleven-o'clock shuttle to Washington after the show and be in your office about twelve-thirty."

"I'll be expecting you."

She hung up and put her head down on her desk. Then she picked up the phone and asked Melba to track down Jeff in Toronto. A few minutes later, he was on her line.

"What's up, Jackie?"

"I know you're in the middle of a shoot, but I have to tell you about my day." She quickly ran through the research she'd done and the phone calls she'd made, ending with the conversation with Travers. "In short, I'm preparing to sell out Julian for the sake of a good story," she said.

"Or you're getting a good story for the sake of selling out Julian."

"That's not fair."

"Sorry. But keep it in perspective. All you did is find a way to get the guy from the CFTC to talk to you. When it comes right down to it, you can't sell out Julian because you don't really know what happened at those meetings in Hong Kong."

"But I know they occurred, and I can name the participants. From what I'm beginning to understand about this story, I think those are connections Julian wouldn't really want made."

"You sound shaken."

"Of course I am. I need you with me tomorrow at the meeting with Travers."

"Jackie, if you really needed me, I'd abandon Doug Smith in a minute and fly down to be with you. But Travers wouldn't let me in, anyway. He wants this off-the-record, you said, and that usually means no producers. If you want, I'll call you later tonight, and we can hash through what you're comfortable telling him and what should remain pillow talk."

"I'm beginning to feel like Mata Hari. Where are you now?"

"In a phone booth on the bottom of a ski slope, waiting for the rain to stop so Doug can interview two members of the Canadian luge team."

Jackie laughed. "Go to it, honey. I'll speak to you tonight."

After the show the next morning, Jackie called Nate Burrows and asked, with some embarrassment, if the writers could switch back to the old system of preparing scripts, at least for this week. They could do their pre-interviews and write the scripts without consulting with her, and she would call in at night to be briefed. "I won't be around during the day today to work on them and I'm afraid I'm also going to be tied up for the next few days," she explained.

"That's what happens," Nate said. "Things get in the way. I suppose you're being paid a fortune to give a speech somewhere. That's why Darlie was never around."

"Actually, it's another story I'm doing for the show."

"Don't worry," he said, slightly disbelieving. "We'll take care of the scripts, whatever's going on."

She flew to Washington and had her meeting with Chairman Travers, just the two of them, behind closed doors.

"I've got the story," Jackie told Jeff on the phone that night. "What Julian's done is legal, but it's ethically deplorable."

"I've never seen a woman work so hard to break up with her boyfriend."

"What do you mean?"

"Isn't that what this is about? You've professed loyalty to Julian, and now you're working desperately to find a reason to leave him."

"I don't think so," Jackie said, annoyed. "This is a professional involvement, not a personal one. You have to give the story it's due, Jeff. We're doing a vital piece here about the proper functioning of commodities markets. Any free market works only when people have full information. Right now, Julian is buying silver and other people are buying silver—and they're working from different sets of facts. We're going to make sure that everyone has the same facts."

"Sounds good," said Jeff amiably. "Any of your sources willing to talk on the air?"

"Some, I think. I'll have them set when you get back. See you tomorrow night."

They hung up and Jackie pulled out her notebook, too keyed-up to go to sleep. She knew what was happening now, and the only question was the best way to present it. Maybe a tape piece and a live follow-up with Julian in the studio? Would she hold back some of the information in the tape piece, try to trick Julian into entrapping himself on the air, as a result of her shrewd questioning?

She had to put the silver story out of her mind. There was a live show to do tomorrow, and that demanded first priority. She got into bed and closed her eyes, but the image still danced in front of her: she and Julian sitting in the studio, lights blazing, live cameras rolling. Julian telling what he knew about the silver market, and her saying, "Yes, Mr. Beardsley, but isn't it true that . . ."

She got out of bed and called Jeff back. "You were right," she said as soon as he picked up the phone.

"About what?"

"I've picked a complicated way to break up with someone."

Julian agreed to be interviewed in his office on Friday morning for the tape piece. Jackie convinced Cawley that the story was critical, needed to be run immediately. Silver had gone from a low of six dollars and change per ounce a few months earlier to over thirty-five dollars as of that afternoon. Maybe it had taken her too long to get started, but she couldn't bear any further delay.

Jackie and Jeff had stayed up much of Thursday night going over her notes, trying to understand the key points of her story.

"It's a clever operation," said Jackie. "Beardsley Enterprises is working in concert with Lem Chen in Hong Kong. Together, they have options to buy about one hundred fifty million ounces of silver this month, and sell about one hundred twenty-five million ounces next month. That leaves twenty-five million ounces unhedged and subject to market fluctuation. Meanwhile, Julian keeps taking delivery on silver, and in the last few weeks, it's become clear that there might be a physical shortage. Those unhedged twenty-five million ounces are worth a lot more than they used to be."

"But there's still the question you said Julian raised a long time ago—how is he supposed to get out without making the price drop?"

Jackie sighed. "That's what I can't figure out. I have a feeling Sheik Fahoud is involved, but I don't have a handle on it yet. Anyway, if a shortage does develop, and someone holding a short position can't meet Lem Chen's demand for delivery, they're likely to go to Julian, who has vast holdings and can pretty much charge whatever he wants."

Jeff nodded. "One warning. I'm not going to let you make any unsubstantiated charges in this report. You may be sure that you're right, but truth is no excuse for character assassination."

"Understood."

"By the way, how did you get all this?"

"I got a lot from Sam, who gave me very classified information. *His* ode to Dana, I think. I faked along until I got the connection between Julian and Lem Chen. Some of it came from Erwin Sewall, who thought I knew more than I did."

"Lem Chen is the name you gave Travers?"

"Yup. I told him the connection, and he opened up his records. They knew something was happening from Hong Kong, but they didn't know who was behind it."

Jackie and Jeff finished outlining the piece, and Jeff got up to leave. "I'll meet you right after the show tomorrow at Julian's office," he said.

"I'm glad you'll be with me. It's going to be a tough interview for me."

He smiled. "I'm glad to be there, but you don't need my strength behind you to do this story, you have your own."

She closed her eyes and held on to him for a moment, then let him go.

When she arrived at the lobby of the World Trade Center immediately after Friday's show, Jeff was already waiting with the crew. They piled into the elevator and rode to the eighty-ninth floor. One of the cameramen made jokes most of the way up, and Jackie found herself relaxing.

Julian was waiting in his office. She introduced him to Jeff, wondering if Julian would make the connection, realize who Jeff was, but instead he shook hands politely and asked Jeff if he wanted him behind his desk for the interview or at the conference table.

"Up to you," Jeff said. Jackie saw that Jeff was struggling to stay professional, but conflicting emotions played across his face.

The crew seemed to take forever to set up. Jackie had asked that there be two cameras on the shoot so that they could get her original questions, rather than having her repeat them on reversals, where much of the impact might be lost. It was an expensive luxury that Cawley rarely allowed, but Jeff had somehow convinced him.

They finally began the interview with Jackie asking the straightforward questions she had originally asked Julian over the telephone.

The preliminaries over, she asked if they were getting to a point in the silver market where demand could outstrip supply.

"Hard to speculate on that," Julian said. He was cool and easygoing—far more so than Jackie.

"The chairman of the CFTC says that some bullion dealers are asking for action against speculators. At least one bullion company may go out of business because it can't make margin payments."

"Beardsley Enterprises is also a bullion company, so we understand the position. I know the company you're referring to, and I've offered to bail them out with a proposal called an EFP—exchange of futures for physicals. I accept delivery before my long positions are due, which cancels my long contracts and their short positions. It will relieve the strain and cut down on their daily margin payments, which is what threatens to bankrupt them."

"And coincidentally reduce the supply of deliverable silver."

"That's correct."

They continued the interview, Julian remaining smooth, Jackie struggling not to get flustered. When they were finished, Julian said he had to leave, and Jeff asked if they could shoot some background shots around the office—the frenzy of the trading room, the computer boards, the excitement of dealing in huge sums of money. "My pleasure," Julian said. "Do whatever Jackie needs. Did you know that you're dealing with the smartest reporter in the business?"

"Actually I did know that," Jeff said stiffly.

Jackie sat in Julian's empty office while the cameramen shot background shots. "Did you get it?" she asked when Jeff sat down next to her for a moment.

"Get what?"

"The story about the EFP. That's why Julian is willing to be on—he wanted to tell the world that he had bailed out another company and saved them from bankruptcy. But Julian didn't do it out of goodwill. The EFP increased his bullion holdings. It's a way of taking more silver out of circulation at no cost to him. The EFP saved one company, but it may bankrupt others that can't find the silver to meet delivery when Lem Chen demands it."

"Want to say that?" Jeff asked.

"Yes, I do." She grimaced. "Monday morning, live on television."

The tape story on the silver market was to run in the seventhirty half-hour on Monday morning. On Sunday night, Laurie Spinner called Julian and asked him if he'd like to come to the studio for one minute of live follow-up, and he agreed.

During the seventy-thirty news break, one of the young pages brought Julian into the studio and he sat down comfortably in the chair reserved for guests. From across the studio, Jackie saw him making amiable conversation with the audio man who was attaching his microphone. Jackie glanced at her notes one final time.

"Everything okay?"

Startled, she turned around to see Bradley looming over her.

"Fine," she said. "I'm just a little anxious about interviewing Julian."

"Just think about what you're doing." Warning lights seemed to flash in Bradley's eyes, and Jackie opened her mouth to respond, then closed it again.

"Thirty seconds back," called the stage manager. "Jackie and Bradley to home base, please."

Jackie had stayed in the edit room with Jeff all night, writing and rewriting her track. She never bothered to go to sleep. At five o'clock in the morning she simply left the edit room and went to the studio. Now she and Bradley moved to the living-room set, sat down next to each other, and had their camera faces ready when the music came up.

Bradley, reading from the prompter, said that Jackie had been out on "special assignment" over the weekend and had come back "with one of the most fascinating and exciting business stories we've ever run on this show. Please watch."

Jackie turned to the monitor, saw the tape beginning with a shot of piles of silver bullion—all that was left in the Comex depository.

"This is a story of silver," said Jackie's voice. *"Or at least the story as well as anyone can piece it together. The key figure in the story is this man, Julian Beardsley, chairman of Beardsley Enterprises. Whether he's a hero or villain depends on your perspective."*

For the next six and a half minutes, Jackie on tape told everything she knew about silver—how bullion was being hoarded to make a false shortage and drive up the price, how Julian and a Hong Kong bullion dealer named Lem Chen had futures contracts coming due in a week, and if they demanded delivery, there could be repercussions that would shake the entire economy.

Across the studio, Jackie saw Julian watching the piece; he seemed momentarily shaken when Lem Chen's name was mentioned, and looked as if he might jump up from his seat. But he recovered.

As the tape was ending, Jackie moved quickly over to the chair next to Julian's. She didn't want him to have time to talk to her before they were back live. As soon as she sat down, the stage manager raised five fingers, dropped one each second, then pointed at Jackie.

"We're back now live with Julian Beardsley," she said, smiling into camera two. She turned to look at him. "Good morning, Mr. Beardsley. This piece raised some questions that we still need you to answer." She took a breath; she was going to be blunt. "You and the Hong Kong bullion dealer Lem Chen both have futures contracts coming due in a week; if you demand delivery, there could be a shortfall that will drive other companies into bankruptcy."

"That won't happen."

"Are you saying that neither you nor Lem Chen will demand delivery?"

Julian uttered a hollow, anxious laugh. "I can't make guarantees one way or another."

"In that case," Jackie said, looking right into the camera, "the only conclusion we can draw is that you and Lem Chen are plotting to corner the silver market. If you succeed, there will be chaos in the financial world."

The director caught Julian's surprised reaction before he cut away to a commercial.

Jackie excused herself quickly after the spot with Julian and joined Bradley at the living-room set for the next piece they were doing.

"Quite a report," Bradley said. "But after commercial I think we should say that some of what was just said may be speculation."

"It wasn't," Jackie said firmly. "Every word was substantiated."

"You made a lot of charges."

"They were all true."

After the show, she found Jeff, who hugged her. "Brave interview," he said. "I'm glad we got it on. Kalina said it's already hit the wires."

"What do they say?"

"That *A.M. Reports* has unveiled major deceptions in the silver market. You apparently get raves."

"You think everybody is going to do this story now?"

"Everyone. And they're all going to call you for information. Good luck. I'm cutting out and going to my house in Hillcrest for a few days. Alone. Call if things get rough."

Julian had disappeared quickly from the studio, and Jackie didn't hear from him again until late in the day. When he finally called, he sounded jovial. "I'm impressed," he said when she picked up the phone.

"Impressed at what?"

"At everything you figured out. I suppose I gave you the key to the puzzle, since you met Lem Chen in Hong Kong, but that's terrific work. I never dreamed you'd get so much."

"I hope you're not upset," Jackie said halfheartedly. "I felt it was necessary."

"Upset? No, honey, not at all. At least not anymore. Commodities markets are a lot like television—image is everything. I'm glad to get a reputation as a man who can control markets, because once people *think* you can control them, you actually do."

She didn't understand. Could this be Julian, man of business and man of ethics? The story had to be damaging to him. Either he would try to get out of the market now, in which case it would come toppling down on him or he could try to take delivery and continue his corner. Would Julian really want the world to recognize such egregious, self-centered behavior?

"What will you do now?" she asked.

"Try to convince you to spend next weekend with me in Paris."

"I meant about silver."

"There's nothing to do. No buying or selling in my future. I don't own much silver anymore."

"How could that be?" She'd watched the wires all day, but the price of silver hadn't changed much, and there had been no major transactions.

"A gentleman from the Middle East has been standing by. He's wanted to enter the market and buy my physical silver whenever I was ready to get out. So this morning we traded. My silver for his oil. Barter. Like trading onions for carrots."

She suddenly understood: it was the final piece of the puzzle, the one that made Julian's position invulnerable. He had manipulated to a point, played the game to see what he could do, but had his out-point ready.

"A deal with Sheik Fahoud?"

"You're even smarter than I imagined, Jackie. That's why I can always forgive you."

She took a deep breath, but instead of arguing, she just said good-bye and hung up the phone.

Now that she knew the truth, she didn't want to be forgiven by Julian Beardsley.

22

Could these be labor pains? Dominique woke up shortly after one o'clock on Tuesday morning. It was a week before her due date. She was having mild cramps, something like the menstrual pains she had experienced as a teenager. It was probably nothing, just the aftereffects of the Chinese food she'd had for dinner. She and Harris had gone out for a late dinner the previous night. When he had asked solicitously if it was all right to eat spicy food in your ninth month of pregnancy, she had just laughed.

"The baby's got to get used to it sometime."

"But what about you? Don't women get heartburn at the end of pregnancy?"

"You read too much, and definitely worry too much."

"I just worry about you."

Harris did worry about Dominique, or at least think about her, calling every day when he was in Washington and flying to New York more and more to see her. The flurry of publicity for his family bill had ended, and recently they were together only because they wanted to be. She was grateful for his friendship—it took away the neediness she might have otherwise felt during the pregnancy and made her realize that her only motive for being with Harris was the way she felt about him.

She decided to go back to sleep, drifted off easily and woke up again at three. The pains were slightly more intense, very different from the false labor she'd had so often in the last few weeks. She pulled out a book of Wodehouse short stories that Harris had left, telling her that she might as well laugh through labor. It kept her mind off her discomfort for about another hour.

What were the signs of real labor supposed to be? A heaviness in the belly, cramps becoming more intense and more frequent. No denying it, this was real. She felt a flurry of kicking from the baby, put her hands on her belly. *Don't be scared, little baby. You're going to be all right.* She had come to enjoy the frequent rhythmic kicks from the baby, liked knowing that she was there. At the moment, it was their only way of communicating, and in this flurry she sensed . . . What? Fear? Excitement? *I'm going to take care of you.*

There was clearly no getting back to sleep now. Her back began to ache, so she got out of bed and walked around. Maybe a warm shower would help. She stayed in the shower a long time, soothed by the water and trying to decide what to do. She had no desire to go to the hospital yet, but she wanted to talk to somebody. Harris had gone back to Washington last night, and Jackie would be on her way to the studio shortly. It wasn't fair to call her before the show. She would wait.

The pains were severe enough that she wanted to crawl back into bed, but she had heard often enough that lying on your back was the worst way to get through labor. So she put on a jogging suit and, at six-thirty when the morning sunlight began to filter into her apartment, she took the elevator down to the lobby. The doorman tipped his hat to her and she smiled, full of her own secret. Outside, she walked over to the East River, pausing now and then to catch her breath and breathe through her pains. There were dozens of joggers and walkers by the river at that hour, and she moved slowly among them. At one point she stopped and clutched her stomach, almost doubled over in pain. Two women jogging by stopped to ask if she needed help. "I'm fine," she said, thanking them. But it was time to get back.

In her apartment, she turned on *A.M. Reports* and watched Bradley interview the astronaut who was supposed to pilot the next space shuttle. There were three commercials and a break for news and weather, and then Jackie came back to interview a soap-opera actress. Yesterday had been a triumph, with Jackie's report on silver and her pointed interview with Julian. Now she was back to more standard fare. Poor Jackie, thought Dominique. All the struggling and triumph, and the proof of her success is that she gets to spend her morning smiling at dumb celebrities.

Dominique remembered her doctor's stressing that everyone's

labor was different; a first baby could arrive quickly, or as was far more common, take about twenty-four hours to make an appearance. She assumed labor would be long, and was in no rush to raise the alarm. She had started doing the Lamaze breathing exercises, getting herself through each wave of pains. Curious, she picked up her stopwatch. The pains were lasting about forty-five seconds and were five minutes apart.

A little before nine, she called the control room, reached Cawley.

"Could you have Jackie call me at home as soon as she's off the air?"

"Sure. Anything special I can help with?"

Dominique paused. "I've been in labor all night. I think it's time to get to the hospital."

"You're joking! Don't hang up. I'll get Jackie at the commercial."

"No, Steve, really. It's not a rush. I'd just like her to come by when the show's over. Does she have promos to do today?"

"Are you nuts? I'll send her out of here the minute we're done. Bradley can handle promos himself."

"Don't do that. I can wait until she's finished."

"No you can't. What does your doctor say?"

"I haven't called him yet."

"Want me to call him for you?"

"I'll wait until Jackie gets here."

Jackie called back about three minutes later. "I can't believe you waited until after the show to call. I'm furious. How close are the pains?"

"About every five minutes."

"I'll be there in fifteen minutes. The limo is waiting outside."

Jackie arrived almost immediately and quickly took control. She called Dr. Page, who said they should go to the hospital. He would meet them there. A moment later, Jackie was holding Dominique's coat and the small bag she had packed, and ushering her into the limousine.

Once in the hospital, they were whisked quickly into a private labor room. For Dominique, the next few hours were a blur, with nurses going in and out, labor intensifying, a fear of losing control. At one point, a nurse strapped a fetal monitor on her, told her to stay in bed. Dominique stayed there for five minutes, then angrily ripped off the monitor and demanded the nurse leave the room. "You won't make a medical procedure out of normal childbirth!" she said, hearing her own voice getting too loud. When the nurse left, Dominique felt herself sweating and groaning, asked Jackie if she thought she was going to have to ask for some Demerol.

"No, I think you should hang in," said Jackie. "You're going to make it just fine."

"What do you know? You've never had a baby."

"You're doing fine, just relax."

"For Christ's sake, I want Demerol. You're supposed to be here to help me, Jackie. Now get it for me."

Jackie patted her hand. "You must be in transition."

"What?"

"Remember? The Lamaze teacher said that when you hate everybody, it means you're in transition. It's almost time to push."

Dominique felt a glimmer of calm, even of hope. Maybe she wouldn't be in labor forever. Maybe the pain would eventually be over.

Thirty minutes later, just as Dominique was beginning to feel an overwhelming sense of exhaustion, she heard Dr. Page say, "One more push, Dominique. One more." Jackie was at her side panting with her, getting her through. Then she was holding her hand and stroking her forehead . . . and suddenly Melanie Sheldon Lane was born.

Dominique never imagined that a room could be as filled with flowers as hers was by the end of the day. Jackie must have spread the word quickly, because there seemed to be large bouquets coming in from everyone at the network. Even Bradley James sent an arrangement. The nurses complained that they could barely get in the door. Jackie's had certainly been the best—a dozen long-stemmed red roses sent to her, and a dozen small yellow ones for Melanie.

Since she had left a message at Harris' office in the Senate about Melanie's birth, Dominique was slightly disappointed as she opened the florists' cards and found none from him.

But nothing except Melanie really mattered now.

Dominique had kept the baby in her room for a few hours

after the birth, feeding her, holding her, falling in love. The nurse suggested then that she take her to the nursery for a while and Dominique reluctantly agreed, realizing that she needed some sleep. When the nurse brought her back later, Melanie was screaming and red-faced. "Good luck," said the nurse. "I think she's going to be a tough one."

Dominique took Melanie from her tiny bassinet and brought her to her breast. In an instant, the baby stopped crying and began to suckle. Dominique felt a wave of calm circling both of them. Melanie sucked hungrily at both breasts, then fell asleep in Dominique's arms. Dominique stroked her and touched her, overwhelmed at the perfection of the tiny being. She was as beautiful as any baby could be, and Dominique wanted to protect her forever. The nurse came in to say that she would take the baby back to the nursery, but Dominique told her that there was no way that Melanie was ever going to move from her side again.

The two of them were dozing on the bed when there was a quiet knock on the door, and Dominique opened her eyes to see Harris peeking in the door.

"Come in," she said quietly.

He came over to the bed, kissed her, and stepped back to look at Melanie.

"What a child. Goodness, Dominique, she's as gorgeous as you are. How are you feeling?"

"Better than I ever have in my whole life. I can't believe I have a baby, Harris. I don't think I feel like a mother yet, but I've never been so in love."

He kissed her again. "I'm sorry I didn't get here sooner."

"Anything important?"

He smiled. "Today was that lunch with the President."

Dominique raised her fingers to her lips. "Oh gosh, I forgot. How was it?"

"Fine, but if I'd thought it through and realized what a beautiful sight I was missing, I would have canceled."

Dominique smiled, stroked the baby's tiny arm. "It is a nice scene, isn't it? I just keep looking and looking at her. She's so perfect."

"Where did she get the red hair?" Harris teased.

Dominique caressed the soft fuzz on Melanie's head, which

really did have a reddish gleam. "That's in case anybody doubted who the mother was."

They talked awhile longer, until the baby stirred and began to whimper. "Do you mind if I feed her?" Dominique asked.

"Of course not. Should I leave?"

"No." She opened her robe discreetly and again the baby took to her breast, quieting as if by magic. Dominique looked up at Harris and explained, "This gives you such a new perspective on your own body and what it was made for."

They sat quietly for a few minutes, then Dominique asked what had happened at his lunch with the President. Harris brushed it off. "We'll talk about it another time," he said. "Your day was certainly more productive than mine."

Dominique told him that she wanted to go home the next day; she couldn't think of any reason to stay in the hospital. She was eager to begin life again, with her baby. "*A.M. Reports* has officially put me on maternity leave, and will welcome me back whenever I'm ready. But you know what? I'm not going back. My agent has already been getting inquiries about my availability. I'm going to wait until I'm ready, and pick carefully."

"You'll be back on the air in no time," Harris said, "and meanwhile, it will be my pleasure to escort you home tomorrow."

"I'd love it," she said.

He reached for her hand, held it gently. "I have to admit that I had a long talk with one of my chief aides today. He was concerned about my coming to see you in the hospital. Leaving with you and the baby will look as if we're a family."

"Oh." She felt a surge of hurt, wondered where this was leading. But she had learned enough from Peter and from the past months to know that she wouldn't press the issue, would gracefully let him go. There was no room in her life anymore for reluctance. "Then I guess you shouldn't."

"You miss the point. I want to."

Now she was confused. "What does your aide suggest you do?"

"Issue an official statement explaining why I'm here. Not to make a big fuss out of it, but just to let anyone who's interested know that you've become an important person in my life."

Dominique looked at him, surprised. "You want to announce that?"

"I deeply want to announce that. First to you, and then to the rest of the world. If it's all right, I'll explain that the beautiful Melanie is not my daughter, but that during your pregnancy I got to know you and to respect you for your principles. And now I've come to love you for yourself. If you'll let me, I'll even suggest that there might be a marriage in the future."

She stared at him, feeling her eyes fill with tears. "Are you really in love?"

He smiled. "Would I lie to my constituency?"

Dominique opened her mouth to say something, then dropped her head down, shook it slightly. Harris came over, put his arm around her. "You're crying," he said.

"Postpartum happiness," she said. "Who wrote the statement?"

"I did, of course. I hope it doesn't sound gratuitous, but I am a public person. Part of the price is that I owe an explanation to my constituents, even when I fall in love."

She tried to find a hand to wipe away her tears, but she was holding Melanie with one hand and Harris with the other, and she didn't want to let go of either of them. Tears bounced down her face, and Harris leaned over to kiss them away. "Did I pick a bad time to say all this?"

"Of course not." She smiled at him through the tears. "Your timing couldn't be better, Senator. I love you."

Jackie had left the hospital shortly after the delivery, realizing that Dominique wanted to be alone with her baby, and also needed some sleep. Jackie did, too—but she had a more pressing need than sleep.

She rented a car and two hours later was ringing the doorbell at Jeff's snug house in Hillcrest. He came to the door, surprised.

"I have a car, so you can tell me to leave anytime."

"Don't be silly. Come in."

She came into the cozy main room, surprised to hear Handel on the stereo and see a fire in the fireplace. "Are you alone?" she asked.

"Of course. My way of relaxing."

"Dominique had her baby today. A cute little girl—Melanie Sheldon Lane."

Jeff's face crinkled in pleasure. "Good for her. Everything go well?"

"Dominique's a trooper. Labor was miserable, but she's so happy with the baby, I'm sure she's already forgotten."

Jeff smiled. "So you drove two hours to be the bearer of good tidings?"

Jackie sighed, and sat down on a comfortable-looking sofa by the fire. "I spoke to Julian late yesterday. He's pleased about the story we did because it gives him an extra dab of power next time he wants to control a market. He's found an ingenious way to get out of the silver market, and is apparently home free. Plus he still loves me."

"So everything worked out perfectly for you," Jeff said, sitting down next to her. "Happy ending."

"Not quite. I need to know where we are now. You and I, I mean."

"Friends and colleagues, isn't that our phrase? I'm happy with it."

"There was a time you wanted more."

Jeff shrugged. "Ours hasn't been an easy relationship, has it? In fact, Jackie, I think you first came to me to escape Julian. You were being devoured by him, and you didn't know how else to get away."

"Was that evil?"

"No. Remember? We made no commitments."

"No-strings affection," said Jackie, smiling. "I remember that's what you called it."

"And that was fine. But a funny thing happened. I fell in love with you, and now I want all sorts of commitments. When we went up to Julian's office the other morning, I wanted to shoot the old bastard. But I promised you friendship, and that you'll always have from me. Julian's not angry, you did the story—and you can be with him now, feeling like your own person."

"I don't want to be with him."

Jeff looked at her, his eyes narrowing. "What do you want?"

"I want to be here, with you. I'm turning to you this time, not to escape Julian, but because . . . because I love you."

"You do?"

"I do."

"I love you too. Even when you're making a fool of yourself over Julian." He put his arms around her, and Jackie realized that she was shaking. She didn't want to talk for a moment, she just wanted to hold him. Wanted him in the same way he wanted her. Why did it take so long to understand? she wondered as she buried her face in his neck.

Jeff leaned back on the sofa, and Jackie moved with him. He pulled back to look at her, his index finger tracing the lines of her nose and cheekbones, the outline of her face. "You'd better think about this," he said softly. "There are a lot of compelling reasons to stay with Julian."

"Should I list them?" Jackie stroked Jeff's face, his chest. "He's rich, he's a friend of Bradley James, he's a genius, and we went to a lot of exciting places together. If I loved him—and I think I once did—all that would be very enticing."

"But?"

Jackie smiled. "But I love you. Enough flip-flopping and waffling. I'm embarrassed about all that, and I'm sorry for it. But all I could think about as I was driving up here for the last two hours was that I want to kiss you."

"You should know that if you do, there'll be a lot of strings attached."

"Haven't I mentioned my new affection for strings?"

She closed her eyes, and Jeff pulled her closer until they were kissing, clutching at each other as if suddenly panicked at the thought that they had almost let go. She felt Jeff's hands under her clothes, caressing her back, sliding down. Her desire for him swept over her, and she felt the passion and hunger returned in his embrace. They made love explosively, giggled at their ardor, then began again slowly, building until they abandoned themselves to incredible mutual pleasure.

Jackie dozed off in Jeff's arms, awoke to see him gazing at her. She kissed him, then said, "It's late. I have a show to do tomorrow."

"You're not leaving," he said, smiling. "We'll have your limo pick you up here tomorrow morning. It will be early, but it's better than going away now."

"I agree," Jackie said, and went to find the phone.

"All set," she said, coming back from the kitchen. "And I decided everyone should know. When I left the phone number with Melba, I said it was Jeff's house. Told her to make sure the rumor gets around."

Jeff laughed, held her tightly as they moved to the bedroom, and made love once more before falling into a blissful sleep. They set the alarm for three o'clock the next morning, but both woke up moments before the alarm went off, their eyelids fluttering, their lips meeting almost before they were fully conscious.

Jackie felt a special comfort in finding herself in Jeff's arms, though she had the curious sensation of waking up hungry for his body, as if their lovemaking the night before had been insufficient to see her through the short night.

"I want you," she whispered.

"You've got me."

"And you've got me. Every bit of me." She kissed him, felt his passion rising, until he gently pushed her away.

"Get me started, and you'll never get to work," he said.

"I don't want to go."

"Of course you do. And you don't have to worry. I'll still be around when you're finished."